the best-kept secrets

OTHER BOOKS AND AUDIOBOOKS
BY SARAH M. EDEN

THE LANCASTER FAMILY
Seeking Persephone
Courting Miss Lancaster
Romancing Daphne
Loving Lieutenant Lancaster
Christmas at Falstone Castle*
also in *All Hearts Come Home for Christmas* anthology
Charming Artemis

THE GENTS
Forget Me Not
Snowdrops and Winterberry
(previously titled *The Holly and the Ivy* in
The Holly and the Ivy anthology)*
Lily of the Valley
Fleur-de-Lis
Snapdragons

THE HUNTRESSES
The Best-Laid Plans*
The Best Intentions
The Best of Friends
The Best-Kept Secrets

THE JONQUIL BROTHERS
The Kiss of a Stranger
Friends and Foes
Drops of Gold
As You Are
A Fine Gentleman
For Love or Honor
The Heart of a Vicar
Charming Artemis

STORM TIDE ROMANCE
The Tides of Time

STAND-ALONES
Glimmer of Hope
An Unlikely Match
For Elise
The Fiction Kitchen
Trio Cookbook

*Novella

CHRONOLOGICAL ORDER OF ALL RELATED
SARAH M. EDEN GEORGIAN- & REGENCY-ERA BOOKS

Forget Me Not	*Romancing Daphne*	*Christmas at Falstone Castle**
Snowdrops and Winterberry	*The Kiss of a Stranger*	*The Heart of a Vicar*
(The Holly and the Ivy)*	*Friends and Foes*	*The Best-Laid Plans*
Lily of the Valley	*Drops of Gold*	*Charming Artemis*
Fleur-de-Lis	*For Elise*	*The Best Intentions*
Snapdragons	*As You Are*	*The Best of Friends*
Seeking Persephone	*A Fine Gentleman*	*The Best-Kept Secrets*
Courting Miss Lancaster	*For Love or Honor*	
Glimmer of Hope	*Loving Lieutenant Lancaster*	

SARAH M. EDEN

the best-kept secrets

A HUNTRESSES REGENCY ROMANCE

Cover image *Woman Wearing Regency Clothes in Field* © Abigail Miles / Arc Angel

Cover design by Christina Marcano © 2025 by Covenant Communications, Inc.

Published by Covenant Communications, Inc.
American Fork, Utah

Copyright © 2025 by Sarah M. Eden
All rights reserved. No part of this book may be reproduced in any format or in any medium without the written permission of the publisher, Covenant Communications, Inc., PO Box 416, American Fork, UT 84003. The views expressed within this work are the sole responsibility of the author and do not necessarily reflect the position of Covenant Communications, Inc., or any other entity.

This is a work of fiction. The characters, names, incidents, places, and dialogue are either products of the author's imagination, and are not to be construed as real, or are used fictitiously.

Library of Congress Cataloging-in-Publication Data

Name: Sarah M. Eden
Title: The Best-Kept Secrets / Sarah M. Eden
Description: American Fork, UT : Covenant Communications, Inc. [2025]
Identifiers: Library of Congress Control Number 2024939258 | 978-1-52442-803-7
LC record available at https://lccn.loc.gov/2024939258

Printed in the United States of America
First Printing: May 2025

31 30 29 28 27 26 25   10 9 8 7 6 5 4 3 2 1

Dedicated to that one time in college when I invented a code name for the guy I had a crush on so I could talk about him on the phone with my mom without my roommates figuring it out, because, before the invention of texting, secrets were far harder to keep.

CHAPTER ONE

Tulleyloch, Ireland
December 1819

EVE O'DOYLE WAS FAR TOO acquainted with chaos to be the least bothered by it. In fact, she felt right at home in the midst of a hubbub. Truth be told, she was usually *at* home when in the midst of a hubbub.

Not even the kitchen at her family home of Tulleyloch was calm. The family's precarious finances had long ago emptied that room of the usual servants employed in a home this size and by a family of the O'Doyles' perceived status. Mother had proven herself an adept cook, and Eve had taught herself to bake, so between the two of them, they'd saved the family a great deal of money.

They were both undertaking those tasks when Nia, Eve's sister, who was only just younger than herself, stepped inside. "I feel it important for the two of you to know that Edmund and Scuff are currently in the yard pretending to be chickens."

Mother met Eve's eye and shook her head with a look that clearly said, "Those boys are nothing short of ridiculous."

"Did our two distinguished Shrewsbury lads explain just why they've chosen to imitate barnyard fowl?" Eve asked.

Nia shrugged as she approached the worktable. "All Scuff would tell me is that they were undertaking 'an experiment.' Edmund then laughed in that way he always does when the two of them are about to shift from 'mischievous' to 'someone send a message of condolence to the king of the leprechauns because he is about to be dethroned as the world's most dangerously mischievous imp.'"

Eve assumed a comically stern expression and looked to Mother once more. "Remind yourself that you were eager to have them home from school."

"I had hoped they would return home the mature sixteen- and fourteen-year-old boys they are."

"Our brothers?" Nia's expression twisted into one of overdone doubt.

In a tone as mock-serious as Nia's, Eve said, "I think Mother must be succumbing to a dreadful fever of some kind that is addling her mind. A very tragic turn of events indeed."

"The entire family's suffering will be significant, I don't doubt." Nia sighed. "There'll be a great deal of fainting."

"Mostly by her," Eve added solemnly. "On account of the fever."

Mother pointed a knife at them but not menacingly. "You two are as bad as the boys."

"Oh, no." Eve shook her head. "We are *far* worse."

Mother laughed as she returned to slicing vegetables for the family's supper. Eve slid a perfectly shaped, deliciously golden loaf from its pan into her cloth-draped hand, then flipped it over to sit upright on the worktable.

"That smells delicious," Nia said.

"Let us hope it *tastes* delicious," Eve answered.

In unison, her sister and mother said, "It will."

Baking was one of Eve's talents—a talent and a passion. But it wasn't considered an acceptable pastime or interest for a lady. Such was the unfortunate nature of her inability to choose commonplace activities to capture her curiosity. No one in the O'Doyle family did anything sedately or with excessive consideration given to meeting others' expectations.

"We've received a letter." Nia held it up.

It was addressed to the both of them.

"Who is it from?" Eve asked.

"Artemis."

Eve laid a cloth over the loaf and moved with her sister into the spill of light from the window, eager to hear what their beloved friend had written.

> *Dearest Huntresses,*

Their group of particular friends were known among themselves as well as in Society as the Huntresses.

> *Plans for our Christmastime house party are at last finalized. True to the forfeit they are required to pay on account of our dear Daria winning this summer's wager, the gentlemen of the Pack*

The Best-Kept Secrets

That was the name the Huntresses' closest friends used, a group of gentle-men their same age who had, of late, become ever more intertwined with them.

> *have worked quite painstakingly—or painfully, depending on one's view of the matter—to bring this about. The previously decided-upon dates remain the same, but they, at last, have secured a loca-tion: Fairfield, the Greenberry family's estate in Surrey.*

"Colm said his parents might be willing to host the gathering," Eve said.

Nia nodded. "And it's near enough to London that Ellie and Daria should be able to make the journey."

Finding a way for all the Huntresses and all the Pack to gather was growing more complicated as their individual lives took them in countless directions.

> *Duke is to meet you in Dunleary, which I am assured is not far from Dublin. He, and an appropriate chaperone, will bring you two to Fairfield for the gathering. As the Pack did vow to make this feasible for everyone, the travel arrangements and expenses have been seen to, though I have not yet managed to wheedle out of my Charlie exactly how the Pack managed that.*
>
> *For now, I will be content knowing that all my Huntresses will be together again, and I will save my energy for planning ways we can amiably torture the Pack.*
> *All my love to you both.*
>
> *Yours, etc.,*
> *Artemis Jonquil*

Eve sighed with delight. "We get to see everyone again."

"Which one is Duke?" Mother asked from the worktable.

"The quiet one who always seems angry," Nia said.

Mother's brow pulled in concern. "Will you not be miserable making so long a journey with a gentleman who's always angry?"

"He always *seems* angry," Eve repeated with emphasis. "'Tisn't true though. And if it further puts your mind at ease, Duke's given name is actually Dubhán."

Mother perked up on the instant. "He's Irish, is he?"

Eve and Nia nodded in unison.

"That must be the reason he's the one accompanying you to Surrey. He'd be departing from Dublin as it is."

That was not actually entirely true. Duke's family *was* Irish, and Eve thought she'd heard that he was born in Ireland, but he'd lived most of his life in England, where his family now made their home. But perhaps he was in Ireland visiting members of his extended family.

"Who do you suppose the 'appropriate chaperone' will prove to be?" Nia asked.

"Perhaps his mother," Eve guessed. "Or Charlie's. She would be lovely to make a journey with."

"If not on this excursion, perhaps on the next." Nia smiled, as clearly delighted with the idea as Eve was. "At the very least, we will see her in London next Season."

Charlie and Artemis were married. There was practically no way anyone among the Huntresses or the Pack could entirely avoid members of either of their extended families.

"We have such larks in London." Eve grinned at the memory of a few of those adventures.

Mother dropped the last of the fish chowder ingredients into the pot over the fire, set the heavy lid over it, then turned back to them. "Have you a minute, Eve?"

"Of course." She walked with her mother out of the kitchen.

Edmund and Scuff ran past as the two women walked down the corridor. The boys were taller than either of their sisters, lanky, and so full of good-natured devilment.

"What are the two of you up to?" Mother asked.

In perfect singsong unison, the boys answered, "Nothing," and continued on their way.

"Strikes fear into the heart, that does," Eve said, grinning as she watched them go.

"They make it a difficult thing, imagining the two of them as gentlemen grown."

"For my part," Eve said, "I assume they'll be very much as they are now, only older. Still mischievous, still entertaining, still pulling each other into often-ill-advised adventures."

Mother looked down the corridor in the direction the boys had gone, though the space was empty now. "Life has a way of extinguishing sparks."

That was a heavier declaration than she usually made. The O'Doyles were known for laughing through difficulty, smiling through trouble. 'Twasn't dishonesty or pretended happiness. They took quite seriously the struggles they had and the reality of life. But laughing helped keep them going. Smiles kept them from abandoning hope.

"Has something happened?" Eve asked, studying her mother's unusually pensive expression.

"Let's gab a minute in the Royal Pavilion." Mother motioned to the door nearest them.

The family had long ago christened the absurdly tiny sitting room, one big enough only for two spindle-back chairs and a side table and nothing else, "the Royal Pavilion." Comparing a space so tiny to an ever-expanding palace so ornate that it was almost unfathomable was very much in keeping with the family's odd sense of the ridiculous.

When Mother closed the door behind them, Eve began to truly worry. "Now you have me fearing someone's dying or something," she said as she sat in one of the chairs.

Mother sat as well. "I'd not wanted to tell you this with Nia nearby. And your father and I had not wanted to send you to your house party with difficulties on your mind."

That was ominous. "*Máthair?*" she pressed when her mother didn't immediately continue.

"The cargo ship your father invested in has not reached any of the ports it was supposed to." Worry pulled at Mother's features. "Several others that departed *after* ours have already reached those ports and continued their journeys. We can only assume it has been lost at sea, along with all the linens and textiles aboard. I have been telling myself that the crew all managed to escape in rowboats or something of that nature and survived whatever catastrophe happened on board. I, of course, know that 'tisn't necessarily the case."

Eve's heart ached at the thought of so many lives lost. She did not take that lightly. But she also knew that the crewmen, whom she also hoped had somehow survived, were not the reason her mother had pulled her into the Royal Pavilion for a private discussion.

"If the ship never delivered any of its goods, then the investment is entirely lost?" Eve posed it as a question but felt certain she already knew the answer.

"Entirely, and with it all the money we invested and all we'd hoped to earn."

If the room weren't so shockingly small, Eve might have risen and paced, which was an odd inclination for her. "How bad is that loss going to prove for us?"

"Fortunately for us all, your father is willing to take risks, but he is not a gambler. He knew that even if this investment failed, we'd not be left destitute.

And without at least trying, our fortunes were unlikely to ever reverse." Mother's response was a little evasive.

"You needn't be afraid to tell me the truth of it. You know me well enough to know that about me, I hope."

At last, Mother offered a bit of a smile. "You've always preferred direct talk and interactions free of obfuscation. Your very sincere and open disposition did worry us a little when you first went to London. Town Society can be very . . . rejecting of those who don't bend when the *ton* demands it."

"We've Artemis to thank for Nia's and my not failing that first Season."

A very maternal sort of affection entered Mother's eyes for a moment. "I am grateful to Artemis for so many things. What an angel she has been."

Few in Society would describe Artemis Jonquil, née Lancaster, as an angel. In Eve's estimation, half the *ton* was intimidated by Artemis, and the other half was jealous. It was, of course, an oversimplification. But those who were fortunate enough to truly know Artemis were well aware of how remarkable she was.

"We aren't at risk of losing Tulleyloch or starving or anything truly horrific like that," Mother said. "But we need to eliminate a significant expense somewhere. Your father and I have discussed it up one way and back the other, and we've but two options. The first is to pull one of the boys out of school."

Eve shook her head. "They both have to find a profession, and neither is likely to manage it without an education, unless you send them into the army. But neither is the least suited to that."

"Their tuition and lodging are expensive," Mother said.

"But it is necessary." Eve, of course, knew that her parents understood that. Thinking out loud had always been her way when she was sorting something difficult. "What is the other option?"

An added measure of hesitancy filled Mother's expression. "We could save quite a lot, nearly half of what we currently spend, if only one of you girls has a London Season next year. Even then, it would be a very curtailed Season."

It was, in actuality, a logical and sensible solution. But the thought of either her or Nia not returning to London dropped like a weight on her heart.

"As the oldest," Mother continued, "it would be expected and entirely reasonable for you to be the sister who returns. No one would give that a second glance. And should you make a match, Nia could return the Season after that."

Eve hadn't made a match during the Seasons she'd had thus far. While she was not one to drown in discouragement because a hope hadn't yet borne fruit, she had to admit her chances of meeting, falling in love with, and marrying the

The Best-Kept Secrets

gentleman of her dreams grew slimmer each year. She would be twenty-two by the next Season. That didn't put her in the realm of old maid, by any means, but it tiptoed her in that direction.

Nia, on the other hand, was younger, and even that one year of additional youth was a helpful advantage.

"Am I correct in assuming you've brought this directly to me because you're wanting me to make the decision?" she asked.

"We wanted you to have the option to make the decision." 'Twas a small clarification, but one that filled the approach with consideration and kindness. "If you feel it's not something you'd like to decide, we'll not be the least upset with you, and we'll sort it out between the two of us."

"There's no need." Eve leaned toward her mother. "Nia needs to be the one who goes to London. She has a better chance of success than I do."

"I wish we didn't have to make this choice," Mother said.

Eve squeezed her mother's hand. "And I am simply grateful that we managed the Seasons we did with both of us in London, and I am doubly grateful that the boys can continue their schooling. Economizing is never a painless endeavor, but this family weathers every storm. We'll certainly manage this one."

Mother looked relieved, which lifted some of the weight from Eve's mind.

"And who knows?" her mother said. "We might, between now and the start of next Season, find ourselves with the income we need. Unlikely, perhaps, but I'm not willing to declare it impossible."

"I don't know, Mother. I've met your children, and I'm not certain they're well-behaved enough to qualify for such a drastic miracle."

Mother smiled, and Eve laughed lightly. The coming months and years would likely be difficult and, at times, a disappointment, but they could most certainly make the best of life, as they always did.

"We've one more thing to ask of you, Eve," Mother said. "And we're aware 'tis a difficult thing."

"What is it?"

"We'd rather Nia not know yet. Not that she ought to be lied to, mind. But we know she'd worry about this, and we'd rather it not dampen her enjoyment of the house party. And we'd rather you not spend the house party arguing with her about which of you's to remain home from London."

"I've not kept secrets from her before." The very idea made Eve uneasy.

"It'll not be forever. Only until you've returned home. That'll afford us time to explain to her, settle her worries, and make all the arrangements we need to take her to Town in the spring."

"If you and Father think it best, I'll not tell her."

After a fierce hug, Mother took the single step required to reach the door and slipped out.

Alone in the small space, Eve released a tight breath. Without a London Season anywhere on her horizon, her chances of making a match were sinking as fast as an ill-fated linen-laden ship. And an unmarried, unlikely-to-ever-be-married daughter of a household was a perpetual drain on a family's finances.

Marriage, love, and a home of her own seemed no longer her future.

Then, what was?

CHAPTER TWO

Writtlestone Manor, Lancashire

DUBHÁN SEYMOUR, KNOWN TO EVERYONE other than his parents and grand-mother as Duke, had completed his studies at Cambridge mere days earlier. He'd left that venerable institution with an admittedly pointless knowledge of Latin, a completed study in moral philosophy that promised to be equally as useless, and a group of friends who had utterly changed the course of his life for the better. It was on their behalf that he had already packed a small traveling trunk and was, in less than a half hour, leaving for Ireland.

"Must you depart so soon?" His mother had been in his bedchamber as he'd put a few things in a small bag to keep with him in the carriage despite the excessively early hour. "You only just returned home yesterday."

"I need to be in Dublin the day after tomorrow," he reminded her.

"Why could not one of the others fetch the O'Doyle sisters? You ought to be here with us for a few days more, especially as you will not be here at Christmas."

Duke set the last of his traveling things in the bag, then moved to sit on the bed beside his mother. "I am sorry to be missing Christmas, especially our annual gathering of greenery."

Mother leaned a little against him. "Who is going to help me choose the greenest branches and the reddest holly?"

"Father has an excellent grasp of color," Duke said.

"But gathering greenery has always been *our* special tradition, Dubhán. It will hardly feel like Christmas without having that time, just the two of us."

He put an arm around her shoulders. "Those are some of my favorite memories, Mother. I will miss that."

"And the Christmas goodies? You'll miss them as well. Your father and I cannot enjoy the gingerbread and shortbread and Christmas pudding nearly as much without you here."

Duke's home life wasn't always ideal, but Christmases were special. His parents were happier. *He* was happier. During those few weeks, he would build enough pleasant memories to get him through the difficult months that always followed. And in those enjoyable interactions, he'd found reason to believe his could be an amicable family. It was a hope he still clung to and leaned on.

"Could you not cut your house party short and return in time to have Christmas here?" Mother pleaded. "It is such a special time for our family."

"This is the last time our entire group will be able to be together, perhaps ever. Being away from our families during Christmastime is not ideal, but it was the only time all of us could gather."

"I, of course, don't wish for you to not see your friends. They have been good to you, which, as your mother, is so very important to me. Surely they would wish to continue being good friends to you by not taking you away from your parents during the holy season."

"This is only one Christmas."

"But Christmas is special, Dubhán. Please reconsider."

"We can have Christmas puddings and cakes and biscuits when I return."

"It won't be the same." Tears clogged her words.

"But we'll be together. That is the important thing." Duke always disliked the placating approach he had to take when Mother was inconsolable. But it was what worked. And not doing what she expected when she was upset simply made her more upset. "I will have all the rest of my Christmases here."

"Until you have a wife and her family wishes for your Christmases to be spent with them." Mother wasn't usually consoled on the first attempt; he ought to have expected further complaint. And predictions of her suffering when Duke eventually married numbered among the many reasons he didn't even entertain the idea of courting anyone. Any lady he brought into this whirlwind of familial wretchedness would be made miserable. "Her family will demand all your time and attention, and I will receive none of it. Marriage has a way of tearing families apart, after all."

"Most would argue that marriage *creates* families," Duke reminded her.

"Your aunt's marriage certainly tore your father's family to bits." Mother crossed her arms in a posture of disapproval. Duke could—and *did*—predict her exact next words. "And she doesn't even care."

"I don't imagine she would have married Uncle Niles if she didn't care."

The Best-Kept Secrets   11

"Of course she cares about *him*. But not about me and the difficulties I endure. She certainly doesn't care about your father. I suspect she has taken actual delight in our suffering these past thirty years."

"Mother, you haven't even known Father for thirty years." Duke immediately regretted the correction. His parents could be very defensive, regaling him with litanies of complaints, declarations of disloyalty, pointed silences that inevitably left him feeling deucedly guilty.

"Twenty-five years," she conceded in sharp tones. "Perhaps in five more years, my suffering will be considered sufficient for my own son to think I don't deserve to be miserable."

"That is not what I meant, Mother." Duke returned to his detestable tone of consolation in an effort to restore their more companiable conversation of a moment earlier. His parents were difficult when focused on their grievances. But when they felt appeased and heard and cared about, there was peace and a degree of closeness among them all. He preferred those times. "Twenty-five years is longer than anyone should spend being unhappy. I want you to be happy. I have always wanted you to be happy, Mother."

"Oh, Dubhán. You are so expert at giving me a measure of peace." Mother's voice quivered with emotion. "How very good you are at helping."

Being rubbish at it had never been a viable option. He was the ambassador, the peace negotiator, the one who redirected their declarations of injustice. He had been since he was very young, and he would continue to be for, he suspected, the rest of his life. But if it kept the household peaceful and afforded him pleasant times and memories with his parents, it was worth it.

"Do you truly have to leave today for Ireland?" Mother asked once again. Apparently, his reassurance a moment earlier that he loved her had not proven sufficient. "Could you not wait another day or more? My heart can't bear to have my only child leave me so soon after returning at last."

Starting the whole mad cycle anew, he repeated, "If I am to fetch the O'Doyle sisters and we are to reach Fairfield in time for the beginning of the house party, then I cannot wait even another hour."

From the doorway, Father said, "I still don't understand why Fairfield, of all places, was chosen. I assume Penelope convinced all of you that she and Niles would be better hosts than your mother and I could be."

Duke undertook an immediate change of tactic. While Mother responded best to repeated reassurances that her place in his life and esteem was sufficiently high, Father calmed fastest when provided with proof that in matters pertaining to his sister, he was not perpetually second best. "Newton and

Toss are in London, and neither can travel far or for long. We had to choose a location near Town."

"I suppose Lancashire *is* quite a distance to travel," Mother conceded.

"I assure you," Father said from far atop his high horse, "Lancashire was not my first choice." Then, under his breath, he added, "We ought to be living at Ballycar."

Ballycar had been the family estate until a few years before Duke was born. Father had fallen on financial difficulties—through no fault of his own, when he recounted the experience, *but* as a result of his poor choices, according to Aunt Penelope's recollections—and had lost the estate and the successful stud farm the Seymour family had run there for generations. Father blamed Aunt Penelope for not coming to the rescue at the time, her finances having been in a better state than his. Aunt Penelope insisted she'd not been as flush in the pockets at the time as Father had believed and that she had done nothing wrong in not trying to pay off all Father's debts.

Through years of listening to and then being required to mediate arguments about that point of contention, Duke had discovered that the Seymour family blamed each other for most every difficulty they'd had in life in the years that had followed.

"Surely someone else in your group lives at a convenient distance from London," Father said. "It didn't *have* to be Fairfield."

"Newton's flat is barely large enough for him and his wife. Toss and his wife live in another family's home while the family is away from Town and are not in a position to offer it for our use." Giving logical explanations for the slights Father felt in far too many aspects of his life helped soothe his wounded pride. For a while, at least. "Charlie is in Northumberland. Scott is in Nottinghamshire. Tobias is in Yorkshire. I am in Lancashire. None of those options is anywhere near London. Colm is the only one whose family home could work. That's why it was chosen."

"We could have returned to Town and let the same house we did during the Season," Father insisted.

"There are fifteen people attending. The London house wouldn't be large enough," Duke said. "Fairfield was chosen for purely practical purposes."

"I find that difficult to believe."

Of course he did.

"Do you truly think I wouldn't have objected if Fairfield were selected as a way of slighting our branch of the Seymour family?" Sometimes reminders of his past fealty helped ease contradictory accusations.

The Best-Kept Secrets   13

Father, at last, looked a little less offended. "You have always spoken in defense of us."

"And always will." It was, in many ways, a matter of survival.

Father's posture stiffened. "I trust you will do so again during this house party when your aunt inevitably begins belittling us to anyone who will listen."

Duke knew full well his aunt would do nothing of the sort. She had enough decorum to not air family grievances in public. Even in private, she was never the instigator of the family rows. She was seldom even a true participant, choosing instead to either silently endure the barbs aimed at her or to defend herself against them when the complaints didn't end in a timely manner.

"I will not allow you or Mother to be unkindly or unfairly treated," Duke promised. It was a promise he knew he could keep because they were seldom the *recipients* of unfair treatment from Aunt Penelope or Uncle Niles.

Father nodded firmly.

Hoping the topic was done with, at least for the time, Duke said, "I need to be on my way."

"I talked with Mrs. Smedley last night," Father said. "She won't be traveling with you to Dublin."

"Is she unwell?" Duke hadn't heard that his former governess had fallen ill or become injured.

Father shook his head and sat on the other side of Duke. "She is as hale as always."

Duke was relieved to hear that, but there was yet another difficulty. "I cannot undertake a several days' long journey in the exclusive company of two unmarried young ladies. Their reputations would be ruined, and I would gain one I'd rather not have."

"That is not what I'm suggesting, I assure you," Father said. "Your grandmother is journeying here from Dublin, having decided to do so with the intention of seeing *you*, but since you will not be here . . ."

Clearly, Duke was meant to piece together what came next, but his father had left too much unsaid to fully grasp his intent. Duke didn't have to wait long to learn the rest.

"As your holiday plans with your friends have robbed your grandmother of the opportunity to see you, which she is taking great pains to do," Father said, "you will travel with her from Dublin. That will afford her some time in your company. I cannot imagine you would deny your grandmother a few days with her grandson. And her presence in the carriage will lend the propriety you require for your journey with the O'Doyle sisters."

Duke shook his head. "Writtlestone is not at all on the way to Surrey. I cannot detour so far without—"

"I meant that you should take her with you *to Surrey*." Father then added with unnerving satisfaction, "To Fairfield."

Fairfield. Father hadn't revoked Duke's arrangement with Mrs. Smedley in order to give his mother time with her grandson but rather to cause Aunt Penelope consternation by sending their mother, unannounced, to her home, a mother who managed to regularly torment her children. Father's interference was an act of petty revenge that perfectly suited the decades-long family feud.

"Do Aunt Penelope and Uncle Niles know that Grandmother is coming to Fairfield?"

Father's mouth pulled tight. He arched an eyebrow. "She is Penelope's mother. What kind of daughter would be horrified at the idea of her mother visiting?"

The issue, if one were being fair, was not with the daughter but with the mother. But Father was never fair in matters involving his sister. And his evasive answer to Duke's question was all the answer Duke really needed.

"Will you at least send word to Fairfield that Grandmother is arriving so preparations can be made?"

Father's expression hardened. "I will write to your aunt when she writes to me, which she never does."

"By not telling her, you are requiring *me* to do so," Duke said.

"I have full faith in your ability to smooth things over. You are very good at that."

Did his family have any idea how exhausting it was to fill that role? He wanted his family to be at peace, to be happy together, but all his efforts felt, and often proved, insufficient.

"Does Grandmother know that I am fetching her?" Duke asked.

"No." That didn't seem to strike Father as odd or inappropriate.

"Does she know she is no longer traveling to Writtlestone?"

Father didn't answer. Duke looked to Mother.

"I spent countless days and endless effort attempting to prepare Writtlestone for her arrival. And the time was running so horribly short." Mother pressed a hand to her heart. "This change of plans has eased a tremendous burden on me, Dubhán. Do you begrudge me that?"

He took a breath and managed to keep hold on his patience. Frustration only ever made things worse. "If Grandmother doesn't know of her new destination,

The Best-Kept Secrets

one I suspect she will not approve of, how am I to convince her to make the journey?"

Father held a hand up. "You need only tell her that you are making the journey back to England with her. It is not untrue, and it will be less likely to inspire objections from her."

"I suspect she will notice when we don't depart Holyhead in the direction of Lancashire."

"The path is the same for quite some time." Father would have struggled to sound less concerned about the situation he was placing Duke in. "I suspect she won't realize until well after you have turned toward Surrey that the plans have changed."

"And that will be the point when I reveal that I have kidnapped my own grandmother at the behest of my father and am taking her to the home of her daughter, with whom she has a strained relationship?"

"Do not be flippant," Father said through tight teeth.

"You wouldn't say it like that, would you, Dubhán?" Mother's voice quivered. "Your grandmother would be livid. And you know how horridly she treats me when she is upset. I would be berated within an inch of my endurance. You would not do that to me, surely. Surely."

"I do not care to lie to my grandmother," Duke said. "But how do I manage this without lying and without Mother suffering a berating?"

"If you tell your grandmother about the change in her journey from the moment you see her in Dublin, she is unlikely to agree to go," Father warned. "And if she does not travel with you, then you cannot travel with the O'Doyle sisters to Surrey."

It wasn't, then, so much a kidnapping as it was a blackmailing. A lifetime of being manipulated and blamed and required to bear the burden of his unhappy family's temporary bouts of happiness had, somehow, not rendered this latest situation less surprising.

"I would have told your grandmother about this change of arrangements myself," Father said, "but I did not know of your journey to Ireland until you arrived last evening. And rather than struggle to scrape together the funds for your journey as well as my mother's, which I will remind you, she planned specifically with the intent of seeing *you*, I found it prudent to combine the two and lessen the strain on my finances."

They weren't poor, by any means, but they hadn't money enough for heedless spending. He could concede that point.

But there was another point he was unwilling to accept. "I will not bring my aunt Penelope an unannounced guest when she and Uncle Niles have already agreed to host fourteen others, a gathering of which I am a part and from which I will be benefiting. I will not further complicate the situation. But neither can I bring Grandmother here when I have given my word to bring the O'Doyle sisters to Surrey. That is unfair to them and would reflect horribly on my integrity."

That clearly gave his parents pause. They had their faults—plenty of them, in fact—but they had always encouraged him to be a person of honesty and to behave as a gentleman ought.

Duke pulled his pocket watch from his fob pocket and checked the time. "I am departing in ten minutes. Talk it through, and let me know the third option you have formulated before I must begin my journey."

He took up his traveling bag and snatched his leather gloves and tall beaver hat from the dressing table. He stepped from his bedchamber and walked down the corridor. He could hear his parents following behind, talking quietly. If he were remaining at Writtlestone for more than those ten minutes, he likely wouldn't have been so short with them.

But he didn't have time for the usual looping discussions. They would sort out an answer; they usually did when he insisted on it, though they were nearly always frustrated with him afterward.

Regardless, Duke didn't have the mental space to sort out *their* difficulty this time. He was plagued by a puzzle of his own, one he needed to keep entirely secret until he had answers. He'd intended to ponder it on the way to Ireland and further mull it over on the journey from Dublin to Surrey. Eve and Nia would likely gab with each other through most of their days on the road. And Mrs. Smedley would have spent those days with her nose in a book; his one-time governess was a prodigious reader.

But Grandmother would be with them instead, which meant Duke's time would be taken up with listening to a litany of complaints, attempting to prevent another Seymour family altercation, and doing his utmost to shield the O'Doyles from it all.

There would be very little time or energy remaining for him to sort out his own difficulties, ponder his own concerns, and, as a result, begin to lay the foundation of a future he could feel excited about.

A footman met him in the entryway with Duke's greatcoat and thick-knit scarf. He helped Duke pull the coat on before handing him the scarf, followed by his gloves and hat.

The Best-Kept Secrets 17

"Thank you, John." Duke wrapped his scarf around his neck. He pulled on his gloves. Taking time to breathe in silence had always helped him maintain his equilibrium and extend his endurance. He set his tall beaver hat on his head, then turned to face his parents, who had only just reached the bottom of the stairs. "Do you have a solution?"

Father nodded. "We will meet you in Epsom at the Wren and Badger. Your grandmother can return to Writtlestone with us, and you and the O'Doyle sisters can continue the hour or so to Fairfield, if that is what you choose to do in the end."

Duke dipped his head. "I will meet you at the Wren and Badger on the thirteenth."

It would, of course, have been far more convenient for Father to meet them at Holyhead or, better still, the village where the road to Surrey diverged from the road to Lancashire, bringing with him Mrs. Smedley to swap out for Grandmother. With a bit more time, Father might have stumbled upon that adjustment. Whether or not he would have chosen it was another matter entirely.

Being away at school as often as he'd been the past years had made Duke's time at home less draining. His parents were usually happy enough at his return that the limited time he'd spent there had been relatively pleasant. They'd taken walks around the grounds, visited the local village, reminisced about family holidays in Ireland and Scotland. And he'd usually returned to school or joined his friends in London before the situation had devolved too much. He loved his parents, but limiting the time he spent with them helped him remember that.

He kissed his mother's cheek and shook his father's hand; those were their usual departing gestures.

"Do not let your aunt berate you while you are at Fairfield," Mother said.

"I won't." Without the tension of warring siblings, his aunt and uncle's house had the potential to be peaceful. His parents' absence would allow Fairfield to be truly tranquil. He was counting on it.

"When Penelope inevitably speaks ill of me"—Father spoke through a tense jaw—"remember that you have promised to defend your parents."

Duke nodded.

There were no declarations of love as he climbed into the waiting carriage. He'd given up on those efforts years earlier. Even when his parents had returned said declarations, the effort had inevitably come with caveats. From the time he was a child, he'd told himself they did love him. He had enough nice memories with them to believe that he was cared about. But having every acknowledgment from them attached to requirements and spoken alongside doubts was harder to endure than not hearing the words at all.

The carriage pulled away from Writtlestone, and Duke slowly emptied his lungs. He had until his arrival in Dublin to think. But he knew it wouldn't likely be enough time. The puzzle he was sorting and the secret plans he was keeping were complex and fraught with potential pitfalls. But it was the only thing keeping him from losing all hope now that his time at Cambridge had come to an end.

He was journeying to Fairfield, which his parents considered enemy territory, and was doing so with every intention of finding a way of asking his aunt and uncle to let him stay indefinitely.

No matter the answer he received, if his parents heard of what he planned to do, they would never forgive him. And that would break his heart.

CHAPTER THREE

"Of all the members of the Pack, Mr. Seymour did seem to me the least likely to forget his traveling companions at a posting inn and not realize his mistake for several counties." Father walked beside Eve and Nia, their arms hooked through his, along the newly completed harbor at Dunleary, where they were meeting Duke. "But see if you two can't manage to make the lad smile between here and Surrey. He seemed to be in desperate need of it."

Father had met the members of the Pack very briefly during the last London Season. Eve's family was firmly ensconced in the gentry, but being Irish was a point against them in the eyes of far too many people in Society. That their financial woes had become almost impossible to hide had dealt their standing another blow. Eve had seen her father treated with arrogant dismissal, disdain, and indifference so significant that it felt dehumanizing. Even those a generation younger than he looked down on him.

But the Pack didn't.

If Eve hadn't already adored that group of gentlemen, she would have been utterly devoted to them for that. There was soul-deep goodness in every last one of them.

"We'll miss the two of you at Christmas," Father said.

"It'll be strange not being at home." Eve had thought on that often since the timing of the party had been decided upon.

"I think you mean 'it'll be *quiet* not being at home.'" Father had always enjoyed teasing, a trait all his children had inherited from him.

"No gathering of the Huntresses or the Pack is ever quiet," Nia countered. "Having both groups together?" She shook her head. "You're likely to hear us all the way from Surrey."

"A joy, that'd be." Father shifted his arms from being looped with theirs to wrapping them around their shoulders and tucking them closer. "I love you girls, you know."

In perfect unison, they said, "We know it."

This was a well-known exchange between them. Their father was not one to leave expressions of love unspoken.

"'Tis a difficult thing for a father, having his daughters grow up." He squeezed their shoulders. "I'll miss you when life takes you away from Tulleyloch and to a home of your own."

Father leaned a bit closer to Nia as he spoke the last bit. Eve suspected he didn't do so intentionally. But he knew that of his two daughters, only Nia was now likely to have a future home and family of her own.

Up ahead along the harbor sat an elegant enclosed carriage. The coachman sitting up front and the tiger standing in back wore perfectly matched livery. The carriage showed not a single sign of wear. Not a scratch marred its deep-red paint. This was a carriage carrying a person of class and distinction.

And standing beside it was Duke.

"Who'd he find to act as chaperone?" Eve said out the side of her mouth. "Queen Charlotte herself?"

Nia looked over at her and lifted an eyebrow. "Why do I feel as though we're about to wish 'twas the queen in that carriage?"

Father let out a low, quiet whistle. "I'm having a touch of that feeling my own self." But then he grinned at them. "Should be an adventure for you, girls."

They'd come near to where Duke waited for them. He offered a very polished bow, which they answered in the expected way.

"A pleasure to see you again, Mr. O'Doyle." Duke had a lovely voice, deep and rich. Eve had always liked it, which she'd felt an odd thing. It was not something she'd ever thought about anyone else.

"And you, Mr. Seymour." They shook hands. "If memory serves, you'll have only just finished your time at Cambridge."

Duke nodded slowly. "You have an impressive memory, sir."

Father shrugged. "I'm pleased to hear at least something about me's impressive." Though Father laughed, Eve suspected he meant the observation more than he let on. Their reversal of fortunes, his struggle to provide for his family, and their tepid reception in London likely all weighed down his view of himself.

"I am certain, sir," Duke said, "were I to ask your family, they could provide me with a list of impressive things about you."

Eve wrapped her arms around her father. "We most certainly could, *Athair*."

Father pulled them close once more, though he spoke to Duke. "These girls are precious to me, so you'll not be surprised when I ask you who it is that'll be looking after them on your journey to Surrey."

The Best-Kept Secrets   21

Looking far from offended or annoyed by the request, Duke dipped his head once more. He then motioned subtly to the carriage. "My grandmother will be making the journey with us."

His grandmother? Eve had not ever heard Duke speak of his grandmother.

Father, however, seemed truly impressed by the revelation, almost awed. "Your grandmother? Mrs. Margaret Seymour?"

"The very same." Duke didn't seem surprised that Father was a bit over-awed. "I cannot imagine anyone would question the propriety of our upcoming journey with her among us."

"Certainly not." The only other time Eve had seen her father so amazed by the mention of another person was when Artemis had first taken Eve and Nia under her wing and, as a result, into the social orbit of the preeminent and infamous Duke of Kielder. Did that mean Duke's grandmother was highly regarded or terrifying? Heavens, Eve hoped it was the former.

Duke checked his pocket watch. He rapped quickly on the carriage door before opening it. To his grandmother inside, he said, "It is time to make our way to the ship."

From within, a very proper, very English-sounding voice said, "I do not care to be standing about in the cold."

"You will be *walking* about in the cold," Duke said, his voice even and his tone one of equanimity. "Surely that must be an improvement."

"Hardly."

Eve exchanged glances with Nia. Their chaperone seemed in less-than-ideal spirits.

"Mr. O'Doyle is here with his daughters."

For some reason, that declaration convinced his grandmother to step from the carriage. Duke helped her with a very masculine grace. His grandmother emerged with an air that leaned more toward aristocratic than merely mannerly.

She wore a flawless, thick reddingote in a deep shade of indigo, with intricate black embroidery details perfectly matched to her black gloves and tall, black bonnet with a large, curling feather in the same indigo as the coat. Artemis, an undisputed arbiter of fashion, would have approved of the ensemble.

Once the older lady had both feet on the ground, Duke pressed on with the matter at hand. "Grandmother, this is Mr. O'Doyle of Tulleyloch in Fingal, and his daughters, Miss O'Doyle and Miss Nia O'Doyle." He then looked at Father, Eve, and Nia and said, "This is my grandmother, Mrs. Seymour of Dublin."

Mrs. Seymour dipped her head a little—a *very* little. Father answered with a deferential bow. Eve managed a curtsy without laughing, though it took effort.

Nia appeared to be struggling in the same way. Overtly pompous displays had always struck them as entertainingly absurd.

The regal *grande dame* eyed them both with an analyzing air. "Are they twins?" The question, Eve could only assume, was directed to the lady's grandson.

Duke must have come to the same conclusion, as he was the one who answered. "They are not twins, and neither are they unable to answer questions."

Mrs. Seymour's lips pursed a bit before her expression relaxed and assumed a more civil set. She turned toward Duke. "I am allowing myself to be petulant again, I fear."

While Duke didn't smile, something in his eyes leaned a bit in that direction. "I have full faith in your impeccable gentility, Grandmother."

The very picture of elegant etiquette, Mrs. Seymour addressed Father. "We will make certain your daughters arrive safely in Surrey."

He dipped his head. "Thank you, Mrs. Seymour."

"Sir," Duke said, "would you be so good as to accompany my grandmother to the ship?"

"Of course." Father offered the lady his arm, showing himself to be as versed in social decorum as any Society gentleman, no matter that they did not always give him credit for being so. The two of them walked slowly toward the waiting ship a few yards down the harbor.

Duke looked to Eve and Nia. "Were your traveling trunks already taken to the ship?"

Trunk*s*, he had said. Plural.

"We've only one trunk between us, and it *is* on board already," Eve said. "Our reticules we've chosen to lug about with us." She raised the hand on which hung her drawstring bag.

If he was shocked by their lack of possessions, he didn't allow even a hint of it to show in his face. He simply nodded and motioned for them to begin walking with him toward the ship.

"Thank you for arranging all this," Eve said. "We'd not have been able to make the journey otherwise."

"The Huntresses bested the Pack quite soundly in last Season's competition. Though I feel I must point out, I was not present for the majority of it, which is likely why we lost."

"And yet, you are the one making good on their debt." Nia sighed quite dramatically.

"I am a saint among men," Duke said dryly.

The Best-Kept Secrets   23

Eve grinned. He had a very subtle sense of humor, one she'd seen emerge now and then when their groups had gathered together. "I have never traveled in the company of a saint before. These next few days ought to be . . . heavenly."

"I should likely warn you about the next few days." Duke's eyes settled on his grandmother stopped just ahead at the point where they would be boarding the ship to take them across the Irish Sea. "My grandmother is not overly happy about this arrangement."

Oh dear.

"Does she not wish to go to England?" Nia asked.

"She'd been planning to, actually. My father was to accompany her directly to our family estate in Lancashire, but he changed the plan in what was, almost literally, the last possible minute. She is not best pleased."

"With your father?" Eve guessed aloud.

"With me, unfortunately."

They'd nearly reached the boarding spot. "Why with you?"

"Shoot the messenger, as it were."

Nia tipped her chin at a defiant angle. "We will not allow her to shoot the messenger."

"And why is that?" he asked.

Eve answered, knowing by instinct what Nia's response would be. "Because the messenger is our only means of getting to this house party."

He didn't smile, let alone laugh, but Eve thought she saw a glimmer of amusement in his eyes.

See if you girls can't manage to make the lad smile between here and Surrey, Father had said. What would it take to get him to not merely smile but to grin as well? An unabashed expression of enjoyment and mirth?

Duke accompanied his grandmother across the short, temporary bridge between the ship and the dock.

Father hugged Nia and Eve in turn. "Enjoy yourselves, girls. Be happy and delighted, and look after each other."

"We will," Nia said as she stepped from the dock and toward the ship.

"Try not to let your mind be heavy," Father said to Eve in quieter tones. "I have not abandoned hope of things turning around for us."

Father always had been very hopeful and optimistic, even in the face of unbeatable odds. He wasn't careless nor foolish, but neither was he easily defeated.

"Something will work out, Father," Eve said. "It always does."

CHAPTER FOUR

No one had thrown anyone overboard during the fifteen-hour journey across the Irish Sea. Duke claimed that as a victory, considering members of his own extended family were often sorely tempted to do precisely that to each other when in each other's company for any length of time. Either the O'Doyle sisters were very patient, or they were plotting a more sinister demise for Grandmother and, quite possibly, for him.

The inn in which they'd eaten a filling supper and would be passing the night before resuming their journey struck the perfect balance between cozy and efficient. Had Father not changed the participants in this journey, Duke could have used the quiet and uncomplicated evening to rehearse the conversation he needed to have with his aunt and uncle upon reaching Fairfield. There were so many ways it could go wrong, and he needed to be prepared for all of them.

Instead, addressing Grandmother's complaints, soothing her ruffled feathers, and shielding Eve and Nia from the bitterness he knew his grandmother was entirely capable of monopolized his time.

"I don't suppose you could have found an inn in Holyhead that serves a meal more sophisticated than potato and leek stew." Grandmother hadn't hidden her disapproval during the meal and still hadn't tired of the topic as they all sat in the comfortable, private dining room, warming themselves by a low-burning fire in a very simple fireplace.

"Cold weather calls for hot, filling meals," Duke said as placatingly as he could manage without sounding patronizing. "The stew was a good choice."

Grandmother was undeterred. "The bread was stale. And the butter crock was only scantily filled. I certainly hope you did not pay anything more than pennies for our stay here, Dubhán. Your father often overpaid for lodging despite my warnings. My children do not always listen to me, though they ought."

"I have paid a fair price for our lodgings, Grandmother, I assure you."

She eyed him more narrowly. "And you do know what a fair price would be? Your father has not always been wise in financial matters."

Out of the corner of his eye, Duke saw Eve and Nia exchange glances. He was accustomed to conversations like this; his parents and grandparents regularly aired their endless grievances to him. But Eve and Nia ought not be subjected to it.

He knew how to stave off Grandmother's complaints every bit as well as he did his parents'. "You have endured much," he said to her, "and with impeccable gentility. I find myself reassured that should anything else less than ideal occur during this journey, we can all depend upon your unwavering civility to ease the way."

Grandmother sat a bit straighter and dipped her head in acknowledgment of the compliment she clearly felt was her due.

In the silence that followed, Duke attempted to turn the conversation. To the O'Doyle sisters, he said, "We will be making an early start in the morning."

Grandmother spoke before either sister could manage even a syllable in response. "Do you suppose the linens will be overly rough? So long a day of travel will be made far more difficult to endure if we have not slept well."

"Your abigail arrived ahead of us, and she has, I do not doubt, been working to secure your comfort," Duke said.

"Weaving the linens her own self, most likely," Eve said quite seriously.

So many Irish families with aspirations and connections in English Society abandoned their accents. Duke very much liked that the O'Doyles had not. Every syllable spoke of their Irish roots.

Grandmother quickly changed topics. "Will you have your own horses for the journey tomorrow, Dubhán, or are we using a hired team?" Grandmother clearly disliked the second possibility.

"We will be using the Writtlestone team waiting for us here," Duke said.

"A *matched* team?" Grandmother pressed.

"They pull well together, but they are not identical."

Grandmother nodded. "For long journeys, a team's ability to work together is more important than its appearance."

"That is very true," Nia said. "You clearly have an understanding of horses, Mrs. Seymour."

"I should certainly hope so. I spent much of my adult life at Ballycar in County Wicklow."

The Best-Kept Secrets 27

"Ballycar?" Nia was instantly enthralled, and Grandmother, Duke knew, would take up the topic with alacrity. The family's former estate and the impressive horses that had once been bred there were a subject on which she could—and *did*—unabashedly brag.

Duke lowered himself onto the well-maintained sofa, grateful for a moment's reprieve from his usual task of keeping his grandmother placated. To his surprise, Eve sat next to him.

"You look worn to a thread, Duke," she said quietly. "Are you worried your linens will be unbearably rough?"

"It is all I can think about."

She grinned at his dry response. Not everyone recognized his humor, but she had from their first introduction. It was one of the things about her that he'd been intrigued by during the house party the previous year. She was clever and funny, intelligent and kind. And beautiful.

"You've finished at Cambridge," she said, pulling him back to the moment.

He nodded. "Only just."

"What did you study?"

"Moral philosophy." He'd known upon choosing the focus of his studies that it was not an obviously useful one. Plenty of people questioned what could possibly have motivated him to pick that emphasis. And he couldn't explain it without laying bare the misery in his family.

"Now you will be a morally philosophical gentleman of leisure?" Clearly, Eve was amused at the idea, yet nothing even hinted at mockery.

"Only imagine how tedious that gives me leave to be," Duke said. "I will spend my days judging others' morality and life choices, likely disapproving of the way they run their estates while not having one of my own, and sauntering about Town, loudly declaring my philosophical judgments."

"You sound eminently qualified to be a spinster, Duke. You are old, have no home of your own, and have no occupation. It's the perfect fit."

"I *am* one and twenty," he pointed out.

In a tone dry as week-old bread, she said, "Ancient."

"I am suddenly suspecting that you might be equally ancient."

Eve pressed a hand to her heart. "How very uncouth of you to suggest such a thing."

"If you are as aged as I, we might combine efforts and open a home for ancient people without estates or occupations," he said. "No applicants under twenty-one need apply. Philosophical judgment would be an added consideration."

"Can you guarantee our days will be spent listening to people complain about stew, linens, and the weather?" Eve asked hopefully.

"Complaints? What could possibly have put the idea of complaints into your mind?"

In a bit of painfully perfect timing, Grandmother's voice carried over to them. "The sky was quite leaden this evening. No doubt, it will rain mercilessly tomorrow. We will all be rendered utterly wretched."

Duke slowly shifted his gaze from his grandmother to Eve. She was biting her lips closed, a clear attempt to hold back a laugh.

"Will you promise me you won't murder her before we reach Surrey?" Duke asked.

"Very well, but the moment we cross into that county . . ." She held her hands up as if to wash them of all responsibility for what would happen.

Duke had never known anyone else with eyes that could be described as silver, but the O'Doyle sisters fit the description. And Eve's were unique even beyond that: a dark ring around the edge of the iris, a sparkle that never seemed to dim, a depth that drew a person in. He'd managed not to stare at her during their friends' previous house party or his very brief visit to London during the past Season. It had been a difficult thing though.

He didn't stare now, but he did watch her, curious and intrigued and confused by the pull he'd felt from their very first meeting. That he couldn't sort it out, he who was known for sorting out *everything*, made the mystery all the more compelling.

"Eve, Mrs. Seymour tells me Fairfield has dozens upon dozens of horses," Nia said.

Eve sighed dramatically. "And we've left our saddles at home. All hope is lost."

Then they laughed.

Eve's eyes crinkled at the outer corners when she laughed that way. And the faintest of dimples appeared to the right of her upturned lips.

Don't stare, Duke. He looked away, but that placed his focus on Grandmother. It was just as well; he needed to fend off difficulties tomorrow, an effort that had to begin tonight, which meant he absolutely would not have time to work on his strategy for Fairfield.

Convincing Grandmother to retire for the night was a crucial part of that. "You need to rest, Grandmother. Tomorrow will be a very long day, and we will depend so much on your equanimity to maintain our own."

The Best-Kept Secrets

"Many people have." Grandmother stood very regally. "I assume you will be accompanying me to my room, Dubhán, as a guard against my being accosted by ruffians on my way."

Duke stood as well. "I have seen nothing at this inn that leads me to believe it is overrun with ruffians."

"It needn't be *overrun*," Grandmother countered. "It takes only one to be accosted."

"She is not wrong," Eve said.

Duke turned his head slowly to look at her, feigning shock.

"I know." She pressed a hand to her heart. "Save it for Surrey."

Those silver eyes danced about. He didn't dare let himself be distracted though. Grandmother could be unbearable when she felt she was not receiving the attention she was owed.

"Let us see you settled, Grandmother."

He led her from the private dining room, the sound of the O'Doyle sisters' laughter echoing after them. This journey would have been an endless stream of entertainment had Grandmother not been made part of it, even with the familial difficulty that awaited him at the end.

One benefit, if he could call it that, of being in company with his grand-mother for the next few days, was the inescapable reminder of *why* he needed to make the precarious request of his aunt and uncle.

If he made his home with his parents, he would spend decades fielding their complaints and soothing their hurt feelings. The difficult moments would far outnumber the pleasant ones if he were never away from his parents. He cherished the happy memories he had with them, even if they were fewer and farther between than he wished. If he had any hope of making more, he needed an escape from Writtlestone. Though his parents frustrated and upset his aunt when they were together, he had enough experience with his aunt and uncle, during visits to London, when they were *not* in company with his parents, to know that they were otherwise very peaceful people.

And he needed some promise of peace.

CHAPTER FIVE

Eve and Nia retired to the simple but tidy bedchamber they had been assigned at the inn. Having already helped each other dress for bed, they were now laying out their clothes in preparation for an early departure the next morning.

"Mrs. Seymour would certainly have a lot to say were she to realize we are acting as each other's abigails." Nia flashed the wide grin the O'Doyles were well-known for.

In her best imitation of an extremely sophisticated English accent, Eve said, "This is shocking! I cannot countenance making this journey with two such shocking people."

They laughed, a sound Eve had grown up surrounded by.

Nia shook her head. "Poor Mrs. Seymour never seems anything but disgruntled with everyone and everything."

"And poor Duke as well," Eve added. "He is, no doubt, used to her bemoanings, but he clearly doesn't enjoy the experience. He looked worn down after only one day of this journey."

"Do you suppose he'll murder her before we reach Fairfield?" Nia turned to look at Eve with theatrically wide eyes.

"No, because he specifically asked me not to do so."

"What if he made his request only so you don't rob him of the opportunity?"

Assuming her aristocratic English accent once again, Eve said, "Shocking!"

With everything ready for the next day, Eve crossed the cold wood floor and climbed into the very inviting bed. She scooted down under the blanket. "You will be relieved to know the linens are not overly rough."

Nia laughed once more as she brought the candle over and set it on the bedside table, then climbed slowly and carefully under the blankets as well.

"What were you and Duke talking about?" Nia asked. "You seemed to be enjoying the topic, whatever it was."

"I told him he would make an excellent spinster."

"You *what*?" The question emerged as a sputter.

"He is twenty-one, unattached, and hasn't a house of his own." Eve pulled the blanket all the way up to her neck, grateful for the warmth. "I believe that makes him a prime candidate for spinsterhood."

"And you told him as much?"

"You know perfectly well that I have a very difficult time *not* saying the things that jump into my mind. It spilled out before I could stop myself."

She could feel the bed shake a bit as Nia laughed. "And what was his response?"

"He joined in the jest. I thought, for the length of a breath, that he might even smile. Father would have been proud."

"Since Duke *almost* smiled, I think we can safely say that Father would be *almost* proud of you."

"I cannot leave it at that. I am determined that Father will be completely proud of me by the time we return to Tulleyloch."

"And leave me as the daughter in whom he is disappointed?" Nia scoffed. "I shall simply have to make Duke smile as well."

"Do," Eve said. "With his grandmother being so vexing, I suspect he will appreciate having a reason to smile, even if he doesn't allow himself to actually do it."

"You think he *chooses* not to smile?" Nia asked.

"I'm not certain. But I don't think he's actually an unhappy person, and he does have a sense of humor. There must be some reason why he doesn't smile." It broke her heart a little to think of the possible reasons why: past sorrows, grief, overwhelming worries.

"When we get to Fairfield," Nia said, "we should corner Charlie and torment him until he tells us."

"I doubt Artemis will allow us to torment Charlie."

"Artemis torments him all the time," Nia insisted.

Eve grinned. "Yes, but he enjoys it when *she* does it."

Nia blew out the candle. The bed moved a little as she settled in.

"I still can hardly believe all the Huntresses and the Pack will be together again," Eve said. "It is a dream come true."

"And I think everyone will be in London at some point during the Season," Nia said. "What larks we will all have together."

The Best-Kept Secrets

"Sounds perfect." It would be utterly brilliant. And she wouldn't be there for any of it.

As she lay in bed, warm and comfortable, her mind was not entirely tranquil. There were so many things she would miss, so many people and connections and experiences she would eventually have to grieve. But so long as the changed future she now faced was required to be kept secret, she had to pretend as if everything were as it had once been.

CHAPTER SIX

THEY WERE HALFWAY THROUGH THEIR first full day in the carriage, and Duke was beginning to ponder the very real possibility of tossing himself out onto the roadside, risking injury for the chance to escape.

"I am not one to complain"—Grandmother made the declaration without the slightest hint of irony—"but it was rather thoughtless of your father to insist that I make a journey several days longer than I had anticipated. He ought to have kept to the original arrangements and permitted me to journey directly to Writtlestone."

Duke most certainly agreed with that. "Let us hope he arranges direct journeys for you from now on." His hopes on the topic were firmly built on the need to keep Grandmother from detouring to Fairfield, where Duke had every intention of being, and that when she did journey to her daughter's home, it would always come with ample warning so he could make himself scarce for the duration of her visit. Perhaps those would be ideal times for him to make brief visits home. His parents might welcome him back if they saw his albeit temporary return as a show of loyalty to them and disapproval of the extended family.

"I intend to confront your father about this disloyalty," Grandmother declared.

"What disloyalty?" He couldn't entirely keep the sudden hint of panic out of his voice. Surely Duke hadn't given away his plan.

Grandmother pursed her thin lips and tipped her chin defiantly. "He has subjected me to unnecessary suffering. He should know how unfairly he is treating his mother."

She was, then, upset about what she saw as *Father's* betrayal, not Duke's upcoming perfidy. Lud, he hoped he could manage to make his end goal less of a mess than it seemed destined to be.

You've navigated complicated situations with your family before, he reminded himself. *You'll manage to do so again.*

"He owes me an explanation as well," Grandmother said. "One does not cause such consternation to one's family without explaining oneself to that family."

Duke was hearing the very complaints that would soon be lodged against *him*, the same denouncements, the same upbraiding. He felt certain his only chance of maintaining a relationship of any kind with his parents was to put distance between himself and them. Yet they would, without question, castigate him for doing so. It was very discouraging.

"Does my son not care that I am being subjected to a much longer journey than I would otherwise have endured? Am I so unvalued as a mother that such a thing seemed perfectly reasonable?"

When Grandmother's complaints shifted toward pointed questions about the possibility of being a dismal mother, Duke knew he was expected to redirect. Unfortunately, he'd found over the years that taking some of the blame on himself worked best. "Father likely would have kept to the original arrangements except that *I* needed to make a journey as well. There would be a great deal more expense in two separate journeys occurring at the same time, something I ought to have considered sooner."

She pondered that a moment and seemed a little appeased. "He has had to be rather careful in financial matters these past years. That, of course, can be laid at Penelope's feet." Duke subtly mouthed the next phrase in perfect synchronicity with his grandmother. "Selfish girl."

"Aunt Penelope is not responsible for Father's difficulties," Duke said.

"She might not have caused them, but she most certainly didn't help when his situation grew precarious."

Duke hadn't been old enough when this bit of family history had occurred to know all the details, but the versions he'd heard from his father, his grandmother, and his aunt did not match. He'd more or less sorted out which bits of truth existed in which retelling of events. But truth was not usually the highest consideration in decades-old quarrels.

"I know that was a very difficult time for you," Duke said.

"The estate that had been my home was taken from our family." Grandmother sniffed. "My son lost his inheritance, and my daughter allowed him to lose it. *Difficult* does not begin to describe my experience."

Duke glanced at their traveling companions. Nia was sitting beside Grandmother on the forward-facing bench. Eve was seated beside him. Neither could

The Best-Kept Secrets   37

possibly have not overheard the conversation, but they were doing a very fine job of hiding any reaction.

Looking at the sisters proved a horrible idea, as Grandmother's attention shifted to them as well. And with her attention came scrutiny.

"I have heard the name Eve before, obviously, but I am not familiar with Nia. Where did your parents find your names?" Asking about a person's name was not unusual or rude, but somehow, Grandmother managed to make the question feel a bit insulting.

"They are our Anglicized names," Eve said. "Too many in English Society cannot comprehend that Aoife is pronounced *EE-fuh* and Niamh is pronounced *NEE-uv*. Rather than explain again and again and *still* hear our names constantly misspoken, the entire family has adopted versions of our names that are simpler for our English associates to manage."

Grandmother turned to look at Nia. "Your name is Niamh? From Irish mythology?"

Nia nodded.

"I've not ever heard that used as a given name."

Nia didn't flinch or look embarrassed. "It was a given name in mythology."

Grandmother shook her head. "But you aren't living in a myth, are you?"

In a quiet, dry voice, Eve said, "At the moment, I'd be more inclined to call it a tragedy."

Duke bit back his amusement. His grandmother's sense of humor was not very reliable. If she thought he was amused at her expense, she would be impossible to endure for days to come.

To him, Grandmother said, "Your aunt and uncle call you Duke."

"Nearly everyone calls me that."

She was unmoved. "But it is not your name."

"I have heard every possible attempt at saying my actual name, but almost never is it actually pronounced *DU-vahn*. And no one can ever spell it. I, too, have chosen to make my name easier on my English friends and neighbors."

Grandmother was quick with a counterargument. "Penelope is Irish. She can say your name. She's simply choosing not to."

"I have never asked her not to call me Duke. If I did, I am certain she would honor that." If only he were equally certain she would say, "Why, yes, Duke, you may stay at Fairfield, no matter that it will make all our lives more difficult."

More difficult. His entire motivation in formulating this plan was to escape some of the difficulty that awaited him at Writtlestone, to preserve what was left of his relationship with his parents.

Grandmother's lips pursed again, a telltale sign that she was about to lodge another complaint. "Your uncle certainly took very quickly to the odd name you adopted."

His uncle Niles had inspired Duke's choice of Anglicized name. But explaining that would require him to spill a secret that was not his to share.

"Penelope ought to have married an Irishman." Grandmother offered the declaration with an indisputable note of finality.

Duke was more than happy to leave the topic there, knowing Grandmother would add to her list of objections to Uncle Niles if given even the tiniest encouragement. She would have found reason to denounce anyone her children married. That same disapproval would, without question, be extended to any lady unfortunate enough to marry either of her grandsons.

"Mrs. Seymour," Eve said, "we met your grandson Mr. Colm Greenberry in London during the Season. He is a very-well-thought-of gentleman."

Duke silently said right along with Grandmother, "Colm is a war hero."

She likely would have launched into the usual recitation of Colm's accomplishments and the myriad ways in which he had made the family proud had not a well-timed carriage stop prevented it.

"It appears we have reached our midday stop." Duke shrugged as if it hardly mattered, but inwardly he wanted nothing more than to bolt from the carriage. "We can step inside the inn for something to eat and to claim a momentary respite from the carriage."

Grandmother pulled back the curtain on the window nearest her. Her mouth tightened into a wrinkled circle. "I do not care for the look of it. I will stay in the carriage."

Duke wasn't going to argue. "I can bring you back something to eat."

"That will be fine." She folded her hands on her lap and sat still as a statue.

Duke kept his demeanor calm and unconcerned as he opened the carriage door. He stepped down. He took a lungful of fresh air. Past experience had taught him that a moment away from his ambassadorial role helped him face more of it. He put down the carriage step, then assisted the O'Doyle sisters from the carriage.

He accompanied Eve and Nia across the inn yard.

"Thank you for your patience," he said. "I am certain this has not been the quietly pleasant journey you would have preferred."

"I don't think either of us has ever been on a *quiet* journey," Eve said. "And we've become adept over the years at ignoring happenings we'd rather pretend aren't part of the experience."

The Best-Kept Secrets

"I am not in a position to ignore those things, I am afraid."

"She is your grandmother," Eve said. "Ignoring her expressions of unhappiness would, naturally, be difficult for you."

Somehow, Eve had managed to make him sound almost heroic instead of pathetic.

"I don't want her to give you a wrong impression of my aunt and uncle before you've even arrived at their home. They are good people. The very best, in fact. Families are . . ." How to finish the explanation?

Eve threaded her arm through his in a friendly and encouraging way. "Complicated," she finished for him.

"Precisely." He looked to Nia walking on his other side. "If you need a respite from sitting beside my grandmother, I can attempt to convince her to move to the rear-facing bench."

Nia shook her head without hesitation. "I don't mind."

They stepped into the inn, and the proprietor greeted them quickly and warmly.

"Mr. Seymour," Duke identified himself. "I sent word requesting arrangements be made for a meal."

"Yes, Mr. Seymour. Yes, of course." The proprietor dipped his head. "I've put it in a basket for you."

"Excellent."

The proprietor turned to go, but Eve stopped him. "Have you a newspaper?"

He looked back. "I do. From London, though it's a week out-of-date."

"Might we take it with us?" she asked.

"If you'd like."

"We would."

He left to go fetch all they'd requested.

Eve turned to Duke, smiling broadly. "There you are, then."

"Why a newspaper?" he asked.

"I assumed you were so desperate for news from London that you would find yourself tucked behind the newspaper for hours and hours and hours."

Ah. "You are providing me with an escape."

"One that is unlikely to put your grandmother's back up." Eve dipped an exaggerated curtsy. "You're welcome."

Shaking his head in amazement and amusement, Duke said, "Where have you been the last twenty-one years, Eve O'Doyle?"

With a grin that lit her silver eyes, she said, "Ireland."

CHAPTER SEVEN

MRS. SEYMOUR HAD FALLEN ASLEEP, making the afternoon hours of their first full day in the carriage far more peaceful than they would have been otherwise. Nia had drifted off as well. Eve was certain Duke was not sleeping behind his newspaper. But he had grown so much more relaxed after his grandmother had gone to sleep that Eve had been very careful not to disrupt his momentary respite.

She'd brought a book with her on the journey and had been enjoying it. But the light spilling in through the windows was growing too dim to continue reading. The strain of trying to make out the words was beginning to make her head ache. She suspected Duke would, at any moment, abandon his efforts to read his newspaper.

The ribbon she'd been using to mark her place in the book had, at some point, fallen off her lap. She didn't see it on the floor or on the bench beside her. It must have fallen into the gap between the bench and the wall.

She slipped her hand into the gap. Her fingers found the ribbon, but when she curled them around it, something sharp stabbed her smallest finger. She quickly pulled her hand free once more. The ribbon fluttered onto her lap, and blood oozed from her wound.

Keeping her voice low so as not to awaken their companions, she said, "Duke, do you have a handkerchief?"

He lowered his paper. "I do." He reached into his breast pocket.

She cupped her other hand beneath the bleeding one, ready to catch any blood that dripped off.

"What happened?" Rather than simply give her the handkerchief, he took her injured hand in his.

"There is something sharp over here. I didn't see what."

He wrapped his handkerchief around her bleeding finger and held tight to her finger, pressing hard but not truly painfully. "You didn't make a sound."

"I didn't want to wake our traveling companions."

"I can't say I blame you for that." The poor man looked embarrassed.

"There's a woman who lives in the village not far from Tulleyloch," she said. "Anyone who happens past her home while she's watching will receive an earful, an extensive recounting of everything that ails or vexes her."

Duke's mouth twisted a little. "That sounds familiar."

"One of the times I found myself caught listening to her, I realized something."

He loosened his hold on her finger, studying the handkerchief wrapped around it. "What did you discover?"

"That she was lonely. She'd no one there to see her struggles and know what difficulties she'd passed through. That makes a person feel very . . . invisible."

Duke pressed her finger once more, even as his gaze slid to his grandmother, still sleeping. "She doesn't have any family in Ireland any longer, and she has a difficult relationship with her children. A lot of her friends have passed away. She likely is a little lonely."

"That realization didn't mean I suddenly enjoyed being harangued with all the complaints the poor woman in the village could toss at me," Eve said, putting her ribbon in her book with her free hand. "Being miserable doesn't excuse treating others poorly. But I found I could be a little more patient with her."

He looked back at Eve once more. "Is that how you have managed to endure my grandmother as well as you have?"

"That, and I am a saint among women."

Duke didn't smile, but heavens, if he didn't look as though he was about to.

"Did you find the ribbon for your book?" he asked.

"It's in my book."

"I understand and fully concur with the wrath that quickly descends upon a person who removes an item marking a reader's place in a book," Duke said, "but I think your finger needs the ribbon more than your book does."

She pulled the ribbon from her book and handed it to him. He tied it around the handkerchief, pulling it tight enough to replace the pressure his fingers had provided.

Duke opened a compartment in the carriage wall beside him and pulled out a stoneware jug.

"While I agree your grandmother's made this a difficult day for you," Eve said with a laugh, "I don't know that hard cider is quite the right thing just now."

The Best-Kept Secrets

He looked back at her, and that same twinkle of an unexpressed smile touched his eyes. "It's water."

"*Inside* the carriage?" She'd never heard of such a thing. Barrels of water were often strapped to the outside but could be tapped only during pauses in the journey.

"I've found having a bit of water inside to be a helpful thing." He then pulled a small tin cup from the same compartment. With a fluidity born, no doubt, of experience, he uncorked the jug and poured water into the tin cup without spilling any despite the carriage's bumping and rocking on the uneven road. He held the cup out to her. "You've cleared your throat a few times in the past fifteen minutes. I suspect you're thirsty."

She gladly accepted it—with her *un*injured hand, naturally. "Do you always address people's difficulties this efficiently?"

Without any indication of jesting or embarrassment, he answered, "I do." He replaced the cork and returned the jug to its compartment.

Eve took a small sip of water. Duke took gentle hold of her injured finger once more, examining the handkerchief bandage.

"Has it bled through?"

"No," he said. "So we may not have to amputate, though I will make no guarantee."

She smiled at him over her tin cup. "What a relief."

Duke sat back once more, but he didn't take up his newspaper. It was too dim for reading now.

"Was there anything interesting in your paper?" she asked.

"Not really," he said. "Parliament recently reconvened in London to address the Peterloo Massacre. But this paper is too out-of-date to include any new information on that matter."

"Do you have an interest in political matters, or did the topic draw your attention because Peterloo occurred in your home county?"

"Both," he said.

She took another sip of water. "Do you mean to enter politics now that you are finished at Cambridge?"

"No."

"But it does interest you?"

"Yes, but a man must own land to stand for a seat in the House of Commons."

Ah. Duke would someday inherit his family's estate, but that did not permit him to pursue a parliamentary career now. "Would you pursue it otherwise?"

"Are you worried about my future, Eve?" He didn't sound offended.

"I like the idea of someone being able to claim a dreamed-of future. I'm hoping there is a way for you to be that person."

"Why would that person not be *you*?" he asked.

"Because I have the unfortunate tendency to dream of impossible things."

Duke's gaze turned studying. "What impossible dream are you nursing currently?"

She shook her head. "I believe I will break with my usual approach and, instead, keep my mouth shut."

"I am a good listener, if ever you do want to talk."

In what amounted to an immediate abandonment of her declaration mere moments earlier, she blurted out a thought as it entered her mind. "Guess."

"You'd like me to attempt to ascertain what you dream of in your future?"

"I would very much like for you to." In her excitement, she motioned broadly with both arms, accidentally splashing a bit of water on her face. "Ah, the state of me." With one hand holding a cup and the other sporting a bandaged finger, she wasn't certain how to address the situation she'd created.

Duke brushed the cuff of his jacket along her cheek, wiping away the water. There was nothing truly romantic or tender in the gesture, yet her heart skipped a beat. He wasn't actually touching her, but he was studying her with his sapphire eyes. She swallowed, finding breathing a little difficult.

"It is a very good thing that *wasn't* cider. Imagine if Grandmother awoke to find you smelling of spirits." She enjoyed hearing his deep, velvety voice, especially when he tucked a hint of laughter into it, as he was doing just then.

Eve shook off the tingling his voice had rippled over her, but she didn't manage to say anything.

Duke reached under the bench and pulled out a carriage blanket. He flicked it out and over her lap. "There is likely at least a half hour before we reach the inn. You should try to rest until then."

Her heart was pounding far too hard for rest. Good heavens, what was happening? This was Duke, a friend, one of the Pack. Yes, he had a voice like a warm blanket on a cold day and eyes so gorgeously blue that they ought to be against the law somewhere, but that didn't mean she was justified in being ridiculous.

"Are you attempting to avoid your inevitable humiliation when you can't guess my ideal future?" she asked.

"You are very confident that I can't sort it out." Heavens, that voice of his. Maybe it *was* the reason she was lightheaded. "I accept the challenge, Eve O'Doyle, but only if you agree that when I guess correctly, you'll tell me."

The Best-Kept Secrets 45

"*When?* That is awfully confident for someone who isn't even certain whether I am soon to lose a finger. Don't you pay attention?"

"Whatever your dreamed-of future is, I would wager it involves teasing people." It was growing too dim in the carriage to see if his eyes were subtly dancing, but she could see what appeared to be an upward tip to one corner of his mouth. For the length of a heartbeat, she couldn't look away. There she went, being ridiculous again.

She shook that off and retook the topic. "If *I* sort out what it is *you* intend to do with your life, will you tell me?"

"Even my own family is unlikely to guess that."

"I do enjoy a challenge," she said.

"How do you feel about an impossibility?" he asked dryly.

That was intriguing. "You think the puzzle will be that difficult for me to solve?"

"I believe the word I used was *impossible*, but I will thoroughly enjoy watching you make the attempt."

She felt her cheeks flush at that declaration. Eve never blushed. She didn't know what exactly had her mind and heart acting so uncharacteristically silly. All she could say for certain was that it was a very good thing they had two days left in this journey, otherwise she might find herself thinking very foolish things.

CHAPTER EIGHT

"A COACHMAN," DUKE TOSSED AT Eve in the same tongue-in-cheek line of inquiry he'd been using since their conversation in the carriage the evening before. He'd discovered she deeply enjoyed the odd game they were playing, and thus, he'd taken to making absurd guesses about her dream-fulfilling future.

"No," she said with a laugh. "Though, in fairness, I would be brilliant."

Don't stare. She was so mesmerizingly beautiful when she smiled that way that he could likely be forgiven for staring a little. Still, he didn't particularly want to have to explain something he didn't fully understand himself, so his wisest course of action was to look away.

Across the carriage, Nia was watching him with obvious curiosity. Grandmother, in a stroke of unexpected luck, was sleeping.

"I cannot for the life of me sort out what it is your repeated questions are meant to be asking," Nia said. "Thus far, Eve has asked Duke, 'Farmer?' 'Barrel maker?' 'Undertaker?' And Duke has asked Eve, 'Pugilist?' 'Thatcher?' 'Anonymous author?' and now 'Coachman?' Then Eve declared she would be brilliant. At being a coachman?"

Eve laughed. The sound would always pull Duke's gaze to her, knowing her eyes would be sparkling and crinkly, her dimple would be evident, and her smile would be dazzling.

"Ooh, I know." Eve turned to him once more. Did she have any idea how startlingly beautiful she was? She held up her finger, a small scab on the pad declaring it last night's victim. "Surgeon?"

"No."

"You never did say what you cut your finger on," Nia said.

Eve pointed to the tiny space between the cushion and the wall of the carriage. "Something down there, though I cannot say exactly what."

"I asked the coachman to attempt to identify the culprit," Duke said. "But I cannot guarantee he has had time to do so yet."

She looked at Duke once more. "Shall I tuck my other hand down there and find out?"

"Only if you have a handkerchief handy, as I do not mean to sacrifice another one of mine."

Her laugh burst forth once more. She immediately clapped her hand over her mouth upon realizing Grandmother had stirred at the sound.

In a whisper, Duke said, "If you wake her, I will tell her it was your fault."

"You would sell me to the enemy?"

"Without hesitation."

She didn't laugh, but she did smile. He liked that nearly as much.

Thunder rumbled outside. Duke pulled back the curtain nearest him. Rain fell fierce and fast, just as it had done all day. They had made slow progress. Now, it seemed, they were to make no progress at all—the carriage came to a stop.

Duke's vantage point offered no view of the road ahead. Whatever might have been on or in the road, he couldn't see.

"The weather has not been overly cooperative, has it?" Nia was watching the same window he was.

"Far from cooperative," Duke said. "But I suppose that is to be expected when one is traveling in December."

Eve took a quick, excited breath. "Writer of almanacs?" she asked him.

Knowing she was once more playing their game, he gave his very solemn usual answer. "No."

"Drat." Amusement added a sparkle to her bright and mesmerizing eyes.

"You two truly aren't going to tell me what these questions are alluding to?" Nia didn't look upset not to be included.

And Eve, matching his tone almost exactly, answered, "No."

That set both sisters laughing, which did wake Grandmother. She, however, remained drowsy enough not to launch immediately into complaints.

The carriage door opened. The coachman stood on the other side, using an umbrella to keep rain off himself and out of the inside of the carriage.

"What's happened?" Duke asked.

"River ahead's running high. We're not permitted to cross the bridge, as there's some concern the water'll wash over and send us toppling."

"And there's no alternative crossing? A more substantial or higher bridge down another road, perhaps?" Duke asked.

The Best-Kept Secrets   49

"None, Mr. Seymour. They say we'll have to wait a day or two for the water to drop again and see how the bridge fairs."

They couldn't proceed, but neither could they remain where they were, in the middle of a sodden road. They needed a place to stay for a day or two.

"When did we last pass an inn?" Duke asked.

"Likely three miles back."

That seemed their best option. "Let's return there. If we are fortunate, there will be available rooms."

The door was closed, and in mere moments, the carriage was being turned around.

"An unknown roadside inn?" Grandmother sounded horrified. "How do we know we will not be murdered in our undoubtedly uncomfortable beds?"

"Because," Eve said, "I am not that lucky."

Duke looked away, biting back a laugh. Letting his amusement show would annoy Grandmother. Giving Nia more things to study in his interactions with Eve might give away more than he was ready to reveal.

The entire three-mile journey back along the road was filled with Grandmother's complaints about the inconvenience and predictions of doom at the inn she was already convinced would be little better than a hovel filled with murderous criminals. By the time the carriage stopped once more, Duke was more than happy to brave the weather if only to be free of the diatribe.

He took an umbrella with him and climbed out. With purposeful steps that he insisted to himself were not the frantic flight of a coward, he made his way to the door of the inn only to find it locked. He knocked, but no one answered. A second knock went likewise unheeded.

His clothing was growing uncomfortably wet with the rain. He quickly walked around the side of the inn and found a small cottage. He knocked at that door.

This time, his knock was successful.

A man, likely approaching eighty years of age and looking quite a bit worse for those years, stood in the dim doorway.

"No one answered my knock at the inn," Duke said.

"Inn's closed. Ain't no one to run it."

That was not the answer Duke had hoped for. "The bridge just up the road is not passable at the moment. I have three ladies in my carriage whom I need to get out of this weather. Could we sit inside while we sort out our options?"

"You'll not have many options. Nearest inn is on the other side of that bridge. Second nearest is hours back on the road. You can stay here as long as you want, but there ain't no one to cook or carry water. And the place needs airing."

Grandmother would not be best pleased. But what choice did they have, really?

Duke dipped his head. "Thank you. I will see the ladies inside, and I will let you know what we decide to do."

The man shrugged. "I'll unlock the front door." The man immediately closed *his* door.

Duke looked back at the carriage, knowing his grandmother would be even more difficult than usual when she realized their situation. And no amount of praising her manners or civility would change that. Perhaps he could simply try swimming across the swollen river and walking the rest of the way to Surrey. Except, once he reached Fairfield, he had every intention of doing far more than inconveniencing his often-difficult family. If all went to plan, he might very well start a Seymour family war.

CHAPTER NINE

THERE WAS NO DOUBT IN Eve's mind that the inn they had just stepped into was abandoned. Heavy burlap hung over several of the windows. The tables and chairs that remained were draped with dust cloths, while the well-worn wooden floor was covered with dust.

The furniture covers would have been placed immediately upon shuttering the inn, making that an unreliable indicator of how long ago the doors were closed. And dust accumulated quickly—the floors and window frames at Tulleyloch grew dusty within days if the family wasn't vigilant. It was difficult to say if the place had been empty for a month or year or even more.

Mrs. Seymour eyed their surroundings with a look of absolute horror. Nia's expression was far more evaluatory.

"This inn's not currently in use, is it?" Eve asked Duke.

"It is not. The man I suspect was once the innkeeper lives in the small cottage beside the inn. He is the one who allowed us in, but he is old and seems frail, which is likely why the inn is shuttered."

"How are we to stay here?" Mrs. Seymour wrinkled her nose in distaste. "The beds, if there are any, aren't likely to have linens. There is dust and dirt. The fireplaces, no doubt, smoke. And who will cook and tend to the beds and all the other things that must be done?"

Eve met Nia's eye. Cooking and tending to beds and such was part of their life every day, though it was not an aptitude the *ton* found acceptable. Revealing their extensive experience was risky. But spending the next couple of days in either an inn that was not functioning or a stationary carriage in a downpour were not acceptable options either.

Eve waved Nia aside. In a low voice, she said, "If you'll go upstairs and assess the situation in the bedchambers, I'll evaluate the state of the kitchen and larder."

"And are we to pretend we are new to this sort of endeavor, or are we undertaking a confessional?" Nia asked.

"Looking for linens, dusting furniture, airing rooms . . . even those who haven't that responsibility every day could likely sort out how to basically accomplish it. Mrs. Seymour won't guess at your role at home simply because you're doing that here."

Nia set her hand on Eve's arm. "But cooking and baking aren't arts that can be acquired suddenly through guesswork. If we've edible food while we are here, Mrs. Seymour and Duke will gain some insights we likely don't want them to have."

Oh, why were Mother and Father requiring her to keep her lost future a secret from Nia? There would be no more Seasons nor true forays into the *ton* for Eve. Should Mrs. Seymour whisper what she learned to others and those whispers somehow managed to reach London from Dublin, *Eve's* chance of making a match wouldn't be ruined; she already had no chance left. It was *Nia's* that needed protecting.

"We'll tell Mrs. Seymour that someone was found to work in the kitchen," Eve said. "She needn't realize *I* am the person 'twas found."

"We can try that." Nia didn't look truly convinced, but she did make her way from the room and up the creaking stairs.

"Where is she going?" Mrs. Seymour asked in tones that indicated she intended to disapprove and only asked for further information in order to feel justified in doing so.

"Nia means to check the state of the bedchambers. It seems wise to know what our situation truly is." Eve kept her expression and words light. "I will go see if there is any food in the larder."

"The two of you intend to stay here?" Mrs. Seymour pressed a hand to her heart.

"As it is our only option beyond sitting in the unmoving carriage, waiting for days until the rain stops, or driving several hours back along the road we've already traversed, hoping to reach another inn before the state of the roads renders us impossibly stuck in mud, yes. We mean to make the best of our situation and be grateful for a roof over our heads." Eve moved to the nearest interior door, unsure which of the exits from the public room would prove the threshold of the kitchen.

The first she tried was a coat closet.

She'd nearly reached the second door when Duke stepped up beside her. "I am sorry the accommodations aren't ideal," he said.

The Best-Kept Secrets

"Our current situation isn't your fault, Duke. And I was in earnest when I said that I'm grateful to be out of the rain."

Relief touched those startlingly blue eyes. So did an undeniable surge of kind concern. "I'll do what I can to make this room usable."

Good heavens, he had a knack for making her blush. She only hoped it wasn't obvious.

His eyes darted back toward his grandmother, offering Eve a moment's respite. "She'll be fractious the entire time we are here. I will do what I can to placate her, but the usual approaches aren't likely to be as effective."

Eve jumped in quickly. "I suspect you're about to apologize for that as well. But her irritability is also not your fault."

"But soothing her vitriol has always been my responsibility. I'm the only one in the family who ever has the least success in doing so."

"Well, I am not a Seymour, and neither is Nia. We place no such responsibility on your shoulders."

Without warning, Duke smiled. But it wasn't a happy or delighted smile but rather one that was almost desolate. A smile, yet somehow, not truly one.

"Wait until we meet up with my parents in Epsom. You will discover that this responsibility is not one I am ever permitted to escape."

"Have you thought about answering their grumblings with a few grumblings of your own? Confuse them a bit?" Eve pulled her eyes wide, as if she had discovered a remarkable strategy.

No smile, but there was a bit of amusement in his eyes. He was something of a puzzle, one she found herself eager to sort out.

When she began her search again, she found that the second door did, indeed, lead to the kitchen. She stepped inside and closed the door behind her.

There was still wood in a basket near the large fireplace. Eve found pots, pans, utensils, and knives. There were spoons and whisks and other implements. She would have equipment enough for cooking. But had the kitchen any actual food?

A door on the back wall proved the opening to the larder. Inside, she found dry beans, containers of flour, and salt. She also found some sugar. She opened the trapdoor in the floor, but the space beyond was too dark for her to tell what she had discovered—a root cellar, most likely.

A quick search of the kitchen revealed a lantern and a small metal tinder-box. The flint and steel fire strikers were inside, as was a bit of dry tinder. That significantly simplified things. She soon had the lantern lit and had made her way back to the trapdoor.

The air grew positively frigid as she descended into the darkness below. She held aloft the lantern, searching her surroundings. There was quite a lot of food and a good variety as well, kept edible by the environs of the root cellar. Everything she'd found in the larder was the sort of foodstuffs that didn't spoil quickly. Still, the inn must have only recently closed—likely not more than a month or so earlier—for so much to still be there and still be fresh enough to eat.

They wouldn't starve while waiting out the weather.

Eve snatched up a basket among the supplies and filled it with onions, garlic, butternut squash, eggs, a crock of butter, and a few apples. If their good fortune continued, there would still be a milk cow on the premises.

She returned to the kitchen and set her basket on the worktable. She then gathered the flour, salt, and sugar. In her gathering, she discovered the larder contained potash. However, she hadn't seen any buttermilk, vinegar, or lemon juice. Without some variety of acid, she couldn't use the potash as a rising agent. And there was unlikely to be any leavening ready for use. She would need to keep to quick breads. Fortunately for her traveling companions, she was well versed in all manner of baked goods.

She eyed the items on the worktable, deciding on her best approach. Butternut squash soup would be filling and satisfying on such a cold day. And she could make farls to eat with it, as that variety of bread didn't require yeast, potash, or a starter. And she could bake the apples for a bit of sweetness to round out their meal.

Far from feeling overwhelmed or overworked, Eve was excited. She liked being in the kitchen, creating delicious dishes and sorting out how to creatively use what she had on hand. At first, her sense of satisfaction had arisen from having a means of helping her family through difficult times. But she'd discovered in the years since that she legitimately enjoyed baking and, to a lesser but every bit as real extent, cooking. And she liked sorting out the *how* and *what* of creating a menu.

She'd lit and built a good fire in the large fireplace when Duke stepped inside. He crossed to her.

"I've built a fire in the public room as well," he said.

"Have you happened to notice if there is a milk cow? I've ideas for supper, but I'll need milk. Cream would be even better."

He shook his head. "But I haven't been out in the yard. Even if there is one, I don't know how to milk a cow."

"Nia and I do." She met and held his eye. "But don't tell your grandmother. Possessing the abilities of a domestic servant is not exactly a prized quality in

The Best-Kept Secrets   55

ladies of the *ton*. Were word to circulate around London, even our connection to Artemis's and Charlie's families would not be enough to prevent us from sinking."

He reached out and took her hand. The simple touch was comforting and reassuring. And as it had done the night before, his touch set her heart pounding. "You can trust me. Tell me what would help, and I'll do it."

"Thank you." She kept hold of his hand. It upended her, yes, but in a way she enjoyed.

"What is it you need?" he asked. "Other than milk and cream, of course."

I need you to stay here and hold my hand and tell me all will be well in the end—that I am equal to carrying these secrets I am tasked with keeping. But she couldn't bring herself to actually say that. *And I need you to look at me with amusement in your gorgeous eyes.* She most definitely couldn't say that. "Tell your grandmother we found *someone* to cook. That way, she'll not realize the someone is *me*, and I won't have to worry that she'll let the secret slip."

He nodded and even squeezed her hand. Heavens, she liked that.

"There is usually a room off the kitchen for the cook's use. I think I will sleep in there. That'll allow me easy access to the kitchen without risking your grandmother seeing me go in and out."

"Or any of the others," Duke said.

"*Others?*" she repeated, confused by the plural.

"That was what I originally came in here to tell you. A family has arrived: a mother, father, and young child. They, too, have been turned away from the bridge."

That increased the risk of discovery. But it also meant she absolutely could not, in good conscience, refuse to see to it that everyone was fed.

"I wonder how many more will arrive," she mused.

Duke shook his head. "Impossible to say. This isn't a very busy road, but there might be more."

"There is a decent amount of food in the larder and root cellar," she said. "I can keep us fed, though I will need to know how many coachmen and servants are here as well. I think we ought to take food to the old man in the cottage as well."

"I emphatically agree. And I plan to make certain he is reimbursed for what we eat."

He was still holding her hand, though she didn't know if he realized it.

"Nia can prepare the needed bedchambers," Eve said. "Will you discover what our newest arrivals are willing and able to do?"

He squeezed her fingers one more time before letting her hand go. "I will see to everything outside of your domain here. And I will do all I can to procure you some milk and cream." He stepped toward the door.

"Duke?" She'd called after him almost without realizing she had.

He looked back at her. "Yes?"

Mercy, those eyes of his. There truly ought to be a law of some sort to save unsuspecting young ladies from being upended every time that indigo gaze rested on them. Of course, then *she* wouldn't be able to enjoy watching his thoughts flit through his eyes, and that would be a shame.

"Thank you," she said, realizing that she hadn't answered his inquiry.

"Perhaps you should save your gratitude until after we discover if I am able to procure you any cream."

"I wasn't thanking you for the cream."

His ebony brows hooked low. "Then, what were you thanking me for?"

She couldn't very well say any of her most recent thoughts about his eyes and voice. So, instead, she just shrugged a shoulder and smiled.

"If there existed an occupation in which a person repeatedly posed riddles to anyone and everyone, that would be my next guess in our game, Eve."

She grinned. "I would be brilliant."

"Yes, you would." A quick smile tugged at his lips.

And she stood rooted to the spot, frozen in place by the impact of that smile long after he'd left the kitchen. Beautiful eyes. A warm voice. An earth-shattering smile. A wonderfully dry and understated sense of humor. Kindness. Intelligence. Thoughtfulness.

If she weren't very, very careful, Duke Seymour would have full claim on her heart before long.

CHAPTER TEN

"Mrs. Seymour has declared that she won't leave her bedchamber." Nia had brought in a bucket of milk earlier and had remained in the kitchen. She helped with the tasks she could, but her abilities were not in the kitchen.

Eve flipped a farl on the hot griddle. "She is requiring you to bring her food on a tray?" Nia looked tired. She really oughtn't be carrying trays about.

"She is requiring *Duke* to do so," Nia said.

That was not surprising. "His family demands a lot of him, and I have the impression that most of those demands are that he dedicate his time and energy to making them happy when they are determined not to be."

Nia stirred the butternut squash soup in the pot hanging over the fire. "That makes me a little nervous about having this house party at the Greenberrys' home. They are his aunt and uncle, after all, and, thus, part of the problem."

Truth be told, Eve was feeling much of that same apprehension. "Colm didn't seem to treat Duke the way his grandmother does, which gives me hope that Colm's parents don't either."

"Duke did say his aunt and uncle are good people," Nia said.

"I cannot imagine Artemis would allow even the gentleman and lady of the estate to cause her Huntresses grief." Eve slid the now-cooked farls off the hot griddle and onto a serving platter. "And should it be necessary, she has taught all of us to fight battles."

"There's to be a war at Fairfield?" Nia laughed a little.

"Mrs. Seymour will be handed over to her son and daughter-in-law before reaching Fairfield. That should prevent war from breaking out." Eve set the serving platter on the worktable. She took up the pleasing but practical soup tureen she'd found among the serving dishes and carried it to the large fireplace. "We'll fill a separate bowl for Mrs. Seymour and one for myself."

Food had already been brought to the stables and to the former innkeeper.

"You aren't going to eat with the rest of us?" Nia ladled while she spoke.

"If our unexpected guests are connected to the *ton*, word of my work in the kitchen might very well make its way back to Society. That wouldn't be good for either of us or our brothers."

The tureen was beginning to feel a little heavy.

"It seems Society would prefer people who have fallen on difficult times starve rather than learn to survive." Nia shook her head. "It's unfair."

"Yes, it is." Heavens, the reality of that had been crushing her these past few days. "That should be enough soup." Eve carried the tureen back to the work-table and set it down. She placed the matching ladle into the thick, autumn-hued soup, the handle settling into a notch in the lip of the tureen designed specifically for it. The lid fit tight enough to offer reassurance that the soup would stay warm and be unlikely to splash out.

She arranged the warm farls on one side of the serving platter, then placed five bowls and spoons on the other side.

In the next moment, Duke stepped into the kitchen. Her pulse tripped about as it had begun doing every time she saw him. "Anything I can help with?" he asked.

Eve pulled herself together. "If you'll carry the soup tureen, Nia can carry the platter. I'll prepare a tray for your grandmother."

Nia took up the platter. "Eve's not eating with us," she told Duke in a tone of tattling.

Duke looked at Eve. Was that disappointment she saw in his eyes? She didn't like seeing disappointment there. Could he not go back to laughter or amusement or pondering? But then again, if he was disappointed not to have her eat with him, that was actually a rather flattering prospect. "I did say I would have to hide in here," she reminded him.

For just a moment, he seemed as though he meant to argue. But he didn't. Which caused Eve a surprising amount of disappointment. She needed him to recognize and agree that she had no choice but to keep her role in the kitchen a secret. It was crucial. Yet she wanted him to want to have her nearby.

"I'll return for Grandmother's tray in just a moment," Duke said, then lifted the tureen from the tabletop.

Please stay. But she couldn't say that out loud.

She instead began preparing Mrs. Seymour's meal: A bowl of hot soup. A perfectly triangular farl. And she scooped a baked apple from the dutch oven set among the coals and placed it in a small bowl. She arranged the needed utensils and a white linen napkin on the tray as well.

The Best-Kept Secrets   59

Duke returned as she finished preparing the tray. "Is that for Grandmother?"

She nodded. "I'm sending a baked apple with everything else. But the rest of the apples can be taken out into the public room once those there have finished their soup."

He stood beside her, near enough for his captivating eyes to draw her in once more. "You are going to take time to eat, aren't you?"

Words, Eve. Think of some words. "I will."

He stayed beside her, not taking up the tray. "I'll come in here and eat with you."

Oh, that was tempting. *Keep your head.* "That would raise too many suspicions. I'm certain the family out there has sorted your social standing as well as Nia's. Should either of you take your meals with the cook, they'd find it odd. Best not risk drawing scrutiny."

He nodded. "I cannot argue with such sound reasoning."

She wouldn't have objected to at least a momentary return of his disappointed look. But she wasn't certain she could have retained her grasp on logic, and she very much needed to.

"Feel free not to argue with the wisdom of helping me clean up after they've gone up to their room. I'll welcome help with that."

He almost smiled; she could tell he did. "Thank you."

That was not what she would have predicted he would say. "What are you thanking me for?"

He lifted one black eyebrow. "I asked you that same question earlier, and you wouldn't answer. I think I will follow your example and launch yet another guessing game between us."

That teasing declaration, tossed out so casually before he left, stayed with her as she ate her own meal, rendering her surprisingly giddy at first. Thankfully, she had herself sorted by the time Duke returned an hour later with his grandmother's empty tray. Eve was in the process of washing the soup tureen and serving platter along with the bowls and utensils that Nia had brought back to the kitchen from the public room.

"The Marlows have retired for the night," Duke said. "Nia is helping Grandmother prepare for bed. I am here to act as a scullery maid."

"That is the answer, isn't it?" She added inarguably too much enthusiasm to her expression, hoping to make him laugh. "All your life you've dreamed of one day being . . . a scullery maid."

"You have sorted me entirely, Eve."

She shook her head. "I doubt anyone has ever sorted you entirely."

The flicker of amusement she enjoyed so much returned to his eyes. "Are you saying I am a mystery?"

"Yes," she answered emphatically.

Some of his amusement dimmed, uncertainty taking its place. "Is that a bad thing?"

"No." She quickly dried her hands on a rag and turned to him. "As someone who is transparent—often to a fault—I envy you a little, that you've learned to tuck away those parts of yourself that you'd rather weren't known to everyone."

"How is it you intend to keep your work here a secret if *not* revealing things is such a struggle for you?" He pulled off his frock coat and hung it on the back of a chair.

"Fate is on my side with this secret." She turned back to the washbasin. "I won't ever interact with the family who is sheltering here with us. And should your grandmother ever raise the topic, I need simply make an offhand mention of either of her children, and she will be immediately distracted."

Duke came and stood next to Eve. "You and Nia have been exceptionally patient with her, and I appreciate that. I suspect you are discovering why it is that all the companions who have been hired to live with Grandmother have eventually thrown up their hands and quit." He rolled back the cuffs of his shirt. "Put me to work, Miss O'Doyle, but with the understanding that I have never done this before and will likely be rubbish at it."

"You didn't talk nearly this much during the last house party nor during your brief time in London," she said. "I am going to take that as irrefutable proof that you find me utterly delightful company."

Something shifted in his gaze. It grew warmer, more focused on her. Even the air around them seemed to change. There was tension and an undefined spark.

Keeping her head was proving more of a challenge than she'd expected.

"You can take up a dishrag and dry off what I've washed," she said, surprised by the steadiness of her own voice. No hint of what she was feeling crept in. "If we put it all away damp, it'll grow musty."

And he did precisely what she'd asked, which broke *some* of the spell wrought by his lack of an answer a moment ago. Had he felt the space between them crackle as she had? Did he feel the lingering effects of it now?

"I took a bit of soup and farls to Mr. Evans," she said as she took up her dish scrubbing once more. It seemed a safe topic.

"Who is Mr. Evans?" Duke asked.

"The owner of this inn. The old man who lives in the cottage."

The Best-Kept Secrets 61

"Ah." He nodded. "I never did learn his name."

"I assured him that any supplies we use, he will be compensated for. He seemed worried about that." She paused her work and risked looking more directly at Duke. Though his eyes were every bit as mesmerizing as ever, she wasn't fully upended this time. "I feel a little guilty that you are bearing that expense. I have only three pounds to my name, and I need that for the servants at Fairfield."

"I doubt very much that Colm will permit you to give a gratuity to the Fairfield staff."

Eve shook her head. "It is expected though. And it is most certainly earned. They will be doing more work than usual and ought to be shown gratitude for it."

Duke set his hand on her arm. The spark in the air returned in an instant. Eve held very still, afraid of breaking the contact and also inadvertently revealing what she was feeling.

"I suspect my grandmother has given you a less-than-favorable impression of my aunt and uncle," Duke said, "but I assure you they are fair-minded and generous. I haven't the least doubt they are offering their staff additional pay in acknowledgment of the additional work."

That wasn't as reassuring as he likely thought. "But it is expected that guests offer gratuities."

"I'll talk to Colm," Duke said. "He'll understand."

She set back to her work, but her mind was far from calm on the question. Duke also returned to his effort at drying what she washed.

"There are a lot of difficult things about being poor," she said quietly, "but the constant humiliation is among the worst."

"I can speak with Colm, or my aunt and uncle, if you'd rather, without embarrassing you," Duke said. "I have a great deal of experience navigating potentially humiliating situations without causing anyone distress."

"But I don't want you to have to do that for me." She set the bowls she'd finished washing on the work top beside the basin. "You shouldn't have to shoulder other people's difficulties. I'll not require it of you."

"But you aren't requiring it; I am offering."

"I have seen how exhausted you are after defending your family to your grandmother and appeasing your grandmother on the matter of her family. And you've mentioned that your parents require the same mollifying of you. And when you talk about that, you don't look just weary; you also look frustrated and sad and . . . lonely." Good heavens, she was getting emotional. "You deserve *not* to feel that way, and I don't ever want to be the reason you do."

His deep voice was soft and gentle as he said, "I suspect, Eve, that you wouldn't ever make me feel that way."

With a shrug, she said, "I could try if you'd like me to."

Duke smiled, truly smiled, and it was breath-catching. Now that he was done at Cambridge and would be a very eligible gentleman-about-Town, he was going to catch every young lady's eye and break quite a few of their hearts.

And Eve was going to miss the entire thing.

"I wish you had been in London longer." She sighed. "You never even danced with me, and I think that is horribly unfair."

He resumed drying the last of the dishes she had washed. "I'll stand up with you next Season. I understand the Huntresses make quite an entrance at the Debenham ball every year. I'll finally get to see it."

Eve was going to miss that as well. It would still happen but without her.

She began setting out a few of the things she would need in the morning to do her baking, hoping the mundane task would provide her some distraction. It helped only minimally.

From his place near the washbasin, Duke said, "You aren't returning to London for the Season, are you?"

Eve shook her head as she set out mixing bowls. "Nia will be at more of a disadvantage in Town than we usually are, which I wouldn't have thought possible."

"Nia will be in London, but you won't?"

Oh, botheration. "This is what I meant about not managing to stop myself from saying things when they flit into my thoughts." She turned back to him, fully frustrated with herself. "I'm not supposed to tell anyone about our changed plans. Not even Nia knows yet."

"I won't say anything to anyone."

She fully and immediately believed him. And there was such relief in having *someone* who knew what was weighing on her and the future she was facing. "Our family's finances have always been fragile, but they've recently been rendered dire. Either I could return to London, or my brothers could return to school. But not both. Edmund and Scuff have to find an occupation when they are grown, or they'll be destitute. And they need an education to do that."

"That is an awful decision to have to make: their futures or yours."

It really was. "I truly am not supposed to tell anyone."

"I meant what I said; I won't tell anyone anything you don't specifically say that I can."

Her sigh of relief was more than just audible; it was soul deep.

The Best-Kept Secrets 63

"May I ask you a question?" Duke asked.

She nodded.

"Why is your brother called Scuff?"

Despite her heavy mind, she grinned. "We all have anglicized names. Edmund's given name is Eamonn. Scuff's given name is Risteárd. At first, he was called Richard, but that transformed to Rich, which then became Itch. Itch turned to Scratch and ended up being Scuff. And Scuff stuck."

Duke smiled. Legitimately smiled for the second time in a matter of minutes. Utterly and wonderfully devastating. Eve needed to think about breathing in order to remember to do it, and her heart quite suddenly forgot what its ordinary rhythm was.

"What does Scuff think of his name?" Duke asked.

"Loves it."

Duke continued drying the clean dishes, and Eve continued fighting her urge to simply stand about watching him, waiting for another heart-stopping smile. If she stood near enough to him, maybe he would hold her hand again. Maybe she could actually make him laugh. She suspected the sound would melt her.

He dried the tureen. "The soup was delicious."

"Thank you." She managed two words, and sensible ones at that. Had he the least idea how much her thoughts and feelings were spinning about, he would be impressed. Best that she push forward and get herself focused once more. "I do enjoy baking, but I don't often get compliments. Mostly because I'm not permitted to confess that I made the food."

"That is an absolute shame." Duke held up the now-dry soup tureen. "Where does this go?"

"Over here." She waved him toward the high shelves that many of the serving items were kept on. "Up in that empty spot there."

Duke stretched up and slid the tureen into place. He was standing very close, near enough to leave her with no doubt that he was strong and athletic and that he somehow managed to smell nice even with all the work they'd done that day.

He didn't walk away immediately but turned toward her. His mesmerizing eyes slowly slid over her face. Eve's breath caught, and her heart leaped into her throat.

"Thank you for your help." The words were whole but whispered. It was all she felt capable of.

He inched the tiniest bit closer. "I enjoy spending time with you." His brilliant blue gaze hovered for the briefest of moments on her lips.

"I enjoy spending time with you." Her voice emerged as little more than a whisper.

"Likely because I am a very gifted scullery maid."

She laughed, which relieved the intensity of the moment. She could think again. "Gifted, perhaps, but currently neglecting your scullery-ing."

Duke bowed at the waist, a perfect replica of the way a footman bowed after receiving instructions from a butler. He returned to his task.

And Eve did her best to simply breathe.

CHAPTER ELEVEN

"You must tell your father, when we see him next, how very intolerable this journey has been." Grandmother wrinkled her nose in that way she so often did. "He will, of course, insist that he is the one most put upon. Do not allow him to diminish what I have endured, Dubhán. Tell him all that I have been put through."

Neither she nor his father would likely give even a moment's consideration to what *Duke* had endured. Father seldom did on matters concerning his mother and sister. Grandmother never did on any matter whatsoever.

"You will see him at the same time I do." Duke set her breakfast dishes on the tray he'd brought them up on. "You could tell him."

She looked shocked, an expression that quickly shifted to offended. *Lud.* "You mean to abandon me? Your own grandmother? My children often dismiss me and my suffering. Surely you would not do so as well, you who have often been the only member of this family to consider my feelings, my needs, my happiness."

And what about mine? Duke's feelings, needs, and happiness had always been set aside when family contention reared its head. Sometimes it felt as though his family didn't notice, let alone care, that they were burdening him with arguments and feuds older than he was.

But Eve cared.

"You don't look just weary," she had said, *"you also look frustrated and sad and . . . lonely."*

He really was weary, frustrated, and sad. But until Eve had said as much, he hadn't realized how lonely he truly was. The Pack had eased that while he'd been away at school. Among them, he was valued and embraced and a welcome part of their family of friends. None of them had ever attached conditions to their acceptance of him. Only when he'd faced the reality of living for decades at his parents' home, where caveats reigned supreme, had he begun to truly appreciate the contrast between the two situations.

Duke placed the last of the breakfast items on the tray. "I need to take these things back down to the kitchen."

"I am impressed with the food this chance-found cook has produced." Grandmother rarely praised anyone. "I've half a mind to extend an offer of employment. My cook in Dublin is not nearly this expert."

"We are fortunate, indeed."

"Your father is, no doubt, paying for all this, though Penelope really ought to be. Her fortunes have fared better than his."

If Grandmother were permitted to chase that thread of thought, it would lead to the inevitable hours-long recounting of past disappointments. Duke hadn't endurance enough for that. From the doorway, he offered an explanation he hoped would end the conversation. "The O'Doyle sisters are compensating the cook, Grandmother."

"Those girls are, I am quite certain, as poor as church mice." Grandmother sounded shocked, and well she might be.

"Poor, yes, but *they* are not complaining." He gave her a pointed but caring look, then closed the door.

Alone in the corridor, he released a pent-up breath. He loved his family. He truly did. And when taken in small doses at a large distance from the extended family, he even had some pleasant times with his mother and father. But they didn't last. Though he'd never been to Fairfield without his parents, he felt certain the bitterness and demands for appeasement were far fewer there and much farther between. He needed that. He needed it desperately.

Duke took the tray back to the kitchen by way of the servants' stairs. It wasn't that he didn't like the Marlows; he did. But he was feeling a little weary of people just then.

He smelled freshly baked bread as he drew closer to the kitchen. Eve was working her magic again. She'd done more than keep them all well fed, which was impressive enough. She'd also made him feel less alone and invisible. She'd made him smile, which was an admittedly infrequent thing.

Upon stepping into her kitchen, he began immediately searching for her. He'd missed her in the hour since he'd last been in the room. One hour. He'd told her the night before that he liked spending time with her. But it was more than that. He thought about her when they were apart, wondered what she was doing, if she was thinking about him too.

The Best-Kept Secrets 67

Eve was asleep in a chair near the fire. She'd admitted when he'd fetched Grandmother's tray to having been up for a few hours already.

Careful to be as quiet as possible, Duke set the items from the tray into the basin of water before setting the tray on the worktable. He'd watched Eve washing the dishes the night before and mimicked what he'd seen then. She'd already cleaned all the other plates and bowls and pots.

Eve O'Doyle was remarkable, though he suspected she didn't realize it. The way she navigated Grandmother without being hurt or hurtful, her ability and willingness to work as hard as she had the past day keeping everyone fed, her strength and courage in the face of a future that had just been snatched from her . . . The more he learned of her, the more amazed he was, and the more intrigued.

He'd come close to kissing her last night in this very kitchen. So exceedingly close. And the look in her eyes had not, to his view, been indifferent. Long after he'd climbed the stairs and retreated to the room he was using, he'd thought about that moment, filled as it had been with the thudding of his heart and the fierce temptation to wrap his arms around her and kiss her.

"You didn't have to wash those." Eve's sleepy voice broke into his thoughts.

He looked in the direction of the fire and saw her walking with sleep-heavy steps toward him. "You washed all the others," he pointed out.

"I don't mind," she said. "I'm certain you and Nia are doing a great deal of work in the rest of the inn."

"There is work, yes, but it is nice to feel useful and to help people."

She reached his side, still looking tired and worn. "Innkeeper, then?"

He didn't know what she meant by that, and his confusion must have shown.

"Is that your dream-fulfilling future?" she asked. "Being an innkeeper?"

He shook his head. "I cannot say I would want to run an inn."

"But you do want to help people and be useful." She didn't pose it as a question. She also didn't talk about that desire of his as if it were a failing or weakness. "That leaves me with only one further characteristic to discover."

He dried his hands on a kitchen rag. "And what is that one further characteristic?"

"Whether or not you are enamored of experimental bread."

He hadn't been expecting that. "Enamored of *what*?"

Her captivating laugh pulled his gaze immediately to her, his heart pounding in anticipation. He'd learned very quickly during this journey that when

Eve O'Doyle was laughing, he didn't want to be looking anywhere other than at her, seeing her silver eyes sparkle, her bewitching dimple make an appearance, her lips turn up in a dazzling smile.

"Enamored of *experimental bread*," she said as if he ought to have known what that meant but with too much amusement in her expression to make her comment anything but teasing. "I found herbs in the kitchen garden that were still alive and usable. It seemed a sign that I ought to use them. I added what I gathered into the bread I baked, and I'm hoping it's worked."

There was something wonderfully refreshing in hearing Eve's lilting Irish voice lending the musical quality of Irish speech to her words. And it made her ever more captivating.

"You'll try a bit, won't you?" She looked hopeful but also a little nervous.

"Of course."

Eve snatched hold of his hand and pulled him to the worktable. It was a simple touch, one she didn't appear to engage in for any reason other than excitement over her baking, yet his heart lurched at the feel of her hand, small and warm, in his.

But it was there for only a moment. As soon as they reached the bread, she slipped free. He knew she needed her hands to cut into a loaf, but how tempted he was to ask her to let him weave his fingers through hers and keep hold of her in that small way. He didn't dare. Instead, he inched a little closer, near enough to hear her breathe and feel her warmth.

She cut a thick slice of bread, then handed it to him, watching him closely.

It smelled divine. Duke took a bite. "Delicious," he said. "Absolutely delicious."

She clasped her hands together in front of her heart. "I'd hoped it would be. I love trying new things and creating my own recipes. I do wish it were something ladies didn't have to be ashamed of."

He tore off a piece of his slice and handed it to her. "I certainly hope you aren't ashamed of this, Eve. It is something far too impressive for you to be anything but excessively proud of."

She took a bite. "It *is* good."

"Very good."

She smelled her bit of bread, looking entirely pleased. "Outside of my family, there are only two people who have any idea that I bake."

"I am honored to be one of those two." Honored. Touched.

"If I had to choose someone to be trapped at an abandoned inn in the midst of a torrential downpour with, I'd put you at the very top of my list, Dubhán Seymour."

The Best-Kept Secrets   69

Duke turned a bit so he leaned a little against the work top and faced her more directly. "What other lists do you have that I can work my way to the top of?"

She thought about it a moment. "I could form a list of people who have Irish names but use interesting English substitutes."

"*Interesting* English substitutes?" He shook his head. "I would say Scuff ought to be at the top of that list."

Eve reached for his hand again, excitement in her expressive face. "You would adore Scuff. He reminds me so much of Charlie and Toss. Both of my brothers do."

"I'd like to meet your brothers." He adjusted his hand so his fingers threaded through hers, just as he'd hoped to. "You said they are still in school?"

She nodded. "They attend Shrewsbury. I realize that isn't as prestigious a school as Eton or Harrow." There was a hint of embarrassment in her tone.

"My father was educated at Shrewsbury."

Her eyes pulled a bit wide. "Truly?"

He nodded. "But even if he hadn't been"—Duke bent a little closer to her—"I hope you know that you need never worry that I will think less of you or your family over something as inconsequential as what school your siblings attend or the size of your house or the depth of your family coffers. Society may set great store by those things, but I don't. I never have."

She smiled once more but this time softly. "Thank you for being so kind to my father when you spoke with him on the docks. Not everyone in the *ton* is."

"Are they unkind to you as well?"

Her shrug wasn't as nonchalant as he suspected she'd intended it to be. "I am poor and Irish. What do you think?"

Duke pressed their entwined hands to his heart. "Tell me if anyone is ever making you unhappy. I'll be in London instead of at Cambridge now. I can actually do something about their unkindness."

"You are very thoughtful. I suspect you don't fully realize that about your-self." Eve had a way of making him feel one hundred feet tall.

"I stand by my offer," he said. And knowing she had worried about being a burden the way his family often was, he added, "And that offer is being made eagerly and willingly."

"And kindly," she said. "But I won't be in London for the Season, for any Season. The Huntresses and the Pack will be. My parents and sister will be. My brothers will be at Shrewsbury. And I—" She blinked a few times, clearly attempting to hold back her emotions. "I'll be left behind by everyone."

A tear slipped from her eye, and without a thought, Duke pulled her into an embrace.

Eve buried her head against him and took a shaky breath. "I don't know why I'm suddenly so overset by this. I understand why it needs to happen, and I'm grateful that some of my family's burdens will be lightened."

"But *your* burdens have been added to." His heart ached for her. "You love your family, and you don't want them to suffer or be unhappy, but that doesn't mean you aren't permitted to be overwhelmed by all that has been placed on your shoulders or to grieve what it is costing you."

Another of her breaths shook with emotion. "I feel as though my entire future was snatched away without warning, and I don't even have anyone to talk to about it. My mother was so clearly heartbroken, and my father looked crushingly guilt-ridden. And I'm not supposed to tell Nia. 'Tis as if I've been abandoned already."

"*I'm* here," he said softly. "I know what you're facing, and I know what it is to feel very alone in carrying a family burden." She was the one who had spotted in his eyes the loneliness he'd not ever acknowledged, even to himself.

"When Nia eventually learns about all this, promise me you won't tell her I cried."

"I won't tell her." He hoped he was offering Eve some comfort and reassurance.

"And if London is unkind, will you look out for her?"

"Like she is my own sister."

She released a slow breath but a steady one this time. "That will help me worry less about her, though I will still miss her terribly when she's in London."

"We will miss you." He silently added, *And* I *will miss you.*

CHAPTER TWELVE

Duke had never before played a game of "move all" with someone as young as the Marlows' little girl. None of the families who lived near Writtlestone ever spent time there—at least not twice—and he hadn't any siblings or any cousins younger than he was, so his opportunities to interact with children had been very limited. He found it an unexpected relief to discover he was not entirely horrible at it.

When the time came for running from one chair to another in an attempt to reach it before anyone else claimed it—the entire substance of the game— the sweet child would giggle as her tiny legs moved as quickly as they could. Duke, taking his cues from her parents, would run past a chair or attempt to sit in it and land on the floor instead. Little Sophia would laugh so much she could hardly continue the game. And as she had four adults happily indulging her with repeated failed attempts at sitting, she never seemed to stop laughing.

Nia proved particularly good with the little girl, likely the result of having grown up with siblings younger than herself. But she was also the first to be eliminated each time they began anew, not only failing to reach a chair before Sophia but also proving slower than all the adults as well. Perhaps that was part of her strategy: quickly place oneself in the position of onlooker and joyful encourager.

The game had been ongoing for nearly thirty minutes when one of Duke's intentionally poor attempts at claiming a chair left him sprawled on the floor and the chair he'd been aiming for toppled. He'd miscalculated a bit.

Little Sophia rushed over to him, concern on her sweet face. "Are you hurt?"

"No, sweeting. I'm not hurt."

She gave him a hug, though her small arms didn't come close to encircling him. And she leaned her cheek against his chest.

Duke wrapped his arms around her. "Do your parents hug you when you're hurt?"

"Yes, to make the hurt feel better."

"It works like a miracle, Sophia," he said.

Across the large public room, Duke spied Eve peeking out from behind the slightly ajar kitchen door. It was a shame she'd spent so much of their time at this inn isolated in the kitchen. He understood her difficulty, but he still wished she could have enjoyed the lighter moments they'd had. He wished she'd been with them more. With *him* more.

And though he was touched by Sophia's sweet little hug, he longed for another embrace from Eve.

Mrs. Marlow scooped up her daughter. "I think it's time for bed, dear. Your eyelids are growing heavy."

Sophia objected but halfheartedly. She wanted to keep playing but was quite obviously sleepy.

"We'll help you put everything to rights in the morning before we all depart," Mr. Marlow said to Duke and Nia. They'd received word that the bridge had been deemed crossable. "And thank you both for all you've done. We would have been in dire straits without you."

Thank you both. Eve had told no one about her baking abilities beyond her family, himself, and one other unnamed person. That likely meant she was seldom thanked or complimented for her offerings. She was being denied that again.

"Our pleasure," Nia said. "I hope the remainder of your journey is less eventful than this bit."

"We will wish you the same," Mr. Marlow said.

"And we're sorry to have not met your grandmother," Mrs. Marlow said to Duke. "I hope she is feeling well enough to travel in the morning."

They'd told the Marlows that Grandmother was feeling poorly rather than inform them that she remained in her room because she felt that keeping company with the young family would constitute an indignity.

The Marlows made their way up the stairs.

"I'm meaning to go offer Eve a good night," Nia said.

Duke nodded. Though he knew the Marlows would keep to their word and help him straighten up the inn before setting off in the morning, he still set himself to the task of returning tables and chairs to where they'd been before they'd arranged them to accommodate the game of move all. Everyone would want an early start. Doing this now would save them time in the morning.

He'd nearly finished when Nia slipped back out of the kitchen and up the stairs. Duke put the last chair back in its place, then crossed to the kitchen

The Best-Kept Secrets

himself. If Eve had already retired to her bedchamber, then he'd go upstairs and settle in for the night. Then he would, no doubt, lie there for hours thinking about her, just as he'd done the night before.

She was still in the kitchen doing her utmost to slip a pot onto a shelf the tiniest bit out of reach.

"I can put that up for you," he said.

She looked over at him. "I would appreciate that. Nia was absolutely no help, she being no taller than I am."

He put the pot easily in its place. "Is there anything else I can do for you?"

Eve shook her head, but her expression was uneasy. "Do you think anyone other than you saw me peeking from the kitchen? The wee girl's giggles were so sweet that I couldn't resist seeing what had brought them on. I oughtn't to have looked. 'Twas too much of a risk."

"I don't think anyone else saw you."

Her sigh of relief was anything but feigned. She took up the broom and began sweeping.

"The Marlows expressed their gratitude for all that's been done while we've been here. I'm extending their thanks to you."

"It has been a lot of work." She continued her sweeping. "But it's also been nice, truth be told. I've relished the challenge of creating things with only what's on hand here."

"A challenge you have excelled at," he said.

She looked at him as she continued her sweeping. "I will bake wonderful things at Tulleyloch while you are gallivanting about London. Remind yourself of that once in a while, in case you're tempted to enjoy yourself too much while I'm not there."

"I wish I knew how to fix this so you could be gallivanting as well."

Eve set her broom against the wall. "Not everything can be fixed, Duke." She walked toward him. "And even those things that can aren't necessarily *your* responsibility to mend."

He smiled a little. "You've told me that a few times these past days."

She took his hands in hers and looked into his eyes. "I'll keep telling you until you believe it."

"I am attempting to," he said. "But escaping the role of family negotiator will require turning the cannons on my family, and I'm not looking forward to it."

"You talk as though you have already lined those cannons up."

Duke hadn't shared his plans with anyone. Even the Pack didn't know the extent of his difficulties.

"Let me begin by plainly stating that my situation pales in comparison to yours."

She waved that off.

"And I further need to acknowledge that the complaining I have done has likely given you an unflattering view of my parents. Life with them is not entirely miserable. When I see them for brief intervals, we get along well. If I am to keep thinking well of them, I cannot be with them all the time. I realize that likely makes me a terrible son."

Eve shook her head. "There is a reason for the universality of the sentiment 'absence makes the heart grow fonder.' Some people *require* fond absences."

There was a lot of truth in that.

"So, are you planning to run away from home?" she asked.

"Essentially. I'm not a pauper, by any means. But my income from my father's estate was never meant to be sufficient for obtaining a home away from Writtlestone. So I am going to ask my aunt and uncle if I can make my home with them at Fairfield." He dropped his gaze to their hands, buoyed by the simple touch. "My grandmother will consider me to have chosen sides, which will make me an enemy to her since she aligns herself with *and* opposes *both* 'sides,' as it suits her needs. And my parents will see this as a betrayal, which has always been at the heart of what they are angry with my aunt about."

"Why stay with your aunt and uncle, specifically, if it will cause such complications?" There was no accusation or dismissal in the question but rather a caring concern.

For the first time since formulating this strategy, Duke felt a little less alone in it. "Asking to be granted indefinite houseroom from anyone other than family would be inexcusable. And my parents would likely make themselves a nuisance at the home of any friend who took pity on me. I would be subjecting people to the very troubles I am attempting to escape."

"But will you be happy?"

He looked up at her once more. "Fairfield is a much more peaceful place than Writtlestone. I'll be able to breathe again."

Eve pulled her hands free of his, and his heart dropped. But almost before he could register the loss, she set her hands gently on either side of his face. "But will you be happy?"

"At Fairfield, happiness will finally feel possible."

The light touch of her hands on his face did odd things to him. His pulse pounded and raced, which he could have predicted, but he also felt calm and his thoughts quieted.

The Best-Kept Secrets

75

Her hands dropped to his chest. "You give so much of yourself to helping others, to securing *their* happiness. You deserve happiness as well."

"That is why my uncle Niles said he went into politics: to help people." He set a hand over one of hers.

She moved a little closer. "You ought to consider following in his footsteps."

"There are a great many obstacles." With his free hand, he brushed a strand of her hair away from her eyes.

"There usually are."

He swallowed. "And complications."

Her gaze affixed to his, she nodded silently.

Duke bent a little closer, the two of them so close that there was no need to speak louder than a whisper. "Things don't always work out the way we hope."

"There's no hope if a person doesn't at least try."

Her silver eyes, so stunning when she laughed, were warm and deep and watching him in a way that pulled him ever closer. Achingly close.

"Aoife," he whispered.

Her eyelids fluttered closed. It was an invitation he didn't ignore. He wrapped his arms around her and stopped pretending her lips didn't tempt him more every time he was with her. He kissed her, slowly and softly. The charge that had swirled in the air the past days rippled around them. And his heart echoed with the pulse of a brewing storm.

The sudden sound of a tree branch blown against a window startled them both. The tension between them didn't abate. She watched him. He watched her. But he wasn't certain either of them breathed.

Her cheeks were a little flushed, but he saw no regret or disapproval in her expression. In fact, he was almost certain a smile tugged at her lips as she returned to her sweeping. He didn't hold back an answering smile of his own.

Neither said much after that but set to cleaning the kitchen. They eventually settled once more into the lighthearted conversation they most often indulged in. There was no true discomfort between them, but he suspected she wasn't any more ready than he was to dissect what had happened and what it meant.

With her domain set to rights, Eve offered a thank-you before stepping into the room she'd been using and closing the door.

And Duke stood alone in this room where he'd well and truly fallen for her, realizing how complicated things had just become. His was a future that would be spent either as a perpetual guest in someone's home or as a man unable to escape the difficulties of his parents' house. He was inextricably tied to a family at war with itself. He knew all too well the battle scars that caused.

He knew he needed to proceed with more than mere caution. He needed to maintain enough emotional space not to overly entwine his heart with hers. But that heart pleaded with him not to push her away.

CHAPTER THIRTEEN

ALL THAT NIGHT AND THE next day as Eve had slept in the carriage, her dreams had been filled with Duke, a warm, quiet kitchen, and a gentle embrace. And that kiss.

She'd worried that things would be awkward between her and Duke. Perhaps he now regretted the impulse, or maybe she'd been rubbish at kissing, and Duke was embarrassed for her. But he'd been busy with the preparations for departure and being the recipient of his grandmother's complaints when they'd first departed, which had been ongoing when Eve had drifted off. Then Duke had been asleep when she'd been awake during the morning bit of their journey. And while she'd slept quite a lot after their lunchtime stop, he'd spent that bit of the journey reading a newspaper.

They weren't interacting enough for her to even know if things were now uncomfortable. And she was a little too tired to try to sort it out.

When their supper arrived at the inn where they were breaking their journey that night, she hadn't the energy to do more than push the food around her plate and focus on keeping her eyes open. She had worked hard in the kitchen the last two days, and that labor had exhausted her.

"I cannot blame Miss O'Doyle for merely picking at her meal," Mrs. Seymour said. "The fare here is not as well prepared as what we had at that dilapidated inn we were holed up in."

"How fortunate we were to have found such a skilled cook." Duke spoke very solemnly, but when he looked at Eve, there was a laugh lurking in his eyes.

Her answering smile was more than just amusement. She was relieved. Their unforgettable kiss, the surprising impulse of a moment, hadn't become a barrier. He could still joke with her, still turned to her with a light and happy demeanor.

"One thing I *can* blame Miss O'Doyle for, though," Mrs. Seymour said, "is how little she helped at that inn. Miss Niamh worked tirelessly to set bed-chambers to rights, often looking entirely done in by the effort. Dubhán carried trays of food and saw to the public room. They could have rested if they'd had more help."

Eve quickly reminded herself that Mrs. Seymour hadn't been told about the arrangement in the kitchen. Knowing how to expertly run a kitchen and prepare meals required years of having done so. A lady could sort out how to make a bed or stoke a fire without having repeatedly done the work of a chambermaid. Eve's work would have revealed their situation to Mrs. Seymour. Nia's didn't. Eve's work had to be kept secret. Nia's didn't. The lady didn't have to be so judgmental, but she was coming at the topic from a place of ignorance.

"I assure you, Mrs. Seymour," Eve said, "I worked quite hard as well. I didn't see you because my duties were all on the ground floor."

"What could possibly have kept you down there?" Mrs. Seymour scoffed. "Dubhán, I am certain, had everything well in hand."

"There was a great deal to do, Grandmother," Duke said. "And Miss O'Doyle worked every bit as hard as Miss Niamh and I did."

"Then, you should have been able to spend more time with me," Mrs. Seymour said. "It was nearly unbearable to pass endless hours all alone."

"You could have joined us in the public room," Duke said. "The Marlows were very good company."

Mrs. Seymour sniffed, which Eve had come to know meant the older woman disagreed but didn't want to continue discussing a topic. And in the next moment, she took up a new topic entirely. "I expect your father has abandoned me because I didn't arrive at Epsom today as I was meant to."

"He is likely confused, and I suspect he is concerned," Duke said, "but I do not believe he will have simply tossed his hands up and returned home."

"And if we reach the inn and he isn't there?" Mrs. Seymour demanded. "What do you mean to do then, Dubhán?"

He means to attempt to escape all the burdens you and his parents place on him all the time.

Duke pushed his own half-eaten meal away. "If my father is not at the Wren and Badger, then we will continue on to Fairfield."

Another sniff. Eve wouldn't miss that sound when their paths diverged. She suspected Duke wouldn't either, though his was too good a heart not to miss his grandmother. If only his grandmother appreciated him as she ought.

The Best-Kept Secrets

79

"Penelope certainly wouldn't be happy about that." Mrs. Seymour appeared already offended at a slight she had not yet received. "She, I am certain, would rather not see me again."

"She has happily welcomed you to Fairfield in the past, Grandmother."

"She has not been happy nor was I truly welcomed," Mrs. Seymour said. "But she didn't lock me out, so I suppose there is a bit of truth to your recounting of the past."

Duke's lips pressed into an almost indiscernible grimace even as his shoulders slumped a bit. He needed a rescue, and Eve knew just how to accomplish it.

"I must say, I am shocked to hear that Mr. Colm Greenberry, who seemed such an exemplary gentleman when we interacted with him in London, has such horrible parents."

That immediately raised Mrs. Seymour's hackles. In absolutely haughty tones, she said, "Colm *is* an exemplary gentleman, and his parents are *not* horrible."

Eve pretended to be confused. "All I know of the Greenberrys is what you have said of them, Mrs. Seymour. And you have said nothing favorable." She stood, necessitating that Duke stand as well. "If you wish people to think well of your family, you might consider *speaking* well of them, as most people will assume you are not an unreliable source of information on the subject." She then addressed everyone as a whole. "I am still quite tired. I believe I will retire for the evening. Good night, all."

And on that parting note, she made her way from the private dining room and up the stairs to the room set aside for her and Nia. As they hadn't a lady's maid to prepare the space for them, no candles were lit. Eve snatched one from a sconce in the corridor and brought it in with her. She lit the candles on the two bedside tables and atop the tallboy before returning the borrowed flame.

Inside the now dimly lit room once more, she closed the door. Only then did she realize she had been very nearly holding her breath. She released it all at once.

She likely shouldn't have scolded Mrs. Seymour. Duke's momentary reprieve from addressing his grandmother's grumblings might very well now turn into an extended effort. But it had been so frustrating hearing him have to keep assuaging her every complaint, undertaking the verbal contortions needed to defend others in his family without offending her. The lengths he anticipated having to soon go in order to secure himself an escape were heartbreaking. She'd wanted to offer him a momentary respite now.

While she undertook the contortions necessary to undress herself—a feat only possible because her and Nia's dresses and stays were specifically designed to be removed by the wearer—her thoughts returned yet again to the kitchen in the abandoned inn. How magical it had proven.

Duke had told her to be proud of her baking. He'd promised to defend her against the unkindness of the *ton*. He'd heard her worries and shown he could be trusted. He'd held her while she'd cried and promised her she wouldn't be alone in her difficulties.

And then he'd kissed her. The same heart-stopping exhilaration she'd felt with the kiss washed over her now at the memory. He'd stood so close. He'd watched her so intently, with a warmth that had been more tense than soothing.

His deep, rich voice had pitched ever lower. And he'd whispered her Irish name as if it were a bit of poetry.

She closed her eyes and breathed. The sound of her name on his lips . . . She would never forget that. Not ever. And being kissed by Duke Seymour was equally unforgettable.

She tucked her feet under the blanket on the bed, sitting up with her book open on her lap. The candle on her bedside table offered just enough light to read, and the thoughts on her mind offered just enough distraction to require that she reread the same page over and over again.

She was still undertaking the futile effort when Nia arrived.

"You did the impossible, Eve," Nia said.

Eve laid her ribbon in her book and closed it. "What impossible feat did I manage?"

"You left Mrs. Seymour speechless."

Eve didn't know if she ought to wince or applaud herself. "For how long?"

"Almost five minutes."

Oh dear. "She was truly upset, then?"

"I think she was stunned more than upset. And once the five minutes of silence ended, she launched back into her litany of complaints. Duke insisted I save myself and run."

"She ought to be more considerate of him," Eve said.

Nia began the task of undressing. "Are you going to tell me what happened between the two of you?"

"What do you mean?"

"You and Duke look at each other as though the moon and stars hang in each other's eyes."

Eve hadn't the first doubt she looked at him that way. She'd never been adept at tucking away her thoughts or feelings. But Duke was an expert at it. She didn't

The Best-Kept Secrets 81

know if she ought to feel flattered that he might be allowing some tenderness toward her to show or if this was an instance of Nia seeing more than was being revealed only because she knew Eve so well.

"I'm needing help with this." Nia motioned to her gown. "I don't know if I'm overly tired or if my mind has decided to live in a state of frustrating stupor, but I cannot seem to unfasten it tonight."

Eve climbed out of bed, wrapped her knit shawl around her shoulders as a guard against the cold air, and crossed to her sister.

"The carriage rides have left me a bit stiff at the end of the day," Nia said. "I ought to borrow Mrs. Seymour's approach and be very vocally upset about it."

"You should," Eve said, making quick work of helping her sister slip free of her traveling dress. "Wait until you feel the sheets. They aren't truly scratchy but neither are they as celestially soft as clouds; thus, you will have every right to be upset about them."

"Perhaps Mrs. Seymour won't grumble about the linens to her abigail tonight," Nia said.

Nia and Eve soon had themselves tucked comfortably in for the night.

Nia, however, did not fall quickly to sleep. Lying on her pillow, looking quite tired, she took up the topic Eve thought she had managed to avoid. "What has you on such close terms with Duke?"

"I came to know him better while we were at the inn."

"So did I," Nia countered, adjusting her position with slow movements, apparently searching for a more comfortable position. "But there's something different between the two of you."

In an uncharacteristic bit of closed-lippedness, Eve didn't offer to her sister all that had happened in the kitchen. She wasn't ashamed of it, neither did she think Nia would run about spreading the tale in every willing ear. Eve wasn't worried about a scandal or Nia laughing at her.

Explaining how she and Duke had grown close likely required revealing at least a little of what they'd talked about. Duke hadn't given her leave to share his plans and worries. Her parents had required that she not share *hers* with Nia.

Ambiguity was likely her best approach. "I am not confirming anything you are hinting at, neither will I deny that I've grown very fond of Duke, very attached to him. But I am refusing to get my hopes up, both for the sake of not wishing to endanger the friendship I have with him and out of a desire not to break my own heart."

"Allow yourself to hope, Eve. We may be poor, but even poor ladies are entitled to a few dreams."

But so many of hers had very recently been whisked away. "I don't mean to abandon the possibility entirely, but I think it would be wisest if I tiptoed toward this dream rather than leaping."

Nia pulled the blanket more closely around herself. "Though you are holding your breath, worried that this tenderness growing between you and Duke will prove as insubstantial as dandelion fluff, *I* am entirely convinced that it won't."

With a grin, Eve said, "My dear sister, I sincerely hope your optimism proves more accurate than my caution."

"So do I, Eve. So do I."

CHAPTER FOURTEEN

IF DUKE NEVER AGAIN TRAVELED with his grandmother, it would be too soon. Most days, she had at least slept through part of the journey, offering him a momentary lull. But on the final leg of their trip, she remained awake and, he was quite certain, never stopped voicing her displeasure with every aspect of life.

That would have been unpleasant enough, but her unending diatribe meant that for the second day in a row, Duke didn't have any opportunity to talk with or laugh with Eve. Though Nia slept on and off, Grandmother never closed her eyes for longer than a blink. Thirty-six hours earlier, Duke had held Eve in his arms and kissed her. He'd *kissed* her. He was still shocked at his own impulsiveness when he thought back on it. But he didn't regret it. He only hoped Eve didn't either.

He'd not been afforded a chance to truly speak to her. Under Grandmother's critical eye, he couldn't so much as momentarily hold Eve's hand.

It was making the needed patience with his grandmother very difficult to come by.

By the time they reached the inn in Epsom where Father would be meeting them, Duke had to work very hard not to rudely bolt from the carriage and announce to anyone within earshot that he had an unendurable passenger he would hand over to the first person willing to take her. Instead, he sat calmly and waited for the carriage door to be opened.

"Would either of you care to step out and stretch your legs for a spell?" He asked Grandmother purely out of civility and Eve as an offered escape. Nia was sleeping.

Grandmother pulled back the curtain and eyed the establishment. "It looks questionable. I would rather stay in the carriage, if it is all the same to you."

Duke had been to the Wren and Badger before, on those occasions when his parents had journeyed to Fairfield for a family gathering that inevitably turned into a battle. It was a perfectly respectable inn, hardly warranting the quick dismissal Grandmother was giving it. This was, more likely than not, her way of punishing him and his father for having inconvenienced her on her journey.

"I would appreciate a bit of fresh air," Eve said.

A stablehand opened the carriage door and put the step down. Duke, sitting nearer the door than Eve, clambered out first. He waved off the stablehand, then turned back to the carriage door and offered his hand to assist Eve. She set her hand in his. Though excessively commonplace and made anything but intimate by their gloves, that small touch set his world to rights again. She had been sitting next to him for a day and a half, but he'd missed her.

Though he thought he kept his relief hidden, Eve took one look at him and grinned. Was he so transparent? Was he ready for her to know how much he'd come to care for her? He'd kissed her, so she must have some inkling. But this was all so new, and it felt frighteningly fragile.

They walked away from the carriage and toward the inn.

"How close were you to tossing your grandmother through the window?" she asked in a low voice.

Grandmother. Eve thought family difficulties were the reason he felt such relief in that moment. It *was* part of it.

"I had abandoned the window entirely," he said, grateful for a topic he didn't feel uncertain discussing with her, "and was planning to kick the door open and give the old lady a shove."

"Duke!" Eve laughed, the sound one of amused shock. As always, he watched her eyes brighten with her laugh, her dimple reappear, her beautiful smile tug at her lips. Her gorgeous, captivating . . . tempting lips.

Pull yourself together. He set his gaze forward once more. They were nearly at the inn doors.

"I hope Nia remains asleep," Eve said. "I don't envy her the diatribe she would have to listen to should she awaken before we return."

It really was frustrating that Eve and Nia had endured Grandmother's penchant for causing distress, but that was what happened when one spent too much time with the extended Seymour family.

"If Nia is truly fortunate," Duke said, "she will awaken only after Grandmother has undertaken her change of carriages."

"We are amassing a worryingly long list of hoped-for outcomes that depend on us experiencing a shocking amount of luck."

The Best-Kept Secrets 85

That was true enough. "I've spent the majority of my life waiting for luck to be on my side. At some point, I'm bound to realize that I need a new strategy."

"Or a questionable arrangement with the fae." She spoke too earnestly to be anything but jesting.

"You are a troublemaker, Aoife," he said.

Her grin shifted to a soft smile. "It is nice to have someone know how to say my Irish name."

"I think the Huntresses would learn if you asked them to," he said. "The Pack would as well."

She shrugged. "I don't mind my anglicized name. I like it, in fact."

"Well, it is a great deal better than Scuff, which I have on good authority is the anglicized name of a certain unfortunate young Irishman."

"The poor lad." She shook her head solemnly.

They stepped inside the inn and were greeted almost immediately by a man Duke assumed was the innkeeper. "How may I help you, sir?"

"I am looking for a gentleman we are meant to meet here, Mr. Liam Seymour."

The man shook his head. "Can't say as I've anyone here by that name. But, then, not everyone tells me their names when they arrive. What's he look like?"

"A lot like me but a generation older."

The man's brow pulled in thought. "We'd a fine couple here yesterday. Didn't stay the night. They took a meal in the private dining room and waited for two or three hours. Then they up and left without a word."

Duke asked the question he knew had to be posed, though he was embarrassed to have to do so within Eve's hearing. "Did they pay for the meal?" His parents weren't dishonest, but they were sometimes a little thoughtless.

"They did."

That was a relief.

"And they gave no indication when they left where they were going?" Duke asked.

"None, sir."

"Thank you."

The innkeeper dipped his head. Duke guided Eve back to the doorway.

"'Twas your parents, then?" Eve asked.

"Most likely."

"And they waited only a couple of hours before giving you up for lost and abandoning the arrangements?"

Duke shrugged. Father wasn't always good about thinking of others, especially when he felt put upon by his mother or sister. And Mother tended to abandon anything that required effort if she felt at all disappointed in the people around her.

"Now what do we do?" Eve hadn't looked away from him. "There's no time for taking your Grandmother to Lancashire."

"Unfortunately, our best course is likely to take her to Fairfield, though she'll be livid." *Blast, Father.* Duke had sworn to Grandmother that Father would not abandon them, that he would be in Epsom to greet them. And Duke had sworn to Father that he wouldn't take Grandmother to Aunt Penelope's home unannounced, but he was now going to be made a liar on both counts. Why was it his father, when given the choice between inconveniencing himself and causing tremendous trouble for Duke, always chose the latter?

He ducked his head back inside. The innkeeper was near at hand still.

"Do you have a horse and rider available to deliver a message?" Duke asked.

The innkeeper shook his head. "Not at the moment, sir. I'm sorry for that."

It had been worth asking, at least. He walked out into the innyard, Eve walking along beside him.

"Will your aunt and uncle be upset at their unexpected visitor?" Eve asked.

"Yes." They had every right to be. "But they will make the best of it. Grandmother, of course, will cause everyone distress. She might even ruin the house party."

"In that case, you have very little to worry about," Eve said casually.

He eyed her with doubt.

"Don't you see? If your grandmother ruins this gathering, Artemis will murder her. Problem solved."

He smiled. He couldn't help it. She lightened him when his mind was heavy and gave him reason for amusement when he was frustrated. He thought about her when they were apart, watched her when they were together, let himself imagine smiling and laughing with her, and, if fate smiled on him, eventually getting to kiss her again.

But first, he needed to bring her and her sister directly into what was destined to become a field of battle.

CHAPTER FIFTEEN

THE PREVAILING WISDOM OF SOCIETY indicated that receiving the cut direct was an experience to be avoided at all costs. However, as the carriage rolled along the tree-lined path toward Fairfield, Eve found she was enjoying the pointed silence from the eldest member of their traveling party.

Though the lady had steadfastly refused to say anything, Eve suspected Mrs. Seymour felt Duke ought to have remained in Epsom, delaying the remainder of his journey indefinitely. Or more likely still, he ought to have discarded his own wishes entirely and made immediately for Writtlestone. Somehow, he had managed to, once again, thwart his grandmother's unreasonable demands without entirely offending her. It was magic how he could turn her unreasonable complaints into opportunities for flattering her and pleading with her to share her wisdom and bestow the gift of her company on the unworthy people fortunate enough to receive her. And he managed it with a straight face. Magic, without question; Eve could think of no other way to describe it.

Nia was still sleeping. That was more worrisome than Eve cared to admit. She and her sister had made countless carriage journeys over their lifetime. While Nia would sometimes slumber a bit during long legs of their travels, the amount of time she'd spent asleep during the last two days of this journey was not insignificant. Eve didn't think Nia was pretending to sleep in order to avoid her seat companion. She seemed genuinely and deeply tired, more than could be accounted for by their work at the abandoned inn. The night before, she'd moved stiffly, struggling to undo her dress, no matter that it was one of the easiest to remove. She'd moved slowly and wearily as they'd prepared for the day's journey that morning. Was she ill?

With that question weighing on her mind, Eve happened to meet Duke's gaze. Somehow, he conveyed a question with only the slightest lift of his eyebrows. He wanted to know if something was the matter.

Eve offered the tiniest of smiles, an answer she hoped he could understand as easily as she had sorted his question. She was not in need of help or reassurance in that moment, but she was grateful that he'd offered.

He nodded so subtly that she would have missed it if she'd not been watching closely. And she recognized his acknowledgment of her response to his silent question.

They'd grown so close and connected during their time at the abandoned inn. As they always did when she thought of the inn, her thoughts filled with their kiss. Their glorious, heart-stopping, wonderful kiss.

The carriage followed a bend in the road, and framed by the carriage window, a grand house came into view. Evergreen shrubs lined the drive as they passed in front of the tall, redbrick home, creating a striking contrast. Every tree, every shrub, the hedgerows and lawn were all perfectly and elegantly manicured.

Eve all but pressed her face to the carriage window to better see the view. "I had no idea Fairfield was this grand. Most everyone knows the larger Greenberry family is significant in Cornwall. I didn't realize they have such an impressive holding in Surrey as well." Tulleyloch was not tiny nor rundown, but it looked like a hovel compared to Fairfield.

"Fairfield belonged to my aunt before she married," Duke said. "It isn't a Greenberry holding."

"But it is now," she said.

"Actually, no. It remained hers after they married, a condition of their marriage agreement."

Nothing short of that shocking declaration could have taken her eyes off the vista outside the window. She looked directly at Duke. "Is that even possible? I've never heard of such a thing."

"It is extremely rare," he acknowledged.

With a sniff, Mrs. Seymour said, "It is inexcusable that Penelope should have all this and her brother is relegated to so ordinary an estate in the north."

Eve swore she saw frustration flit quickly through Duke's eyes as he looked at his grandmother before his expression became conciliatory once more. "Regardless of the circumstances of estates and inheritances, it is for us to show the guests at Fairfield that the Seymour family can be depended upon to be pattern cards of gentility."

His grandmother sat up straighter and more stiffly, something Eve would not have thought possible. "I am *always* complimented on my impeccable manners and enviable ability as a hostess."

Duke dipped his head. "I know you are, and I am depending on it."

The Best-Kept Secrets   89

Mrs. Seymour actually smiled at him. Hers was a smile that didn't fit her face, though, as if her features were so unaccustomed to the expression that they had to be forced into it. "You can depend on me, Dubhán."

The carriage reached the top of the drive and stopped at the exterior vestibule. Eve took a tight breath. She'd felt out of place at Brier Hill during the last house party, and it was smaller than Tulleyloch. Fairfield, indeed, was no place for a comparatively insignificant Irish lady with no money or future.

The Huntresses are here, she reminded herself. Her dearest friends. And this was likely the last time they would all be together. She would not squander even a moment on such worries.

Eve reached across and gave Nia's knee a quick pat. Another was required to wake her.

"We've reached Fairfield," Eve said. "I suspect a footman will open the door at any moment. Best shake off the sleep."

Nia blinked a few times. "Could we tell the footman I've swooned and he'll need to carry me inside?"

"Only if he is particularly handsome," Eve said.

Nia smiled as she smoothed her clothing. Mrs. Seymour looked completely horrified. A quick glance at Duke, however, revealed that he was holding back his amusement.

I will make you laugh out loud, Dubhán Seymour. And smile fully. Mark my words.

Nia was handed down first. Mrs. Seymour followed. Her immediate listing of complaints to, Eve assumed, the footman stopped the disembarkation.

"Do I have to go inside?" Duke said with a sigh.

Eve turned and looked at him. "I have absolute faith in your bravery, Duke." She leaned toward him and pressed a quick kiss to his cheek.

Her timing was good; a mere moment after she turned back to face the carriage door, the footman pivoted to look inside.

Eve was handed down. She moved to Nia's side and hooked her arm through her sister's.

"This is a very impressive home," Nia whispered.

"I admit to being a bit intimidated." Eve kept her voice equally as quiet.

Duke, now out of the carriage as well, joined his grandmother and led the procession through the exterior vestibule and into the grand entryway. It was elegant without boasting the least hint of opulence, a simplicity that somehow stood as a greater testament to the owners' prosperity than a space filled with expensive belongings would have.

"Good heavens," Nia whispered, looking around with an expression of overawe that matched what Eve felt. "Do you suppose Colm realizes that most of the Huntresses live uncomfortably near to the cliff of poverty?"

"Either he does, and he likes us anyway, or once he discovers the truth, we'll learn a few things about him that we might rather not know."

The awe in Nia's eyes shifted to something closer to mortification. Neither of them had ever loved that their finances didn't bear scrutiny, but they'd not felt embarrassed by their meager finances whilst with the Huntresses. Eve was feeling a little overwhelmed at how much worse their situation was now. But Nia wasn't aware of that change. What, then, had her suddenly conscious of their indigence?

They followed Duke to where Colm stood beside a couple of the same generation as the Huntresses' and Pack's parents. These, obviously, were his. He bore a striking resemblance to both of them. And the combination was inarguably handsome. He and Scott Sarvol, who had married Gillian, another of the Huntresses, were the sort who constantly turned heads, the sort of handsome that seemed almost impossible.

"Welcome to Fairfield," Mr. Greenberry said. "We're pleased you've arrived."

They all exchanged bows and curtsies.

Mrs. Greenberry smiled at her newly arrived family members. Her expression was a little strained but not surprised. "Mother. Duke. 'Tis good to see you both." She was Irish; it was woven subtly in every syllable she spoke.

"His name is Dubhán," Mrs. Seymour said tightly.

"I call him by the name he has asked me to use." The explanation was calm, no sharpness present, yet no one could miss the tension in her explanation.

Duke jumped in, addressing Colm. "Thank you for convincing your parents to host this. I hope you have adequately warned them about the chaos they have invited."

"Chaos is always more fun when it is unexpected." Colm grinned, which would have been enough to render a few young ladies in London incapable of speech for several long minutes. "Mother, Father, these lovely young ladies are the O'Doyle sisters." He motioned to Eve. "Miss Aoife O'Doyle and"—he motioned to Nia—"Miss Niamh O'Doyle."

Their Irish names, and perfectly pronounced. That seldom happened in England. Eve enjoyed hearing it, but it hadn't nearly the impact Duke's whispering of her name had had.

"Miss O'Doyle is generally called Eve," Colm added, "and Miss Niamh is known as Nia."

The Best-Kept Secrets

"Irish girls." Mrs. Greenberry could hardly have looked more pleased. "I've not been back to Ireland in far too long."

"'Tis a place that calls to the heart no matter how far away that heart resides," Eve said.

"My wife's accent grows heavier when she's in company with other Irish people," Mr. Greenberry said with a happy warning. "By the end of this house party, I will not be able to understand her at all."

Though Mrs. Greenberry and Colm laughed, Mrs. Seymour did not appear at all amused. But, then, she never did. She looked as if she meant to say something, and that something was unlikely to infuse additional happiness into the exchange.

Duke spoke before she could. "Aunt Penelope, have you heard from my father? He was supposed to meet us at the Wren and Badger in Epsom, but he and Mother had already departed when we arrived, and the innkeeper didn't know where they'd gone."

She looked at her nephew with empathy in her eyes. "They are here. I didn't realize they hadn't left instructions that you be told of their location, otherwise we would have sent word to the inn."

"Where is Liam?" Mrs. Seymour demanded.

"I believe he is in the drawing room with the other guests," Mrs. Greenberry said.

"*Guests?*" Mrs. Seymour scoffed. "You relegate your only brother to a mere *guest?*"

"I believe, Grandmother," Duke said, "she used the word *other* on account of the O'Doyle sisters being guests."

Whether or not that was true, it was a rather ingenious bit of placating. Duke truly was an expert at this, which made Eve feel a little sad.

"Colm," Mr. Greenberry said, "accompany the O'Doyles to the drawing room."

"I suspect there is a 'with all possible haste' hidden in that request," Colm said.

"If you have such a suspicion," Mr. Greenberry said, "I wonder that you have not snapped to." When Mr. Greenberry smiled, his resemblance to his son grew.

Colm responded to his father with a perfectly executed salute. His years in the army were obvious in that moment. With an elegant grace that had likely been terribly out of place during his time fighting in the war against Napoleon, Colm stepped over to where Eve and Nia stood. He offered them each an arm.

"Ought we to run?" Eve asked under her breath with a feigned air of worry.

"Likely," he said, "but that would ruin the effect, do you not think?"

"And what effect is that?" Eve asked.

"Huntresses don't retreat," he said.

"Oh, but we *do*. All the time." It was, after all, one of the battle tactics Artemis had taught them, and it had proven remarkably useful over the years.

Colm looked over at Nia. He stopped himself from saying whatever he'd been about to say and made what sounded like an almost unintentional change of topic. "Are you feeling well, Miss Nia?"

"This journey has been more taxing than I expected it to be." Nia's answer was a little quieter than was usual for her.

"Then, our very first order of business upon reaching the drawing room will be to procure you a place to sit."

Color crept up Nia's neck and to her cheeks. "Thank you."

Either she truly didn't feel well and was embarrassed, or she was every bit as in awe of this elegant home as Eve was. It was hard not to be a little embarrassed in thrice-mended gowns when in a house that could, without warning, host royalty.

As they walked away from the entryway, Eve glanced back at Duke. He was, yet again, in the middle of family tension. Colm had been offered an escape, but Duke hadn't been. Was he ever offered one?

Duke glanced at her, and she gave him a look very much like the one he'd given her in the carriage, one that silently and subtly asked if he was in need of anything. He answered with a tiny shake of his head. He might have added something to it, but her path to the drawing room turned a corner, and she could no longer see him.

"Duke was nervous about your grandmother coming here," Eve said.

"With good reason, I'm afraid." Colm sounded as happy as ever, but with a hint of dismay underlying his words. Was any member of the Seymour family not weighed down by the difficulties among them? "You will, I hope, not think me unfeeling if I say that I hope Duke's parents and our grandmother do not remain long."

"Far from unfeeling," Eve said. "Family connections can be complex, and I suspect that with the Pack and the Huntresses here, things are complicated enough already."

Colm nodded his agreement, though his gaze was on Nia again. She was being very quiet. Even he, who hadn't known them overly long, must have realized how odd that was for her.

They stepped into yet another undeniably elegant space. On the silk-draped walls hung large portraits, clearly painted by masters of their art. The furniture

The Best-Kept Secrets   93

was of the highest quality. The rugs stretching over the polished wood floor were vibrant and intricately patterned.

"At last!" There was no mistaking Artemis's voice, though she'd spoken only two words. "I was moments from assembling a hunting party and rushing out in search of you."

The inarguable leader of their band of friends pulled Eve and Nia without apology or hesitation away from Colm and hugged them each in turn. Though she could at times be dramatic to the point of theatrics, her treatment of the Huntresses was imbued with sincerity.

Her husband, Charlie, was well-known for being both friendly and mischievous, and one of the best-hearted people anyone could possibly meet. He stood among the others gathered a little farther inside the room but turned to look at Eve and Nia. "What happened to delay you?"

"All the rain washed out a bridge on the road," Eve said.

"Good heavens." Daria pressed a hand to her heart. "While you were on it?"

They'd not have arrived at all if they'd been on the bridge during the deluge. Daria had a tendency to ask questions with obvious answers. Some in Society were unkind about that. The Huntresses, however, delighted in everything about her.

"The bridge was ahead of us on the road, and we were forced to stop and wait for it to be passable again," Eve said.

Artemis pulled them over to the group, where they were inundated with words of welcome and hugs and friendship. It was little wonder Eve's and Nia's time among London Society had been as pleasant as it had despite their low standing, country of origin, and utter lack of resources. With friends like these, a person was wealthy indeed.

Toss, Daria's husband, assumed the look of an unrepentant troublemaker. "Anyone care to place a wager on who was grumpiest about the delay?"

In perfect unison, the Pack, except for Colm, said, "Duke."

Eve laughed lightly. "I will have you know, Duke was not grumpy."

And standing a bit apart from them all, a woman said, "Of course he wasn't. My Dubhán is always very helpful and considerate."

"Oh bother," Charlie whispered. "I'd forgotten they were in here."

They proved to be a couple of likely the same age as Mr. and Mrs. Greenberry, with the husband bearing something of a resemblance to their hostess and a strong resemblance to Duke. These were, no doubt, Duke's parents.

Borrowing a page from Duke's book, Eve struck a note of conciliation. "He was more than merely helpful in the unexpected difficulty," she said to his mother. "He was very competent and calm. I don't know what we'd have done without him there."

Duke's mother beamed. His father looked undeniably proud.

Her voice still a little too quiet, Nia asked Artemis, "Where is Lisette?"

"She is expected tomorrow," Artemis said, studying Nia with a hint of concern, though she didn't press the matter. "Lisette's was the longest journey, and we can only hope she did not have to contend with any troublesome bridges."

"'A troublesome bridge' is actually a rather fitting description of the Channel," Eve said.

Artemis smiled ever more broadly. "It is good to have the two of you here. You always keep things lively."

Lively. When the Season rolled around again, the Huntresses would be in London enjoying the liveliness of it all. And Eve would be at Tulleyloch, gaining an aching familiarity with loneliness.

CHAPTER SIXTEEN

"OF COURSE YOU MAY STAY as long as you need." Aunt Penelope was doing an admirable job hiding her frustration.

Grandmother was making no such effort. "I notice you did not say we were *welcome* to stay."

Aunt Penelope took a single breath, something Duke had seen her do when keeping her temper in check. "The omission of that word was not intentional nor is there a message in it."

"Yet you did omit it," Father said, arms folded across his chest.

Through tight teeth, Aunt Penelope muttered, "Liam."

The family confrontation was occurring in a sitting room out of sight *and*, Duke hoped, out of earshot of the others in the house.

"The house is quite full at the moment and will be chaotic for at least a fortnight," Aunt Penelope said. "You might find that uncomfortable if you are in the midst of it overly long, so you needn't feel obligated to endure it. That is all I was attempting to say."

"Then, why didn't you?" Grandmother's offended sniff was not one of Duke's favorite sounds, yet it was one of the most familiar.

"I did say that." Aunt Penelope spoke slowly and precisely.

Good heavens, they were going to murder each other in the middle of a Huntresses and Pack house party. This gathering would be legendary in all the wrong ways.

He would have to step in and steer the Seymours away from disastrous waters again. And he would have to do it here, at Fairfield, where he'd been imagining creating a haven for himself.

But before he spoke, an unexpected sight in the window he was facing caught his attention.

The Pack.

Undertaking a theatrical reenactment of something.

Toss stood stiffly with his arms at his side, while Newton and Charlie pretended to punch him. Scott strutted about, occasionally taking a jab at the others as he passed. Fennel and Tobias, with an absurd lack of synchronicity, pointed alternately at the group gathered outside the window and at Duke. Colm stood a bit to the side, laughing at them all.

Duke shook his head at their absurdity but was inwardly grateful for it. The Pack's antics over the years had formed most of his absolute favorite memories.

Charlie threw his hands up in a dramatic show of annoyance that Artemis herself would have been hard-pressed to match. Then the Pack began all over again with a performance assuredly meant to be identical to the first but falling apart even more quickly. They dissolved into laughter on the other side of the glass.

They were entertainingly ludicrous.

Charlie held his hands up to the others, signaling that they should stop their efforts. He then stepped right up to the window, so close he could have leaned forward and pressed his face to the glass and, looking directly at Duke, pointed at himself and the rest of the Pack, then pointed at Duke. He held up his fists in a pugilistic stance, pretending to jab his fists at an imaginary foe. Then, still holding Duke's gaze, he used two fingers on his left hand to mimic the movement of walking.

"How ridiculous is he likely to get if we pretend we didn't understand that?" Uncle Niles had apparently been watching.

Duke answered his whispered question with a whisper of his own. "He excels at being ridiculous."

"Which either pleases or annoys his brother-in-law. The Duke of Kielder is very fond of the word *ridiculous*." Uncle Niles glanced over at the family group eyeing each other tensely. "We should sneak out while they're distracted."

"You would abandon Aunt Penelope?" Duke asked, still keeping his voice low.

"She can take care of herself." His smile was so proud and besotted that no one seeing it would think for a minute that he was actually leaving her in a time of need.

Careful to keep very quiet, they slipped from the room and into the corridor. Only once they were sufficiently far from the sitting room did they dare speak.

"You don't mind that Colm and I told the Pack about Penfield?"

Uncle Niles shook his head. "When my friends have visited over the years, we've spent a lot of time at Penfield. It ought to host a crowd again."

The Best-Kept Secrets 97

They cut across the grass leading to the spot outside the sitting room windows where the Pack had been acting as a theater troupe. The men were still there.

"I thought for a moment that we would have to resort to semaphore to get our point across," Fennel said. "And I am afraid to think who among us would have been forced to use his small clothes as a flag."

In a quiet and stern tone, Uncle Niles said, "I'm told you have fallen prey to a rumor that there is a corner of this estate that houses a building of questionable purpose."

The Pack exchanged nervous but intrigued looks. They didn't know Uncle Niles well enough to recognize his humor.

"Is the rumor true?" Newton asked.

Uncle Niles's mouth turned slowly into a troublemaker grin. With a lift of his eyebrows, he nodded.

Whoops of excitement met his admission. Whoops which, apparently, caught the attention of those inside. Aunt Penelope had turned fully to face the window, watching them with her head tipped to the side at an amusedly vexed angle. Grandmother didn't appear to know what to think of the display, though she was unlikely to approve. Father was mortified and Mother confused.

"Flee for the hills, lads," Uncle Niles said. "It's our only hope."

And with that encouragement, they bolted, laughing as they went. They slowed only once past the formal garden and on the path that began on the other side.

They continued in clumps, following Uncle Niles and Colm, who led the way.

Fennel walked alongside Duke. "I didn't realize your uncle is so funny. I've seen him only a couple of times though. In London."

"He's quieter when he's away from Fairfield. I've always liked visiting him here. I feel as though I get to know him better every time I do."

"It must be nice for him that he feels so at home . . . at home." Fennel had inherited his family estate while still at Eton, after the untimely death of his father. He didn't talk about the late Mr. Kendrick often, but what he had shared was, in a word, horrifying. And it was obvious, to hear Fennel speak of his estate, that he still associated it too much with his father for it to be a comfortable place.

"Cambridge was a welcome escape from home for me," Duke said. "You have that still."

"Actually, I am considering not going back."

That was news to Duke. "Why is that?"

"I'm not an academically minded person, and I don't need further education to run my estate. Now that I'm the only one of the Pack still there, I haven't any real reason to stay."

"But that will mean living at Bryony Hall." That, Duke knew, was not a peaceful prospect for the Pack member they all thought of as their little brother. "Can you endure it?"

"What choice do I have?" He shrugged a little. "I'm certain my sisters would let me visit them, but that would provide only a temporary reprieve." His expression was contemplative but not defeated. That was a very good sign. Fennel might have been the youngest of them, but he had a wisdom and maturity that belied his age. "Do you ever feel as if your path has been chosen for you and you have no choice but to walk it, and yet you feel completely at loose ends?"

"I felt that way for a very long time," Duke said.

That pulled Fennel's gaze to him as they continued following the Pack. "*Felt?* Past tense? Then, you found a solution?"

"Whether or not it proves to be an actual solution has yet to be seen." Duke was less sure of his plan than he had been a mere few hours earlier. "But there's something to be said for trying to find an option, even when life seems to have left you with none."

Fennel nodded and seemed very preoccupied throughout the rest of their walk to Penfield.

Their destination was just as Duke remembered it. A long building built of brick in the same color as Fairfield. The front of the building had no windows. A fence wrapped around it from either side, forming a full ring around the back garden. Anyone seeing it would assume it was a farm building, unexceptional and uninteresting. But it was anything but.

Uncle Niles unlocked the door and motioned them all inside. Duke and Colm had, of course, already seen the inside of Penfield, but Duke couldn't help noticing the resemblance his friends bore to a group of schoolboys being led into a candy shop.

Duke and Colm helped Uncle Niles pull back the curtains on the windows at the back of the large space, then light the lanterns strategically set around the room. The back of the house was not accessible from the outside, the fence cutting it off from wanderers, meaning no one could see inside from there. They had done that on purpose.

The Best-Kept Secrets

"This is better than Gentleman Jackson's." Newton looked around with that evaluating gaze he'd developed long before beginning his law studies but that they all knew would serve him well in his chosen profession.

"I'd make certain to tell Jackson I'd bested him in this if I didn't prefer he not know about it." Uncle Niles opened a cupboard, inside of which were strips of fabric for wrapping knuckles, towels for wiping away sweat, even trousers for changing into to prevent one's regular clothing from becoming torn or stained.

He opened another cupboard and pulled two buckets from it, setting them on a longboard along the near wall. He then set beside them a basket containing bits of chalk in varying lengths.

"The buckets are for water," Colm explained. "There's a well in the back to draw from."

"And the chalk?" Fennel asked.

"Marking the ring on the floor."

"We're fighting each other?" Was Fennel excited about that or not? It was difficult to tell.

"A little sparring if anyone would like," Colm said. "But there are plenty of hanging sacks of hay or cotton to pummel if you'd rather. And we can take turns holding up hand cushions for each other to hit. Anything you could possibly hope for in a boxing salon."

"This is brilliant," Tobias said.

The Pack began perusing the cupboards, looking at the newspaper clippings in Uncle Niles's memento book, talking excitedly about how often they planned to retreat here during the house party.

To his uncle, Duke said, "Thank you for this."

"You're welcome." Then, with an ill-concealed laugh, he added, "Just make certain they know the rules."

Ah. "Pack," he called out, getting their attention. "My uncle has reminded me of the need to inform you of a few requirements for using Penfield. They are very important, so listen closely." They watched with rapt attention. "The first: No one tells the Huntresses." Nods of agreement filled the room. "The second: *Absolutely* no one tells my parents or my grandmother."

"That was never going to happen," Charlie said with wide-eyed emphasis.

"And the last: no obvious pugilistic injuries. Not all of you are good liars, and the jig would be up instantly."

Scott laughed. "In other words, we've all been sworn to utmost secrecy, encompassing not merely our words but our very appearances."

Duke nodded solemnly. "No boxer's blow could ever land with the stinging ferocity of a lady's look of disapproval."

With avid agreement to that sentiment, the Pack began choosing what they meant to do during this visit to Penfield.

Tobias pointed to a page in the book of mementos. "This is Martin, the Bath Butcher."

"It is," Uncle Niles said.

"Did you ever see him fight?" Tobias sounded amazed at the possibilities.

"I did."

"Was he as good as legend says?"

Uncle Niles nodded. "He was a fierce fighter."

"Did you see a lot of the legends of that time?"

"Most of them, I daresay."

"Mendoza?" Tobias asked.

Uncle Niles nodded.

"Humphries? Harry the Coalheaver?"

Another nod.

"The Cornish Duke?"

"Yes. I attended his fights as well."

Tobias whistled appreciatively. "The Cornish Duke didn't fight in many bouts compared with the others. To have actually seen one . . ." He shook his head in amazement before more of the pugilistic trappings of the place claimed his attention.

With Tobias moving on to other interests, Uncle Niles let himself laugh silently. Duke did the same. Niles Greenberry was known as an effective and efficient member of Parliament, one who would be returning to the House of Commons in January. He was considered the least notable of his group of impressive friends. Many who did not know him or Aunt Penelope well speculated whether so outgoing and capable a lady as she was was bored with a gentleman whom they considered sedate and comparatively dull.

How little people understood him.

Uncle Niles hadn't merely *attended* the legendary Cornish Duke's fights. He *was* the Cornish Duke, having fought under that epithet and in disguise to hide his true identity. Duke, when he'd decided to choose an Anglicized name for himself, had chosen what he had in honor of the uncle in whom he'd found support and a listening ear.

Duke had long suspected that the reason Fairfield was a more peaceful place than Writtlestone, despite the Seymour family upheaval, was owed in large part to Uncle Niles's preference for tranquility. Which only added to the uncertainty Duke felt at the prospect of—once Father, Mother, and Grandmother left—requesting that his aunt and uncle sacrifice a portion of that peace for the possibility that Duke might have a modicum of it himself.

CHAPTER SEVENTEEN

GRANDMOTHER, FATHER, AND MOTHER MADE it through supper without yelling, throwing anything, or poisoning each other's food. And Aunt Penelope managed to look only slightly likely to murder them in return. That, in Duke's estimation, was both miraculous and reason for a rare bit of familial optimism. The night might not be a complete disaster. The uninvited individuals would leave for Lancashire in the morning, and all would be well again.

Duke trailed behind the Pack, his uncle, and his father as they made their way toward the drawing room, where the ladies had already assembled. He was still a few doors from their destination when he heard what sounded like his name being whispered.

He stopped and listened more closely. Then he heard it again. He looked around for the source and found Eve standing in a doorway, motioning him over. *Odd.*

Curiosity compelled him there every bit as much as the excitement of being in her company again. She tugged him a bit away from the doorway when he stepped inside. The room was lit, and the door was open, so there was no true impropriety in the arrangement.

His inward smile diminished when he saw an unmistakable look of distress on her face. "What's happened?"

"I'm worried about Nia. She didn't feel equal to joining everyone at supper. When I looked in on her while the other ladies went to the drawing room, Nia hadn't eaten a single bite of anything from the tray that was sent to her. And she's asleep again."

Duke took Eve's hand. It was a gesture meant to comfort her, but he'd also missed holding her hand. He was grateful for a chance to do so again. "If Nia's feeling poorly, sleep is likely the best thing for her."

"Except it's so unheard of for her to be as tired as she has been the past few days, especially today." Eve paced away a little, which pulled her hand from his. "In the past, whenever we've been reunited with the other Huntresses after an absence, she is bounding with energy, staying up far too late, gabbing and learning the latest from all the others. Instead, she took to her bed within an hour of our arrival."

This was a significant change, then.

"I think she ought to be seen by a doctor, but I know she won't admit it, and I know why." Eve wrung her hands just above her heart, her entire posture one of nervous worry. She met his eyes but only for a moment. In that moment, he saw unmistakable embarrassment. "I need to ask you a favor." She stopped directly in front of him and looked up at him once more, a hint of franticness now in her expression. "But you have to promise not to tell Artemis. She'll turn this into a crusade, and that would be disastrous."

"Tell me what you need, Aoife. I will do whatever I can."

She took a tense breath, her hands still clutching each other. "Even if your prediction proves true about Colm and his parents not allowing us to leave a token of acknowledgment for the servants, we—we still don't have enough to pay a doctor. If I tell any of the Huntresses that, they'll begin asking questions about the true state of our finances, and I'll be faced with the impossible choice of either lying to them or revealing the truth to Nia and breaking my promise to our parents."

"Your parents ought not to have required you to keep this from her. I suspect you do not care to withhold confidences from your sister."

"From *anyone*," Eve said, shaking her head. "I've told you of my tendency to speak without thinking overly much. I find myself doing an awful lot of thinking lately." Her hands stopped twisting around each other but remained clutched in front of her heart. She held his gaze with a pleading one. "Would you—" She took a bit of a shaky breath. "Would you pay the doctor?" She immediately and frantically added, "I will reimburse you, I promise. I don't know how, but I will manage it eventually."

He took her hands in his, lowering them. "You don't need—"

"You're going to say that I don't need to worry about repaying the debt, that you've money enough and are happy to pay the bill." She shook her head. "But I am tired of always taking and never being in a position to give to others. If I make good on this debt, then I will, for once, not be a leech, bleeding dry everyone around me."

The Best-Kept Secrets 105

"*Always taking?* You do remember the inn, don't you? Without your cooking while we were there, all of us would have been in dire straits. You certainly weren't bleeding anyone dry then."

Her hands shifted into a more comfortable position in his. She hadn't pulled away. His heart pounded out a pleased rhythm.

"Perhaps instead of remaining at Tulleyloch while my family attends the Season, I should find myself a position as a cook at someone's house." She smiled at him, but there was too much worry in the expression for him to believe the jest was anything but forced. She was trying to keep her spirits up in the face of anticipated humiliation.

"I was not going to say that you didn't need to worry about reimbursing me for the cost of the doctor but, rather, that you needn't worry about the cost at all. When a guest at a home grows ill, it falls to the host to fund the services of a man of medicine. No one would expect you or Nia to take on that obligation."

She looked hesitantly hopeful. "Truly?"

In all honesty, there was a small fraction of a chance that he was remembering that incorrectly, but he didn't think he was. He would sort out a means of discovering the established protocol without betraying Eve's confidences. Should paying the doctor, in actuality, be the responsibility of the person who was ill, Duke would quietly see to it.

"Do you feel the doctor ought to be sent for tonight?" he asked.

"I'm not so worried that I don't think it could wait until morning." She squeezed his hands and even smiled a little, though not quite enough for her dimple to reappear. "Thank you for this. I just knew you'd help me, but I felt guilty asking, seeing as your family burdens you so much with demands on your time and energy."

"There is a great difference between you asking me if I will help you and my family's unwavering requirement that I help them."

She narrowed her eyes. "Are you saying I should be more demanding?"

She had the most uncanny ability to bring him right to the brink of laughter. Not many people did.

"Are you not allowed to laugh, Dubhán Seymour?" she asked, much to his surprise. It was almost as if she had read his thoughts. "You assume a look now and then that I can describe only as 'inclined to laugh but not permitted to.'"

She was sorting him rather easily, wasn't she? He liked that she seemed so interested in doing so. "I don't laugh out loud very often. It has never been in my nature to do so."

"But you aren't unhappy, are you?" She seemed to genuinely want him to be happy.

"I am not any more unhappy than anyone else."

With a soft smile, she asked, "Are you happy right now?"

He was with her again, seeing her smile, holding her hands. "Right now, I am decidedly happy."

Then Eve did something he never thought he'd see from the lively Irishwoman: She blushed. And that blush set his heart racing and his mind back to their final evening in the inn.

He brushed his free hand along her cheek, mesmerized, as always, by her expressive silvery eyes. She slid closer but with the air of one who didn't realize she'd moved. They were drawn to each other; there was no denying that.

And her lips were as tempting as ever.

But before he could so much as lean closer to her, voices echoed in the corridor. Eve stepped back, her hands dropping free of his.

"This could be difficult to explain," she whispered.

While theirs wasn't a truly inappropriate arrangement, provided his inclination to kiss her was not inadvertently revealed, explaining the reason for their private conversation would be difficult without revealing the secrets she'd been sworn to keep.

He motioned her over to the wall the door was on. They stood side by side, their backs pressed against the wall. They wouldn't be spotted unless someone stepped inside and peeked around the door.

"But musical magic, of all things?" Grandmother's disparaging tones could not be mistaken. "Surely we could spend our evening in a more sophisticated manner."

"This gathering is for the young people," Aunt Penelope replied as calm and even as ever, though Duke knew well the telltale sounds of tension in her voice. "It's for them to choose the evening's entertainment."

"You would relegate your duties as hostess to a child?" Grandmother was likely wrinkling her nose the way she so often did.

"Mrs. Jonquil is not a child. She is perfectly capable—"

"How very like you, Penelope." That was Father, which meant the discussion in the corridor might soon be a full row.

Duke glanced at Eve, hoping she wasn't as horrified as he feared she would be. She was concentrating, but for once, he couldn't read her expression in the least.

"And just what is it you mean by that?" Aunt Penelope asked.

The Best-Kept Secrets

107

"Finding ways to benefit from the efforts of others," Father said. "The horses you snatched away from Ballycar, your greediness regarding Fairfield, now this."

"The horses I brought here were mine," Aunt Penelope said tightly. "Fairfield was always mine. And this house party is not about you, Liam. Neither is it about you, Mother. Nor myself or Niles."

"Then, what, pray tell, *is* it about?" Grandmother asked haughtily.

"For the first time since Colm returned from war, he has a group of friends he is at ease with, who accept him *as* himself. And he has brought them here, something he hasn't done since joining the army. And when he is with them, I see less of the hardened soldier and more of my Colm. If these young people want to play musical magic or move all or any other game you two consider beneath you, they will have free rein to do so."

"Colm is a war hero," Grandmother said. "He doesn't need childish—"

"You haven't the first idea what Colm needs," Aunt Penelope declared firmly and fiercely. "Or Duke."

"His name is Dubhán," Grandmother snapped.

"I call him what he asks me to call him," Aunt Penelope repeated to her. "I have found that listening when he speaks is a very enlightening experience. You should try it sometime."

"How dare you, Penelope." Father was clearly upset.

Eve's neutral expression slipped into a wince. More often than not, Duke's family managed to make everyone uncomfortable.

"Someone should stand up for your son," Aunt Penelope said. "These are his friends, too, and they have remained his friends despite this family's absolute inability to keep the peace among ourselves. What will happen when you have cost him every connection he has, Liam? Do you think he will thank you for the lonely future that would stretch out in front of him? War isn't the only thing that hardens a person."

"If his friends are so flighty as to abandon him because his family isn't perfect, then he could likely do better." Mother added that observation. Good heavens, they were all going to come to blows.

"I do not for a moment think they will be driven away," Aunt Penelope said. "Duke is a protector; he always has been. At some point, he will decide that he cannot bear to watch our animosity hurt his friends. What remains to be seen is if he will save his friends by cutting them off or by cutting *us* off. And lest you all think otherwise, I include this entire family in my use of the word *us*."

Duke was all but holding his breath. There was a painful truth in what his aunt was saying. He'd never invited the Pack to spend a school holiday at

Writtlestone, not wanting to subject them to the inevitable misery. His current decided-on approach was going to be distancing himself from his parents.

"If the young peoples' choice of entertainment is not to your liking," Aunt Penelope said, "you needn't join in. You can retire to your bedchambers and ponder on the question of when you mean to leave."

The click of shoes on the floor echoed an angry rhythm, growing quieter. Duke would guess it was his aunt who had stormed off.

"She laid the blame for all this at our feet," Mother said.

"She never does acknowledge how implacable she is." Grandmother clearly didn't realize stubbornness was a trait one often inherited from one's parents. "If not for me, I daresay, Penelope would have long since destroyed this family."

If not for *Grandmother*? They had demanded his entire life that Duke save the family, and either they didn't even realize what he'd done for them, or they simply chose not to give him credit for it.

"I'm of half a mind to remain at Fairfield," Father said, "if only to show her that she can't dictate what I do." He sounded just peevish enough to make good on the threat.

"Half a mind?" Grandmother repeated. "I'm of one mind on the topic. Penelope has seen herself as the head of this family for far too long, but I do not answer to her."

"*We* do not answer to her," Mother said.

"You two may include yourself in this if you wish," Grandmother said a little dismissively. "Penelope clearly thinks she has won this battle already. She will soon enough realize this battle is only just beginning."

Three sets of angry footfalls sounded after that.

"Do you think they will really make trouble?" Eve asked.

Duke wished he could honestly say no. "The Seymours have had some legendary battles over the years. They are never pleasant."

"But they have, thus far, kept their quarreling mostly behind closed doors, or at least away from everyone else," Eve said. "There was some snipping and grumbling during supper but not *overly* much. Perhaps that will continue to be their approach." Though she phrased it as a statement, there was an obvious question in it.

"I hope it is," was the most reassurance he could offer, and even it rang hollow.

"They are going to wreak havoc on the house party, aren't they?" Discouragement had entered her voice and expression.

"My family generally manages to ruin most everything." They had, after all, only just ruined a tender moment he'd been enjoying.

The Best-Kept Secrets 109

"No wonder you're hoping to achieve a bit of distance from the feud," she said. "Of course, even here you clearly can't entirely escape it."

"I cannot fully do so without having a home of my own," he said. "And I haven't sufficient income for that."

A hint of misgiving touched her expression; he realized quickly the likely reason why.

"I am not stretched thin, nor will I be burdened should I be called upon to pay a doctor after all," he assured her. "Paying for a residence is a much larger expenditure."

"You would tell me, wouldn't you, if I were asking too much?"

"Of course I would."

But she didn't seem convinced. "Your family asks too much of you, and you don't tell them."

"They will likely begin suspecting as much when I 'join the enemy,' as my parents and grandmother are likely to describe the situation, and potentially bring to Fairfield a larger battle than the one my grandmother is now planning."

"And they truly intend to stay at the house party, no matter that they weren't invited?" An anticipated misery clouded her usually bright and joyful eyes. "How do your aunt and uncle usually act during these battles?"

She had more than enough worries weighing on her. It was inexcusable for his family to add more.

"Uncle Niles usually steers clear of the fray." Duke had always envied him that. "Aunt Penelope manages a tense calm, for the most part. Family gatherings aren't precisely pleasant for either of them."

"Your grandmother sounded as if she means to intentionally escalate hostilities among and with her children."

A twist of dread clutched at his stomach. "She will almost certainly do precisely that."

"This is likely my last time among the Huntresses and the Pack, and it's going to be miserable." The disappointment in her eyes skewered him, though he didn't think it was truly aimed at him. She stepped toward the door. "I think I'll follow Nia's lead and get a bit of rest."

"Tell me if you decide she ought to have a doctor before morning," Duke said.

"I will. Thank you." Eve left with so little of the joie de vivre she usually had.

This was what time with his family did to people. Eve had managed to endure nearly a week with his grandmother, but one evening with the rest of the quarreling Seymours had visibly and heartbreakingly dampened her spirits.

"Duke is a protector," Aunt Penelope had said. *"At some point, he will decide that he cannot bear to watch our animosity hurt his friends."*

That animosity had already caused Eve pain and had done so here, where he was supposed to have been free from the bickering for a time. He had no expectation of Fairfield being an unbroken idyll should his aunt and uncle allow him to live with them. But he'd not even had a single minute of freedom from the feud since his arrival.

He was never going to truly escape it.

Aunt Penelope was absolutely correct. Duke would do what he must to protect his friends from his family.

CHAPTER EIGHTEEN

"WHAT WILL HAPPEN WHEN YOU have cost him every connection he has, Liam?"
Aunt Penelope's question—her *prophecy*, if Duke were being entirely honest about how it felt—had echoed again and again in his thoughts all night long. And the reality of it all had crashed down on him that morning as he'd dressed. He had fully expected to attend this house party as Duke, member of the Pack. But if he were to have any hope of keeping his family from making his friends utterly miserable and ruining this rare time of all being together, he needed, instead, to spend the next two weeks being Dubhán, peace negotiator of the Seymour Family.

It is horrifically unfair.

"Do you think he will thank you for the lonely future that would stretch out in front of him?" Aunt Penelope had also asked Father the night before.

Lonely *future.* As if all this hadn't already cost him connections and moments of camaraderie. He'd missed some of the school holidays the Pack had spent together because he'd needed to go to Writtlestone and he didn't dare invite his friends there. When Father had visited him at Eton and Cambridge, Duke had arranged for the two of them to be extremely busy so there would be limited opportunity for Father to interact with anyone.

Living with his parents when they were in London would mean never having his friends there. He'd have to do his utmost to avoid connecting enough with anyone new that they would not call at his parents' home. And he'd likely not have the privilege of joining the same gentlemen's club as Father. All this had Duke's thoughts begging houseroom from his aunt and uncle even when in Town.

Now, with his parents' and grandmother's decision to remain at Fairfield, he would have to spend this house party as the peacekeeper rather than being permitted to relax and participate fully. This was his first social foray since ending his time as a student. It was a new beginning of sorts, yet his old difficulties had followed him through the door.

"Good morning," Colm said, approaching him with curiosity.

That morning after finishing his breakfast, Duke had placed himself next to the door everyone used when making their way out to the stables. His cousin, being a Seymour and thus an avid and skilled equestrian, would without question be planning on a morning ride. Hovering near the exit was Duke's best chance for talking with him.

"Before you leave for your ride," Duke said, "I have two favors to ask, which I realize is a little presumptuous." They were cousins, but they were also not well acquainted and didn't interact often.

"No harm in asking," Colm said, still watching him with an inquisitive look. Though Colm was not truly a hardened person, at least from Duke's limited time with him since Colm's returning from war, there was an authoritative air to him that a person couldn't miss.

"The first is a little odd," Duke said, "but mostly because I'm not certain precisely what it is I'm asking for."

A quick nod of acknowledgment. "That *is* odd."

"I unintentionally overheard a conversation between your mother, my father, and our grandmother last night," Duke said.

Colm's mouth pulled into a tense line. A lifetime of their family members being at odds with each other hadn't exactly been a delight for either of them. "Were they arguing again?"

"Of course they were." He didn't bother hiding his annoyance. "I wish I knew how your mother maintains as much of her composure as she does during these altercations."

"How *Mother* stays composed? Duke, you are the Unshakable Dubhán. I've wondered for years now how you manage to keep the peace as well as you do." With a hint of a smile, Colm added, "We could have used that gift on the Continent while Napoleon was frolicking around Europe."

There was just enough lightness in Colm's response to ease Duke's mind. He found he could jest a bit as well. "I *did* prove myself an excellent spy last night."

Colm looked intrigued. "Did you?"

"I overheard your mother say something that I think you ought to know." Duke felt strange making the request he was about to, but he'd heard heartbreak in Aunt Penelope's voice last night. "The undefined favor I'm going to ask is that after I tell you what she said, you do something about it."

The Best-Kept Secrets 113

"With the *undefined* part being that you don't know what precisely I ought to do," Colm guessed with a flicker of a smile. "What did she say?"

Duke had debated all night how to approach this. He didn't want Aunt Penelope to continue being unhappy and worried. But he didn't want to transfer that distress to Colm. "That, essentially, she's a little worried about you."

All hints of Colm's smile disappeared, though he didn't look upset or offended. "Worried about *what* in regard to me?"

Duke wasn't going to tell Colm that he was breaking his mother's heart or that she felt like she'd lost her son to the ravages of war. Those ravages were likely still tearing at him. "She wants you to enjoy this house party, but she worries that you won't now that my parents and our grandmother have decided to remain."

Colm breathed tensely. "They're staying?"

"Unfortunately." This was an approach to the matter that didn't require Duke to tell Colm all the pain he'd heard in Aunt Penelope's voice. "She said this was the first time you've had friends at Fairfield since returning from the Continent, and I suspect she wanted everything to be as close to perfect as she could manage."

"And she's worried that I won't bring friends around again if—when the Seymour family's bickering causes the inevitable upheaval?"

"Yes, and that you'll be made unhappy by it. Aunt Penelope very much wants you to be happy."

Colm's jaw worked in a movement that spoke of uneasy contemplation. "She looks at me sometimes with an expression that tells me she knows I'm not as happy as I used to be. War does that to people, Duke. It breaks something in a person that makes happiness a little hard to keep hold of."

Maybe he shouldn't have even tiptoed toward this. Wanting to ease Aunt Penelope's worries might have led him to cause Colm pain, which wasn't at all what Duke wanted. Everything about the extended Seymour family felt impossibly complicated.

"I am glad the Pack and the Huntresses are here," Colm said. "And even with the eruption of hostilities you and I can easily predict between our parents and grandmother, I will still be pleased to have our friends here."

Duke hoped that proved true, but he knew perfectly well how destructive the family's feud could be.

A flicker of a smile tugged at Colm's lips. "I will make certain my mother knows how pleased I am to have this house party at Fairfield."

"I think she would appreciate that." And Duke hoped he'd done the right thing in turning Colm's thoughts toward that expression of gratitude.

Colm leaned against the doorframe. "What was your other favor?"

"This one requires you to keep a secret," Duke warned.

"Understood."

Duke rested his shoulder against the other side of the doorframe. "Eve told me last night that she thinks Nia ought to be seen by a doctor."

"Gads." Colm's posture grew rigid once more. "She's that ill?"

"Eve thinks she might be."

Colm nodded. "Nia didn't seem like herself yesterday."

"I don't know where the nearest reliable man of medicine is."

"Dr. Wilstead in Epsom. I'd trust him with the lives of anyone I care for."

"Excellent. Will you send for him?"

"Of course." Colm's gaze narrowed a bit. "But I suspect that isn't the thing you need me to keep secret."

"Eve was embarrassed to admit that they haven't money enough to pay a doctor. She's been worried about the gratuities expected for the servants." Duke didn't feel he was betraying her confidence in mentioning that. What he had already understood about their financial situation before Eve's further revelations would have told him as much. "While everyone, the Huntresses especially, knows the O'Doyles are quite thin in the pocketbook, Eve was so clearly embarrassed by her inability to afford those two things that I am certain we oughtn't reveal it to the others. But we also need to find a way for the sisters, without being further humbled, to be relieved of those expenses."

Colm dropped a hand on Duke's shoulder and steered him back down the corridor, clearly not intending to go for his ride as he'd originally planned. "No gratuities will be owed to the servants, from *anyone*. Mother and Father arranged for that, knowing quite a few of the Huntresses and the Pack are stretched thin. See if you can't communicate as much to Eve."

"I will." Duke was breathing a bit more easily.

"And my parents would likely be offended if any of their guests thought a doctor summoned to Fairfield would not be recompensed *by Fairfield*. So, Eve has no reason to worry on that score either."

Relief washed over Duke. "I told her that would be the case, though I wasn't completely certain. I would have paid the doctor if need be, but Eve insisted that if I did, she would repay me over the years to come, which she absolutely cannot afford to do. I'd hoped you would be willing to help me work around that."

"Consider it worked around. I will send for Dr. Wilstead. The estate will pay for his services and for any medicines he says Nia needs. Eve has nothing to be concerned about except looking after her sister."

"Thank you," Duke said.

"I am newer to this group of friends than you are, Duke, but they all matter to me. It's been too long since I've allowed myself to really care about people." A little emotion had crept into his admission, but Colm pushed it out of his expression. "Don't you dare tell my mother I said that."

"I'm good at keeping secrets," Duke assured him.

Colm answered with a crisp nod. Duke watched his cousin continue down the corridor, no doubt to ask the butler to have a message sent to Dr. Wilstead in Epsom. *"It's been too long since I've allowed myself to really care about people."* The friendship Colm had with the Pack and the Huntresses was helping him find some happiness and connection, helping him heal a little after the brutality of war. If their family caused distress to Colm's newfound friends, he would lose this chance to solidify those bonds of friendship. Duke couldn't sit idly by and allow that to happen.

Duke stood in the corridor, a bit to the side of the door to Eve and Nia's bedchamber. Dr. Wilstead had arrived a few minutes earlier and was checking on Nia. Duke wanted to be close at hand should anything be needed.

"Dr. Wilstead can be depended on, Eve. I promise you." Aunt Penelope was inside. She'd offered variations on that reassurance more than once already, a sure sign that Eve wasn't hiding her worry very well.

"Nia is almost never ill," Eve said. "And on the rare occasion when she is, she won't admit to it. She had a miserably sore throat a couple of weeks ago, and though we could all hear it in her scratchy voice, she still insisted she was fine."

"We Irish are a stubborn people, aren't we?"

"Stubborn enough not to admit we're stubborn," Eve said.

A moment passed in silence. Duke was sorely tempted to peek inside, but he would not invade their privacy that way. Part of him wasn't certain he was within his rights to be as near to doing so now as he was.

"I knew she had been tired," Eve said, "but she told me this morning that she's been in pain as well. Something about the long carriage ride increased her suffering enough that she could no longer pretend all was well."

Duke thought Nia had done a good job, actually. He'd not guessed she was hurting. That she was exhausted had been obvious. But he had seen no indication that she'd been in pain.

From behind him, Colm walked almost silently to where Duke stood. "The doctor arrived, I heard." He spoke quietly.

Duke nodded. "He's in there now. Thank you again for arranging this."

"Of course. What has Wilstead said?"

"Nothing yet. I suspect he is still in the midst of his evaluation."

Colm met Duke's eye once more. "You've likely not long before the Huntresses hear that Nia has required a doctor. Do you mean to stand guard and prevent them from breaching the threshold?"

Duke raised his brows. "Do *you*?"

Colm held up his hands in a show of denial. "I tiptoed uncomfortably close to death enough times in the army not to wish to repeat the experience."

"You think Artemis would murder you?"

"Readily and eagerly." Though Colm made the declaration with an air of somberness, there was laughter in his eyes.

"Do the Huntresses frighten you?"

"Absolutely," Colm said without hesitation.

They could hear Dr. Wilstead's voice from inside the room. "A word, Miss O'Doyle."

Duke grew instantly still and listened. Colm did the same.

"How long has your sister had this rash?"

A rash? That was not a good sign at all. Depending on what type of rash, Nia might be horribly ill indeed.

"I will not tolerate her neglect." Grandmother's well-known shrill tones carried over to them. "It is an embarrassment to the entire family."

"What is stuck in her craw now?" Colm muttered under his breath as they turned to watch their grandmother approach.

"I suspect she will tell us without prompting."

Grandmother stormed toward them, her eyes on the doorway. Duke moved to stand between her and her apparent destination. Nia needed to rest, not be subjected to a Seymour squabble.

"Penelope is in there instead of seeing to the rest of her guests, and I mean to remind her of her duties."

Duke reached back and pulled the door closed, preventing their grandmother's voice or her presence from intruding further upon the sickroom.

"The younger Miss O'Doyle is not feeling well," Colm said. "Mother is acting as a support to the older Miss O'Doyle, who is understandably concerned about her sister. That is the perfect thing for a hostess to do."

Grandmother ruffled up on the instant.

Duke would do best to head off whatever was coming before it burst forth. "The time you spent teaching her how to look after guests in her home has

The Best-Kept Secrets   117

clearly proven beneficial now. All the guests will be singing the praises of the Seymour family."

Colm very clearly bit back a laugh. He obviously knew Duke was soothing Grandmother's ire with a bit of exaggeration.

"Would you be so good as to make certain the breakfast items have been refreshed?" Duke said. "Not all the guests have risen yet, and I do not have to tell you how important it is that they not find stale offerings when they do."

Grandmother gave a firm nod. "I suspect that hasn't been seen to. I will do so at once." She made good on her declaration and stormed off only slightly less snappish than she had been when she'd arrived in the corridor.

"That was a near-run thing," Colm said. "She almost bullyragged her way inside."

"Our parents and grandmother all being at Fairfield is likely to lead to more disasters like the one we only just narrowly avoided."

Colm released a tense breath. "Unfortunately, I've been having the same thought. The Seymours can't manage to be entirely at peace, can we?"

"I've never known the family to accept a ceasefire." Duke rubbed at his forehead, tension and frustration expanding ever more inside him.

"Makes you feel sorry for anyone who has to spend any amount of time with us." Colm set himself on the other side of the closed door, likely intending to keep watch over that end of the corridor.

"Our friends will leave here grateful that they aren't required to endure a lifetime among the Seymours."

A lifetime among the Seymours. Colm hadn't, Duke felt certain, meant the observation to be pointed, yet it struck Duke with piercing emphasis.

Duke was making plans to reduce the amount of "this" that he would have to endure during his lifetime, knowing it wouldn't ever be fully eliminated. And any lady he brought into his life would have to endure it as well. The arguing and petulance. The demands for appeasement. The barbed comments and thinly veiled criticisms. The embarrassment when other people witnessed the combative connections in the Seymour family.

Courting a lady would bring her into the periphery of that purgatory. Actually marrying her would permanently tie her to it.

He supposed he had always known that to an extent, but he'd not dwelled on it overly much. There'd been no reason. But there was now.

The growing infatuation he had for Eve couldn't be allowed to grow. Even setting aside the precariousness of his housing situation, something no lady should be pulled into, the life he had to offer was one inextricably connected to conflict and unhappiness, with a family he suspected would treat her as poorly as they treated each other. It was, he knew all too well, a dismal prospect.

Eve deserved better.

CHAPTER NINETEEN

"IT IS IMPORTANT THAT YOU not overexert yourself," Dr. Wilstead told Nia as he walked attentively at her side toward the drawing room. "But it is also important that you move about—*sedately*, mind—keep your spirits up, take some fresh air each day. The trickiest aspect of that will be striking the appropriate balance between rest and movement."

"How does one go about discovering that balance?" To Eve's relief, Nia didn't sound as exhausted as she had before the doctor's arrival, though she was certainly not her usual self.

"Unfortunately," Dr. Wilstead said, "usually by getting the balance wrong and paying the consequences."

"I do not like that methodology," Nia said.

"I don't blame you," was the doctor's kindly spoken response.

Eve plumped a cushion on the sofa, placing it in what she hoped was the exact right spot to give her sister optimal comfort. Eve had felt so helpless that morning, hearing the doctor diagnose Nia's illness as rheumatic fever, worrying over what that meant, hoping Duke was right that the Greenberrys would pay the doctor's fee whilst simultaneously feeling guilty about that.

Dr. Wilstead saw Nia seated and looked her over, no doubt checking her coloring and the clearness of her eyes and all the other symptoms doctors were forever studying in their patients.

"How long is this likely to last?" Eve asked.

"With rheumatic fever, duration is difficult to predict. Many people feel markedly better in only a few weeks."

Hearing the words *rheumatic fever* fall from Dr. Wilstead's lips in the room she shared with Nia had driven fear directly to her heart, but this declaration gave her hope.

Then he snatched it away by adding, "Many others are afflicted for years."

For years. Nia might be ill *for years.* Heavens above.

To Nia, Dr. Wilstead said, "You are young but not a child, and healthy. And by your own recollection, you have not had rheumatic fever in the past. All of those things are marks decidedly in your favor."

But was it enough?

"I am in a rather lot of pain," Nia said, and her expression revealed the truth of that.

"I have sent down to the Fairfield kitchen a recipe for a very effective tisane that should relieve much of that without making you sleepy. Keeping your spirits up is important. At night, you can take the powders I will have delivered to your room to help you sleep."

"But I don't have to remain in my room for the entirety of the house party?" Nia pressed.

The doctor shook his head. "Your activity will need to be limited, but it needn't be curtailed entirely. Rest whenever you feel you need to. I will be here at Fairfield for the next few days to make certain you are doing as well as you ought. After that, I will return as needed to check on your progress."

"Thank you, Dr. Wilstead," Nia said.

As he turned toward the door, he motioned for Eve to walk with him. "She is doing well," he said in low tones, "but rheumatic fever is not to be taken lightly. Should she show any signs of heart distress, I am to be sent for immediately, even if I have already returned to Epsom."

Heart distress.

For years.

Eve nodded, doing her utmost to hide the worry that surged at his firmly delivered instructions. Everyone knew rheumatic fever could cause tremendous damage to the heart, but no one seemed to know how to predict if it would or how to prevent it from happening.

Keeping her voice low, she asked Dr. Wilstead, "You said she could be ill for years. Is Nia likely, then, to need a doctor's care after we return to Ireland?"

"When are you planning to return?"

"In about two weeks."

Dr. Wilstead nodded. "She will not be recovered by then. She might still be too unwell to travel."

Eve summoned the closest expression she could manage to calm and collected, while inwardly she was anything but. "I'll not risk her health by forcing her to travel, but if the house party has ended . . ." She didn't have an immediate answer to the dilemma.

The Best-Kept Secrets

"If you are unable to extend your time at Fairfield," he said, "there are several very reputable inns in Epsom that you could remove to while she continues her recovery. I can look in on her there."

They couldn't afford to pay for the doctor's services or the medicines Nia needed, let alone pay for a drawn-out stay at an inn. Eve would have to find an answer to that difficulty should Nia not be recovered enough to return home. And since the doctor didn't believe Nia would be truly well before returning to Ireland, there would be continued expense after they were at Tulleyloch.

How were they ever to manage it?

"How likely do you think it is that Nia will be ill for years upon years?" Eve asked the doctor.

"I think it more likely that she'll recover in a few weeks and emerge quite healthy and not terribly worse for the experience." A bit of warning entered his expression. "I, of course, cannot guarantee that."

Eve nodded. "I understand."

She wished Duke were here. He'd not merely told her that she could talk with him about her worries and uncertainties, but he'd also shown himself to be a wonderfully kind and considerate listener. He was reassuring and comforting. Just being with him helped her feel better no matter what was weighing on her.

Doing her utmost to wipe the worry from her expression, she returned to where Nia sat on the sofa. "If that doctor hadn't said you were to join in a bit of the revelry to come, I think I would have demanded a different man of medicine be summoned."

Nia's smile helped ease some of Eve's worry. It wasn't as broad or easy as it usually was, but neither was it weak nor forced. "I don't know how much 'revelry' I will manage, but I would be cruelly disappointed not to at least be permitted to watch."

"Shall we demand that Charlie undertake some very diverting mimicry for your entertainment?" Eve suggested. Charlie had a shocking knack for portraying in mannerisms and voice a great many people with incredible accuracy.

"We should demand that *everyone* do all I ask for my entertainment."

"Excellent plan. I shall implement it immediately."

They laughed, Nia lightly, Eve with an eye on her sister. A moment's silence descended on them.

"Do you think Dr. Wilstead was making light of the situation?" Nia asked after a moment. "I have never felt this ill before. Not like this. I'm—I'm a little worried."

Eve took her hand. "I think he was being entirely forthright. There is a chance that you'll grow more ill or have a prolonged recovery, but he doesn't seem convinced that either is inevitable."

Nia pulled her shawl a bit more tightly around her shoulders. "But Dr. Wilstead is staying here at Fairfield for several days. I don't think he would take such precautions if he was confident in my recovery."

It was a very logical evaluation, yet Eve didn't think Dr. Wilstead had been dishonest. "The fact that he hasn't said he will remain for *weeks* tells me he knows you will feel quite unwell for a few days but expects you to greatly improve after that."

Nia leaned a little against her. "I don't want to be excluded from the party."

"It would hardly be a party without you."

Artemis Jonquil had ever been one to make a dramatic entrance. That she glided into the room just as Eve made that declaration further proved the fact. "Nia most certainly *will* be part of this house party, even if we have to hold the entirety of it at the foot of her bed."

"That'd be terrible crowded, that would." Nia's bit of humor did much to reassure Eve. Somehow, they would weather this unexpected storm.

Charlie poked his head into the room. "A carriage is coming, Artie."

"It must be Lisette." Artemis turned bright, hopeful eyes on them. "Are you equal to rushing with us to the windows in the entryway to peek out like vagabonds?"

"I am always eager for vagabondish peeking," Nia said.

They walked sedately, on account of Nia's aching body, from the drawing room to the entryway. All the other Huntresses, aside from the one they were anticipating, and the entirety of the Pack were gathered at the two tall windows, looking out. Even Duke, who did not always participate in their ridiculousness, was doing so now.

Colm fetched a chair and set it at one window, motioning for Nia to sit there. Eve silently chastised herself for not having thought of that. Thank the heavens Nia had so many people here who cared about her.

Into the absurdly immature tableau, Mr. and Mrs. Greenberry arrived.

"I would be shocked," Mr. Greenberry said, "but this is precisely the sort of thing our friends would have done at your ages."

"We believe the final Huntress has arrived," Artemis said. "A carriage has stopped in front of the house."

"I hate to disappoint you," Mrs. Greenberry said, "but I know whose carriage that is, and 'tisn't who you think."

The Best-Kept Secrets 123

As one, the group turned and looked at her, but she offered no further explanation. The Greenberrys stepped through the door as a footman opened it, and walked out to meet this mysterious new arrival. No longer satisfied with just *watching* the goings-on, Eve, as she suspected the rest of the group was doing, strained her ears to hear what was said as well.

The carriage door was opened, and a lady was handed out. She was of the same generation as the Greenberrys, very elegantly and tastefully attired. She was pretty in a graceful way.

Next, a gentleman, also of the Greenberrys' generation, emerged from the carriage. His brand of elegance tended more toward simplicity, but it suited him perfectly. Who was this striking couple?

The newly arrived lady said something to Mrs. Greenberry in French. Though Nia had something of a grasp of that language, she was nowhere near proficient.

In a low whisper, Duke said, "She asked, 'Has she arrived?'"

Eve glanced back at him, not having realized he'd come and stood near her. She smiled quickly at him, her heart leaping at the chance to see his gorgeous eyes light up with a smile of his own. They didn't, but he also didn't look upset.

Duke continued his translation. "My aunt just replied, 'Not yet, but she is expected at any moment.'"

The elegant gentleman also spoke in French.

"Then, we are not too late?" Duke translated. His uncle's response to that, he explained was, "You are not. And it wasn't—" He had to think for a moment. "Nothing was said to her." The new arrivals looked immediately relieved.

"*Merci*, Penelope," the French lady said. "*Merci beaucoup*, Niles."

Eve didn't need help understanding that.

When his aunt replied, Duke took up the translation once again. "I only wish we could have found a means of arranging this sooner."

Arranged what *sooner?* It was all so mysterious.

The Frenchman spoke to Mr. Greenberry. Duke once again translated. "It is better that this is . . . done later than we hoped than . . . for it not to be done at all."

Eve leaned a bit back, so she could speak to Duke. "Translator?"

He looked confused.

"Your dreamed-of future is as a translator, isn't it?"

He allowed only the tiniest and briefest show of amusement. "No."

"Then, perhaps as a solver of mysteries. Have you been able to sort what it is they are talking about?"

"I haven't." His tone was a little distant, a little impersonal. Odd.

"Are they talking about Lisette?" Daria asked from her place of watching, her husband, Toss's, arms around her. "Lisette *is* French."

"And soon to be arriving," Gillian added.

The Greenberrys walked beside their French friends back to the doors and into the entryway. The new arrivals spotted the crowd of curious onlookers and, far from shocked, laughed.

"They are like our Gents, are they not?" the French lady said, shifting seamlessly to English.

"And our Gents' ladies," the gentleman Eve assumed to be her husband replied.

"Monsieur Fortier." Toss stepped out from among them and shook the gentleman's hand enthusiastically. "I didn't realize you were going to be at Fairfield."

"A pleasure to see you again, Mr. Comstock."

Eve had heard of the Fortiers. They had helped Toss sort out a difficulty with his brother and his chosen profession. They had invested in a property of Gillian and Scott's, allowing it to be brought to rights without draining what little funds the young couple had. And no one seemed to know why they would do so much for people they didn't know and to whom, as far as those beneficiaries could tell, they had no connection.

"These are the Huntresses, *oui*?" Mme Fortier said, watching them all with a fondness not usually shown to complete strangers.

"*Oui*." Artemis stepped forward. "All of us, save one."

Everyone's eyes pulled wide as Mme Fortier wrapped her arms around Artemis in a hug that could be described only as motherly. "*Merci beaucoup, Mme Jonquil. Merci. Merci.*"

Artemis looked utterly baffled. What was happening?

Eve turned to Duke, hoping he might have some explanation, but he wasn't standing near her any longer and wasn't looking at her.

"*Merci* to all of you wonderful Huntresses." Mme Fortier stepped away from Artemis as she looked over the group with obvious gratitude. But gratitude for what? No one else seemed to have any better idea than Eve did.

M. Fortier spoke next. "I can tell all of you, we did not see another carriage on the road this morning, meaning the arrival you are awaiting is not likely to reach Fairfield immediately."

With a huzzah, Charlie declared, "To the drawing room, friends!" then rushed in that direction as if storming a fortified city.

"He is very like his father was," Mme Fortier said.

The Best-Kept Secrets

Charlie stopped his forward march, spun around, and bowed deeply to the Fortiers before resuming his energetic exit.

With a smile that was somehow both amused and sad, M. Fortier said, "So very like him."

The Pack and Huntresses followed Charlie's path. Eve helped Nia stand, and Colm quickly saw to the chair Nia had been using. Duke passed by on his way to the drawing room.

"I can only imagine what mischief Charlie will get into this next fortnight," Eve said to Duke.

"We'll soon find out, I suppose." The response was not unfriendly, but he kept going rather than walking with her as she had fully expected him to.

"Is Duke upset with you?" Nia asked as they slowly walked toward the drawing room.

"I don't know." In her confusion, that was all Eve could manage to say. "I don't know."

CHAPTER TWENTY

Artemis was waiting for Eve and Nia just inside the drawing room when they arrived. She hooked her arm through Nia's. "If that horrid doctor had said you could not participate in this house party," Artemis said as she walked with Nia to the sofa, where space had been left for her to sit and rest, "I would have declared him my mortal enemy and vanquished him with all possible haste."

"What a relief that you aren't to be excluded, Nia," Daria said.

"Especially for Dr. Wilstead," was Toss's dry remark.

"What shall we do while we wait for Lisette?" Artemis asked.

"A game," Charlie said in an immediate and enthusiastic suggestion.

"One we can play sitting down," Eve requested, earning a smile of gratitude from Nia.

"We'd need to move the chairs into more of a circle," Ellie, one of the Huntresses, said, "but we could play short answer."

The group quickly took up the suggestion and adjusted the furniture as needed. Artemis remained seated beside Nia. It was like seeing a glimpse of the Season Nia would have without Eve. She wouldn't be alone. She wouldn't be neglected. That did Eve's heart a great deal of good.

As everyone took seats to begin the game, Eve was able to sit beside Duke. After days of sitting next to him in the carriage, it was an arrangement she found comfortingly familiar. And as it always did, her heart flipped about at being near him.

Nia was chosen to begin the game. She turned to Artemis, seated on her right, and asked, "Who is your favorite Huntress?"

Laughter and grins popped up. The answers given could not be more than one syllable; that was one of the rules of the game. And of the Huntresses, only Rose and Eve had one-syllable names. Which would Artemis choose?

She proved more clever than that and answered, "All."

Her response was booed, but only on account of "all" being a very useful answer in this game, and according to another of the rules, it could now not be given by anyone else.

Artemis turned to Charlie, who had predictably sat beside his wife. "Who is your favorite member of the Pack?"

Four Pack members had single-syllable names, but Eve didn't think Charlie would simply pick one of them.

Giving Artemis a triumphant look, he answered, "None."

The Pack vocally approved.

Eve was on Charlie's right side, meaning the next question would be posed to her. She grinned in anticipation.

"Which character of Greek mythology is the most troublesome?" he asked.

Greek mythology? Eve had given very little thought to the topic, beyond reading about Artemis's namesake after becoming one of that lady's dear friends. A few names flitted through her mind but none that was a single syllable. Ought she to think of a sidestepping answer, as Charlie and Artemis had done with their questions?

But then she remembered. "Zeus!"

Charlie sighed as if disappointed. "I was so looking forward to hearing you attempt to say, 'Artemis,' in a single syllable." He earned a laughing shove from his wife for that comment.

Eve turned to Duke. Those beautiful eyes of his. She would never grow tired of looking at them. "Which of Charlie's brothers is more clever than he is?"

Duke shook his head solemnly. "An unfair question, as the only accurate answer would be 'all.'"

The group laughed. A flit of humor twinkled in Duke's deep-blue eyes as he looked at his friends. It was so good to see him light and happy. But when he looked back at her, some of that lightness dissipated. Was he upset with her, as Nia had wondered? Eve could think of nothing that had happened.

To her game question, Duke answered, "Most." And then he turned to Toss to continue the game. He hadn't lingered on her even long enough to see if she appreciated his answer. Something clearly *had* happened. Three nights earlier, he'd kissed her. Now, he barely acknowledged she was there.

"Which instrument," he asked Toss, "is played by the most intelligent people?"

That earned Duke approving laughter. Toss was an exceptional musician, but his instrument of choice was the pianoforte, which was four syllables too

The Best-Kept Secrets 129

long. No matter his answer, Toss would be declaring himself lacking in intelligence, the prospect of which was making him laugh even harder than everyone else.

"Pianoforte," Toss declared.

"That's *five* syllables," Newton said at the same time Artemis said, "You've managed to lose on your very first turn."

Looking excessively proud of himself, Toss said, "Well worth it." That set everyone to laughing yet again.

Hilarity was near constant when this group of friends was together. This gathering was no exception. Of course, it absolutely helped that the Seymours, other than Duke and Colm, were not in the room. That was unlikely to be true most of the next fortnight.

"Ask Daria a question," Artemis instructed Toss, "then sit there and ponder what a troublemaker you are."

As jovial as ever, Toss turned to Daria. "Which Pack member is, without question, the greatest, most loving, handsomest, most talented, exceptionally amazing husband?"

Daria grinned. "Toss!"

Shouts of "No fair" and "Foul" and a fair number of boos answered that. But Toss put an arm around his wife and looked out at all of them smugly.

In the midst of the good-natured teasing, the group heard carriage wheels outside.

"Lisette!" Artemis jumped up and made for the door of the drawing room, the rest following suit.

But Mrs. Greenberry stood on the other side of the threshold. "I must ask you to wait a moment."

"But this will be Lisette arriving," Artemis said. "We've not seen her in a year."

"Please," Mrs. Greenberry repeated. "It is very important that this not be interrupted."

"That *what* not be interrupted?" Eve pressed.

Mrs. Greenberry stood firm. "Something of paramount importance that must go perfectly, or it will be an absolute tragedy." There was too much sincerity in her expression for her declaration to be an exaggeration.

"We can see through windows," Daria declared excitedly.

The Huntresses exchanged looks before rushing to the drawing room windows facing the front drive. Nia moved quite a bit more slowly, allowing Eve a chance to ask their hostess one more question. "Watching won't cause difficulties, will it?"

"Not if you aren't obvious about it." She glanced behind herself in the direction of the entryway.

Someone in the group opened two windows a crack. The sound of the coachman talking with the footman who'd met the carriage carried over to them.

The Pack had gathered at the windows as well.

Eve joined them all there, standing next to Duke. "Mrs. Greenberry said we have to be careful not to draw attention to ourselves," she warned them all.

Quieter than she suspected the lot of them had *ever* been when together, they watched and listened. Eve found her attention divided between Duke beside her and the scene outside. Duke didn't seem to be experiencing the same quandary.

M. and Mme Fortier stepped out of the house, stopping beside the carriage. They motioned for the footman to open the carriage door.

From within the dark interior, Lisette was handed out. She was decidedly the most gorgeous of all the Huntresses, which was no small feat when one considered how shockingly beautiful Artemis was, but there was a fragileness to Lisette's beauty, added to by the slightness of her frame, that made her seem like something exquisitely precious that could be whisked away at any moment without warning.

"Is that your Lisette?" Colm asked in a whisper.

"Yes," Artemis answered at the same volume.

Outside, Lisette's gaze fell on the French couple, and she immediately burst into tears. *Good heavens.* Mme Fortier pulled Lisette into an embrace. M. Fortier brushed his hand tenderly and soothingly over her dark hair.

Lisette spoke to the couple in French. Eve hadn't ever been overly embarrassed at her lack of education in that language, but now, she was downright frustrated.

"'How did you know I would be here?'" Duke once again translated for Eve.

She took his hand, hoping he would feel in the gesture the expression of gratitude she wished it to be. He gave her hand a quick squeeze—a *very* quick squeeze—then pulled free. Eve told herself not to take that personally.

He kept translating. "Mme Fortier is saying, 'We have been watching for two years now, hoping for an opportunity.'"

An opportunity for what?

"Lisette says, 'Mme Dupuis is with me.'"

"Oh no," Eve whispered. Lisette's dragon of a chaperone had made the last Huntresses' house party a sometimes frustrating affair.

The Best-Kept Secrets

131

"M. Fortier says, 'She has—tormented you long enough.'"

Eve watched as the Frenchman, who'd given the impression of being very genial and sedate, turned toward the carriage with a suddenly hard expression. He spoke to whomever was inside, Mme Dupuis, no doubt.

"He says, 'No need to get out. This can be accomplished in here.'" Then he stepped into the carriage.

Mme Fortier walked with her arm around Lisette back into the house and out of view. Mrs. Greenberry was still standing guard at the drawing room door, not allowing them to greet their beloved Lisette.

"What do you suppose that was about?" Eve asked no one in particular.

Artemis answered, "I have absolutely no idea."

CHAPTER TWENTY-ONE

It had taken every bit of strength Duke had had to pull away when Eve had taken his hand. He would miss that simple touch. But reality had met him here on his very first night at Fairfield. He'd imagined that if he made his home here, he would have control over when and how often he saw his parents. He would be afforded some peace and a refuge from the Seymour family feud. But his parents had descended on Fairfield without invitation and without warning. The feud was erupting anew, and there was no preventing it. He might manage to claim some time away, but there would be no actual escape. Ever. And he could offer no actual peace to any lady who threw her lot in with his.

There was no point in permitting his and Eve's connection to grow and deepen. It would be cruel, in fact, to do so.

"M. Fortier has climbed back out of the carriage," Artemis said.

Everyone leaned closer to the windows, watching. Duke could only just make out the edge of the carriage. Moments later, the horses were set in motion, and the carriage pulled away, not toward the stables but back down the drive.

"Mme Dupuis was still inside," Eve said. "Where do you suppose she's going?"

"I haven't the first idea," Nia answered.

"Clearly, the Fortiers are not strangers to Lisette," Artemis said as she stepped away from the window, her expression one of contemplation. The rest of the group wandered away from the windows as well.

"They *are* all French," Daria said.

Duke was near enough to Eve to hear Nia whisper to her, "I think I'd best go lie down. I'm suddenly feeling awful."

Eve looked at him, and he saw worry in those expressive eyes. He couldn't not help, but he also didn't want to see her hurt in the end. Somehow, he would find a way over the coming weeks to toe that line.

He set a hand under one of Nia's elbows, with Eve wrapping her arm around Nia's waist. All the Huntresses were watching. The Pack looked no less concerned.

"I simply need to lie down," Nia said, "mostly owing to the horror of discovering that Toss is an unrepentant cheat at short answer."

The bit of humor seemed to set everyone's concerns at ease. Everyone except Eve.

It's not your place to comfort her. She has difficulties enough without pulling her into yours.

As if to reinforce his self-chastisement, Grandmother's voice reached them as they passed through the doors and into the corridor.

"Nowhere to be seen," she grumbled far too loudly. "And from all I can discover, the newest arrival has not even been shown to her bedchamber. Penelope ought to know better than this."

Grandmother, Father, and Mother were making their way toward the drawing room.

"Two friends of hers arrived," Father said. "As always, her own enjoyment is all Penelope can think of."

In the next instant, their eyes settled on Duke and the O'Doyle sisters. He wished he could depend on his family to be gracious.

"I thought all the young people were in the drawing room," Mother said, eyeing the sisters with a hint of disapproval.

"They are, Mother."

Before he could say more, Father spoke over him. "And you have abandoned your friends? That is not like you, Dubhán."

"I am assisting the Misses O'Doyle." He attempted to continue walking, but his family was making a very sufficient blockade.

"I can guess which of the sisters has imposed upon you," Grandmother said. Clearly speaking to his parents but studying Eve with a disapproving air, she said, "The eldest Miss O'Doyle was nowhere to be seen while we were attempting to survive at that horrid inn. Dubhán worked ceaselessly. Miss Nia must have climbed the stairs dozens and dozens of times. But where was Miss O'Doyle?"

Small splotches of color splashed Eve's cheeks, a blush of embarrassment, if Duke had ever seen one.

"I told you, Grandmother, that Miss O'Doyle worked very hard, simply not in a capacity that you saw."

The Best-Kept Secrets 135

Grandmother was unappeased. "She never looked in on me, never offered me a good morning. She never even passed the door to the room I was in. I watched; I would have seen her."

"May I please be permitted to continue helping my sister to our room?" Eve sounded dispirited. "She is not feeling well."

"Little wonder, after working so hard and with so little help at that inn," Father said.

Duke slipped his hand away from Nia's elbow. "Best keep going," he said to the sisters. "This might continue on for some time."

They took the escape offered and moved around their confronters.

"Penelope really ought to be the one assisting her guests, Dubhán," Mother said. "It shouldn't fall to you."

"When we find her," Grandmother said firmly, "we will tell her. Come along, Silvia. We will sniff her out."

When they walked away, Duke and Father alone stood in the corridor. The complaints and demands for appeasement would begin shortly. They always did.

But Lisette turned the corner and came into view, walking in their direction. Perhaps Duke had found an escape.

In French, knowing Father would feel quite proud of the education he had provided his son, Duke greeted her. "Welcome, Miss Beaulieu. The Huntresses and the Pack are most anxious to have you with us again."

In her usual quiet and delicate way, Lisette answered in her native tongue as well. "Thank you, Mr. Seymour. I am eager to be with them as well."

He motioned her toward the drawing room and, under the pretense of accompanying her, left his father behind.

The Huntresses rushed to the door the moment Lisette appeared there. If she'd harbored any doubts as to her importance to her friends, they would have instantly vanished. She was pulled into one embrace after another. There were even a few tears of joy.

"I am attempting not to be jealous," Artemis said, "but the Fortiers being permitted to greet you first nearly undid my ability to be civil."

"I did not know they would be here." A hint of emotion touched Lisette's words.

"Are they still here?" Scott asked.

Lisette looked over at him, wariness written all over her face. "They are." Duke wasn't sure any two syllables spoken in English had ever been so obviously

French. "But, *s'il vous plaît*, do not ask them questions about . . ." She didn't seem to know how to finish her request without, apparently, giving away the very thing she did not wish to be brought up.

"I had only hoped to thank them," Scott said. "Their kind generosity allowed Gillian and I to marry, and we don't even know them."

"They are the very best of people," Lisette said.

"When I first met them," Daria said, "they were kind and amiable. Once they knew I was a Huntress, they were inarguably excited to meet me. I never could sort out what difference that made."

"I think they are pleased that I have friends." Poor Lisette looked embarrassed. "They care a lot about me."

"Because you are French?" Daria guessed.

Lisette smiled but not in a way that indicated she was laughing at her friend. "Because I am their niece."

And with that simple declaration, a great many bits of information began to make sense. Lisette and the Fortiers were family. No matter that Duke's family argued, they *did,* on some level, care what happened to each other. They'd all worried over Colm while he'd been at war. Duke had received letters from his aunt and uncle and grandmother whilst away at school.

The Huntresses pulled Lisette entirely among themselves, diving directly into the task of catching up on all that had happened to each of them. The Pack had always been close as well. The flat they'd shared at Cambridge had been filled with laughter and support and camaraderie. And no matter if he did secure a place with his aunt and uncle or had to spend his time in London at his parents' London residence, he fully expected to enjoy those parts of the Season when this group of friends were all together.

Except Eve.

She was going to lose these precious moments with them.

And he had already lost her.

CHAPTER TWENTY-TWO

EVE PINNED A FEW LOOSE bits of hair back in place, hoping she looked mostly presentable. She was tired and half-tempted to insist that she should remain in her bedchamber looking after Nia. But as her sister was sleeping and was likely, according to Dr. Wilstead, to continue doing so for the remainder of the night, that excuse would not hold water.

There was a light rap on the door. Eve crossed and opened it, finding Lisette standing on the other side.

"Lisette." Eve gave her friend a hug. She'd not had the opportunity to greet Lisette in the hours since her arrival, having been fully occupied in the sickroom. "'Tis a grand thing seeing you again."

"I am so happy to be with the Huntresses again. And the Pack, as I am told the gentlemen have named themselves." Lisette had always been soft-spoken. People who didn't know her well might think she was shy, though she wasn't. "I am told Nia is ill. Is she equal to having a brief visit?"

Eve shook her head. "She is sleeping. The doctor believes she will sleep all night."

"Well, we must not wake her." Lisette looked a bit disappointed.

The Huntresses were all so dear to each other, and they missed each other terribly when they were apart. Eve didn't know if that offered her more comfort or more heartache as she faced a lifetime away from them.

"May I walk with you to the drawing room?" Lisette requested.

"Certainly." Eve closed the door, careful not to make noise. Mrs. Greenberry had assured her that her own abigail would look in on Nia periodically throughout the evening. "It appeared, from our vantage point by the windows, that M. Fortier sent Mme Dupuis away. Did he truly beard the dragon so handily?"

Lisette nodded. "He is quiet and reserved, so most people do not realize that he has . . . What is the phrase used here?" How Eve wished she spoke

French so her friend needn't search about for the English word. "He has a backbone of steel. My aunt even more so."

"Are they to serve as your chaperones during the house party?" Eve asked.

"Yes, and they will be *une grande* . . . improvement. Everyone will like them very much." Lisette looked more than merely relieved or pleased; she looked ecstatic. Mme Dupuis had been a gloomy cloud over the last house party, but Lisette had been subject to that gloom without escape for years. "I have every hope that they can fill that same role in the coming Season during those gatherings or outings my parents will not be participating in."

"You will be in London for the Season?" Though it was a question, Eve could hear in her own voice that she'd stated it more as a declaration. She couldn't help it. Lisette had been denied a London Season the past two years in a row, and 'twas horribly unfair.

"*Oui,* and I am so very happy."

Eve hooked her arm through Lisette's. "We will have the most wonderful Season." Only as the words spilled from her lips did Eve realize her mistake. The Huntresses would, indeed, have a glorious time in London. But Eve wouldn't be there. *They* would have the most wonderful Season. She would be left behind.

Unwilling to dampen Lisette's much-deserved excitement, Eve pushed all thoughts of loneliness from the forefront of her mind. She felt she was doing an admirable job of not showing her distress as they stepped into the drawing room to await the announcement of supper.

All the other guests and their hosts were inside, mingling and gabbing. The elder Mrs. Seymour stopped Eve and Lisette. The sniff ought to have warned Eve that nothing good was to come of this encounter.

Still, she was caught off guard when Duke's grandmother said, "That is the same blue gown you wore for supper last night. Do you not consider being a guest at Fairfield to be honor enough to make it worth your while to put in a bit of effort?"

Mrs. Seymour had been quite a complainer during their journey, but she hadn't, until that day, truly become insulting.

Eve didn't know entirely what to make of the change. "I fear," she said, "this is the only gown I have that would be appropriate for supper. All my others are day dresses."

"You have only one?" Mrs. Seymour gave every indication of shock. "It seems I was correct, then."

"Correct about what, Mrs. Seymour?" Eve hated to ask, but she suspected the lady would be upset if she didn't inquire.

The Best-Kept Secrets

139

"Dubhán told me that you and your sister paid the cook at that empty inn. It was hardly fair that he and his father were funding the entirety of that trip, and I told him as much. But he insisted you two had seen to that bit." Another sniff—*heavens*, Eve had come to severely dislike the sound. "I do not know why he would lie to me about that, but he obviously did."

"Nia and I *did* make certain the cook was compensated." Eve knew it was a bit of a misleading explanation, but she was also perfectly aware of the reason Duke had offered it in the first place. It was a good tactic, and she would continue on with it.

"You couldn't have," Mrs. Seymour insisted. She snatched hold of Mrs. Greenberry's arm as she happened past and pulled her into their conversation. "How much, Penelope, is a cook at an inn likely to be paid for two days' worth of meals?"

"I really haven't the first idea, Mother."

With a huff, Mrs. Seymour said, "It needn't be an exact answer, merely an estimate."

"I couldn't even provide you with that," Mrs. Greenberry said. "I have no experience with such a thing."

"How much do you pay your cook?" Mrs. Seymour asked.

With a look of patience wearing thin, Mrs. Greenberry said, "That is a rather gauche topic to discuss in a drawing room."

Eve whispered to Lisette, "We'd best make our escape while we can."

Lisette did not require being told twice. She slipped away. Eve, however, wasn't fast enough.

Mrs. Seymour took hold of her arm the same way she had with her daughter moments earlier. "I told you during our journey that my daughter was difficult, did I not? And now you see it for yourself. I am attempting to sort the answer to a very simple question, and she not only will not offer basic information, but she also accuses me of lacking manners. Do you not now agree that I am very poorly treated by my children?"

"I do not know either of them well enough to answer definitively." How she hoped that elusive answer would suffice. She would rather not be made part of a squabble.

"Liam." Mrs. Seymour called her son over, and he obeyed with all possible haste. "Your sister is being difficult again. And she has, in some way, used her influence as hostess of this gathering to convince Miss O'Doyle to make light of the misery it is causing me."

"That is unfair of you, Penelope," Mr. Seymour said.

"It is also untrue," Mrs. Greenberry answered tightly. "And it is inexcusable of you, Mother, to put Miss O'Doyle in such an impossible situation."

Mr. Seymour's expression turned a bit thunderous. "Where is Dubhán? He will settle this."

While they searched the faces around them for their designated negotiator, Eve slipped away, hoping her lack of height would help render her difficult to spot. She stopped across the room, next to Artemis and Charlie.

"They are exhausting, aren't they?" Artemis subtly nodded toward Duke's family.

"Like trying to run through ankle-deep mud." Eve was beginning to appreciate Duke's eagerness to gain some distance from his family.

"How is Nia feeling?" Charlie asked.

"She's sleeping, which Dr. Wilstead says is expected and important for her recovery. Of course, if Mrs. Seymour, the elder, is to be believed, Nia's best chance of avoiding future illness is for me to stop being so selfish and lazy."

"She said that to you?" Charlie didn't look shocked at the possibility.

"She says a lot of things," Eve answered. "They all do."

"It is rather surprising, isn't it, that Duke and Colm are such lovely people?" Artemis shook her head in amazement.

"I've spent time with Mr. Greenberry away from the rest of his family," Charlie said, "and he is far more like Duke and Colm than the others are. He was a good friend of my father's, actually. So was M. Fortier."

"Truly?" Eve hadn't heard that. "And yet you didn't seem to know the Fortiers' connection to Lisette."

"I learned about it at the same time everyone else did: earlier today."

Artemis's expression turned to one of confusion and contemplation. "It's almost as if their connection were intentionally kept a secret, yet Lisette spoke of it openly when she arrived. There is a mystery in all this that I am determined to sort out." To Eve specifically, she said, "Lisette has indicated that she will be in London for the Season. Is that not wonderful? We will have a Season with *all* of us present for the first time in years."

"A wonderful prospect indeed." But not destined to actually happen. Lisette, at last, would be with them. But Eve wouldn't be.

The butler arrived at the door to the drawing room. He gave a quick nod, Eve assumed to Mr. and Mrs. Greenberry.

Their host addressed the gathering. "Let us all proceed to the dining room."

Duke's grandmother moved with chin held high to stand near her son-in-law. To the room in general, she said, "Last evening, we took a very careless

The Best-Kept Secrets   141

approach to our evening meal. I believe true decorum is actually called for. As such, I will walk in on the arm of our host."

"If we intend to undertake this meal on the most formal footing," Mrs. Greenberry said, "then Mrs. Jonquil will walk in with her host, and Mr. Jonquil with myself."

"I will not be supplanted by children simply because they are the leaders of a ragamuffin band of mischief makers."

Fortunately for the older lady, that "ragamuffin band of mischief makers" found the descriptor funny rather than offensive. Enough smiles popped up around the room to put to rest any concerns that the Pack and Huntresses would be up in arms over the slight.

Duke moved to his grandmother's side. He patiently explained, "Mr. Jonquil is the son of an earl. As such, he outranks everyone in this room. By rights, he and his wife would have the distinction of walking to supper with their host and hostess. Propriety dictates that."

"I do not need a lecture on propriety." She tipped her chin at a defiant angle and sniffed. "We will, of course, do things properly. Penelope will most certainly take great pleasure in seeing me relegated to a lowered standing."

Behind her, Eve heard Tobias mutter, "I'd wager a pony that your mother will murder your grandmother before the week is out."

Colm replied, "I'd double the amount on a wager that Mother would find ample people willing to help."

Mrs. Greenberry had warned her brother and mother that if they did not find a way to coexist peacefully, they ran the risk of eventually losing Duke. As Eve followed the procession into the dining room, she couldn't help thinking Colm was hanging in the balance as well.

She wasn't in a position to offer any real reassurance to the elder of the Seymour grandchildren. And Duke seemed to not enjoy her company as much now as he had during their journey. He was with the Pack and had their loyalty and companionship; he hadn't as much need of hers.

All the Pack and the Huntresses would be in London for the coming Season and might very well learn the same lesson: that Eve wasn't overly necessary to any of their happiness.

CHAPTER TWENTY-THREE

Duke felt certain he could watch Eve drive a gig every day of his life and never grow tired of the sight. He could say that about watching her do most things. The bite of cold air pinked her cheeks. And her dimpled smile, lighting her silvery eyes, drew him in as he suspected it always would.

Colm had suggested that they all go for a ride, Fairfield being a horse-breeding estate and boasting an incredibly large number of remarkable horses. When Eve had pointed out that Nia was unlikely to be feeling well enough to ride but would also be heartbroken to be left out, Colm had swiftly solved that difficulty with the suggestion of a light gig.

Eve had thanked Colm profusely, and Duke had stifled the urge to land his cousin a facer. Jealousy was a new experience for him. That wasn't to say that he'd never had competition when his interest had been captured, nor that every tendre he'd experienced had always fully and immediately been returned. But until now, he'd been able to more or less shrug and move along when his head was turned by someone whose head was turned by someone else.

But Eve was different. She didn't merely turn his head; she captured his every thought and resided in every beat of his heart. And a happy outcome was so utterly impossible that being near her filled his soul with a painful sort of hopeless longing that couldn't be shrugged away.

"With a bit of ingenuity, we could have tucked you into the gig too." Colm's voice directly beside him startled Duke out of his distraction. His cousin kept the white mare on which he rode perfectly in step with Duke's mount.

"What do you mean?" Duke asked.

"I mean that rather than watching Eve drive past, looking as though she's hauling your heart around with her, you could be sitting beside her."

They continued riding alongside each other, both experienced enough equestrians to manage the thing with very little thought.

"You are operating under the assumption that I want to be sitting beside her."

Colm shook his head. "I am horrified to discover that a cousin of mine is this thickheaded. Tragic." He bent a bit away and called out to the front of the group. "Fennel. Take the fork to the left."

Up ahead, Fennel signaled his understanding.

Speaking to Duke once more, Colm said, "You watch her a lot, and never with disinterest."

"That doesn't matter," Duke said.

"Why on earth not?"

"Because I'm not willing to cause her sorrow, and any lady who throws her lot in with me will be caused precisely that. Our family was bickering before supper last night, and who did they pull in to fix it? Me. When I arrived with Grandmother a few days ago and your mother was understandably frustrated, you were offered escape, and I was required to remain and arbitrate the inevitable argument. If I am at Writtlestone for more than a week, the days become utterly filled with my father's bitterness over how his life has played out and my mother's unhappiness with it all." He was worn to a thread and often feared that thread would snap. "I cannot ask any lady, let alone one I care deeply for, to be part of a family like ours, neither can I require her to build a life in a place I know will drain the happiness from her. But I haven't income enough for a home of my own, so escaping that place of misery means living as a perpetual guest in someone else's home."

"An arrangement you are not at liberty to extend to someone else," Colm made the connection.

"Precisely." Duke guided his horse to the left of the fork as they reached it. "I was foolish to let myself even begin any semblance of a tendre for Eve. But I am not such a selfish villain that I would let that grow into something that will hurt her in the end."

"War taught me a lot of things, Duke, not all of them good. But among those lessons was this: battles often feel the most hopeless in the moments before the tide turns." His cousin was attempting to offer him hope, but he wasn't certain there actually was any.

They reached the others and dismounted. Fennel took possession of Duke's horse. Fennel's estate bred horses just as Fairfield did; he was fully capable of seeing to the animals and would enjoy it as well.

Tobias was holding the horse at the front of Eve's gig. Duke crossed to them and, with care, helped Nia descend. Ellie was there in an instant to offer support to her friend. Duke turned back to the cart.

The Best-Kept Secrets 145

Eve smiled at him. He kept his expression neutral as she climbed down from the cart. With her feet on the ground, she looked up at him once more, a hint of tenderness in her gaze. He wished he could let himself return it. Wished he could put an arm around her. Wished . . . a lot of things.

"A footman who specifically hands ladies down from carriages and gigs?" The teasing quality of her question told him she was continuing with the game they'd started during their journey to Surrey.

"No." It was his usual answer, but he wasn't enjoying the diversion as much as he had before.

The Pack and Huntresses pulled items from the back of the gig: a few small chairs, a lot of cushions and blankets, and a basket of food.

"Make certain Nia gets a chair," Eve called out to Newton and Scott as they passed, each carrying two chairs. "And a blanket," she said to Gillian, that Huntress having several blankets in her arms.

While the group arranged all that had been brought, Eve remained near the gig, watching her sister with ill-concealed concern. Duke knew he ought to follow the others' lead and set himself to a task, but he couldn't seem to convince his feet to take him anywhere.

"I hope this doesn't prove too much for her," Eve said. "Nia has been so discouraged, but she has also been crushingly tired." Eve looked more than a little tired herself. "Everything will be fine in the end, won't it? Tell me I'm not foolish to believe that."

He wanted so badly to hug her in that moment, as he'd done in the inn kitchen. She seemed to need an embrace as much now as she had then. But he couldn't indulge in that any longer. A few kind words were all he could reasonably risk offering.

"A wise person very recently told me that battles often seem most hopeless in the moment before the tide turns."

"Then we'd best prepare ourselves for a significant turning of the tide because I am feeling . . . well, not hopeless but definitely helpless." She looked over at him. Her silvery eyes were smiling but also sad.

Duke clasped his hands behind him and kept his distance. "I'm confident you'll sort something out."

Her eyes narrowed a little, and her mouth tugged downward. "Thank you." But there was confusion in the response.

He was making a muck of all this. He had to get them back on more neutral footing, and that meant returning to a more generally affable connection. Things needed to go back to the way they had been before the journey from Ireland and the magic of the abandoned inn, but he wasn't at all sure that was even possible.

CHAPTER TWENTY-FOUR

"You will miss the start of the evening's festivities." Nia's quiet objection managed to only further convince Eve that returning to their room after supper to be with her sister had been the right choice.

"You are going to miss *all* of this evening's festivities," she pointed out.

Nia opened and closed her eyes slowly, her eyelids heavy with illness. "It is not your fault that I am laid low."

"And it is not yours either." Eve took Nia's hand as it rested on the coverlet.

"I did very little today," Nia said, "yet I'm utterly spent."

"Dr. Wilstead did say you would struggle for a time to sort out what your limits are. Today, you have discovered, surpassed your current limits."

"I sat in a gig, then sat on a chair, then returned to the house and sat on a chaise longue. How can a day filled with *sitting* be beyond my endurance?"

"You know as well as I do that sitting in a gig is not the same as sitting on a chaise longue. Tomorrow, we'll keep to the house, and you'll feel better. You'll see."

Nia's mouth turned down in an expression of sorrowful worry. "I'm going to ruin this house party for everyone."

Eve squeezed her hand. "No, dear. Duke's family is doing that."

Nia smiled a little. "That has surprised me. Duke and Colm are so peaceable and easy to get along with."

"Perhaps they are because they have seen the consequences of being the opposite."

"I think Mr. and Mrs. Greenberry, at least, aren't ordinarily the sort to fight and feud." Nia kept her eyes closed as she spoke, looking closer and closer to drifting off to sleep. "Why would they be so much at odds with their own family?"

"I don't know," Eve said honestly. "What I do know, though, is that our family will never, ever become that. Because there is nothing we wouldn't do for each other."

"Will you do something for me?" Nia asked.

"Of course."

"Once I fall asleep, will you rejoin the party? I will sleep so much better if you do."

Eve suspected that was a bit of a Banbury tale, but she also didn't think her sister had the energy for even a friendly disagreement. "I will," she promised.

Nia's next breath was the slow and deep sort that accompanied the arrival of sleep. She needed her rest. Eve remained in her chair beside the bed for a time, waiting until she was absolutely certain Nia was deeply asleep. Then she rose, carefully slipped her hand from her sister's, and quietly left the room.

Eve returned to the drawing room, where a game of cross questions was underway. She managed to catch Mrs. Greenberry's attention and wave her hostess over.

"Forgive me for pulling you away from the game," Eve said.

"Not at all. Is your sister in need of something?"

"She's sleeping, which is the best thing for her. But I have a question for Dr. Wilstead."

Mrs. Greenwood smiled kindly as she motioned for Eve to walk with her from the room. Just outside the door, a footman sat at his post. He rose upon seeing them. "William, will you ask Dr. Wilstead to meet Miss O'Doyle and me in the north sitting room?"

"Yes, Mrs. Greenberry." He hurried away to see to his assignment.

"I hope you will forgive the presumptuousness of deciding for you where the conversation will occur," Mrs. Greenberry said, "but I acted on my suspicion that you did not wish for the rest of the party to be privy to your discussion with Dr. Wilstead."

"I appreciate it."

Mrs. Greenberry watched her as they walked. "How are you holding up, dear? We so seldom think of the toll an illness takes on those who care about and for the one who is ailing. But I have been that person, and I know how that feels. How are *you*?"

"Overwhelmed and worried," Eve confessed. "And I'm not sleeping well, so I'm tired."

"I know you and Nia requested a room to share, but if it would help you get the rest you need, you can be provided a room of your own."

The Best-Kept Secrets   149

Eve had never had a room of her own. She and Nia had shared from the time Nia had been born. "I will let you know if I decide to accept your generous offer."

"Please do."

They were only in the sitting room for a few minutes when Dr. Wilstead arrived. Mrs. Greenberry stepped to the side of the room, giving Eve a bit of privacy.

"What can I do for you, Miss O'Doyle?" Dr. Wilstead asked.

"You've said that Nia will still be ill when we return home to Ireland."

He nodded. "Better than she is now, but even if she avoids the more severe version of rheumatic fever, she will be ill for several months."

Several months.

"And no matter the length of this bout of illness, it is imperative that we watch her for signs of damage to her heart. That is the most dangerous aspect of rheumatic fever, and we must act decisively and quickly should we see any indications of it."

Eve swallowed against the lump in her throat. "Decisively and quickly" were not very comforting words. The doctor had said he thought Nia unlikely to be ill for years to come, but clearly, he harbored very real concerns for her.

"I will, of course, let you know if I see anything at all that is concerning," she promised him.

"And in the name of full honesty, even with treatment, any damage done to her heart cannot be reversed. We can lessen it but not entirely stop or undo it."

"It would be permanent?"

He nodded.

"Would it be . . . fatal?" She could hardly get the word out.

"It can be," he admitted, "which makes treatments all the more crucial."

"I need an idea of what the medicines she will require are likely to cost once we've returned home. I realize that is difficult to say, since what they cost here is different from our corner of Ireland. But even a vague idea'd be quite helpful."

"I will make a list and give you my best estimation."

"Thank you," she said. "And please give it to me and not to my sister. I don't wish to burden her with worries."

"Of course."

As Dr. Wilstead made his way out of the room, Eve felt a sense of relief. She would have information, which would help her know what she was facing. But she also felt an added weight. The doctor's estimate would almost certainly exceed what the family could scrape together.

Mrs. Greenberry joined her once more. She didn't offer pity or platitudes. She didn't press for details about Eve's situation, and she didn't ask Eve to lay bare her worries. She simply smiled and walked with her out of the room.

"I suppose everyone will understand if I don't join in the festivities," Eve said. "I think I would rather lie down and try to rest." She would be breaking her promise to her sister, but she *had* left the room when Nia had fallen asleep, and she *had* gone to the drawing room where the evening's entertainments were being undertaken. So she had fulfilled her obligation, in a sense.

"A good idea," Mrs. Greenberry said. "And we do have guest bedchambers that are not being used. Please do tell me if having a room of your own would be helpful."

"I will. Thank you."

They parted ways at that point, Mrs. Greenberry walking in the direction of the drawing room and Eve making her way toward the stairs.

It is imperative that we watch her for signs of damage to her heart.

Act decisively and quickly.

The most dangerous aspect of rheumatic fever.

She tried to breathe through each successive thought, but she didn't manage it overly well. And in her distraction, she almost didn't hear Duke and his father approaching before they were nearly already in view.

"All I am asking," Duke said to Mr. Seymour, "is that you do what you can not to quarrel with Grandmother or Aunt Penelope around the other guests. It reflects badly on the family, and I cannot imagine you want that."

"Why is it you aren't scolding your grandmother? She instigated tonight's difficulties."

Duke rubbed at his mouth and chin. "I realize she is difficult, but one of you will have to be the more noble person, and I am holding out hope that it would be you."

"I have always been the more noble person in this family. The *most* noble, I daresay."

"Is it *noble* to call your mother a banshee in the midst of a parlor game?" Duke asked.

His father actually smiled a tiny bit. "I ought not to have said that, I'll admit."

"Please at least try to keep the peace," Duke said.

The momentary look of amusement disappeared from his father's face. "I will if they will." And on that petulant declaration, he stormed off in the direction of the drawing room.

The Best-Kept Secrets 151

Duke remained behind, rubbing the back of his neck as he sighed.

"Did he really call your grandmother a banshee?" Eve asked, moving to where he stood.

"It isn't the first time." He looked away from the path his father had taken and at Eve instead. "We didn't think you would be rejoining us tonight."

"I'm not," she said. "I needed to talk with Dr. Wilstead." She expected Duke to ask how Nia was or if something had happened. He'd been so quick to offer assistance or a listening ear when she'd touched on difficult topics before. But he didn't this time. "He is still concerned about Nia, as am I. And he confirmed that she will need powders and medicines for months to come. I am attempting to ascertain what that is likely to cost. I think I'll feel less helpless if I know, but I might also feel more overwhelmed."

She slipped her hand in his, needing the reassurance that touch had always brought. But he pulled his hand free. He'd done that the past couple of days, but she'd always been able to explain it away. In those instances, something or someone else had pulled him away. Or he'd been worried about embarrassing her by that small token of affection when others were around.

Eve couldn't think of an excuse that applied in this moment.

"While I am still a little frustrated that my parents asked me to keep our situation secret from Nia, I'm feeling a little grateful that they did. If she knew how dire our finances were, she'd be worrying on top of ailing, and that wouldn't do her any good at all." There was such relief in being able to talk with him about this. She felt less alone. "What are the chances, do you suppose, that Dr. Wilstead's estimate will be within my family's reach?"

"I don't know." The hints of distance and aloofness she'd caught in his words and posture of late were impossible to miss in those three words. "I don't have the answers, Eve."

"I don't expect you to." Heavens, she was confused. "I just need someone to talk to."

"I can't be that someone," he said in what almost sounded like an apology.

Her confusion was turning to bewilderment. "But you said at the inn that I could always talk with you."

He took a step away, in the direction of the drawing room. "I shouldn't have." He shook his head. "I'm sorry, Eve. I really am."

"But you—" She swallowed hard. "You are the only person who knows. There is no one else I can talk to."

"I'm sorry." He held his hands up in a show of helplessness. "You'll have to sort this out on your own."

Afraid of bursting into tears, she pressed her lips closed and silently nodded.

"I didn't act as I ought. I never should have—It was a mistake," Duke said.

"Which part?" Seldom had her voice emerged so small and uncertain.

He sighed. "All of it." He shook his head. "I know I keep repeating this, but I feel like it has to be said: I *am* sorry. I really, truly am." He hesitated for the length of half a breath, then turned and left her there.

The one confidant she'd had in all her troubles, the person who'd let her cry in his arms, who'd held her and comforted her, even kissed her—and he'd left her there.

I can't be that someone.

Sort this out on your own.

He'd pushed her so fully away. She was losing more than a listening ear and a support in her troubles. Watching him walk away, she felt her heart shatter.

She'd told him at the inn that she felt as if she were being left behind by everyone already. And he'd promised her he wouldn't abandon her, that he would still be there. But he wasn't.

It was a mistake. All of it.

Eve didn't know how long she stood there, shock gluing her to the spot. He'd more than just walked away; he'd told her he shouldn't have offered his support in the first place. How could she make sense of that?

His sincerity had been palpable when he'd said he was sorry. He was too good a person not to regret the pain he must have realized this was causing her, and he was too much a gentleman not to wish that this adjustment in the connection had never been needed in the first place. But his regret at the pain of that moment didn't lessen her confusion.

She had not yet moved from the place where he'd left her when the elder Mrs. Seymour happened past. She paused on her way to the stairs and gave Eve a quick look-over.

"The blue gown again?" was all she said and kept walking.

Mrs. Seymour knew why Eve wore the same gown each night. Eve herself had told her she didn't have any other options. There was no need for the comment, no reason beyond cruelty. And the cruelty was pointed and well-aimed.

Eve's emotions were too fragile and too raw in that moment to push the mortifying comment out of her mind. The humiliation that often accompanied being poor hurt, as it always did, yet it wasn't what hurt most in that moment.

Being abandoned was far more painful.

CHAPTER TWENTY-FIVE

Duke had dithered long enough. He needed to stop standing at the figurative crossroads and start actually walking into his future. And he would find a way of convincing himself that he wasn't utterly crushed by the fact that Eve couldn't walk that path with him.

Keeping his distance from her, physically and emotionally, was agonizing. He'd seen the hurt in her eyes as he'd told her the night before that he couldn't be the one she turned to with her worries. And he'd watched his words land a more stinging blow than he'd intended when he'd told her that all they'd shared during their journey to Fairfield had been a mistake. That, he felt certain, would haunt him for years to come.

Rather than go for a morning ride, he made his way to Penfield, having heard that his uncle meant to spend the morning there. The door was locked when he arrived, so he pulled out the key from the hiding place Uncle Niles had revealed to the Pack on their first day and let himself in.

He opened the drapes on the back windows, then lit various lanterns, the early morning sun not being strong enough this late in the year to adequately light the space.

Duke undertook the preparations he'd memorized during visits to Fairfield over the years, when he had joined his uncle here. He soon had a borrowed pair of trousers on, his shirt off, his knuckles wrapped in strips of fabric, and his gaze firmly on a hanging bag of hay ready to be pummeled while he waited.

His family was squabbling, as always, but doing so in front of others, which they usually managed to avoid.

He landed a fist against the hanging bag.

Father and Grandmother had declared their intention to remain at Fairfield specifically to make trouble for Aunt Penelope.

He landed another punch.

Though he hoped he was about to secure for himself a future that offered some respite from family discord, it was far from the dreamed-of future he and Eve had jokingly attempted to guess for each other, because none of the paths stretched out in front of him included her.

Two more punches.

The door opened, and Uncle Niles stepped inside. "Good morning, Duke."

"Is it?" Another punch.

Uncle Niles hung his hat and coat on hooks near the door. He then walked around and stood on the other side of the bag of hay. He set his shoulder against it. They'd done this before; Duke knew his part. He lifted his hands into a fighting position once more. He gave the bag a quick jab.

Uncle Niles had a way of looking at him that said without a single word that he saw far more than he ever let on.

Duke landed another blow on the hay bag. "My family is driving me mad."

"I suspect the Pack and the Huntresses feel the same way."

"I managed to shield my friends from our family's brokenness for years only to have it spill out all over this house party." He punched the bag far harder this time. "And my only chance for having a bit of peace is—" He eyed his uncle hesitantly.

"Talk while you punch," Uncle Niles said. "That often makes it easier."

"Makes which part easier: the talking or the punching?"

"Both, I suppose."

Duke stepped back from the bag. "I actually think better when I pace."

Uncle Niles nodded. "There's plenty of room."

Duke began his pacing. Still at the hay-filled bag, Uncle Niles landed a series of perfectly executed blows, an almost graceful dance.

"I wish I could have seen you fight," Duke said.

Uncle Niles grinned. "The Cornish Duke wasn't half bad, if I do say it myself."

"I don't know how you kept it a secret from your family." From what Duke had been told, not a single member of the enormous extended Greenberry family had ever discovered Niles's alter ego.

"In the end," Uncle Niles said, "I ran away from home."

That stopped Duke's pacing on the instant. "You did?"

"I realized that remaining at home meant abandoning the life I wanted to live. I did my best to try to make everything weave together happily, but in the end, it wasn't possible. So I left and lived for a time with a friend."

Uncle Niles had left home because living there hadn't allowed him to claim the life he'd wanted. Of all people, Uncle Niles would understand why Duke needed to request what he'd come to Fairfield to ask.

The Best-Kept Secrets 155

"Did your family ever forgive you?" Duke heard the unease in his voice.

Uncle Niles clearly did as well. He stepped away from the hay bag and motioned to the sofa. "Have a seat, Duke. I know you think better when pacing, but I suspect you need to do more talking and less thinking."

There was truth in that.

He sat, feeling nervous and hopeful.

Uncle Niles tossed Duke the shirt he'd pulled off upon arriving. "You'll grow cold sitting there not moving about."

Duke stood to pull it on, then dropped back onto the sofa. Uncle Niles sat beside him.

"What is weighing on your thoughts, Duke?"

"I can't live at Writtlestone." He slumped back. "I love my parents, but living with them is difficult at best. Whenever I am home, Father talks multiple times a day about his perceived ill-treatment and unfair life. Mother brings up equally as often how put-upon she is and how much happier life would be for her if Father hadn't been so badly treated. And I have to try to soothe those battered feelings over and over again. And if I don't do a good enough job of it, they grow petulant and sometimes insulting. The speed and aptitude with which I play the role of placater and ambassador is seen as not merely proof of whether I love them enough but also evidence of whether I am worthy of being loved by them. I can only endure that a few days at a time, but I no longer have Cambridge to escape to when it inevitably becomes too much."

"Lud, Duke. I didn't realize things were that bad."

"I can't do it every day for the rest of my life. I just can't."

"When Ballycar had to be sold, Penelope was heartbroken, but she was also furious. It was her childhood home. It had been the Seymour family home for three generations. It was her last connection to her father, an inheritance she had helped secure and build upon while she'd still been at home." His eyes took on that far-off look of someone taking a moment to walk through the past. "Not long after that happened, she and I were here at Penfield." With a besotted smile, he said, "Your aunt can throw a deuced great punch." He lingered on that thought for a quick moment before returning to what he'd been talking about. "Penelope said she was afraid that if she dwelled on it, the loss of Ballycar and the blame her brother had put on her for it, would turn her bitter and angry. She'd lost enough, and she didn't want to lose herself as well."

"I wish I'd known my father before losing Ballycar. It would have been nice to be his son first and foremost instead of . . . whatever it is I am to him."

"I wish, for your sake even more than his, that Liam had decided not to let that loss gnaw at him."

"How often does Aunt Penelope talk about Ballycar or her frustration with my father or Grandmother's treatment of her and Father?"

"Almost never," Uncle Niles said. "She'll sometimes talk about a horse she had as a child or memories of her father at Ballycar. And now and then, she'll wonder aloud what her brother or mother are doing. But she's managed over the years to create a separation between the difficulties in the Seymour family and her life from day to day. I think, in all honesty, it saved her."

"I don't think I could endure a lifetime at Writtlestone," Duke said. "But though we aren't poor, Father's finances never recovered from losing Ballycar, though that happened before I was even born."

"But you've been paying for that loss your entire life, in more ways than one."

"I've spent many years telling myself that after I was finished at Cambridge, I'd find the resilience to endure a lifetime at Writtlestone." But instead, he was giving up already, hoisting the white flag. "I never did have the fighting spirit that Colm has, as Grandmother has so often pointed out."

"Do you know why she says that?" Uncle Niles asked.

"Does she need a reason?" Duke answered dryly.

"I think *you* need the reason. Your grandmother belittles you and offers unflattering comparisons to Colm because she knows it will hurt her son. It drives Liam to try harder to earn her elusive approval, not realizing even after a lifetime as her son that she approves of no one."

Uncle Niles was usually rather quiet, keeping on the outskirts of family difficulties. This was blunt talk.

"She belittles Colm in her comparisons with you in order to punish her daughter. And ever since our Luke died, your grandmother has taken to unfavorably comparing Colm to *him*. That change was not difficult to decipher; your grandmother realized it would hurt Penelope more."

"Grandmother is entirely capable of being peaceful, or at least not unkind," Duke said. "I don't understand why she so often chooses cruelty."

"I fear she has allowed the habit to take deep hold, and she no longer notices how that continues to change her."

Change her? "Did she used to be kind?"

Uncle Niles thought on that a moment. "By the time I met her, she was already rather inconsiderate and had no qualms about turning her children against each other in the hope of receiving greater attention herself." It was, by far, the most unapologetic conversation Duke remembered having with his uncle on the topic of the Seymour family.

The Best-Kept Secrets   157

"I was frustrated when Father said I had to travel with Grandmother to this house party. I was worried about how she would treat the O'Doyle sisters." He'd decided that referring to them together would be less revealing to anyone listening than if he talked about Eve specifically. "Grandmother wasn't truly horrible on the journey, but she wasn't pleasant either."

Uncle Niles nodded. "There is a reason your aunt and I haven't been to Dublin in years. A person can love his family and desperately need distance from them as well."

It was the perfect return to the topic Duke needed to finally tackle. "I need distance too. It is the only pleasant future I can hope for any longer." He certainly couldn't hope for one with Eve. Her continued guesses about his dream-fulfilling future would all be wrong, no matter what they were, because she wouldn't be part of them. "I'll understand if what I'm about to ask is too much, considering how hard Aunt Penelope has worked to find peace and distance from the family's troubles." He took a quick breath. "Could I stay at Fairfield? Live here instead of at Writtlestone?"

Uncle Niles dropped a hand on his shoulder. "You are always welcome here, Duke. Whether you want to be with us permanently or temporarily, there is *always* room for you."

"I'm asking to live with you," he clarified. "Part of the household."

Uncle Niles nodded.

"Instead of at my parents' home."

"I understand."

Did he though? "My parents will likely be furious. They will, no doubt, blame and attack Penelope for my 'defection.'" That had given Duke even more pause than the disapproval he himself would receive from them.

"When was the last time someone in this family fought a battle *with* you, Duke, rather than leaving you to trudge through the muck alone?"

"Likely never." Why was answering that question proving an emotional thing?

"I think it's past time that changed." Uncle Niles nodded firmly. "I suspect you think I never stand up to any of them."

"I wouldn't say *never*."

Uncle Niles smiled a little. "Penelope has pleaded with me repeatedly over the years to not rebuke them in front of others, even you. And while I haven't always managed to abide by that request, I've done my best. But no public dressing down is not the same as no rebukes at all."

"You have chastised them without witnesses?"

"More times than I can recall. It helps for a little while."

"Nothing ever helps for long." Duke sighed. "And if I push back too much, they're even more bitingly angry when they eventually do react."

Uncle Niles nodded slowly. "To buy us all a bit of time before the inevitable arguments arise from this, I would suggest you go with us to London when I return in January to take my seat in Parliament. You would be staying with us, but I don't think your parents would realize that it was part of a more permanent arrangement."

Duke stood also. "I'd like that. And I would enjoy hearing what you're doing in Parliament and what Parliament is doing in general."

"Do you have an interest in politics?" Uncle Niles asked.

"I don't know what I would do in that arena, but I do find politics intriguing. And I like the idea of being in a position to do some good."

Uncle Niles smiled. "The gentleman who has acted as my political secretary during my previous times as a member of Parliament is looking to pursue his own political ambitions, and he and I have agreed it is time to train a replacement for him."

"Truly?" That caught Duke's attention.

"Learn from him what the position involves. If you find it's to your liking, then we might have shockingly easily solved a difficulty for both of us. Though I must warn you it is not a pursuit that will secure a gentleman enough income for a leisurely future."

Duke nodded. "I understand. I have known gentlemen who have worked in that capacity. Thrice-mended coats were the order of the day."

Uncle Niles had walked back to the bag of hay. "I wouldn't leave you in that state, Duke. Even if the position earned you only pennies, which I assure you it won't, you'll have a roof over your head that you needn't pay for." He gave the hay bag a succession of perfectly executed jabs. "You'll be in a position to tuck a few of those pennies away while still having ample funds for a new coat should yours grow threadbare."

"I can't guarantee I'll be anything but rubbish as a political secretary." Duke joined him near the bag. "But I can promise I'll work hard."

"I wouldn't have extended the offer if I'd thought otherwise." Uncle Niles dropped an arm around Duke's shoulders. "If you discover that you don't care to keep the position, there will be no hard feelings, I promise. And you'll always have a place with us, no matter what you choose to pursue in the end."

"Thank you." Duke didn't know what else to say. He'd stepped into Penfield that morning without a place to live where he could feel at peace. And he'd

The Best-Kept Secrets 159

undertaken a guessing game with Eve about his future pursuits but had had no answer she could even stumble upon because he'd had no dreams beyond getting away from Writtlestone, no occupation that he felt was at all within his reach.

And now, he had both.

He just didn't have her.

CHAPTER TWENTY-SIX

EVE AND NIA HAD BEGUN their first London Season already at a disadvantage nearly four years earlier. By the third ball they'd attended, Eve had been deeply discouraged. All around, people had whispered in not-quiet-enough voices about their overly plain gowns and about how obvious it was that they were out of their element. Less than a fortnight into their first foray into Society and they were already sinking.

In the midst of the cruel dismissals, word had begun circulating that Artemis Lancaster had arrived. The presence of Society's reigning diamond guaranteed that the ball would be deemed *the* Society gathering of the night.

The Queen of Society, to Eve's shock, made her way to where the rejected Irish sisters were huddled together. And she was wearing a gown of lovely but decidedly ordinary fabric with very little adornment.

Artemis arrived beside them. "How lovely to see you both." She smiled at them as if they were dear friends rather than literal strangers. "I'd hoped you would be in attendance tonight." She hooked her arms through each of theirs and began a slow circuit of the ballroom, all eyes and ears on them as they passed. "You must tell me who your modiste is. She clearly doesn't need to hide poor craftsmanship behind gaudy adornments and ridiculously lavish fabrics."

That comment caught quite a few peoples' attention.

"It is not, after all, the done thing this year, to look as though one were standing in the middle of a trimmings shop during a windstorm and emerged covered in frills and frippery."

More whispers followed that. Artemis continued leading them around the room, letting such comments reach eavesdropping ears. She had stayed with the O'Doyles all evening. And she'd favored more simple gowns throughout the remainder of that Season, which Eve had known was purely to ease the way of two poor Irish sisters who had had nothing but plain gowns.

162   SARAH M. EDEN

They'd been Huntresses ever since.

Looking over the faces of her friends now, gathered in a sitting room at Fairfield, Eve couldn't entirely keep her thoughts away from that long-ago night and the miracle Artemis had worked for her and Nia and the blessing this group continued to be in their lives.

"Rose and I have so many ideas for further increasing the appeal of Miss Martinette's," Artemis said. She and Rose, who was also one of them, though she didn't spend much time among them, had secretly opened a dress shop in London. "Our goal is that within three years, our shop will be not merely a place for obtaining gowns but also a sought-after location in London for the *ton* to see and be seen."

"The Almack's of dress shops?" Ellie asked with a laugh.

"We would never sink so low as to be compared to Almack's." Artemis managed the response with a strong feigned haughtiness but also with the right amount of earned dismissal—Almack's was not what it had once been—that no one in the group could help but laugh.

It had become tradition that each of the Huntresses be provided with a dress from Miss Martinette's ahead of Christmas and a gorgeous gown at the start of each Season. Nia and Eve were so close in size that they were able to share gowns, which helped tremendously.

As Eve ran her fingers lightly over the soft, floral-print muslin of the dress she had been given, she felt such a contradiction of emotions: Gratitude that her friends knew how to support each other without making anyone feel pitied or pathetic. Sorrow that she would see so little of them in the years to come. Happy for Nia that she would have *two* new dresses with this gift. Loneliness at knowing she herself wouldn't have need of anything new or fine or flattering. Hope that Nia would be well enough to enjoy the Season when it began again. Worry over Dr. Wilstead's warning about the potential for damage to Nia's heart.

"Is it not to your liking?" Lisette asked quietly as she sat beside Eve.

"'Tis inarguably beautiful," Eve answered.

Artemis had apparently been listening even while inspecting the fit of the gown she had brought for Gillian. "You might as well confess what is on your mind, Eve. We've all noticed your thoughts are elsewhere. And we have our suspicions there is more to your distraction than Nia's poor health."

"You'll think me ridiculous," she said.

"When have we ever objected to 'ridiculous'?" Gillian grinned.

Eve did need to share some of her worries. There were far too many things she was carrying alone. She'd told Duke about her changed future and the difficulties

The Best-Kept Secrets 163

associated with it, and that had helped while he'd been willing to support her. She didn't dare share that with anyone else, having confessed it to him entirely by accident. She'd promised her parents not to spill the secret, especially to her sister. Telling the Huntresses of it would require them to keep the truth from Nia as well. She couldn't pass that burden on. But she'd felt so abandoned and discarded after Duke's rejection the night before that she'd hardly slept. Having some support from the Huntresses would help her feel less alone, even if they couldn't know everything.

"I think Duke is angry with me. Or irritated."

"He is certainly irritated with his family," Ellie said.

"Who of us isn't?" Daria immediately covered her mouth with her hands. From behind them, she said, "Oh, that was terribly rude."

"But accurate," Artemis said.

Their smiles and laughter helped ease some of Eve's tension.

Lisette, in her usual soft manner, asked, "Why is it you think Duke is upset with you, in particular?"

Heavens, this was going to turn into a confession whether she wanted it to or not. Once she started talking about it, she was unlikely to entirely prevent herself from telling them all her feelings for him. Being guarded was not, or at least had not previously been, a skill of hers.

"Duke was truly lovely during our journey here. He was kind and attentive. We talked easily about everything imaginable. We laughed about so many things." Those memories had been so delightful but now mostly made her want to cry. "He held my hand." Her newfound ability to not spill all her secrets came to the rescue; she managed not to tell them that he'd held her and even *kissed* her.

"You've fallen a bit in love with him," Gillian said.

There was little point in denying that. "More than a bit. And I thought the experience was a mutual one. But not long after we reached Fairfield—not immediately, but after a little while of being with everyone—he didn't want to stand near me, and he didn't smile at me like he had."

They were all watching her now with mingled expressions of concern and offense on her behalf.

"He hasn't been unkind," she was quick to assure them. "At least I don't think he has been deliberately. I know I said I thought he might be angry with me, but now that I'm finally talking about it, I don't think that is quite right. I suspect he either realized I had come to believe there was more between us than he'd intended, and he's attempting to prevent me from misunderstanding further, or upon reaching the house party, he had time to think on things a little more and realized that . . ." She swallowed quickly. "Realized that I am not really to his liking after all, beyond being a friend, at least."

Lisette set her hand on Eve's. The other Huntresses drew nearer to her as well, gathering around her.

"Do we need to vanquish him?" Artemis asked, clearly only half in jest.

"He was a little . . . blunt the last time I spoke with him," she acknowledged. "And it was not enjoyable having things laid out so plainly, but I truly do not believe there was any *intentional* cruelty in his rejection." It was still agonizing. "It is hardly his fault that he doesn't have the same . . . feelings that I do. A person can't be forced to love someone. And while I wish I could say otherwise, I think if he hadn't been very direct about things, I probably would have gone on believing that we were viewing each other in the same way."

Artemis sat on Eve's other side and put an arm around her shoulders. "But bluntness and directness, even if not *intentionally* hurtful, still are not always kindnesses."

Eve took a deep breath for what felt like the first time since talking with Duke in the corridor the night before. The pain wasn't gone—she suspected it wouldn't be for a very long time, if ever—but she felt a little less overwhelmed by it.

"He and I could still be friends, don't you think? I would be devastated if we weren't still friends, at least."

"I think so," Artemis said. "There may be some awkwardness at first, but I do think you two can get past that."

Except if that awkwardness lasted beyond a fortnight, there would be no chance of getting past it. Eve would be permanently at Tulleyloch, and she'd not ever see Duke again. She didn't want her last interactions with him to be uncomfortable or unhappy. There had to be a way to salvage the time she had left.

He'd always been comfortable being her friend. And this was a gathering of friends. If she pushed aside all the hurt and the hopes she'd begun to let herself entertain, they could walk away from each other as friends.

"What else is worrying you?" Ellie asked. "There's clearly more."

All the Huntresses were well aware that the O'Doyle family was far from plump in the pocket. It was the reason the Pack had arranged for Duke to make the journey from Ireland with them. Eve could talk a little about her concerns on that score without betraying the recent change in their situation.

"Dr. Wilstead says that Nia will need medicines and doctors' care even after we've returned to Ireland. I'm not certain how we will manage to pay for that."

Lisette squeezed her hand. Artemis tightened her embrace.

The Best-Kept Secrets   165

Eve continued. "I'm more worried, though, that Nia is likely also concerned about that. She needs to be able to rest, to worry about nothing beyond recovering." Eve hadn't admitted that worry to anyone yet. "If I can think of something that might help stretch the family budget, I could offer that reassurance to Nia. Dr. Wilstead says it is crucial that she rest as much as possible."

"Does the doctor think Nia is growing more ill?" Daria asked.

Eve shook her head. "But he has emphatically told me that I need to watch for any indication that her heart might be struggling. Rheumatic fever can cause tremendous damage to the heart. Permanent, fatal damage." She'd thought about this almost constantly since Dr. Wilstead had made his diagnosis. Speaking the words out loud was somehow both relieving and worrying. "If I can free her of even this one burden, she'll be able to rest better. I need to give her that."

"Perhaps you have a previously unrevealed talent for fashion," Lisette said. "You could open a rival shop and race Miss Martinette's to be *the* place to be seen in Society."

They all laughed, and Eve found she could as well.

"I fear I will have to obtain my funds some other way," she said. "Alas, I've no hidden fashion abilities."

"What hidden abilities *do* you have?" Ellie asked.

"Only one. But it does have to be kept secret, as the *ton* would disapprove as wholeheartedly as they would a lady running a dress shop."

With dry humor, Gillian said, "If only there were a way for you to feel confident that we could keep that particular variety of secret."

That set them laughing again. How good they were for her. "I know I can trust Daria, at least. She already knows this secret."

Daria smiled broadly, excitement pouring from her. "I haven't told a soul."

"I hope you mean to tell the rest of us, Eve," Artemis said.

She'd wanted to tell them for years. Keeping secrets was not her natural inclination. She was currently keeping two very large ones from the Huntresses. There would be such relief in getting back to carrying only one at a time.

"I bake," she said.

"And she is very good," Daria said. "The scones we had at the very first gathering I planned during the Season were baked by Eve."

"Those were marvelous." Ellie's eyes pulled wide.

"They certainly were." Artemis looked impressed.

"I learned to bake as a means of saving the family money," Eve said. "It lowers our expenses, but it doesn't generate income. Even if I thought there were people near Tulleyloch who would buy baked things from us, there would be no explanation we could offer to explain how we'd come by the scones or cakes or whatever it might be."

"That *is* a complication," Gillian said.

"Baking might not be your answer to this difficulty," Lisette said, "but there is an answer. I have full faith that there is. And among all of us, we will stumble upon it."

"In the meantime," Artemis said as she stood, "we will enjoy these gorgeous gowns"—she dipped a theatrical curtsy—"and think of ways to torture the Pack since Eve has told us we aren't allowed to vanquish Duke specifically."

Eve knew Artemis was teasing, so she wasn't at all worried that Duke would actually be mistreated or that the Huntresses would reveal in any way what she had told them about the state of her heart. And while telling them didn't remove the ache that resided there or the pain of having been abandoned after he'd promised to be a support in her struggles, it did help her breathe.

"And," Artemis continued, "while we are tormenting the Pack, I propose that we make certain to also celebrate the unexpected absence of Mme Dupuis."

Lisette smiled softly, even as the Huntresses all cheered. Eve put an arm around her and hugged her fiercely.

"We won't ask you for details of how or why your aunt and uncle dispensed with her so quickly and thoroughly," Gillian assured Lisette. "We are simply so happy that you are free of her."

"And I am happy that we are *all* free of her," Lisette said. "What suffering she caused at the last house party."

"Do you think she will be with you again in London?" Artemis asked.

Lisette pressed her lips closed and didn't answer.

Artemis reached over and set her hands atop Lisette's. "I hadn't realized that was more than I should have asked. I really won't press you more on any of this. I promise."

But Eve suspected Artemis would continue to wonder, just as she knew all the Huntresses would, what was rumbling under the surface of Lisette's family.

CHAPTER TWENTY-SEVEN

DUKE WAS WANDERING ADMITTEDLY AIMLESSLY around Fairfield. He had time to himself and wasn't entirely sure what to do with it.

He was excited by the prospect of making his home here, of traveling to London with his aunt and uncle. Eve would have been happy to hear he'd been granted his sought-after respite. And he would have loved to tell her that she might have been unintentionally correct when guessing that his dream-fulfilling future included politics. In the end, it might not be his lifelong pursuit, but it would soon be providing him with a purpose and a small income. She would celebrate that with him, and she would understand his excitement.

But he couldn't let that happen.

His feet took him to the library. It seemed as good a destination as any, so he stepped inside. Perhaps Uncle Niles had a London newspaper to peruse.

Turning toward the desk, he found not a paper but Eve. She sat in the leather chair, arms folded on the desktop, her head resting on her arms, asleep. There was no one else in the room. The door was open, so he hadn't intentionally intruded on her privacy. But now that he had, what ought he to do?

She couldn't possibly be comfortable in her current position. She would likely awaken with a horrible crick in her neck. Perhaps he should wake her and give her the chance to go lie down or at least move to a more accommodating chair in the room. He stepped up to the desk but stopped himself before actually nudging her.

Was he violating his own insistence that distance be kept between them? He didn't want to again be the cause of the pain he'd seen in her eyes the last time they'd spoken. If he opened the door to a renewed tender connection only to have to close it once more, he'd hurt them both.

His eyes fell on a bit of parchment on the desk, a lead pencil nearby. On it was written a short list.

Only two meals each day
Nia also misses the Season
Sell some possession have nothing of value
Pull Scuff from Shrewsbury he'll need a profession
Pull Edmund from Shrewsbury

It was clearly a list of possible ways for her family to further economize. She must have been even more worried about the O'Doyles' finances than she had been when they'd spoken about it on their journey. She'd not, at that point, been talking about curtailing what the family ate.

Duke rubbed at the back of his neck as he paced away. He wasn't in a position to be a confidant, yet if she was this worried, she likely needed one. He also couldn't violate her trust by telling anyone else what she had told him about her situation.

"*'Tis as if I've been left behind by everyone already.*" She'd said that while they'd been at the inn. There'd been such sorrow in her voice. And loneliness. Even he had stepped away from her since then.

What ought he to do now? He didn't want Eve to feel entirely abandoned. But he wouldn't break his promise not to spill the secrets she'd told him. And he couldn't risk implying renewed promises of a future that he couldn't follow through on.

He'd maneuvered through the complications of his family for twenty-one years, but he didn't know how to navigate this.

He lowered himself onto a chair, one facing away from her. He would likely be able to think more clearly that way. But the chair scraped against the floor as he sat, and the noise woke her. He could see just enough of her out of the corner of his eye to know she had sat up straight.

Now what did he do? Ought he to quickly reveal he was there and attempt to make an expeditious, if embarrassing, exit? She might be angry that he was in the room. If she was about to leave, then keeping mum might be his best bet.

"This is what happens when you don't sleep." For a moment, he thought he'd been spotted. But then he realized she was talking to herself. "Perhaps Mrs. Greenberry's suggestion was a good one, after all."

What had Aunt Penelope suggested?

That question was quickly brushed aside as he realized his hesitation to decide whether to reveal himself or hide had, in the end, made the decision for him. She would be terribly embarrassed if she knew he'd overheard her having a self-directed conversation.

The Best-Kept Secrets 169

"Miss O'Doyle." And now, apparently, there was a second potential witness to his bungled decision-making. "Dr. Wilstead asked that this be given to you."

"Thank you."

He heard footsteps, a pause, then footsteps again that faded into the corridor. Duke could only just catch the slightest glimpse of Eve, standing near the desk. She was holding what looked like a folded piece of parchment.

"Well, Dr. Wilstead, how impossible is this number going to be?" She held the note but didn't unfold it. "I need to know what I'm facing, but I suspect you are about to deal me another blow."

Duke should have left when he'd had the chance. Now he was trapped, intruding.

"And if you could hear me talking to myself, you'd likely recommend I head to Bedlam instead of Dublin." He heard her sigh. "But I don't have anyone else to talk to about this. I—I have to sort this out on my own."

That was one of the last things he'd said to her. He hadn't intended to be cold or unfeeling, but hearing his words repeated, he felt the sting of them. And he was being unfair again, listening to her private conversation, no matter that doing so hadn't been his intention.

He heard the sound of stiff parchment unfolding. A moment's silence was followed by a whispered, "Good heavens." It was not the sound of someone who had just received good news. "We could never economize enough for this."

Duke couldn't be an eavesdropper any longer. He shouldn't have continued as long as he had. Careful not to scrape the chair legs again so as not to startle her, he stood and turned toward her. But her back was to him, so she still didn't know he was even there.

He moved around the chair, which placed himself between her and the door behind her. He could have slipped out. But she was hurting, and no matter that he knew he needed to keep a distance, he couldn't simply walk away.

"Eve?"

She spun around. His heart lurched to see tears clinging to her lashes.

"Is there anything I can do?" he asked.

She swiped firmly at her eyes. "No."

"Are you certain?"

Eve stood evermore stiffly. "I'm certain." She snatched her list from the desktop. "I sort my difficulties on my own now." She moved quickly past him.

He didn't turn to watch her leave. His heart couldn't bear it. "I miss you, Eve," he whispered. "But I don't know how else to protect you from my family."

He stood in the silence for a drawn-out moment. He'd imagined many times since latching on to the possibility of staying at Fairfield how quiet and peaceful his aunt and uncle's home would be. It had been one of the most appealing things about the idea. That stillness felt more burdensome than freeing just then. He had a direction and a potential purpose for his future, but he felt lost.

He dragged himself from the library. Not far down the corridor, he came upon his mother wearing her all-too-familiar expression of pained offense.

"Dubhán, you will never countenance what I have just endured."

Lud. Had Grandmother said something? Had Mother encountered Aunt Penelope and felt she'd been shown insufficient graciousness?

"Miss O'Doyle passed by," Mother said. "But when I offered her my warmest greeting, she responded with nothing but a halfhearted nod and smile so fleeting it could not possibly have been sincere." Mother's chin quivered a little. "No doubt your grandmother said unflattering things about me during the journey from Dublin and poisoned Miss O'Doyle's opinion of me."

In this, at least, Duke could be of some help to Eve. "Miss O'Doyle's sister is quite ill. Her concern for Miss Nia would, almost without question, render her thoughts distracted. We would do well to show her compassion during what must be a very difficult time."

That seemed to give Mother at least a moment of pause. Duke took full advantage of that pause and walked away. But he wasn't quick enough.

"What *did* your grandmother say about me during the journey from Dublin?" Mother asked, hurrying to catch up with him. "You heard her last night repeatedly referencing my 'pathetically nervous disposition.' The things she says about me when I am present are unkind; I can only imagine what she says that I do not hear."

"You say a great many things about her that she doesn't hear," Duke reminded her.

"Only acknowledgments of how unkind she is to me." Mother pressed a hand to her heart, walking alongside him. "Surely you are not going to begin disregarding her treatment of me."

"Of course not, Mother."

She shook her head. "You were quite harsh with your father two nights ago when she was complaining about every aspect of the evening's activities."

That night's row had culminated in Father calling Grandmother a banshee. Duke had taken him to task for it, yes, but Duke had been well within his rights to do so. He shouldn't have had to, but it had needed to be done. "I

The Best-Kept Secrets

171

was careful to discuss the situation in private. No one was privy to our conversation."

"But I am certain they guessed. And your aunt and grandmother, no doubt, were pleased to think he was being humiliated."

"Neither of them has mentioned it."

"Your father has." Mother set a hand on his arm and stopped their forward progress. "He will need to talk about this. No one outside of the two of us ever listens. And he is particularly helped by you. When this gathering has concluded, we'll have time to talk about it all."

If Duke were to return to Writtlestone, that would monopolize his energy for months. He would actually miss his parents. He loved them. And during the increasingly rare times when they were focused on something other than past defeats, perceived wrongs, and family tensions, he enjoyed being with them. But Mother's declaration drove home once more how crucial distance was between himself and his parents.

"I suspect my friends are ready to begin the day's activities," Duke said. "I am going to seek them out."

"But what if your father needs to speak with you?" Mother looked shocked at the possibility of Duke not dedicating his every waking moment to the fiasco of the Seymours. "What if your grandmother is unkind to me? What if Miss O'Doyle not acknowledging me proves to be an intentional slight? What are we to do if you are with your friends when your *family* needs you?"

"This gathering was planned specifically for these friends, including me, to be together. I ought not be prevented from taking part."

She looked hurt, though he didn't know whether the possibility that she was being inconsiderate or the possibility that he would *not* abandon the reason for his journey in order to assuage his parents' injured sensibilities caused her offense. No matter her reason at first, if he didn't disrupt the thought, she would soon be bemoaning that she wasn't a good enough mother and that he didn't love her as a son ought.

"As you said, after the gathering has ended, Father will have ample time to discuss his experiences, as will you. I am certain you have the fortitude to be patient until then, though I acknowledge that your patience will be sorely tried."

She squared her shoulders. "I have endured worse," she declared. "And I can be counted on to be long-suffering."

Duke pressed a quick kiss to his mother's cheek. "In exchange for your forbearance, I will tell you that the library was empty. You will find a great deal of peace and many books to choose from in there."

She didn't seem convinced, but at least she was distracted. Duke walked away again, this time managing to escape. His parents would have plenty to say during their return journey to Writtlestone; not the least of those grievances would be the fact that Duke was not journeying with them. There was every chance they would follow him to London.

He followed the corridor around a turn and found his aunt standing in a doorway, watching him with a look of concern and compassion.

"Is it always like that, Duke?" She subtly indicated the direction he'd come from and the conversation she had apparently overheard.

"No. Sometimes it is much worse."

She stepped up to him and took his face gently in her hands—a feat, as she was quite a lot shorter than he was. "If I'd fully realized just how much you've been burdened by all this, we'd've long ago brought you here to stay."

"Uncle Niles told you?"

She smiled. "Almost the instant he returned from Penfield."

"Thank you for letting me stay," Duke said.

She dropped her hands to his upper arms, still looking directly into his eyes. "There is peace in this house and in our London home. You'll find respite with us. The harmony here is a bit shattered at the moment, but it always returns."

"I am increasingly desperate for it."

Aunt Penelope did something next that Duke couldn't even remember his own mother doing in years: she wrapped him in a loving, maternal hug. After a lifetime of being broken by the family's animosity, he felt he finally had a chance to piece himself back together.

CHAPTER TWENTY-EIGHT

THE PACK AND THE HUNTRESSES had settled upon a parlor game for that night's entertainment. Nia felt equal to participating in something sedate and quiet, and everyone wished for her to be part of the festivities as much as she was able. Unfortunately, all the people gathered at Fairfield would be participating.

Duke wasn't overly worried about his aunt and uncle being disruptive. And he suspected the Fortiers would not cause difficulties either. But his parents and grandmother were another matter entirely.

"Do we place the warring parties on the same team or on opposing ones?" Charlie asked Duke under his breath as everyone was settling into the drawing room.

"It won't matter," Duke said. "They'll make trouble no matter which we choose."

"I'm beginning to understand a little better why you never seemed eager to return home during school holidays." Charlie shook his head.

Duke nodded. "The trouble they cause never ends."

"You know that you are always welcome at Brier Hill, don't you?"

Duke smiled a little. "I know, and I'm grateful to you and Artemis for that. For now, I'm heading to London after the house party and will stay there with my aunt and uncle."

"And when the Greenberrys leave London?" Charlie asked.

"They've said I can stay here, which I intend to do."

Charlie didn't look surprised, but he did seem a little wary. "Do your parents know yet?"

"No. And I likely won't tell them until the last possible moment."

Charlie nodded with emphasis. "Maybe wait until they're home and send a letter."

It wasn't a bad idea, actually.

Duke's gaze wandered, as it had all evening, to Eve. She sat beside her sister on a sofa. Nia looked spent, but so did Eve. Was anyone comforting *her*? She needed a respite from everything weighing on her. Duke was being granted that by his aunt and uncle, but Eve seemed to be drowning.

There had to be something he could do that would help in the moment without hurting in the long term. There had to be.

"What game are we playing this evening?" Grandmother's disparaging tone indicated that she would be unhappy no matter what had been chosen.

"We have decided on three kingdoms," Ellie said with a perfect mixture of excitement and deference. That might help lean Grandmother toward graciousness.

"An entirely unchallenging game." Grandmother proved Duke wrong in an instant. She meant to be petulant.

They'd been freed of Mme Dupuis's presence, who had shown herself entirely capable of ruining even the most enjoyable of games. How frustrating that Grandmother was filling those shoes so readily.

"I hope you will be on our team, Mrs. Seymour," Newton said in what they had labeled his "barrister voice" while at Cambridge. "You must be very adept at Three Kingdoms to find it so simplistic."

Grandmother seemed to sense that there was a hidden criticism in that but couldn't quite identify it.

To Father and Mother, Scott said, "We are forming the opposing team. I hope you'll join us."

With her brow drawn, Mother said, "I don't know that an American would be overly adept at games of wit."

"True," Father said without hesitation.

Shocked silence settled over the room, all eyes on Duke's parents. Uncle Niles's lips were pressed together in an obvious struggle to keep quiet. Somehow, Mother and Father managed to make things worse than had seemed possible.

Newton came to the rescue once more. "The Seymours can be on our team."

Scott turned to Colm. "Do you harbor any unexpressed doubts about American intelligence?"

Colm smiled broadly. "None whatsoever. Consider me a stanch member of your team."

Far from looking abashed at their own inexcusable behavior, Mother and Father ruffled up, whispers passing between them about how very typical it was for a Greenberry to side against them.

The Best-Kept Secrets 175

The teams were quickly formed after Mother and Father's blunder. Duke made certain that he was on the same team as his parents since that would make it easier to rein them in if need be. *If.* He'd long couched his concerns about their behavior in terms of *possibility* rather than *inevitability*, though the latter was far more accurate.

Charlie was elected to be the first guesser and, as such, walked with bouncing step into the corridor, closing the door behind him. The Pack and Huntresses all turned in near unison to Artemis.

She laughed. "You are hoping I will think of something my Charlie will never guess?"

Nods answered.

"He is one of the most intelligent people I know," Artemis said. "There is very little that he cannot sort out."

"Likely because he's not American," Toss said, almost keeping the laughter out of his voice.

"That should be what Charlie has to guess," Daria said. "'An American.'"

They all immediately agreed that that was a good option. Duke watched his parents for signs of offense, but they sat in displeased, somewhat haughty silence.

Charlie was brought back into the room, grinning with excitement. Games were among his favorite activities. He'd always been incredibly diverting. He eyed the gathering, likely debating the person to whom he ought to pose his first question. After only a moment, he chose Daria.

"To which kingdom does the thing thought of belong?" Charlie asked.

"Animal," she answered before clasping her hands over her mouth. From behind her hands, she said, "I do hope that answer does not give offense."

Gillian leaned a bit toward her. "Not the least offense. It is the correct answer, after all."

"Correct but potentially offensive." Charlie's eyes narrowed in thought, but his smile didn't fade. He spun around and questioned Tobias. "The thing thought of is a person?"

Tobias laughed. "Some would say so."

That brought laughter from the group. Scott good-naturedly declared that answer "misleading and offensive." His objections, of course, led to even more laughter.

Charlie turned directly to their resident American, studying him a moment. "How specific did the group decide to be?" he said quite obviously to himself.

"This is rather a juvenile game, isn't it?" Father grumbled to Mother in a voice not quite quiet enough.

Being the clever person he was, Charlie quickly turned that comment around. "Just juvenile enough for me to have sorted the answer after only two questions. The thing thought of is 'Americans.'"

Charlie's teammates cheered. The opposing team made a show of being quite disappointed, but there were smiles all around.

M. Fortier leaned a bit toward Uncle Niles and said, "His father's whimsical nature and his mother's intelligence."

Uncle Niles nodded. "Quite a combination of the two."

What would people say Duke had inherited from his parents? Few people were ever permitted to experience anything beyond his parents' bitterness.

"Who should go next?" Daria asked. "Someone from our team this time, I think."

That was the pattern of the game.

"Mrs. Greenberry," Charlie suggested. "My mother's told me she is quite clever. I think I'd like to discover how accurate the tales really are."

"Far be it from me to prevent Julia from being exalted in her son's eyes." Aunt Penelope rose and, to the laughter of her husband and friends, made her way from the room.

"What should be chosen?" Fennel asked.

"Nothing too difficult," Father said. "We'd hate for her to embarrass herself."

"She won't," Colm said. "The dowager's assessment of my mother's intelligence is not inaccurate."

"I've known her longer than you have," Father countered.

"Have you though?" Uncle Niles muttered.

Duke jumped in. "Let's choose a thing for her to guess. Perhaps something outside of the animal kingdom this time."

"Might I suggest a knife?" Grandmother said. "One for stabbing someone in the back."

Duke, who sat near enough to her to be heard without raising his voice, said firmly, "Stop."

She looked at him with wide eyes. Did she truly think he wouldn't object?

Father's gaze shifted to Uncle Niles, who gave him a hard look of clear warning. Had there already been a not-in-public conversation between them? Or was Uncle Niles telling him one was forthcoming should things not calm down?

"What about hay?" Lisette suggested to the group. "Being such an accomplished horsewoman, Mrs. Seymour ought to think of it, but if she doesn't, it will be quite a lark for her to realize she ought to have."

The Best-Kept Secrets

"Excellent idea," Artemis said.

Everyone agreed. Grandmother, Father, and Mother didn't actually offer their thoughts. While their petulance was irritating, at least they were not choosing to be further insulting.

Aunt Penelope stepped inside once more. Her smile dimmed only when her gaze happened past her brother, sister-in-law, and mother. But she didn't allow her gaze to linger there. Generally speaking, ignoring whichever members of the family were currently part of the warring faction kept skirmishes from immediately breaking out. Aunt Penelope's willingness to help Duke, in essence, run away from home would trigger a battle soon enough.

She turned to Mme Fortier. "To which kingdom does the thing thought of belong?"

"*Legume*," the Frenchwoman answered.

Duke glanced at Eve. She didn't have any real grasp of French. He wished he were sitting closer to her so he could translate. She looked at him in the exact same moment. He'd translated for her a few times during the house party, and it seemed that she'd turned to him now for help again. He smiled, relief washing over him. But her expression grew ponderous once more, and the same pained sadness he'd seen in her eyes as she'd left the library returned.

"How are we to know if they are cheating if their answers are not offered in English?" Mother demanded.

Mme Fortier's composure didn't slip in the least. "I did not realize I had spoken in French. My answer was *vegetable*."

Grandmother sniffed, the small sound overflowing with disapproval. Good heavens, they were being particularly difficult tonight.

Aunt Penelope turned to Nia. "Is the thing thought of that belongs to the vegetable kingdom a plant, as opposed to fungi or lichen or something of that nature?"

Vegetable was the term used in the game to encompass living things that were not animals, though it did not truly reflect all things that fell into that category. Aunt Penelope was wise to further narrow her options.

Nia nodded. "It is." Her answer was quiet but steady. It was good of Aunt Penelope to so intentionally include Nia; she had missed out on so many things.

To Eve, Aunt Penelope asked, "Is this plant that belongs to the vegetable kingdom of the edible variety?"

Eve's eyes pulled wide even as a laughing grin spread across her face. She looked to them all. "How do I answer that?"

"In the least helpful way possible," Duke suggested.

That set Aunt Penelope's team to good-natured shouts of disapproval, and the opposing team to cheers and applause.

"I believe I shall borrow an answer from Tobias," Eve said, "and reply to your question with, 'Some would say so.'"

Duke didn't think he'd seen Aunt Penelope look so entirely delighted since this house party had begun. Her tender kindness to him that morning had further endeared her to him. He wanted to see her shed some of the weight of this family feud.

Nia, likewise, looked pleased to be taking part, which was a relief in itself. Knowing her happiness would help Eve worry a little less added to Duke's feeling of relief. An evening of parlor games was proving a brilliant idea.

"I will choose to assume that Miss O'Doyle's answer is an indication that this particular plant is edible but not in all instances or to all creatures." Aunt Penelope began looking them all over, searching out the next person to whom she would pose a question. She settled on Duke. "Is this plant, which I suspect is eaten by some creatures, consumed by people?"

"Not by *wise* people," he answered, finding a means of being just obscure enough to be slightly unhelpful.

But before his aunt could good-naturedly object or the rest of the gathering laugh, Father spoke up. "So, perhaps by Penelope."

"Liam—" Uncle Niles cut himself off at just his brother-in-law's name.

"Father, stop." Duke didn't manage quite as quiet a rebuke as he had with his grandmother.

His correction proved too little too late though. Much of the amusement in the room dimmed.

Aunt Penelope turned back to Uncle Niles. Though Duke couldn't see her face, the look of loving concern on Uncle Niles's told him his aunt was not so unaffected by the insult as she often went to great pains to appear.

"This sometimes-edible plant is consumed by animals, I can deduct. Is it eaten by domesticated animals?"

"Yes, dear." No attempt at silliness or subtlety from Uncle Niles.

"You have but one more question, Penelope," Grandmother said. "I believe this will prove beyond your ability."

"This is a group which has shown itself prone to choosing things pertinent to the evening's discussions or the people involved. The thing thought of is a plant that is eaten by domesticated animals. As I am one of 'the people involved' and I have been associated with one particular 'domesticated animal' for more

The Best-Kept Secrets 179

years than our younger participants have been alive and those animals are quite known for eating a very particular plant, I will guess"—she looked directly at her brother and mother—"hay."

Everyone applauded. Everyone except Duke's parents and grandmother. They were so infuriating at times.

"Someone from *our* team now." Charlie managed not to sound desperate to move on, but Duke knew him too well not to hear hints of it.

"Eve should be next," Nia said. "She's quite good at this game."

Words of encouragement followed, and Eve acquiesced in her usual good cheer. She slipped into the corridor and closed the door.

"What should we have her guess?" Colm asked Nia.

"All the O'Doyles are excellent equestrians."

"Something to do with horses, then," Uncle Niles said, sitting with his arm around Aunt Penelope, whose spirits were noticeably dampened.

"What about a horse *thief*?" Father grumbled, eyeing Aunt Penelope sidelong.

"Father," Duke said in a voice of warning.

"A horseshoe," Fennel suggested.

"Excellent." Tobias rose and moved toward the door, no doubt wishing to begin the guessing before Duke's family could cause more consternation.

Eve stepped inside. She was smiling. The expression had its usual mesmerizing effect.

To Newton, she asked, "To which kingdom does the thing thought of belong?"

"Mineral," Newton said.

She spun around and faced Aunt Penelope. "Does this thing of the mineral kingdom follow the pattern you discovered in bearing some connection to the group here tonight or to myself specifically?"

With a look of pride, Aunt Penelope said, "Indeed. Well puzzled, Miss O'Doyle."

Eve spun once more. It was good to see her so obviously cheerful. She'd had so much on her mind of late. Her eyes met Duke's, and he couldn't hold back a smile, though she didn't fully return it.

"Does this thing of the mineral kingdom, which has been selected, perhaps, because of a connection to this group, happen to be a knife, as was suggested earlier?"

Amused chuckles sounded.

"I'm afraid not."

She narrowed her eyes in a theatrical look of contemplation. "It truly isn't?"

"Nay," Duke answered but with just enough hint of "neigh" to turn the chuckles to outright laughter.

Even Eve smiled at him. That dimple of hers tugged at his heart once more. "It's to do with horses, then."

In a very clearly enunciated grumble, Grandmother said, "Cheating is to be the order of the day, it seems."

"It's only a game, Grandmother," Duke said.

"An already juvenile game that has to be made embarrassingly simple for simple-minded girls."

Stunned silence settled immediately over the room once more. Shock rendered Eve pale, even as blotches of color spread over her cheeks. She looked horrified. Even more than that, she looked hurt.

Uncle Niles moved, clearly meaning to stand and, likely, break his word to Penelope to keep quarrels behind closed doors.

Duke stood, saving him the trouble. "It is time for you three"—he motioned to his parents and grandmother—"to retire for the night. Come along."

"Come along?" Father scoffed. "We are not children to be ordered about."

"You are behaving abominably, Dubhán," Mother said.

"*I* am?" Were they so mired in bitterness and a desire to punish Aunt Penelope that they didn't even realize how horrible *they* were to everyone else? "I am far too tired to argue with you about this, and I have less than zero desire to enact a scene in front of so many people who ought not be subjected to this."

"You do not usually resort to dramatics," Father said in tones of dismissive bother.

Duke held his father's gaze with a hard one of his own. "Do I look as though this is a mere performance?"

For the first time, the offenders seemed to actually believe him.

"I will walk with you," Duke said firmly.

They rose, watching him with varying looks of surprise. He motioned to the open door, then followed them through it.

"You cannot be in earnest, Dubhán," Grandmother said as they walked down the corridor. "This is unseemly."

"Do not lecture me on uncouth behavior, any of you." He took a breath to keep hold of his calm. The corridor deposited them in the grand entryway at the foot of the equally grand staircase. "The things you have said tonight would have been merely embarrassing if they hadn't also been unkind. And I have never, in all my time in Society, heard anyone speak to a lady of the *ton*

The Best-Kept Secrets 181

the way you"—he looked at his grandmother—"just did to Miss O'Doyle. I will endure a lot of things from the three of you, but not that."

"She is an insignificant girl from a family considered unimportant even in Irish circles," Father said. "Mother's comment was, perhaps, overly harsh, but it isn't as though she spoke a bit severely to royalty."

Another quick breath to keep his temper in check. "Two things the three of you need to understand. The first: I do not care how 'insignificant' you consider any of my friends. I will defend every last one of them against any unkindness you show them."

Mother's hand was, of course, already pressed to her heart in a show of injured sensibilities. Grandmother appeared surprised but plotting. Father only looked more annoyed.

"The second is this," Duke said, "and listen well because I will offer no further warnings. You have, both directly and indirectly, caused Miss O'Doyle pain, and you have done so at a time when she is away from her family and worried for her sister. At a time when you ought to have felt some flicker of human kindness, you have chosen to be cruel."

For once, his warring family was silent.

"One word, one look of unkindness toward Eve O'Doyle," he said, "and I will have you tossed bodily from this house."

"Dubhán!" Mother's voice rang with shock.

"Do not test me on this, because I will follow through." He held his ground. "I will do what I must to protect her from you."

"After all these years, you are siding against me." Father looked at him the way one would a bucket of milk that had turned sour.

"You consider my insistence that you behave like a gentleman to be 'siding against you.' How has this become the person you are?" Duke shook his head. "Find something to fill your time this evening away from my friends. And if by morning you cannot discover within yourself the civility to treat Miss O'Doyle as you ought, then make arrangements to return to Writtlestone."

He gave a single dip of his head before turning around. Duke was not an outwardly emotional person. He never had been. But in that moment, he felt a tremendous urge to go straight to Penfield and pummel bags of hay for hours while shouting to the heavens all the frustrated anger he felt. But he had just as strong a desire to lower himself to the floor and cry like a child, to grieve a lifetime that had been stolen from him by a family at war with itself and parents whose selfishness he was finally admitting to himself exceeded their willingness to simply love their son.

He followed the corridor back toward the drawing room, his spirits flagging. This was supposed to have been a joyful gathering of all his dearest friends.

As he came within view of the drawing room door, he saw Eve standing just outside it, watching his approach.

His heart dropped to his feet, pinning him to the spot. "I am so sorry, Eve. I've tried to shield you from them, and I've tried to put as much distance between them and you as I could, but it's not enough. This is who they are. This is what they do."

"You can't stop them from doing the things they apparently *always* do in the end." She'd stepped a little closer, but his heart ached at the remaining distance between them, both literally and figuratively.

"I don't want them to keep hurting everyone."

"And I don't want them to keep hurting *you*."

No one else had stepped out of the drawing room. It was the closest to a private moment he'd had with her since their first evening at Fairfield. "My aunt and uncle have said that I can make my home with them indefinitely."

She looked genuinely pleased for him. "You will have your respite."

He nodded. "And not a moment too soon."

"But do you know what will lift your spirits even more than that good news?" He welcomed the teasing he heard in her question. It was a glimpse of what they'd shared before, of what he'd had and lost. "Winning this game of three kingdoms. You see, I am about to guess *horseshoe*, which I am confident will earn our team a point."

"I certainly do not want to miss that," he said, managing a fleeting smile.

He followed her into the drawing room, wishing he could hold her hand as he'd once done, or at least walk at her side. She didn't seem to intend to hold against him the unforgivable behavior of his parents. He was grateful for that.

But she was clearly not at ease as his friend any longer, and that broke his heart.

CHAPTER TWENTY-NINE

"I FIND I'M RATHER GLAD that it's raining so much today." Nia sat beside Eve on a sofa in the drawing room, their eyes on the windows. Artemis, Ellie, Gillian, and Daria were at a nearby table, laughing their way through a friendly game of whist. Lisette was elsewhere in the house with her aunt and uncle. The Pack was, no doubt, up to some mischief or other.

"Why is it you are so pleased with the wet weather?" Artemis asked.

"Because I haven't the energy for an outing, but I would feel awful if everyone remained in the house on account of me. But I'd also be sad if I were left behind."

Eve nodded. How well she understood that. She would not be with their friends for their future larks and adventures, and she was already mourning that. But she wouldn't want them to not enjoy themselves simply because she wasn't there.

"Will you have enough vigor to join in our games tonight?" Daria asked.

"I don't know," Nia said. "I was spent by the time I went to bed last night. I think it was a little too much exertion for me."

Nia's coloring wasn't worrying. She'd assured Eve several times already that she wasn't experiencing palpitations or lightheadedness. She was worn out, easily tired. But, Eve continually reassured herself, Nia's heart didn't seem to be affected.

"I suppose we will just have to hold tonight's festivities at the foot of your bed," Ellie declared. "There is nothing else to be done."

They all laughed at that, teasing Nia and each other. Dr. Wilstead had said Nia needed to keep her spirits up. The Huntresses were miraculously good at that.

Since receiving Dr. Wilstead's estimate of expenses, Eve had been spinning in her mind the question of how to find the money to see her sister well again.

Lying in her bed early that morning, the answer had come as a sudden bolt of understanding.

Eve needed to find employment. While she certainly had the knowledge and ability to be a very good cook or baker, such a thing was not acceptable for the daughter of a gentleman. The only options truly open to her were governess and lady's companion. She would be separated from her family, pulled from Society, and taken away from her friends regardless. She didn't particularly wish to add the crushing isolation that governesses experienced to that list of losses. As a companion, she would have the company of the lady she worked for. And she wouldn't be relegated to dark corners or the confines of the nursery when there were visitors, and she wouldn't take all her meals alone. Being a companion *was* the better option, provided she could find a lady in need of a companion.

Deep-pitched, boisterous voices floated in from beyond the door. In near-perfect unison, all the Huntresses present said, "The Pack." And a moment later, the gentlemen poured inside, laughing, shoving each other, and grinning.

Eve immediately found Duke. He looked content, which she hoped meant his parents and grandmother hadn't rung a peal over his head for tossing them from the drawing room the night before. He had endured a lot from his parents and grandmother, but it was only after they had insulted *her* that he'd put a very public and vocal end to their behavior. She wanted to thank him, to tell her how touched she was, but he'd insisted on this distance between them. He likely wouldn't welcome her narrowing it even for a well-deserved expression of gratitude.

"Nia." Charlie eagerly led the gentlemen to the sofa. "Just who we were looking for."

"You were looking for me?"

They all nodded eagerly. Tobias, Newton, Scott, and Toss all held out small plates, a different baked good on each.

"We've just been to the kitchen, where we shamelessly stole a variety of delicacies for you," Charlie said, "and we have subsequently committed ourselves to extremely irresponsible wagers regarding which of the options you will declare your favorite."

Wonderful, thoughtful gentlemen, every last one of them. Though they'd made a friendly game of their offering, Eve knew perfectly well they'd done this as a means of lifting Nia's spirits.

"As I am not part of this wager," Eve said, "I will step aside and let Nia ponder her answer without running the risk of unduly influencing her." She

The Best-Kept Secrets 185

rose and moved away from the sofa, allowing her sister to receive all the attention and kindness she deserved.

Eve hadn't gone far at all when Duke separated from his friends and walked toward her. That was decidedly unexpected.

Eve very nearly held her breath.

"How is Nia today?" Duke asked quietly.

"Not any better. I don't want to assume that means hers will be a severely prolonged illness, but I am worried about that. And I keep watching her for signs of heart distress, which terrifies me." What was she doing? She was supposed to be carrying this by herself, not burdening him with her troubles.

But Duke didn't look upset. "How are *you* holding up?"

"I have a lot I am attempting to sort out. But I think I am closer to doing so."

From her place on the sofa, Nia declared that the gingerbread was her choice among the offerings the Pack had brought her.

Colm immediately turned to the rest of the gentlemen. "Just as I insisted, yet not one of you agreed. I will be making good on those wagers, my friends."

With a theatrical sigh, Toss said, "We really should have given heed to the wisdom he has gained in his old age."

"It isn't a matter of age, young one," Colm said very solemnly—a little *too* solemnly. "It is, rather, the benefit of a life strategy that I have honed over the years."

"And what strategy is that?" Scott asked with a grin.

"Paying attention." Colm took the plate from him, then turned to Nia and presented it with a flourish. "Your gingerbread, Miss Nia."

The Pack laughed at Colm's antics. Nia smiled and blushed a little. It did Eve's heart good to see.

"I wanted to warn them that Nia likely has very high standards in baked treats," Duke said quietly, "but I didn't dare run the risk of tipping your hand."

"I told the Huntresses about my . . . hobby. I hadn't intended to, but I'd very recently lost my confidant." She didn't dare look at Duke, not trusting herself to keep her emotions in check. "I wanted so badly to be seen by someone."

From the whist table, Artemis said, "I hope the Pack realizes we will absolutely abandon you to the ire of the Fairfield cook once your pilfering is discovered."

"You would leave us to such a cruel fate, and after we've only recently escaped the clutches of Mme Dupuis?" Charlie was up to his usual theatrics.

"Will you at least weep when you eulogize me and my tragic end at the hands of an offended chef?"

From the doorway came an unexpected answer. "Your wife might weep for you, but your brothers would mock your kitchen-related misfortunes." Everyone spun about to find Charlie's mother standing there, watching them all with a look of maternal fondness. The loving radiance she exuded was undimmed by the black she always wore.

"Mater!" Charlie rushed to her and pulled his mother into a hug.

Artemis was there an instant later. Scott moved only slightly less swiftly. Daria and Gillian joined in. Before long, everyone was surrounding the newly arrived dowager countess, whom all the Huntresses and the Pack called Mater, just as her sons did. Eve hung back, sitting once more beside Nia, who looked too tired to do anything but nibble at her gingerbread.

"This house party keeps growing larger and larger," Eve said. "Christmas will be very merry indeed."

Nia nodded, the movement slow and weary.

"Do you need to lie down?" Eve asked.

"Could I lie down here? I think I'm too tired to climb the stairs again."

Eve saw her sister comfortably situated on the sofa with a warm throw spread over her. She was paler than she had been even a half hour earlier.

"Any palpitations?" Eve asked her quietly.

"No." Nia closed her eyes.

Eve pressed her hand to Nia's forehead. Nia was a little feverish.

Dr. Wilstead had said Nia's fevers would ebb and flow for weeks or months. And if the fevers did reach her heart, they would need to begin treatments immediately. Eve couldn't drag her feet. She needed to start looking for a position now.

She didn't know many people, not of the generation most likely to hire a companion. Finding that elusive future employer would be difficult and take a great deal of time. But she didn't have that luxury.

"You look worried," Nia said softly, having opened her eyes a little once more.

Eve quickly produced a smile. "My thoughts were wandering, is all."

"Could those thoughts wander to finding another blanket?"

Eve tucked the blanket Nia already had more firmly around her. "I'll procure you an entire pile of blankets."

"And more gingerbread?" Nia's eyes were only half open.

Eve leaned close and lowered her voice. "Is it as good as *my* gingerbread?"

The Best-Kept Secrets   187

"No."

"Good answer." Eve rose and crossed to where Colm stood. She set a hand on his arm to get his attention. "Nia is asking for another blanket, but I don't know where to find any."

He looked over at Nia. "The room isn't actually very cold." He sounded as concerned as Eve felt. "Should I send for Dr. Wilstead? I don't think he's left Fairfield."

"He did look in on her this morning," Eve said. "But if he is still here, having him check on her again wouldn't be a terrible thing."

"What else can I do?" Colm asked.

"You sound like Duke."

Colm shrugged. "He and I *are* the pride of the Seymour family." There was a hint of a laugh in the declaration.

"As the pride of the Seymour family, perhaps you could pilfer a bit more gingerbread."

He snapped a salute. "Miss Nia will have all the blankets, gingerbread, and medical attention she could possibly want."

"Thank you."

Colm set to action. Knowing she could trust him to do all he'd promised, Eve took a moment to think. Mater might know of someone looking for a companion; the Jonquils had connections all over the kingdom. The Greenberrys and Fortiers did as well. She could begin there to look for a position.

Though their hostess had been very gracious and hadn't begrudged Nia the help she'd needed, Eve didn't feel entirely comfortable asking for yet another favor. Neither did she know how much of her situation she could trust to Mrs. Greenberry's discretion.

But Duke would know.

If she could phrase her question in a way that didn't set his back up again, she might learn what she needed to move forward with confidence. It was entirely possible that she would mismanage the balance between speaking with a friend and burdening him with her troubles. And if she did, he might very well respond with that blunt directness that still caused an ache in her heart when she thought back on it.

But she would be asking only for a little information, not for any true assistance. Surely he wouldn't object to that.

She turned toward him. In so doing, she discovered he was actually already looking at her.

She subtly motioned him over, and he immediately joined her a bit apart from all the others. She took a quick breath to solidify her determination and to brace herself should this not go well.

"I know I'm not meant to bother you with my worries and spill my thoughts in your ear"—she spoke quickly in the hope of getting past the barriers she anticipated—"and I really am working to sort my own difficulties. I truly am. I simply don't know something that I need to know and that I think you *do* know, and I can't find it out if I don't ask you."

Duke set a hand gently on her arm. "Eve, I didn't—"

Daria walked past them in that exact moment, blankets in her arms, and said to Eve, "Colm had these brought for Nia with instructions to tell you when they arrived."

The interruption was ever so brief, but it was enough to set Duke back a step, his expression and posture more reserved once more.

"What is it you need to know?" he asked.

Eve kept her courage up and pressed forward. "I have an idea for addressing my family's situation, and my likelihood of success will increase if I have your aunt's thoughts on a critical aspect of it."

Duke looked tempted to ask for details, but he didn't.

"I don't know her well enough to be certain if she would be willing to help me. And I'm not certain if I can trust her enough to tell her anything about my circumstances."

"My aunt Penelope will help you in every way she can. And she will keep confidential anything that you ask her to."

A bit of hope returned to her heavy heart. "Truly?"

"You have my word, Eve."

"Would you—" For a moment, she'd forgotten the situation. "Never mind."

"Would I *what*?"

She shook her head. "I've already overstepped myself. I'll not ask more of you."

"Please do." There was something mournful in the request, and she ached to hear it.

"I was going to ask if you would be willing to be with me when I ask for your aunt's help. You needn't stay while I talk with her, but being there when I ask might be helpful."

"Of course. Of course." His posture straightened, and his gaze focused. "You need only tell me when you'd like to talk with her, and I will join you."

It was a glimpse of the Duke she missed so acutely. He'd been entirely out of reach. She'd felt rejected and tossed aside. But she had a bit of him back, at least for a time. And she meant to cherish that while she had it.

CHAPTER THIRTY

EVE STOOD OUTSIDE THE GROUND-FLOOR sitting room that afternoon fighting her growing nerves. She had not previously been prone to trepidation, but these past couple of weeks had seemed to change that. Carrying secrets, being brushed aside after confiding in someone she had trusted, and having her entire future snatched away without warning had left wounds. She didn't yet know how many of those wounds would become scars.

Her heart floated and calmed when she spotted Duke walking toward her. His rejection at the beginning of the house party still ached, but she'd seen regret in his eyes since then. She couldn't entirely believe that he disliked her or was indifferent or truly wanted nothing to do with her.

She didn't know all the answers, but she still trusted him enough to tiptoe toward them.

His smile was tentative. She could feel that hers was as well.

"Your aunt is in the sitting room," she said. "But so is Mater and Mme Fortier. They've been together all afternoon, and I suspect that's unlikely to change."

He nodded. "You don't want to interrupt."

"I don't—I don't want to keep annoying people with my problems."

The regret she'd so often seen in those deep-blue eyes returned once more. "I was never annoyed, Eve."

She wanted to feel relieved, but she didn't. "But that's not really better, is it? I'm not irritating; I'm just not worth talking to."

His brow angled low. "That isn't true at all."

"Then, what is? Because I'm so very confused by you, Duke."

"My family hurts everyone who wanders into their sphere, and I was already seeing that impact you." He released a breath. "I was *and am* trying to save you from it, and distance is likely the best way."

"Did it never cross your mind to talk with me about what was worrying you?" she asked. "Or, at the very least, tell me why you were abandoning me after having promised that you wouldn't? You just walked away when I needed you, and you didn't even tell me why."

Duke's eyes dropped. "I went about this entirely wrong, didn't I? In trying to prevent pain, I instead caused it. I am sorry, Eve. I truly am."

He was sorry for the rejections he'd dealt her the past few days, but he didn't say he no longer considered the closeness that had grown between them or the kiss they'd shared "a mistake." She had *some* of those elusive answers she'd been longing for. In time, she hoped to have all of them, but she felt certain now was not the time to push for more admissions from him.

"Are you still willing to go in with me when I talk to your aunt?" she asked.

"Of course." His response was fervent and sincere.

Her nervousness began to ebb. "How well do you know Mme Fortier? I think she could also be helpful in this matter, but I cannot say if she would be willing or simply inconvenienced."

He met Eve's eyes once more. "I can ask my aunt."

"I would appreciate it," Eve said.

"Thank you."

She hadn't expected that. "Thank you?"

"For still having a little faith in me," he said. "It's more than I deserve."

She did have faith in him. But she also felt uncertain. Asking his aunt for a moment of her time and helping Eve know how to approach the coming conversation would be legitimately helpful. It was also a comparatively safe thing to trust Duke with.

Duke opened the sitting room door, and they stepped inside. Heavens, she was nervous. If these ladies helped her, and she hoped they would, her future away from home, away from Society, away from the Huntresses would be that much more real.

"Please forgive the interruption," Duke said. He looked to his aunt. "May I speak with you for a moment?"

"Of course." Mrs. Greenberry stood and walked with her nephew a bit aside. They began whispering.

Eve stood awkwardly as she waited.

Mater didn't allow it to last long. "How is your sister feeling, Miss O'Doyle?"

"She is sleeping," Eve said. "And feverish again, unfortunately. Dr. Wilstead has chosen not to return to Epsom. She is more unwell than any of us would like her to be."

The Best-Kept Secrets   193

"My son Corbin had rheumatic fever when he was twelve years old," Mater said. "It worried me so deeply."

Mother would be worried, too, when she learned of Nia's illness.

"Corbin has endured no lasting effects." Mater spoke firmly and comfortingly. "Rheumatic fever is a frightening illness but not a hopeless one."

Eve nodded, grateful for the encouragement, especially as it had been offered without dismissal of the reality of the illness or belittling her worries.

"*S'il vous plaît*," Mme Fortier said, "tell us if we can do anything for you or your sister."

"I will, thank you."

Duke and Mrs. Greenberry returned to the group.

He moved to Eve's side and spoke quietly. "My aunt says she would trust these ladies with her life, that people have, in fact, done just that. And she says she hopes you will allow them to help you in whatever way they are able."

That should have lifted some of the weight from Eve's mind, but her thoughts remained distressed. "I'm grateful that they're willing to be of assistance, but I wish I didn't need them to, not in this way."

"Would it help if I stayed?" Duke offered.

A flicker of hope in her heart told her the answer. "If you're willing."

"More than willing."

Eve straightened her shoulders and nodded. There was no point in delaying any longer. The ladies were watching her expectantly.

"Do sit with us." Mater motioned her over.

Eve took the offered seat next to Mater. Duke remained standing, placing himself near the windows.

"I'm certain you've sorted out that my family's not well off," Eve said. "But— and this bit isn't widely known, so I'd appreciate it not being whispered about."

"Of course," Mater said.

The other ladies nodded their agreement as well.

"Our situation has grown worse lately. And now, with Nia being ill and facing months of needing a doctor's care and treatments, things are dire." Eve took a deep breath, pushing it out slowly. "I need to find a position that will earn me a bit of money that I can send back to my family. I am hoping that you three might know of a lady looking to take on a companion. I realize I am hardly in a position to be particular, but I would prefer a lady who isn't cruel or inclined to be too much of a taskmaster."

"I think you are entitled to greater consideration than that, Miss O'Doyle," Mrs. Greenberry said.

194 SARAH M. EDEN

"I haven't the luxury of waiting for an ideal option."

Duke was watching her with a pained look from his place near the window. "You'll at least wait for one that isn't abysmal, won't you?"

"That is why I wanted to talk with"—she looked at the three ladies—"the three of you. You know more people than I do."

Mme Fortier laughed, the sound fittingly graceful. "We know more *older* people, I believe you mean."

Eve shrugged. "I wasn't going to actually say it out loud."

The ladies all laughed at that. Duke smiled a little.

"Your mother might know ladies nearer to your family home," Mrs. Greenberry said.

Eve's heart dropped. "She might, but she doesn't know the change in Nia's health, so she wouldn't realize how urgently I need to make whatever arrangements for employment I can."

"You haven't written to her?" Mrs. Greenberry asked.

Eve shook her head. "My family couldn't possibly pay the postage on a letter."

"Eve, my uncle is a member of Parliament," Duke said. "He can frank letters. Your family would not have to pay any postage to receive them."

She swallowed down a surge of emotion. "Do you think he would do that for me?"

"Absolutely," Mrs. Greenberry said.

"I've wanted to send a letter, but I couldn't strain the family finances that way."

Duke crossed to the door. "I will have the arrangements seen to immediately." And on that firm declaration, he stepped from the room.

"In your letter," Mrs. Greenberry said, "be certain to tell your mother that we have room enough for her to stay here and be with your sister. She needn't worry about that."

"We cannot afford to receive letters," Eve reminded them. "There isn't money enough for a journey. Even if there were, she needs to be at Tulleyloch with my brothers. And I need to sort out a means of seeing my family through these painfully lean times."

"Well, Julia," Mrs. Greenberry said, "I suspect I know what you're thinking, but I do have to wonder what you think the chances of success are this time."

"Considering I haven't managed the thing in more than thirty years of trying . . ." Mater made a show of deep pondering. "I can see no reason not to expect absolute success."

The Best-Kept Secrets 195

Eve looked at each of them in turn, confused.

"This is the risk one runs when sitting amongst friends who have known each other as long as we have," Mrs. Greenberry said. "Too many discussions are undertaken without the least context offered to those listening."

Mater turned to face Eve more directly. "The first time I attempted to take on a companion was in 1787." She motioned to Mme Fortier. "It was Nicolette, in fact. And while she did accept the offer, in the end, she married Henri instead. Our friend Violet Barrington made the same offer to Penelope." Mater nodded to Mrs. Greenberry. "But she married Niles instead."

"You ought to have noticed the pattern by then," Mme Fortier said.

"Alas." Mater sighed dramatically. "A few years ago, I took on a dear young lady who grew up on a neighboring estate to ours, and she was my companion for mere weeks before marrying Artemis's brother. Then I offered the position to Sarah Sarvol, but she decided to marry my son Harold instead."

"Even I am beginning to see a pattern now," Eve said, letting her amusement show.

"Oh, it continues." Mater shook her head. "This past Season, I arranged for Daria to take on that role."

Eve remembered that. "Because her parents were going to force her to go live with a tyrannical relative."

"Because I have very much wished for a companion these past years," Mater said. "And I would have enjoyed having her stay with me. But she married Toss instead. And here I am still without a companion."

Eve's heart pounded out a hopeful rhythm even as her mind warned her to be cautious. "But you do wish for one?"

Mater nodded. "The offer I made thirty-two years ago was extended to allow Nicolette a means of escaping a very difficult situation. But the attempts I have made in more recent years have been undertaken because I genuinely would enjoy having someone make her home at the dower house and travel with me to London and the various parts of the kingdom where I have children or friends I'd like to visit."

"I like to travel," Eve said. "And I believe I can accurately and honestly say that I'm an easy person to get along with, unlikely to be a difficult addition to your household." How she wanted to believe the issue of earning money had been solved so swiftly.

"Yes," Mrs. Greenberry said, "but how likely are you to abandon the idea in favor of getting married? That does seem to be the usual outcome of anyone accepting Julia's offer."

"Quite *un*likely," Eve said with a laugh.

"I suppose Monsieur Duke jumps to secure letter franking for you only because he disapproves of the current Royal postal system?" Mme Fortier suggested dryly with a smile in her eyes.

"There was a time when I thought the wind might be beginning to blow in that direction." Heavens, Eve was back to her old way of spilling her thoughts as she had them. "But he's made it clear in a few ways and a few different moments that he's not so inclined to see things that way any longer. Maybe he never did to the extent that I thought."

The three ladies exchanged looks that, she suspected, were very communicative from their perspectives. She, however, wasn't certain what they were silently telling each other.

"I intend to spend this Christmas season here with my dear friends," Mater said. "You and I can work out all the details and arrangements needed."

"I do need to keep this a secret for the time being," Eve said. "Nia doesn't know the extent of our family's difficulties, and I am not at liberty to tell her yet. I don't know how I would explain to her my employment intentions without breaking my word to my parents."

Mater gave Eve's hand a quick squeeze. "Set your mind at ease, my dear. Your sister will have all she needs while she is at Fairfield. We'll keep this arrangement a secret until you tell us otherwise. And when Nia is ready to return home, you will be in a position to help her and your family."

"And you aren't making this offer out of pity?" Eve didn't think she could bear that.

"I am offering for two very important reasons: because I would enjoy the arrangement and because I am certain my friends will forthwith place a wager among themselves as to how long I will keep my companion this time, and I look forward to hearing what absurd forfeit they decide upon."

"For the sake of our entertainment," Eve said, "I hope, no matter what their guesses are, that they are wrong enough to have to pay that likely ridiculous forfeit." Her heart was lighter than it had been since the day she'd stepped into the Royal Pavilion with Mother.

"So do I," Mater said.

CHAPTER THIRTY-ONE

"Nia's parents haven't been informed that she is ill because the family can't afford to receive letters." Duke had, at last, managed a private conversation with his uncle. "I told Eve I would ask if you would frank a letter for her so she can write to her parents."

"If I had realized she hadn't written home, I would have offered myself when Miss Nia first took ill."

Uncle Niles sat at the elegant desk in his library. Duke sat across from him.

"None of us knew," he said. "Eve confided in me that her family's finances don't bear scrutiny. But even I didn't guess that things were this bad."

"It makes your father's three decades of anger over his comparatively easy situation all the more frustrating, doesn't it?"

Duke couldn't imagine their struggles making the O'Doyles bitter and angry. "You said my grandmother has changed over the years. Did my father used to be different?"

Uncle Niles nodded. "When I first met him, he was . . . unsure of himself but always trying to convince others that he was self-assured. It was a little vexing, but he wasn't like he is now. And there was already some tension between him and Penelope, but even seeing that, I wouldn't have predicted the fracture that later split their family."

"I wish I had known him then," Duke said.

"So do I." Uncle Niles's expression was pensive. "I've found myself wishing a number of things had been different. And I wonder lately if maybe all this was allowed to go on too long and hurt too many people."

Duke stood, a tense twist in his stomach. "Even knowing they can be unkind, I was still shocked at how they spoke to Eve. And all three of them believed I was overreacting when I told them not to rejoin everyone else for the remainder of the evening. I cannot comprehend how they could possibly *not* realize that they were so clearly in the wrong."

Uncle Niles leaned back in his chair, his hands woven together and resting on his middle. "Perhaps because until now, when they have said unkind things to each other, to Penelope, to myself, to Colm, to you, they've been tiptoed around."

"Kid gloves are the only way to keep the squabbles from becoming battles," Duke said. "I don't think I could have endured Writtlestone all these years without constantly soothing their ruffled feathers."

"What changed?" Uncle Niles asked. "This time, you didn't soothe feathers; you ruffled them."

Duke had thought about it more than a few times. "I've spent the majority of this house party doing everything I can to prevent them from hurting Eve. And they still managed to. I think I was as frustrated with myself as I was angry with them."

"What happened between you?"

Duke sat on the window seat. "I told them their behavior was abominable. They disagreed and haven't spoken to me since."

Uncle Niles smiled. "I meant between you and Miss O'Doyle. When you first arrived, the two of you were all smiles and tender glances. And then suddenly, you didn't seem to want anything to do with her. She looked confused at first, then dejected."

"Dejected?"

"You've been quite thoroughly breaking her heart, Duke." Uncle Niles narrowed his gaze a bit, the look one of scrutiny. "Yet, you pushed back for the first time against your parents and grandmother in defense of her. You came in here to ask a favor on her behalf. I'm not entirely certain what to make of the contradiction, and I suspect she isn't either."

Duke rubbed at the tension in his temples. "I have been trying to protect her."

"From the Seymour family animosity?"

"And from a future that wouldn't be what she deserves. I—" Pacing seemed his only option. "I've always liked Eve. She's interesting and clever, and she's always been enjoyable to talk with. I didn't realize until we reached Fairfield how much that friendship had grown into something deeper. A life with me is inextricably tied to the kind of treatment she endured during three kingdoms. And though I'm making my first strides toward a future away from Writtlestone, it isn't—I'm not—"

"Establishing your Writtlestone-distant life will take time," Uncle Niles finished for him.

"I know how it feels to have people who are supposed to care about me make promises that they don't keep—that they *won't* keep." His parents had told him countless times that they would leave aside discussions of their grievances during his school holidays. They'd often promised to be civil when discussing their family in the company of others. Father had promised not to disrupt this house party but instead take Grandmother directly to Writtlestone. All those promises had eventually proved empty. "I don't want to do that to Eve. Keeping a distance and putting a stop to what was beginning to grow between us seemed best."

"I think she has shown herself well able to navigate difficult things. Perhaps instead of protecting her, you should start trusting her."

Duke's steps took him back past his uncle's desk. "I do trust her, but I also love her too much to tie her to the misery I know she would experience connected with us."

Uncle Niles stood and crossed into Duke's pacing path. He looked at him, holding his eyes with the firm, intelligent, caring expression that seemed so ingrained in him. "Did you hear what you just said?"

"*Misery*? Believe me, I long ago discovered the proper adjective for life with my parents."

"No." Uncle Niles set a hand on his shoulder. "You said you *love* her."

Love. He had said that. The accuracy of it, the truth that underlay it swelled in his heart on the instant. He loved Eve. How had that happened? "Two weeks ago, I would have, honestly, said she was a friend."

"Some of the very best love stories begin as tales of friendship." His Uncle didn't seem as struck by Duke's discovery as he himself was. "It is noble of you not to want to see her hurt. But you are already beginning to forge a new path for yourself that does not have to inevitably include that. You'll be living away from Writtlestone, which will grant you distance in which to find your footing and discover if that distance is enough to lessen the pain your parents and grandmother too often inflict. There is every chance you will discover an aptitude for and enjoyment of politics, which will give you a purpose and focus. Your friends, Duke, are very much like mine were at your age and still are: family in all the ways that matter." Uncle Niles held his gaze. "Don't abandon a life of love and happiness because the path to reaching it isn't going to be quick or easy."

He couldn't remember his father ever taking time to give him encouragement and direction and needed clarity. He'd offered advice now and then, and he did listen when Duke spoke of his ambitions or concerns. But their discussions never remained off Father and his grievances for long. Duke was beginning to realize how much he had, in essence, raised himself.

He squared his shoulders. "That life is a possibility worth fighting for."

"Yes, it is." Uncle Niles made his way back to his chair, though he didn't sit immediately. "I hope you plan to work hard for it as well, because I make a point of severely overworking my secretaries."

"I will endure my suffering with as much dignity as I can manage." Lud, it felt good to be lighthearted for a moment.

And he was still grinning when Eve stepped into the library.

"Here you are." Seeing her dimple made him realize how seldom she had smiled the last few days.

"You've been quite thoroughly breaking her heart, Duke." Uncle Niles's declaration rang anew in his mind.

She moved quickly toward him but stopped when she spotted his uncle. "I've interrupted, haven't I?"

Uncle Niles shook his head. "You are most welcome, Miss O'Doyle."

"Which actually puts me in mind of something I need to tell you," Duke said. "I asked about having a letter franked."

Eve watched Uncle Niles with hesitant hopefulness.

"I must apologize," Uncle Niles said, "for not thinking to ask you sooner if you'd been able to send word to your parents. I will happily frank any letters you wish to send, Miss O'Doyle. Please do not hesitate to write to them."

"Thank you, Mr. Greenberry." She then turned to Duke. "I had such a wonderful conversation with the three ladies." Those captivating eyes of hers danced and sparkled once more. "I've been so worried that the only options available to me were horrible ones."

"I cannot imagine they would propose anything truly awful."

"Your aunt said that Nia can remain at Fairfield until she is well enough to travel, no matter how long that takes." Eve sighed. "I've been worried that the journey would prove too much and she would grow worse. But I also wasn't in a position to ask if she could remain."

"I wish you'd told me you were worried about that," he said. "I could have assured you that my aunt and uncle, and Colm, for that matter, would not only have insisted that she remain but would also likely have been a little hurt that anyone would think they would toss out an ailing person."

Eve gave him a dry look. "And when could I have asked you, Duke? While you were refusing to acknowledge my existence? Or ought I to have waited until after you told me to solve my own problems?"

The Best-Kept Secrets 201

Uncle Niles didn't quite manage to hold back a snort of laughter at that. "She's not wrong."

Duke couldn't argue with that. "Would it help if I told you my idiocy was inspired by a noble cause?"

Eve smiled once more, amusement dancing in her eyes. "Noble stupidity *is* better than the alternative, I suppose."

"I am legitimately sorry for that 'noble stupidity.'"

Though she didn't stop smiling, there was still hesitancy and a little pain in her expression, and it struck him right to the heart.

"You're still wary," he acknowledged. "And that's fair. I'm simply grateful you haven't disavowed me entirely."

"If I had, I wouldn't be able to tell you that I have secured a position already."

"You have?" A multitude of reactions swam around in his mind: relief, excitement, nervousness, confusion.

"Mater has been looking to hire a lady's companion," Eve said. "She offered the position to Daria during the Season, and we all assumed it was nothing more than an act of generosity to help her escape her parents. But Mater said she was and is still in earnest."

"A miracle," Duke said. "And I cannot imagine any lady treating her companion with greater love and kindness than Mater will."

Eve clasped her hands together, pressing them to her heart. "I would, of course, still rather be at Tulleyloch, but this will save my family. And that is worth having to be away from them."

As if speaking of family conjured them, Duke's parents chose that moment to barge into the library. Whatever Father intended to say as he entered died on his lips. He and Mother eyed Eve with obvious misgiving.

Mother spoke first. "I realize the door is open, but this arrangement still seems a bit more isolated than ought to be permitted."

"Mr. Greenberry is in here," Eve answered without sounding the least cowed by the clear criticism. She motioned to Uncle Niles at his desk.

Mother and Father looked that way in near-perfect unison. Uncle Niles offered the smallest dip of his head in acknowledgment. Then they looked back at Duke and Eve, their gazes lingering a little too long on her.

"My uncle can provide you with the ink and parchment you need to write the letter you'd hoped to write." Duke was grateful to see understanding immediately fill her gaze. He'd offered her an escape, and she took it.

With Eve across the library, talking with Uncle Niles, Duke looked to his parents. "I am assuming you came searching for me specifically."

"We have thought about and discussed your behavior last evening," Father said.

"*My* behavior?"

Mother's expression turned mildly reproachful. "You were embarrassingly dramatic."

I won't have to live with this every day. There was some comfort in that.

"But," Father said in placating tones, "we also acknowledge that we ought to have been more courteous. And I could have been more firm with your grandmother when she began making unkind remarks."

It was an unexpected concession. "Both of those things would have helped."

"We are not unreasonable people, Dubhán." Father undermined the declaration a little with the defensiveness of that response.

"We cannot guarantee your grandmother will be courteous, but we will be." Mother managed to sound even more defensive than Father had.

They weren't doing much to convince Duke to believe them. But he hoped they really did mean to try. Changing his residence wouldn't entirely sever his connection to his parents, so having them choose to be less hurtful would be a very helpful thing.

"And if Grandmother does choose to be unkind again," Duke said, "will you be *firm* with her this time?"

"Do you intend to ask your aunt if *she* will be firm with our mother?" Father asked.

"My aunt is not the one I am talking to at the moment."

Mother set a hand on Father's arm, apparently stopping whatever he was about to say. "We will not cause you further distress, Dubhán. We promise."

Promise. He would believe that if it actually proved true.

CHAPTER THIRTY-TWO

"I'D HOPED THE WEATHER WOULD be more cooperative," Duke said as he guided the hooded gig Eve was riding in with him carefully around a bend in the muddy road. "At least the rain's not pouring down any longer."

Eve wasn't uncomfortable nor overly bothered by the weather. She was, though, extremely curious. "The weather isn't ideal for a leisurely jaunt, which leads me to suspect you've a destination in mind."

He kept his expression a little too neutral. "Perhaps."

"And you're not meaning to tell me where?"

He shook his head. "I've exerted far too much effort since yesterday afternoon arranging this without your discovering the secret. I won't be tricked into spilling it now."

It was, perhaps, a bit of a bending of propriety, the two of them alone in a gig. But truly only a bit. Such a thing was not unheard of at a country house party. And no one at *this* country house party would lob accusations or start whispers. Almost no one.

"Do your parents know about this secretive outing?" She hadn't missed the disapproval in their eyes when they'd looked her over the day before in the library.

"Definitely not."

As quickly as she'd grown nervous, she felt relieved. "Is there a reason you planned a mysterious outing?"

"I realized, talking with you in the library yesterday, that you've spent far too much of this house party unable to claim even a moment's calm. I think you deserve to spend a little time enjoying yourself."

"We're aiming for another abandoned inn, aren't we?" She laughed.

"Better even than that," he said. "The washed-out bridge."

He pulled the gig to the side of a quaint cottage and beneath an overhang attached to the side of it, precisely the right size for the gig and the horse. They weren't more than a five-minute drive from the house, yet Eve hadn't seen this building before.

"Where are we?" she asked.

"When buyers come to Fairfield to undertake business, they generally bring quite a few of their own stablehands, horse handlers, and drivers. My aunt came to the realization ages ago that providing the visiting stable staff their own accommodations separate from the extensive staff at Fairfield was far less disruptive. This is where they stay so they can make their way to the stables when asked to do so by their employer."

That was rather ingenious. And as there were no buyers at Fairfield at the moment, the cottage would not be in use. But puffs of smoke emerged from the chimney. Someone was there.

Duke handed her down. A walkway of flagstones had been laid, beginning on either side of where the gig sat and extending all the way to the door of the cottage. It meant they could make the short walk without being up to their ankles in mud.

They'd not gone a single step when the door opened, and Artemis and Ellie waved to Eve.

"I'd not thought I could be more intrigued than I was," Eve said.

"They helped me arrange all this."

She looked up at him as they approached the door. "All *what*?"

"You'll see."

No matter that she was still a little uncertain of him, her heart flipped around at the sight of his smile.

Duke led her past their greeters and into the cozy, well-appointed cottage. The visiting staff who stayed there must be deeply pleased with their accommodations. To one side of the door was a sitting area, clearly comfortable furnishings gathered pleasingly around a low-burning fire.

Eve looked in the other direction toward a small kitchen area with a fire already lit in the fireplace. Several crates sat on the worktable. Duke motioned her in that direction.

She crossed to the worktable and peeked inside the crates. Goodness. There was flour, sugar, eggs, and butter. She found baking tools alongside jars of spices and dried fruits. A great many unexpected cooking treasures.

"You told me that the Huntresses knew of your interest in baking, so I enlisted their help," Duke said.

The Best-Kept Secrets

205

Eve looked from Duke to Artemis and Ellie and back. "This is for me?"

"For the remainder of the house party," Duke said.

"Where did you get all this?" She had all she would need to bake any number of dishes.

"I stole it."

Eve spun about, surprised by Duke's declaration. But there was amusement in his eyes.

"We made a request of the Fairfield kitchen," Artemis said. "And the request was approved by Mrs. Greenberry, done so without anyone knowing why or for whom we were requesting it."

"I can truly use any of this?" Heaven help her, she was growing excited.

"Every last bit," Duke said.

Eve began pulling items from the crates. "What ought I to bake first, do you think? There are so many possibilities."

"Whatever you wish," Duke said. "And whatever you don't choose today, you can bake tomorrow or the next day, whenever you choose to come back."

"We *have* demanded to be recompensed for our time and efforts with something delicious," Artemis said as she and Ellie took seats beside the other fireplace.

"Ah, something delicious." Eve nodded very solemnly. "I had intended to go in the opposite direction."

Duke hung his greatcoat on a peg near the door, then hung his hat atop it. He laid his gloves on the narrow table nearest those pegs. Eve was so excited by the prospect of baking that she'd not even remembered until he'd pulled off his outercoat that she was still dressed for the out of doors. She unbuttoned her wool pelisse, and he helped her slip it off. While she untied her bonnet, Duke hung up her coat. Her bonnet joined it, then her gloves took their place beside his.

She couldn't help a little bounce in her step as she returned to the worktable. "There are so many possibilities." She took up the task of emptying the crates once more. "What is your favorite baked treat, Duke?"

"Nothing particularly impressive."

She looked over at him. "Things don't have to be impressive to be enjoyed."

"I have never been able to resist shortbread biscuits."

Eve assessed her ingredients. "I have everything to make shortbread. Oh, there's even dried lemon zest. Perhaps I could make Shrewsbury biscuits."

He moved to stand by her. "I'm not familiar with those."

"A shortbread biscuit, but with lemon, caraway seeds, rose water, and sometimes dried fruit."

Duke nodded toward the assorted items. "You have lemon and dried currants."

"I suspect I could adjust the usual approach to make something delicious even with some of the ingredients missing." This was exciting. "I should make some bread as well. Then, when I return, it'll be a bit stale, and I could make bread pudding. That is Artemis's favorite."

"An excellent plan, Eve." He pulled off his frock coat and draped it over a chair. "What can I do to help?" He pushed back the sleeves of his shirt. "Bearing in mind, of course, that I have never baked anything in my entire life."

"You even thought to obtain aprons." She pulled them out of one of the crates. "We'll not return with telltale flour on our clothes."

"We should ask Artemis if telltale flour is destined to be all the rage in London fashion next year."

They turned in unison to look at her across the way.

"No." She managed to look entirely haughty while somehow still conveying that she was laughing along with them.

Eve set to work making the Shrewsbury biscuits. Duke did whatever she asked him to do. And while they worked, they talked.

"This feels like being back at the inn," she said.

He was concentrating very hard on his task of working butter into the flour mixture. "I don't know how much help I was to you in that kitchen. Or *this one*, for that matter."

"Oh, you are decidedly useless in the kitchen."

Duke smiled. How she loved that smile.

Eve chopped the dried currants. "I would love to bake every day. I could create my own recipes and discover which herbs make the most delicious bread. And I would love to learn how the French make such uniformly layered pastries. There's some trick to it that I haven't yet sorted."

"Never you fear, Eve. I happen to be an expert at pastry." He preened for the length of a breath, then, as if confused, asked, "We are talking about *eating* pastries, aren't we?"

She burst out laughing. "You are no help at all, Dubhán Seymour."

Eve happened to glance across the room in that moment. Artemis and Ellie were watching them with curiosity.

"You will adore Shrewsbury biscuits," Eve assured them.

"And what about Duke?" Ellie asked.

"He said he likes shortbread."

The Best-Kept Secrets 207

With a not-quite-hidden smirk, Artemis said, "Oh, we were talking about the biscuits, were we?"

There was no mistaking what Artemis was implying. They thought Duke "adored" Eve, or at least liked her in a way beyond friendship. A quick glance at Duke revealed that he hadn't missed the comment. And though he didn't look confused or embarrassed, he did look uncomfortable.

He had only just begun showing his playful side again, teasing her and smiling with her. There was more warmth between them again. She didn't know that they would return to the tenderness of their time at the inn or the first day or so of this house party, but she didn't want to lose what she had only just regained.

She pointed at them with her knife. "Watch yourselves there, you two. You'll be noticing I'm accidentally armed."

Artemis smiled broadly. "All the Huntresses know what it means when Eve's voice grows excessively Irish."

Ellie laughed. "It means we're in trouble."

From beside her, Duke said so quietly that he might not have even realized he'd vocalized the thought, "I like the Irish in her voice."

Eve continued her chopping, pretending she hadn't heard, not wanting to embarrass him and not wanting him to pull away again.

"Does this look as it ought?" Duke turned the bowl he held toward her to reveal the contents. He'd incorporated the butter enough to make a very crumbly dough.

"It's perfect."

Bless him, his expression immediately filled with pride. "I would have been satisfied with, 'You didn't ruin it.' How fortunate to discover, instead, that I am a baking prodigy."

"But terribly *un*fortunate for your uncle."

"How so?"

She shrugged. "His newly hired political secretary is likely to abandon him and join a troupe of traveling bakers instead."

"Are there troupes of traveling bakers?"

"There *should* be." She scooped up a handful of the now-chopped currants and dropped them in the bowl. "And the moment one is formed, I assume joining said troupe will be the fulfillment of your elusive dreamed-of future."

"No," he said with another smile. He nodded to the currants now in the bowl. "Do I stir those in?"

Eve nodded as she scooped up the rest. As she dropped them into the bowl, her hand brushed against his. So briefly. So lightly. But a surge of warmth rushed from her fingers, along her arm, and directly to her heart.

She kept her gaze on the bowl. If she looked up and didn't see any reaction at all to the unintentional and fleeting touch, it would probably break her heart. She was letting herself begin hoping for things, which she realized was an enormous risk so soon after having her hopes dashed. By *him.*

"Were you able to finish the letter for your parents?" he asked as he stirred the thick dough.

"Yes. I finished it last night. It is such a relief to know that they will be aware of Nia's illness." She moved the pan she'd chosen for the shortbread over to where they stood. "The O'Doyles excel at supporting each other, even if we have to do so at a distance."

"I've seen that between you and Nia. I sometimes wonder, if I'd had a brother or sister, if we would have had a connection like the two of you do." His wistfulness brought her gaze to him once more. The laughter in his eyes was gone, and she missed it immediately. "But my parents would likely have tormented this hypothetical additional child the same way they have me, which would have made the last decades even worse."

"Although, this imaginary sibling of Duke could be nicknamed Earl or Viscount, which would be enormously entertaining," Eve said.

His smile bloomed immediately. "I should tell my parents that I've decided to abandon Duke, as they've so long insisted I should, and will henceforth be called Marquess. They will be so pleased."

"Better yet, tell them you will now answer only to Scuff."

He laughed, his eyes dancing with genuine delight and a tender vulnerability that she felt certain few people were permitted to see. She had been among those privileged few during their journey from Ireland. That she was once more filled her heart with hope.

CHAPTER THIRTY-THREE

THE ELDER MRS. SEYMOUR HAD sat petulantly among those gathered in the drawing room that night ever since the ladies had departed the evening meal. Her daughter had made one valiant attempt to urge the lady to set aside whatever grievance she was currently nursing, but to no avail. Her son had done the same when the gentlemen had joined them and had been equally unsuccessful. His attempts, though, had led to a tense exchange of words with his mother, his wife's disapproving commentary, and vague references to his sister's inability to create a hospitable environment for a house party.

Eve had seen Duke push down and tuck away the obvious frustration and disappointment he felt. How could they not see the pain they caused? Worse still, Eve found herself wondering if they did see it but were too selfish to stop hurting him.

The guests were playing whisper down the lane, a less-common parlor game but a decidedly entertaining one. The person chosen to begin whispered to the person nearest, who then whispered what they heard to the next nearest. As the whispers proceeded around the room, the message inevitably changed, resulting in a humorous and often nonsensical collection of words at the end.

The message transformations thus far that evening had been delightfully entertaining. Even the often-warring Seymours had allowed their enjoyment to show.

The most recent whisper around the room ended with Daria. Looking utterly confused, she shared what she thought she had heard. "A man saw his feet with turnips."

Among the laughter that followed, M. Fortier revealed what he had actually said to begin the whispers. "At tea, we had delicious biscuits."

That inspired further laughter. Absolutely nothing in the original sentence had survived the journey around the drawing room.

"The biscuits *were* delicious," Toss said. "Though now I am desperate to sort out the mystery of this man and his turnip feet."

Mr. Seymour was seated next to Duke. "They reminded me of Shrewsbury biscuits."

"I believe that is what they were," Duke said.

Eve saw an opportunity for a more encouraging conversation than usually happened. "I understand you attended school at Shrewsbury, Mr. Seymour."

"I did." Mr. Seymour's features pulled with tension. "I realize the other gentlemen here attended much more exalted institutions, but—"

"My brothers attend Shrewsbury." She jumped in before he could turn her comment into yet another reason to be upset with everyone. "We are so proud to have two Shrewsbury lads in the family."

He didn't seem to know how to respond to that. Uncertain silence was not a terrible option when compared to the other ways he'd behaved during this house party.

"I believe it is your turn to begin the whispers, Mr. Greenberry," Daria said.

"I predict he will whisper something to do with Parliament." Mater's teasing expression brought entertained smiles to the faces of her generation. Aside from Duke's parents.

"Not for another few days," Mr. Greenberry said. "Until we leave for London, I reserve the right to speak of any- and everything else."

"A few days?" Eve repeated. "Are all of you leaving for London so soon?"

Mrs. Greenberry nodded. "A few days after Christmas. As a newly seated—*re*seated—MP, my husband needs to be in attendance at the official opening of Parliament."

Eve looked at Duke. Was he leaving with them? Likely, since his path forward was entwined with his uncle's. She wasn't in a position to ask about that with so many people about. She didn't know if he had yet informed his parents of his future plans.

"I do not know if Nia will be recovered enough to depart Fairfield so soon."

"She will not need to leave," Mrs. Greenberry said. "You and your sister are to remain as long as is necessary for her health."

"Alone?" Duke's mother's shock could not have been more apparent.

"Lady Lampton will be staying with them," Mrs. Greenberry said as calm as can be.

"But no member of the family?" Duke's father clearly didn't think the dowager countess's presence would be sufficient. "You would relegate your duties as

The Best-Kept Secrets   211

mistress of this estate and abandon your guests? One of whom is still too unwell to join us in the evenings?"

"Father." Duke's quiet voice echoed with a strong warning.

Mr. Seymour recognized the reminder. He snapped his mouth shut and folded his arms across his chest.

"I am remaining at Fairfield," Colm said. "My parents need to depart at the end of the planned length of the house party. But I will stay behind."

This was a new revelation to Eve. But neither Mater nor the Greenberrys seemed surprised by it.

"You will be denied a return to London?" Duke's mother pressed a hand to her heart. "A young gentleman as well-liked as you must certainly wish to be in Town rather than kept in such isolation."

For the first time in at least thirty minutes, the elder Mrs. Seymour spoke. "It is unfair of your parents to rob you of your opportunities, Colm. A hero such as yourself should have everything he wishes to have."

"I am glad to hear it, Grandmother," Colm said. "Because what I wish is to remain at Fairfield after the house party is over."

Mrs. Seymour senior sniffed. Duke kept his expression neutral, but Eve saw the exasperation that flitted through his eyes.

"I have decided on a phrase for our next whisper around the room," Mr. Greenberry said.

With an unpleasant twist of his mouth, Duke's father said, "It is whisper down the lane, Niles. The name is nearly as simple as the game."

"And the players," Duke's grandmother muttered.

Even a terribly unobservant person would have been immediately aware of the discomfort in the room intensifying.

"'The name is nearly as simple as the game' was the phrase I was going to whisper," Mr. Greenberry said as if thoroughly disappointed to have had his secret spilled.

Colm smiled broadly. Even Duke looked a little less on edge.

"I'm sorry, dear," Mrs. Greenberry said, "but you will have to choose something else."

"It's a shame he didn't 'choose something else' thirty-two years ago," Duke's father said dryly.

"From what I've been told," his mother chimed in, "he *did*, but she wouldn't accept it."

The small hint of light that had tiptoed into the room dissipated once more.

"Stop," Duke said quietly but firmly.

"We have said nothing that is untrue," his mother insisted.

"You are being rude."

"It is Penelope's history we recounted." Duke's father was all indignation. Eve was feeling a swelling of that same emotion. "If it is so objectionable, that cannot be laid at *our* feet."

With a tense sigh, Duke rubbed at his forehead. His posture drooped in resignation. His parents were draining every bit of happiness from him, and Eve couldn't bear to see it any longer.

"You promised," she blurted, the Eve who quickly spoke her mind making a bold and sudden reappearance. The unexpected declaration turned all eyes to her, but she didn't care at all that she was about to make a spectacle of herself. "I heard you promise your son just yesterday that you wouldn't squabble or pick at your family, that you wouldn't be rude or uncivil, that you would adhere to the most basic level of politeness."

His father attempted to interrupt, but she didn't so much as pause to breathe.

"Is that all your son is worth to you? Thirty-six hours of vaguely keeping an incredibly simple promise?"

"His grandmother—"

"Didn't make that promise," Eve cut across Mr. Seymour once more. "He shouldn't have to ask her to. He shouldn't have to ask any of you not to cause him embarrassment or struggle or unhappiness. He deserves at least that much."

She knew everyone in the room must have been staring at her, but she couldn't look away from the Seymours. She was far too bewildered and riled to stop now.

"Your son is remarkable. He is loyal and kind, clever and funny, thoughtful and dependable. He cares about people and does all he can to help those who need him. He makes people better simply by being part of their lives. You should love him, but instead, you treat him like rubbish."

Duke's mother looked horrified at the accusation. Mr. Seymour stood, likely intending to give her a piece of his mind, so Eve rose as well, tipping her chin defiantly.

"He wants so badly for there to be peace in his family that he endures your mistreatment. He bears those blows repeatedly. And I keep watching to see if you"—she eyed his mother and grandmother quickly as well—"any of you will ever decide to care about the pain you are causing. But you don't. He is—" Emotion broke her voice. "He is so easy to love. You could manage it

The Best-Kept Secrets 213

accidentally, but instead, you hurt him. That cannot be anything but a choice you are making over and over again."

For the first time, his mother began to look a little uncomfortable.

A tear slipped from Eve's eye. She swiped it furiously. "You don't deserve him. And I suspect it'll not be long before he realizes that. You will lose such a wonderful and remarkable person from your lives, and it'll be entirely your fault."

Another hot tear escaped. Eve turned quickly to the rest of the room, though she couldn't bring herself to so much as glance at Duke.

"I am sorry to have disrupted the game." She swallowed against the rawness of her emotion-clogged throat. "I am going to go check on my sister now." Then she spun on her heel and left the drawing room, nothing more to say and no energy remaining with which to say it. She moved swiftly down the corridor, making good her escape.

How she hoped she hadn't made things more difficult for Duke. No one ever championed him when his parents and grandmother mistreated him. And no one ever confronted them with their own terrible behavior. She simply couldn't listen to it any longer.

She'd reached only the first step of the staircase leading up to the guest wing when a voice called out from behind her.

"Aoife." Duke. He was moving swiftly toward her.

"I likely shouldn't have said anything to them," she said. "But they are so thoughtless and unkind to you. I couldn't bite my tongue any longer."

He'd reached the base of the stairs, standing on the floor directly in front of her. Standing as she was on the first step, she was nearly eye to eye with him. And those gorgeous eyes of his were focused entirely on her.

"Please don't be angry with me," she whispered.

His mouth tipped up in a slow-spreading smile. "You were brilliant." He slipped his arms around her. "And in case no one has told you"—he leaned closer, his deep, captivating voice growing tenderly quiet—"you are also astonishingly easy to love."

He closed the minute gap between them, enfolding her in the warmth and shelter of his embrace. And then he kissed her. His lips were as soft as they'd been at the inn. Eve folded her arms around his neck and poured into her answering kiss every moment of longing and every hopeful hum her heart had beat out since the last time he'd kissed her.

She'd worried that he might break her heart. But she felt in that moment his unwavering promise to cherish it.

CHAPTER THIRTY-FOUR

Duke rode out with Colm the next morning. His parents and grandmother had turned the delight of a house party into something dreadful, but he was grateful to be coming to know his cousin better.

"You ride well for a Cambridge man," Colm said as they walked back into the house.

"And when you were splattered with mud this morning, you kept your tongue very civil for an army man."

"If Eve asks, tell her I have treated you exceptionally well." Colm slapped him on the back. "I have no desire to be on the receiving end of her next well-deserved condemnation."

"Your mother has called Father to account a few times, and Grandmother certainly delivers her fair share of criticisms to all of us, but that was a stinging rebuke for the ages." Duke shook his head in amazement. "Eve is truly remarkable."

"I hope you told her as much."

Duke couldn't help the hint of smugness that tiptoed into his smile. "I believe I managed to deliver the message."

Colm's laugh echoed around them as they reached the stairs. "I hope your next message will be something similar to 'I've lost my heart to you entirely, Eve O'Doyle. Marry me, or I will waste away in a state of desperate, unmitigated longing.'"

"*Unmitigated* is not a very romantic word to include in a marriage proposal." Duke shook his head. "I'm certain I can think of something better."

Colm paused and turned to look at him. They'd made it halfway up the stairs to the first landing.

"Then, you *are* planning to propose?" Colm asked.

"Things haven't reached that point yet."

"Why on earth not?" Colm actually sounded a little offended, though whether on Duke's behalf or Eve's, he wasn't entirely certain.

"Your parents have offered me an escape from home, but I don't yet know how much of an escape from my parents this change of residence will afford me. Until I know how often I will see them and how much grief they will still manage to cause, I cannot tie her to that life."

"If it helps, life at Fairfield and the London home is entirely peaceful the vast majority of the time," Colm said.

"But those times when it isn't are because my parents or our grandmother is here."

Colm sighed and nodded.

"Once the dust has settled and I know what the landscape will look like, I can ask her if she'd be willing to share a future with me—assuming, of course, it hasn't proven so awful that the question is rendered moot."

Colm began making his way up the stairs once more, and Duke kept pace with him. "I will hold out hope that everything works out so well that I find myself with another cousin sooner rather than later."

"You have hundreds of cousins on the Greenberry side." Duke knew full well, as did most everyone in Society, that the Greenberrys of Cornwall were an enormous family.

"If you include second cousins in the count, I probably do." Colm tossed him a smile. "But on the Seymour side, it's only you and me now."

"I miss Luke and Róisín." Duke looked over at him as they continued past the first landing, aiming for the second, the floor on which all the bedchambers were located. "I can't even imagine how much you miss them."

"I sometimes feel as though I lost my entire family when my brother and sister died. My parents haven't been the same since then."

"You joined the army almost immediately afterward."

"That is not a coincidence," Colm said quietly.

"I never thought it was."

They continued upward in silence, the sort that accompanied comfortable deep thought.

After a moment, Duke spoke again. "Thank you for volunteering to stay at Fairfield when your parents and I leave for London. Eve seems less worried knowing Nia will have time to recover."

"I lost a lot of friends in the war, Duke. I don't intend to lose any more." Colm seldom spoke with any specificity of that time in his life. "And these

The Best-Kept Secrets 217

friends you've allowed me to share with you have fast become like brothers and sisters. I've needed that."

They reached the second-floor landing, where they were greeted by Grandmother's shrill voice. "This is unacceptable, Penelope. I should no longer be surprised at how often you let your own pride undermine you. Shameful."

Colm sighed. "I don't know how my mother endures their treatment. Anytime Father attempts to intervene, she pleads with him not to, which frustrates him and confuses me."

They stopped in the corridor, both looking warily ahead at the family gathering. Duke's and Colm's parents stood with Grandmother, no one looking happy about the arrangement.

They approached the combatants. Grandmother, Father, and Aunt Penelope stood nearest each other wearing expressions of distrust. Mother stood a bit apart, watching them anxiously. Uncle Niles paced in the open doorway of the bedchamber Grandmother was using, watching the group with equal parts concern and frustration.

"We have lost everything your father worked so hard to preserve," Grandmother said to Aunt Penelope. "If not for your selfishness, we would have our land still."

"If you cannot feel sorrowful for Liam's loss," Mother said, "I would think you could at least grieve for Duke's. Writtlestone could never be Ballycar's equal."

"Of all the members of this family," Aunt Penelope said, "Duke is the one my heart aches for most."

Father folded his arms across his chest. "Are you going to lecture us now about how we don't love our son? We had plenty of that last evening."

"Yes, but did you actually listen to any of it?"

"You always were cruel," Mother snipped.

"And selfish," Grandmother added. "I hope Ballycar rests on your conscience, Penelope."

Duke glanced at Colm, who was looking more like a war-hardened soldier the longer this confrontation dragged on.

"The family estate was lost the way most things are," Aunt Penelope said firmly and calmly but with a tense edge to her voice. "Through bad luck and bad decisions, neither of which was mine."

Father didn't let that explanation go without comment. "That's how things are lost, are they? Then, whose bad decisions are the reason Luke and Róisín were lost?"

Shock descended on the instant, with all eyes on Father.

"What the devil?" Duke whispered in disbelief.

Tears pooled in Aunt Penelope's eyes, heartrending pain in her expression. Duke took a step toward her, the mediator in him sparking to life, his mind whirling, not having heard his father say anything so brutal to his sister before. Colm moved in the exact moment Duke did. But neither of them managed more than a single step before Uncle Niles's authoritative voice cut into the tense moment.

"I have held my tongue from the moment you arrived, Liam, because my wife pleaded with me to. Repeatedly." He moved with slow, menacing steps toward Father. In that moment, Duke could, for the first time, see in his usually sedate uncle the potently dangerous prizefighter he had once been. "She does that every time, you realize. She tries to save you from yourself. Tries to save Colm and me from you. But as you well know, I never manage to bite my tongue indefinitely. And after what you have just said, I don't intend to do so *ever* again."

Colm's voice emerged as tense and menacing as his father's. "My brother and sister will not be used as weapons against my mother."

Father's eyes met Duke's for a fraction of a moment, before flitting to the angry Greenberry men once more. "I shouldn't have said—"

"I have not the least interest in your excuses." The white-hot anger that flashed through Uncle Niles's eyes sent even Duke back a step. "If I ever hear you speak of my children again, I will do far more than toss you out of my house."

Colm crossed to his mother's side and put his arms around her.

"The subject of *my* son was thrown like a spear at me last evening," Father said defiantly. "None of you came to *my* defense. No one comforted *my* wife."

Duke at last found his voice. "Do not use me as justification for what you said. Mocking a mother's grief? How could you be so cruel?"

Uncle Niles was still glaring at Father. "Your carriage will be leaving Fairfield in one hour, and you will be in it whether or not you have finished your packing."

Grandmother never had been one to ignore a chance for abandoning a family member who didn't currently hold the upper hand. "That really was badly done of you, Liam. You can hardly be surprised that you're being asked to leave."

Uncle Niles turned immediately to her, though he didn't walk in her direction. "You are leaving as well."

The Best-Kept Secrets

219

Clearly offended, Grandmother pressed her hand to her heart. "I am Penelope's mother."

"A mother who couldn't be bothered to be here while Penelope buried her children. A mother who insults her more often than she comforts. You have hurt her long enough, and it will no longer be endured. It should not have been endured this long."

"Penelope," Grandmother said, "talk some sense into your husband."

She swiped at a tear but faced her mother directly, Colm's arm still tucked supportively around her. "You came from Ireland to visit Liam at Writtlestone. It's time you finished your journey."

Grandmother didn't seem to believe what she was seeing and hearing. "But it is almost Christmas."

Colm gave a single, crisp nod of his head. "You can consider your departure a Christmas gift to your remaining grandchildren."

Mother turned to Duke. "Explain to your grandmother that Colm didn't mean grand*children*. You would not side against your own parents and grandmother."

"Of course he wouldn't," Father said. "Your aunt and uncle have tossed us all out, Dubhán. You had best gather your things."

A month ago, he would have dived into the fray, searching for a means of smoothing the conflict between them all. He might even have left with his parents in the name of keeping the peace. Today, he said, "I am remaining at Fairfield."

Father and Mother looked surprised, but that lasted only a moment.

"We cannot blame you for wishing to finish your little party," Father said, "but after that—"

"No." Duke shook his head. "After that, I am going to London."

Uncle Niles led Aunt Penelope away. Colm walked alongside them. Before going too far, Uncle Niles said over his shoulder to Father, "One hour, Liam."

"Dubhán." For the first time in Duke's life, his father seemed legitimately concerned that his behavior would bear consequences.

"I don't know what it will take for you to finally let go of all this bitterness," Duke said, "but I hope you find a way." Retreating to his bedchamber was not his best option. They might follow him there.

"You truly aren't leaving with us?" Mother asked, her worry appearing to lean more toward regret than it usually did.

"I am staying here." He would have considered telling them then that Writtlestone would never be his home again, but he couldn't be certain it wouldn't put their backs up once more. They were leaving, which everyone at Fairfield needed them to do. And they appeared to at last be pondering the damage they had done, which *he* needed them to do.

It was too little and far too late for him to change course and consider making Writtlestone his home again. But it was some hope that the future might not be entirely filled with inescapable animosity.

He turned and walked back to the stairs, dragging himself downward. Would this confrontation, this moment of hard truths, truly change anything? His parents might be so angry that they'd choose never to see him again. Or they might be so determined to feel justified that they would hound his heels, demanding, as they'd done for years, that he take their part. Only time would tell. But for the moment, he had a bit of a respite and the possibility, however slim, that things might change for the better.

This had needed to happen. And he hated that it had. And it hurt so deeply. *I need Eve.*

But he didn't know where she was or how to find her. He wandered for more than a quarter hour before finally crossing her path.

"Duke." She smiled at first, but her expression turned quickly worried. "What did your family do?"

"I shouldn't be surprised that you could guess the source of my current discontent."

She crossed to him. "You only ever wear this particular look of heartbreak when they have been wounding you." Eve reached up and gently touched his face. "I wish I knew how to take that pain away."

He truly breathed for the first time since hearing his father speak so hatefully to Aunt Penelope. "My parents and grandmother are being thrown from the house entirely."

"It is about time."

Duke sighed, releasing some of the tension he was carrying. "I don't know if this moment marks a real change or a temporary reprieve."

She slipped her hand from his cheek to his chest. "Temporary or not, it is much-deserved."

He set a hand over hers, pressing their hands to his heart. "Until I know how they will behave, what my future interactions with them will look like, I can't—I won't know if—"

"You cannot begin fully planning your future until you know what role your parents, and to a lesser extent your grandmother, will play in that future," she said.

The Best-Kept Secrets

221

"Precisely. And I will only have those answers after seeing how they move forward. That will take time."

"You now have a peaceful home to live in and an occupation," she said, "so you needn't panic that you haven't time for watching and waiting and deciding."

"That's true." And it was reassuring.

"And *I* have Mater's company to look forward to and will have income enough to help my family restore Nia's health, so I'm not panicked about the future either."

Hearing her speak of her future and his tied together in any way warmed him to his core. He was beaten down, but he wasn't defeated.

"For now, we'll trust that the future will sort itself," she said. "What are you needing to sort things a bit in the present?"

"I think a hug would help." He felt a little foolish making such a juvenile request. But it was what he needed.

Eve wrapped her arms around him. He held her in return, closing his eyes and enveloping himself in the comfort she offered and the tranquil happiness he felt when he was with her. And he didn't think he would ever forget her fierce defense of him the night before, the succinct way she had declared that he didn't deserve the treatment he had for so long endured from his family. He had sometimes struggled to believe that himself.

"I love you, Aoife," he whispered. "I hope you know that."

"I do." She looked up at him without breaking the embrace. "And I think I know what else you love." There was mischief in her silvery eyes.

"What is that?"

"Baking. And I know just the place where you could indulge in a bit of it *today*."

He smiled. Mere minutes after having to finally abandon hope of his parents changing or wanting to stop hurting him, he smiled. Bless the heavens for Aoife O'Doyle. "I think I would thoroughly enjoy that."

"Excellent." She rose on her toes and pressed a kiss to his cheek. "And I hope you know that I love you, too, Dubhán."

CHAPTER THIRTY-FIVE

CHARLIE AND ARTEMIS HAD SERVED as "chaperones" during Eve and Duke's second time baking in the cottage kitchen. Charlie had entered a request for ginger biscuits. Only when those biscuits, along with the bread pudding Eve and Duke had also baked that morning, were set out along with tea that afternoon did Eve realize why Charlie had asked for what he had.

"Ginger biscuits are my favorite," Mater said, clearly delighted.

Eve looked at Charlie sitting between his wife, whom everyone knew favored bread pudding, and his mother, who was also getting her favorite treat. He looked deeply pleased at their excitement.

To Duke, who sat next to her, Eve said, "Charlie looks happy enough that one would think 'twas *his* favorite foods being offered today."

"You have made an ally there, Eve. Few things will earn a person the undying gratitude of the Jonquil brothers faster than helping them do something kind for their mother, wives, and children."

"And for each other?" Eve guessed.

He nodded. "Their family is the most loving and loyal I've ever met."

She took his hand. "I want so badly for you to spend some time with my family, Duke. My parents will fuss over you in the best way. And I predict Edmund and Scuff will idolize you immediately before coercing you into joining their endless mischief."

He lifted her hand and kissed it. "I would enjoy that immensely."

From across the room, Daria said, "I think the bread pudding has nutmeg in it. I love nutmeg."

"*C'est délicieux*," Lisette said before having another spoonful of the pudding.

"*C'est très délicieux*," her aunt said.

"That sounded like *delicious*," Eve said to Duke.

He smiled at her. "Lisette said it was *delicious*, and Mme Fortier said it was *very delicious*."

"I am determined to sniff out what everyone's favorites are and try to bake them all before the house party ends," Eve said.

Duke bent closer and spoke quietly. "You should consider telling Mater about your baking."

A bubble of hope expanded on the instant. "She might allow me to bake at the dower house without giving away the secret."

"Precisely."

Mater rose and took a plate with two ginger biscuits on it across the room to Scott, who had just stepped inside.

"Thank you, Mater." He gave her a quick one-armed hug, then sat with his wife.

"I think I will talk with her now," Eve said to Duke before rising and crossing to her.

"We have had such delightful tea goodies these past days," Mater said, taking another bite of a biscuit. "We'll all leave Fairfield with very high expectations."

Eve motioned her a bit aside. Mater looked intrigued.

"There is something I think you should know since I will be living with you for some time. It is yet another secret, so—Actually, all the Huntresses already know, as do Duke and Charlie. But it still does need to be kept from essentially everyone else. I do so hate to ask you to keep another secret."

Mater squeezed her hand. "Do not feel the least badly about it."

Eve nodded, then pushed forward. "Because of my family's financial woes, we have all needed to develop skills most in the *ton* never do. My contribution to the household was doing the baking, and I found I enjoy it. I also discovered I have a talent for it. I actually miss baking when I'm away from home."

Quick as that, a look of complete understanding entered Mater's eyes. She gave Eve a hug, whispering, "By the time we arrive at the Lampton Park dower house, I will have sorted a way for you to bake whenever you'd like without risking your secret becoming known."

"Thank you." Eve hugged her tightly in return.

"Do you promise you will bake ginger biscuits now and then?" Mater smiled.

"Every single day if you'd like."

"Excellent." Mater stepped back but then hooked their arms and began walking with Eve at a leisurely pace around the drawing room, allowing for a private conversation. "Do you know how to bake any Spanish delicacies?"

Eve shook her head. "But I do love to learn new things and new recipes."

The Best-Kept Secrets   225

"One of my daughters-in-law is from Spain. I would love to offer her a bit of home when she next visits Lampton Park."

"Could we find a way to ask her about the Spanish treats she enjoyed?" Eve asked. "That would at least give me a place to begin."

"I think we could nudge some information from her." Mater laughed. "We will be the Bow Street Runners of baking."

"We should wear red aprons!"

Mater laughed, pulling a laugh from Eve as well. Being a lady's companion hadn't been her intended path in life until very recently, yet she found herself increasingly pleased with her new position.

"And if you aren't one who objects to travel," Mater said, "perhaps we might travel to Spain to try a few delicacies for ourselves."

Eve turned wide eyes on her. "I have long wanted to taste baked items in their countries of origin. I could learn so much from doing so."

"Truly?" Mater looked almost emotional. "I have wanted to travel for years now. It was always my plan once my boys were grown, but I can't seem to retain a companion long enough to do so."

"We should start planning *now*," Eve said excitedly.

"I haven't been to France in more than fifteen years," Mater said, "and I've wanted to return to Paris."

Paris. Good heavens. "Could we visit a pâtisserie while we are there? I have dreamed of doing that in Paris."

"We can visit dozens of them." Mater looked as excited as Eve felt.

"Have you ever been to Ireland?" Eve asked.

Mater nodded. "Not in many years though."

Eve squeezed her arm. "We should visit there as well."

"I will make certain you see your family regularly, Eve. Whenever you'd like."

"While I am grateful to you for that," Eve said, "I'd suggested Ireland because there's no more magnificent place in all the world."

"We'll add it to the list."

Eve clasped her hands together, grinning with absolute delight. She was not only going to be able to bake while living with Mater, but she was also going to get to travel.

"Of course, we need to make time for being in London during the Season," Mater said. "At least for a few weeks."

"Truly?" Eve had resigned herself to never participating again. She had grieved missing every moment her friends had together. Her heart ached at not being able to see Nia enjoy her time there.

"I, for one," Mater said, mischievously, "refuse to miss the Debenhams' ball."

Eve could hardly believe how the proverbial tide had turned, and so quickly. "Thank you."

It was an entirely different future than she'd ever imagined for herself, yet it was inarguably bright.

From the doorway, Gillian spoke. "Look who's decided to join us."

Eve, along with the rest of the room, turned in that direction. Gillian stepped inside with Nia on her arm.

"I feel a little better this afternoon," Nia said. "And I've missed so much of this party."

While nearly everyone in the room assisted Nia to a seat, Dr. Wilstead appeared in the doorway, watching her. He looked more observant than worried, which set Eve's mind a bit at ease, though not entirely.

"Go speak with the doctor," Mater suggested. "You'll feel better if you do."

Eve nodded at the wisdom of that, then followed through with the suggestion.

"I hope that she really is feeling better," Eve said to him upon reaching where he stood.

"She is, though not as well as I would like. She is extremely tired and has admitted to me that she is in constant pain."

"Oh mercy," Eve whispered.

"But her spirits remain buoyant, which is promising." Dr. Wilstead looked away from his patient and at Eve.

"What about her heart?" That was what worried Eve most.

"It still sounds strong," Dr. Wilstead said. "But her fever keeps returning."

"Progress but also struggles," Eve said.

The doctor nodded. "I believe she will need another month before she will be well enough to safely travel."

"How long before she could *comfortably* travel?" Eve didn't want her sister to be in agony.

"That is more difficult to predict. I understand you will both be able to stay here for as long as she needs."

"Yes. The Greenberrys are very generous."

"They are."

"As are you," Eve said. "We are so near to Christmas. You must wish to be home for the holy day."

"I don't mind, Miss O'Doyle. There is a lady in the area I enjoy visiting with." A bit of an unexpected blush touched the doctor's expression. "And Fairfield is an enjoyable place to be."

The Best-Kept Secrets 227

Eve's gaze slipped to Duke. He was sitting with the Pack, smiling and happy. He'd been pensive during the first part of their baking adventures that day. His parents had been departing Fairfield during that time. He'd not wanted to return to the house to see them off, but he'd also seemed anxious not to be there when they left.

She didn't fully understand his attachment to them. They knowingly caused him pain. Yet he worked so hard to maintain that connection. Why would he cling to that? She didn't understand, but she loved him. And for his sake, she would walk with him while he navigated something that felt almost impossibly complicated. And she would hope that in the end, Duke was granted enough separation from his parents' cruelty to give him faith that he and Eve could move forward into the future together.

CHAPTER THIRTY-SIX

CHRISTMAS EVE ARRIVED WITH HARDLY anyone in the group even realizing it. Duke's time had been divided between planning and preparing with his aunt and uncle for their pending departure for London and baking with Eve in the mornings. He'd also done all he could to help her look after her sister, who had taken a bit of a turn for the worse, even after Dr. Wilstead's more optimistic evaluations of late. And he found himself wondering about his parents—if they had regrets, if they would ever actually change.

All that meant he, as much as everyone else, had lost track of the date and was caught entirely unaware when Artemis announced that they would all be going out to gather greenery for Christmas boughs, wreaths, garlands, and such.

Time had gone so quickly. The house party was nearly over.

Dr. Wilstead seemed a little unsure of Nia's participation in the outing but agreed that she could go along, provided she was bundled against the cold, not required to exert herself in any way, and vowed to be very forthright with the rest of the group regarding how she was feeling as the excursion went on.

Three of the estate wagons, each with a generous layer of straw laid inside, awaited them outside the doors of Fairfield. They were obviously very utilitarian vehicles, but the white horses pulling them would not have looked out of place at the front of a royal carriage. Duke had heard stories of the impressive horses bred at Ballycar before it was lost, but nothing could compare to the famous snow-white horses at Fairfield.

"Oh, Eve," Nia whispered to her sister. "They are the most beautiful horses I've ever seen."

"And you've not even seen *most* of them," Eve said. "An enormous stable full of pure-white horses."

Duke stood at Eve's side, where he tried to be whenever possible.

"Do you suppose I'll feel well enough before our time at Fairfield ends to . . . to actually ride one?" Nia sounded hesitantly hopeful but also entirely exhausted.

"We'll make certain of it," Eve said.

But Nia didn't look convinced. "We have no control over how long I will be ill."

"I intend to threaten Colm if he attempts to send us away before you've had your dreamed-of ride," Eve countered, earning a smile from her sister. "As everyone here now knows, I am more than capable of speaking my mind when I decide to."

Duke set an arm around Eve's middle, pulling her gently against his side. "If you do threaten him, let the Pack know. They'll help you follow through on whatever consequences you deem necessary."

"But Colm is *part* of the Pack," Eve said with a laugh.

Duke pretended to be caught unaware. "I knew I was forgetting an important detail."

"Did you also forget that he's your cousin?" Nia asked.

He dropped his mouth agape. "I have a cousin?"

Eve leaned a bit against him. "I love when you laugh."

"I didn't actually laugh."

She smiled. Heavens, that dimple of hers. "You laugh with your eyes."

There was an unexpected amount of revelation in that simple declaration. Duke was not one for laughing out loud often, but that didn't mean he didn't laugh *inwardly* quite regularly. And Eve had sorted that about him. He wasn't certain anyone else ever had.

Duke pressed a kiss to the top of her head.

"I do hope I am placed in a different wagon than the two of you," Nia said with a theatrical show of nausea.

Eve laughed again.

Duke drew her ever closer. "I love when *you* laugh."

"That is fortunate, because I laugh *often.*"

It was one of the many things he loved about her. She brightened every room she was in and lifted his spirits with ease.

"Friends." Charlie's voice echoed through the entryway. "Allow me to cut through the drudgery that inevitably accompanies festive activities to propose a ruthless competition. It is Christmas, after all."

Artemis shook her head, barely hiding a smile.

"We depart as three teams, each in its own wagon, and vow to gather an assortment of Christmas greenery that will outshine that obtained by the other

The Best-Kept Secrets 231

teams." Charlie seldom looked as excited as he did when formulating a bit of entertainment. "Three wagons. Three teams. Only one winner."

"What will the prize be for the winning team?" Newton asked.

"Is not the pride of winning enough for you lot?" Charlie pretended to be shocked.

In perfect unison, Colm, Toss, and Tobias shouted back, "No!"

Charlie turned to Artemis, a look of inquiry on his face.

But she shook her head. "This is *your* scheme, Charlie. I'll not rescue you from it."

His grin firmly in place, he looked over at his mother. "Any brilliant ideas, Mater?"

"My most brilliant idea: to never side against Artemis."

The Huntresses cheered that declaration. Eve's shoulders shook with a laugh.

Charlie, good gun that he was, grinned through it all. "I may not know at the moment what the prize will be, but I will think of something. And that something will be well worth the effort to win."

"Are we to choose teams, or will you be assigning them?" Scott asked.

"I propose that Mr. and Mrs. Greenberry be the head of one, M. and Mme Fortier will be the head of the second, with Mater the leader of the third. The . . . more experienced generation can undertake whatever machinations they deem necessary to create the team they each wish for."

Aunt Penelope, standing near Duke, asked him a little under her breath. "'More experienced generation'? By that, he means old, I assume."

"I'd assume the same thing," Eve said.

Duke nodded. "The Jonquils have a tendency to walk about with their foot permanently in their mouth."

"Quite a trick, that." Uncle Niles shook his head. "It must be brutally injurious to one's back."

With Duke's parents and grandmother gone, there was so much more lightness to his aunt and uncle. To himself as well.

"I hope you will join our team, Nia," Aunt Penelope said.

"If you'd like me to."

Aunt Penelope put an arm around Nia exactly as a mother would a child who'd been ailing. "We'll see you settled in our team's wagon. And as we pass Colm, we'll ask him to join our team. He knows Fairfield better than any of the other participants, other than his father and I. We will have a clear advantage."

The two "more experienced" participants and Nia walked toward Colm, standing near the door.

"Unfair," Duke called after them with a grin.

"Your aunt has been so attentive to Nia," Eve said. "I'm so very grateful to her."

"She lost two of her children to illness. I think she worries when other people are ill, but I think she also wants very much to help in any way she can."

Eve leaned more fully into his one-armed embrace. "You are like your aunt and uncle in a lot of ways. You will fit into their household perfectly."

"I always did feel more at home at Fairfield than at Writtlestone, though I made absolutely certain to never so much as hint at that in front of my parents."

Teams were being organized all around them. But Duke was perfectly content standing with an arm around Eve. Outside of this group of dear friends, he would not have been permitted the show of affection. And in mere days, they would be counties apart for months. Even when he saw Eve again in London—Mater would be making the journey for a brief time during the Season—they would be among Society, and the rules of propriety would be far more strictly enforced. Duke meant to hold her while he could.

Mater, with Charlie and Artemis in tow, moved to join them. "Care to be on the third team?"

"I would be honored," Duke said in the same moment Eve said, "That would be brilliant."

"We tried to recruit Fennel," Charlie said, "but he was too busy explaining to the Fortiers why he should be on *their* team. Traitor!"

"Scott and Gillian would be a good addition to the third team," Eve said.

Mater leaned a bit closer and lowered her voice. "You and I are proving shockingly well suited, my dear Eve. I had the same thought and already asked them."

"Perfect."

There really was something bordering on perfect in the way the teams had divided themselves. Toss and Daria had joined the Greenberry team, as had Tobias. He was Daria's brother, and he and Colm had become particular friends very swiftly during the Season. Newton and Ellie had joined with the Fortiers, a good fit for Lisette's quieter demeanor. Fennel had been accepted by their team, and while he could absolutely be as riotous as the rest of the Pack, he could also be perfectly sedate.

And Mater had assembled a team that allowed her to spend time with her son, with Scott, whom she considered a son, and with Eve, who had been most recently brought into the circle of Mater's loving embrace. And the rest of the

The Best-Kept Secrets 233

team were the people who deeply loved her children and honorary children. Duke hadn't the first idea if they'd any chance of winning the competition, but he found he wasn't overly bothered by the possibility either way.

"If we hurry," Charlie said, "we can select the best team and wagon for ourselves."

As they walked through the door, Duke said, "Every vehicle, whether serviceable or fashionable, is excessively well maintained at Fairfield, and every horse is beyond compare. We'll not claim any advantage that way."

"Then, we must choose the best driver among us," Artemis said.

"That's likely Duke or Eve," Scott said.

"Excellent." Charlie pulled his features into a melodramatic expression of relief. "They can sit up on the driver's bench and gaze longingly into each other's eyes as much as they wish, and the rest of us won't have to watch it."

"I hope at least one of them plans to gaze longingly at *the road*," Scott said dryly.

Gillian and Artemis exchanged quick glances before bursting immediately into laughter. Mater looked sorely tempted to join them.

Duke didn't mind, and he suspected Eve didn't either. Everyone who remained at the house party was happy for them. Even their teasing was done in the spirit of love and friendship.

They were soon situated, with Duke and Eve on the bench, a warm blanket spread over their laps. Eve didn't particularly want to drive, so Duke took the reins. The others sat in the back of the wagon, watching the trees and hedges for signs of Christmas greenery. Duke felt certain that he knew which area of Fairfield his aunt, uncle, and cousin would aim for in their search. He had a different location in mind.

"This has been such a lovely house party," Artemis said from the back of the wagon. "I am so pleased that *all* the Huntresses and the Pack are here."

Charlie added, "And that Mme Dupuis is *not* here. She would have made this absolute lark utterly miserable."

"I only hope Lisette isn't chastened by her parents for her chaperone's dismissal," Gillian said.

"She won't be." Mater spoke too firmly and with too much confidence for her response to be a mere guess.

"Lisette prefers not to talk in any detail about this," Artemis said. "At first, I was simply curious, but I'm lately finding myself a little worried, primarily because *Lisette* sometimes looks a little worried."

"Set your mind at ease," Mater said. "You will, in time, know what it is your friend isn't telling you and why she and her aunt and uncle are being so close-lipped about it."

"You are telling me to be patient?" Artemis asked with what sounded like a laugh.

With the same amusement, Mater answered, "I wouldn't dare."

Duke had often, over the years, wished his family were as loving as Charlie's. Eve was being brought into the Jonquils' warm embrace. He couldn't possibly be more grateful for that.

"Draw up, Duke," Artemis said. "There's mistletoe in that tree."

Duke brought the graceful team of horses to a stop.

"She's correct," Eve said, looking up into the nearby tree.

"Brilliant, Artie," Charlie proclaimed.

They all began climbing out.

"That looks to be holly in the hedgerow." Gillian motioned a bit farther ahead.

"Let's go gather some." Artemis rushed off with her, a basket at the ready.

Scott and Charlie pulled from the back of the wagon the stepladder and garden shears placed inside for just this purpose, then eagerly crossed to the tall tree.

Duke remained on the bench, keeping watch over the team.

"I believe I've discovered your dreamed-of future." Eve snuggled closer to him.

"Have you?" He shifted the reins to one hand and set his other arm round her.

"Wagon driver," she said with a laugh. "Don't deny it."

"If every drive ended this way, I'd absolutely be living a dream."

"Are you saying that *I* am your dream?"

Duke kissed the top of her head. "That is precisely what I'm saying, Aoife."

Mater climbed up and sat on Eve's other side, the driving bench now entirely full. "While I have a moment alone with the two of you, we need to have a quick conversation."

"About what?" Eve asked.

"As we have already established," Mater said, "I have a vast history of losing my intended lady's companions to the more pleasant, at least in their estimation, prospect of marriage. I suspect the wind is blowing in that direction for the two of you."

Their current arrangement surely would give any onlooker that impression.

The Best-Kept Secrets 235

"Should you decide to follow the established pattern, Eve," Mater said, "please know that I will be incredibly happy for you. Know also that I will tease you mercilessly about abandoning me."

He could feel Eve laugh. He liked that.

"I also felt I ought to assure you that I will remain at Fairfield for however long Nia needs to remain, regardless of whether or not the two of you inform me that Eve will be jaunting to London to join Duke and leave me to make my way to Lampton Park alone."

"I don't know if this will set your mind at ease or sink your opinion of my family lower than it no doubt already is," Duke said, "but I do not yet know how my parents will behave or how they will treat me and those connected to me after all that occurred here. Until I know what I would be asking Eve to endure, I cannot, in good conscience, ask her to do so."

"Niles told me what your father said to Penelope." Mater spoke quietly. "It speaks well of you that you hesitate so much to expose Eve to that degree of cruelty."

He tightened his embrace. "I am learning to accept that Mother and Father will never be truly kind. I've managed to secure some distance from them, but how long that will last or how much peace that will actually afford I cannot possibly guess."

Mater nodded. "You can't know until you experience it."

Eve looked up at him. "How long do you suppose it will take to have a better idea?"

"I wish I had a good answer for that." He truly did. Not knowing how long they'd be apart was nearly as difficult as not knowing if his parents would prevent that wait from ending happily. "I need to see how they behave when I tell them I'm making a home with my aunt and uncle. I have to see what they do when we cross paths in London and what their course of action is when the Season is over. I don't yet know how they will react when I don't return for Christmas next year." That bit gave him the tiniest moment of regret. Christmastime had been one of the few clusters of pleasant experiences with his parents. But they'd managed to ruin this one. "I don't yet know how they will react to my decision to tiptoe into the world of politics or what they might do to cause difficulty there." He hoped Eve could see that he wished things were different. "It could be years. I hope not. But I cannot deny that it very well might be."

Though the question had been Mater's, he offered the answer to Eve. "All my estimates tell me that I will likely need three or four years."

Eve didn't cry or rage or demand that he make everything right immediately. She actually smiled. "In those three or four years, you won't have to live at Writtlestone, which is a wonderful thing for you. And Mater and I will travel to our hearts' content and see so many sites. And we'll be in London for a portion of the Season, so I will see you then. And we can write to each other."

"You aren't going to demand that I fix this?"

"You *are* fixing it," she said. "Just because doing so will take time doesn't mean it won't work."

She was remarkable. Living without her for potentially years would be excruciating. But knowing they could have a life together would make all the effort and waiting that lay ahead of them well worth it.

"Might I make a suggestion?" Mater sounded as if she meant to make it regardless. And then she did. "Should you decide in the near future that you mean to more formally declare your intention to eventually marry, you would do well not to make that declaration publicly nor to sign marriage contracts yet."

"Are you afraid one of us will change our mind?" Eve asked.

Mater shook her head. "A years' long engagement would lead to whispers in Society, and neither of you is currently on such firm social footing that those whispers wouldn't do damage."

"A secret engagement?" Duke quickly appended. "Eve has been burdened with quite a few secrets of late. I wouldn't want to add to that burden."

"It sounds to me," Mater said, "as though you two have a lot to discuss."

The greenery gatherers were making their way back to the wagon. Mater alighted once more, exclaiming over their offerings as they all retook their places in the back of the wagon.

"I'm going to miss you while we're apart these next years, Duke," Eve said.

"I will miss you too." He pressed a kiss to the top of her head.

He took up the reins in both hands once more and set the horses in motion.

Eve leaned against him, an arrangement of tenderness and trust. He would more than just miss her while they were apart over the years to come; his heart would be left in her keeping.

CHAPTER THIRTY-SEVEN

THE PACK HAD TREKKED TO Penfield for a spot of Christmas Eve pugilism while the Huntresses were turning the morning's collected greenery into kissing boughs and garlands and other decorations.

Charlie and Duke were sparring inside the chalk circle they'd drawn.

"All I ask is that you avoid socking me in the mouth," Charlie said. "My Artie's making a kissing bough, and I'm planning to show my undying support for the endeavor."

"But a well-placed jab would shut you up for a bit, which would earn me the undying support of everyone here at Penfield."

A chorus of laughter and good-natured ragging followed. Charlie seemed to be the most amused of anyone. Being his friend was a never-ending delight. He was never dismissive of the Pack's struggles or dreams or hopes. He supported them in every imaginable way while also managing to make them smile and laugh regularly.

"Don't let Duke fool you," Colm said, lounging at his leisure on the sofa. "Everyone knows he plans to make ample use of the kissing boughs himself."

Seated beside him, Tobias said, "Kissing *himself*. How will he manage that?"

"It will be an awe-inspiring Christmas miracle," Colm answered.

"What was that?" Fennel stepped over to the sofa, managing to look confused. "A nausea-inspiring Christmas miracle?"

Duke looked back at Charlie. "I think you've been a bad influence on our youngest Pack member."

"Poppy doesn't need a bad influence." Charlie grinned.

From the hanging bag of hay, which Scott had been pummeling while Newton braced it and Toss looked on, Scott said, "The very mature, married component over here would like to point out that the lot of you are shockingly juvenile."

"*I* am part of the married component of the Pack," Charlie said, pretending to be hurt by the oversight.

"Scott specified the *mature* part of the married section of the Pack," Newton said.

With a dramatic sigh, Toss stepped away. "That removes me from membership."

Duke couldn't imagine his life without this group of friends. "Will there be any room in that 'mature' group for someone who isn't married?" he asked. "I'll be in London, after all, along with Newton and Toss."

"I thought Toss just disqualified himself from the mature section." Colm made a show of being confused.

"What is your evaluation, Tobias?" Charlie asked. "Toss is your brother-in-law, after all."

"That is a trap I am not about to fall into." Tobias shook his head. "Daria and Toss are the only members of my family I don't mind spending time with."

"A glowing recommendation," Duke said dryly.

And again, the gentlemen laughed and teased.

To the room as a whole, Fennel asked, "Will all of us be in London this Season?"

While almost everyone nodded, Scott did not. "We'll have to be absent this coming year. But retrenching significantly during 1820 will, we hope, mean that from 1821 onward, we'll be breathing quite a bit easier."

Then, perhaps this wouldn't be the last time they were all together.

The door to Penfield opened, revealing Uncle Niles standing on the threshold. "Your ladies are beginning to ask a lot of questions about where the lot of you have disappeared to. Best hop back over to Fairfield before they form a Christmas Eve hunting party."

Charlie sighed. "We really should have forged this close connection with a group of thickheaded ladies instead of clever ones. We'd get away with a lot more."

"But what fun would that be?" Toss gave Charlie a shove as he walked past.

Within a few minutes, they were all dressed once more, coats pulled on, and out the door.

Uncle Niles had brought a wagon. "Hop in," he instructed, climbing onto the driver's bench. "I'll have all of you back to Fairfield before the Huntresses can say, 'I suspect the Pack have been involved in clandestine boxing.'"

In the end, not a single one of the Huntresses offered up any guesses as to the Pack's activities when they arrived in the Fairfield drawing room. The ladies

The Best-Kept Secrets

239

motioned grandly to the adornments they had created and used to decorate the space.

Duke, without having to even ponder a destination, made his way directly to Eve's side. She took his hand without hesitation.

"It's very festive in here," he said. "The Huntresses have been hard at work."

"We enjoyed it," Eve said.

Artemis eyed everyone triumphantly. "The Pack are welcome to offer us both a hearty congratulations and your unending gratitude."

"For what this time?" Scott asked.

"We decided amongst ourselves which team won the greenery gathering competition this morning," Artemis said. "And I am deeply disappointed to say that it was not my team."

"Which one?" Duke asked.

"The Greenberrys' team," Lisette said.

That inspired whoops of excitement from Colm, Tobias, and Toss, and a grin from Daria.

Duke lowered his voice and leaned toward Eve. "Nia's not here for the celebration."

"She's sleeping. This morning's excursion depleted what strength she had."

"Is Dr. Wilstead worried?"

Eve shook her head. "He said her heart still sounds very strong." Her next breath shook a little, but she looked more relieved than concerned. "And setbacks like this are to be expected. Dr. Wilstead said, so long as Nia rests, she'll regain her strength."

He raised Eve's hand to his lips and kissed her fingers. "That's good to hear."

From among the group, Daria said, "We've been so curious, Charlie, what prize you decided on for the winners."

"Only the most brilliant of prizes." Charlie looked absolutely giddy, which usually meant a bit of absurdity was about to be unleashed on them all. "Each of us on the losing teams will draw a portrait of someone from the winning team."

It was, as predicted, absolutely absurd. And everyone looked as entertained as Duke was by the idea. Indeed, mere moments passed before they were all provided with parchment and lead pencils as they planned their works of art.

Duke hadn't the first idea if anyone in the group had the least artistic ability. But quality was not the point of the undertaking, and he was absolutely certain the Greenberrys' team would be surprised if any of the offerings they received from their defeated opponents were at all impressive.

Duke, while doing his utmost to draw something that he hoped at least vaguely looked like a human being, spoke with Eve, who was bent over her own piece of parchment. "Who are you planning to draw?"

"It is a secret, Duke." She looked up at him, her eyes dancing.

He tipped a corner of his mouth upward and allowed his gaze to turn a bit flirtatious, a bit warm. "Is there no way I could convince you to spill *that* secret?"

"You could certainly try." Her whisper was undeniably bewitching.

But Charlie broke the spell when he chose that moment to pretend to be struggling not to be ill.

"You're ruining Christmas, Charlie." Duke gave him a pointed look that he knew was too filled with amusement to be effective.

They'd not been at their drawings for more than a few minutes when yet another disruption occurred. The butler arrived in the drawing room with a silver salver containing three sealed letters. The first he presented to Mme Fortier, the second to Artemis. The final letter, he handed to Eve.

A quick look at the written address and she said, "It is from home. Thank goodness."

Duke didn't even pretend that he was paying the least attention to his drawing efforts. He watched Eve for indications that the letter contained bad news or that she needed additional support while reading it. He glanced toward the other two ladies who had received letters to reveal that their husbands were watching them as closely as he was Eve, both men wearing expressions that matched what he was feeling: a desire to be helpful if help was needed and a hope that the letters they were reading contained good tidings.

Eve's expression lightened as her eyes darted repeatedly across the page. Duke had so little experience with letters from home being anything but discouraging that he was almost more surprised than relieved.

She stood, her letter in one hand and the drawing she'd been working on in the other. "I need to go speak with Nia, assuming she's awake." She leaned toward Duke and kissed his cheek. "Good luck with your drawing."

"You say that as though you don't think I have the talent to create a masterpiece with ease."

Her beguiling dimple appeared once more. "Read into it what you must, Duke."

He watched her leave the room, and he smiled broadly and without feeling the least odd at the uncharacteristic outward show of delight. She was a balm to his soul. Being granted a place in her heart was a remarkable feat.

The Best-Kept Secrets

241

"Mother and Father shouldn't have asked you to keep this from me." Nia was sitting up in bed, Eve sitting beside her, having just finished explaining their family's true financial state. "I understand why they did. They want so much for us to enjoy our time with friends. But you should not have needed to bear this burden alone."

"I wasn't entirely alone. Duke sorted it out shockingly quickly."

"During our journey from Ireland, I'd wager. A bond grew between you two. I was so afraid of getting in the way of that. He's such a good person, and you're so happy when you're with him."

"Is that why you didn't tell me you were feeling poorly until you could no longer hide it?"

Nia nodded. "I probably should have told you sooner."

"And I desperately wanted to tell you about all this sooner. Only upon receiving the letter from home granting me permission to do so did I feel I could without breaking the promise I made to our parents."

"When do you intend to tell our parents about your new position?"

Eve had also told Nia about her arrangement with Mater. "In the letter I will send them next. I need to finish it before Mr. Greenberry leaves for London so he can frank it."

"How strange it will be without you at Tulleyloch or with us in London." Nia's mouth turned down. "Of course, I may not be well enough for a Season next year. Dr. Wilstead said some people don't recover significantly for a year or more. Some never truly do."

Eve squeezed her hand. "He does seem optimistic that you *will* recover and recover well. We can accept the possibility of less ideal outcomes without believing those outcomes are inevitable."

Nia smiled sincerely and genuinely. "I do feel optimistic; I promise I do. Being this tired and weak is not something I am at all accustomed to, and it sometimes feels as though I'll never escape it."

"When you are feeling equal to doing so," Eve said, "we will take rides in the gig with a succession of different horses so you can see as many of the famous Fairfield Whites as possible. And before we leave, we will make good on that hope of yours to actually ride one of those glorious horses yourself."

"Else the Pack will vanquish Colm on my behalf?" Nia said with a laugh. "Fortunately, I don't think they will have to."

"Neither do I. He is as good as gold; they all are."

Nia leaned against her. "I don't think we can ever thank Artemis enough for making us part of the Huntresses. She changed our lives for the better."

"For the absolute best."

"You'll have to make certain to send her an invitation to the wedding." There was mischief in Nia's voice.

"The wedding?"

"Do not think, Aoife, that I have been so ill that I haven't made note of the fact that Duke's devotion to and affection for you has not merely continued since our arrival at Fairfield; it has grown and deepened."

"There is not, at present, an understanding between us," Eve pointed out.

"Trust me, *everyone* understands what is happening between the two of you."

That was undoubtedly true. "Duke's parents are terrible."

"Also something *everyone* understands," Nia said dryly.

"He doesn't yet know how they will respond to his change in residence and his new role as political secretary for, as they so caringly put it, 'the enemy.' He's afraid they'll still manage to make him and everyone around him wretchedly unhappy."

"Would their unkindness actually convince you to walk away from him?" Nia asked.

"No," she said, smiling inwardly. "But he needs to know that I chose a life with him with full understanding of what that means. And I've patience enough to make certain he has that reassurance."

Tears shimmered in Nia's eyes. "You really do love him."

"So much."

Her sister smiled at her. "Then, in a year or two or however long is needed, I will be very happy for him to be my brother."

"Not nearly as happy as I will be."

"Will the wait be worth it?" Nia asked.

Eve closed her eyes and smiled. "Absolutely worth it."

CHAPTER THIRTY-EIGHT

Upon deciding to hold their house party during the holy season, the Huntresses and Pack had made an unbreakable commitment to each other that absolutely no gifts would be exchanged.

Eve knew this was a way of saving those without financial means from feeling any pressure to obtain gifts and experiencing any embarrassment at being the only ones without offerings. But as Christmas morning gave way to Christmas afternoon, she knew with certainty that the arrangement hadn't been a concession at all. Being together was the greatest gift she could think of. She was surrounded by her very best friends. Everyone was being thoughtful of Nia but not in a pitying or suffocating way. The holy day was peaceful while also filled with laughter. And Duke had spent the entirety of it with her, holding her hand, sitting beside her, talking about anything and everything.

She wouldn't have him with her for long. He and his aunt and uncle were leaving for London in only a few more days. She wouldn't follow for months. *Months.* Though she'd set a goal for herself not to dwell on his looming departure, she couldn't entirely clear her thoughts of it. And she must not have kept her sorrow from her expression, as Duke regularly drew her closer and whispered, "I will miss you as well."

They were sitting together, listening to Toss and Tobias trade entertaining tales from their various school experiences, when Artemis tiptoed over to Eve and Duke.

"I've come to steal you two for a moment," she said quietly.

Careful not to disrupt the storytelling, they followed Artemis out of the drawing room and to the nearby sitting room. Charlie was inside, as was Mater. And Artemis shut the door behind them, which was decidedly unexpected.

"I have had yet another brilliant idea," Artemis said, taking a seat beside Charlie. "There have been so many that I'm certain you have lost count."

Charlie grinned at her, clearly delighted by his wife's theatrics.

"But to share that brilliant idea," Artemis continued, "I first need to make Duke aware of something few people know."

"I am intrigued," Duke said.

With a nod, Artemis answered, "You should be."

Mater's smile was as amused as Charlie's but heavily infused with an undeniably maternal bent.

"This cannot go beyond this room," Artemis warned Duke.

"My secret keeping can be depended on," he said.

"As you know, the Huntresses are particularly fond of Miss Martinette's dress shop."

Duke shook his head. "I did not know that, but I do now."

Artemis looked surprised. "We spent countless hours there during the Season."

Eve jumped in. "And Duke spent only a week in London."

"True." Artemis nodded her head. "I suppose your ignorance on the matter can be tolerated this time."

With that look in his eyes that Eve knew to be laughter, Duke said, "How magnanimous of you."

"Miss Martinette's is not merely *the* place for fashionable ladies to obtain unparalleled gowns," Artemis said, "it is also overseen by a proprietress who does not actually own or run the shop."

Was Artemis truly going to reveal this secret? It was so tightly kept that other than Charlie, none of the Pack had been told.

"You have met Rose Narang," Artemis said.

"I have," Duke answered.

"She and I secretly own and run Miss Martinette's dress shop."

Nothing but shock registered on Duke's face. But his expression quickly shifted to one of a person sorting a puzzle. "If Society knew of your role at the shop, it would be a disaster for both of you."

"And everyone connected to us," Artemis added.

Duke turned to Charlie. "This is how your finances are stretching further. I was baffled, honestly. I didn't think publishing mathematical papers came with much financial reward."

"Fortunately," Charlie said, "no one outside of our nearest and dearest had any idea that our budget was so strained to begin with, so they'll have even less idea now or moving forward that anything has changed."

The Best-Kept Secrets 245

Artemis was focused once more on Eve. "Rose and I have been discussing some changes at the dress shop."

Eve nodded. "You said as much at the very beginning of this house party."

"One of the changes we have considered is converting the alcove near the front door of the shop into a very exclusive tea room. Ladies who come to order dresses or for fittings could enjoy little delicacies while they wait, which would elevate their experience and further set our shop apart from others. But ladies could visit *just* the tea shop without an appointment at Miss Martinette's, and in so doing would see our dresses and establishment in person, which we believe would encourage more people to place orders at the shop."

Eve listened intently, feeling the undeniable sense that something was about to change for all of them.

"We had assumed that our best approach was to place a daily order with Gunter's, as is often done." Artemis shook her head. "But that rather undermines our aim of setting ourselves apart, to create an experience that can be had only at Miss Martinette's. Then you confessed early in this gathering that you are, in fact, a baker, and I have tasted for myself how remarkable a baker you are."

Duke, watching Artemis intently, squeezed Eve's hand.

"I wrote to Rose that very day," Artemis said. "We have developed a very extensive code, which allows us to discuss potentially sensitive topics with no fear that others will read or understand them. This secret of yours, Eve, remains safe."

Eve could hardly breathe, excitement warring with her hesitation to open herself up to possible disappointment.

"The letter I received yesterday was from Rose," Artemis said. "We would like to propose that you open a tea shop on the premises of Miss Martinette's. It would be yours to guide and run, though you would likely need to do so with the same secrecy and misdirection that we utilize. Mr. Layton has been invaluable in sorting the complexities of our endeavor and has said he would be happy to do the same for a tea shop. And while I imagine a tremendous amount of tea will be served, Rose and I are of the opinion that it will become known as, in essence, a pâtisserie that also serves tea."

Almost too amazed to speak, Eve whispered, "I would have my own pâtisserie."

"You would have to be very secretive about that," Artemis reminded her. "Being a lady's companion is perfectly acceptable in Society. A lady running an actual business isn't *at all*." She leaned forward and took Eve's free hand. "And though the first year will be leaner than those that follow, your pâtisserie would provide you income that you can add to what you receive as a companion. That will allow you to help your family give Nia the care she needs while still having money to set aside for other things."

Eve took a quick breath, her mind and heart leaping about.

Charlie watched Duke. "Living with your aunt and uncle isn't a terrible prospect, but it might be nice not to have to do that for the rest of your life. Eve's income, combined with yours, could make that possible down the road."

"Once we know how my parents will behave," he said, his smile more amazement than anything else.

"In the meantime," Mater said, "Eve would need to be in London from at least the beginning of March until the very end of the Season."

"We'd have months together instead of weeks." Eve swallowed down a lump of emotion.

Duke turned to Mater. "That would mean you would likely need to be there as well."

"A change that will delight my friends to no end."

"But will it delight *you*?" Eve pressed, looking at her with concern. "That would mean far less time spent at Lampton Park."

"I've needed something to nudge me into the next stage of my life, to discover what is next for me." Mater actually looked a little excited. "I believe this is just the thing. And the traveling we wish to do could be undertaken in the autumn, after the *ton* has left Town for their country estates. It would work out rather well, actually."

Eve could hardly believe how much had changed in one brief conversation.

She squeezed Duke's hand. "We wouldn't have to be apart for endless months." Eve shook her head in stunned amazement. "I would be in London, spending time with our friends. And I could bake every day. Every single day."

"Your dreamed-of future," Duke said with a smile.

She leaned closer to him and whispered, "A future with you is my dream. Always."

He kissed her forehead and wrapped his arms around her.

"While this path doesn't come with a guarantee," Mater said, "it comes with a great deal of hope. And hope combined with love, be it the love of family or friends or the person with whom you wish to spend all your life, is a powerful thing."

From the moment Mother had told Eve of the painful change in the family's situation, making do had been the best that had seemed possible. Making do. Getting by. Now she stood with Duke, looking ahead to a future filled with hope and love.

CHAPTER THIRTY-NINE

THE WEATHER WAS FINE THE next day, so Eve suggested that she and Duke walk to the baking cottage, and he was happy to do so. He welcomed any opportunity to spend time with her.

He held her hand as they walked. It was such a simple gesture, yet he would miss it terribly. Even when they were together again in London, they wouldn't have the freedom they'd enjoyed at Fairfield.

"Mater says that Mr. Layton will most certainly be able to sort out a location for the baking to be done for the tea shop," Eve said as they walked. "I will likely need at least one other person to work there with me. Mr. Layton helped Artemis and Rose find skilled and trustworthy employees, so I do believe he can help me with that as well."

"I am happy to meet with him on your behalf while I'm in London if you'd like." Duke wanted to do all he could for her.

"I would appreciate that. There may be decisions that need to be made more swiftly than letters can be sent back and forth." She smiled up at him. Lud, he was going to miss her alluring dimple. "So many things need to be done, and it is a bit overwhelming, but I'm excited and eager to see this all come together."

"So am I." He was hesitant to express the concern that still troubled him, but it would be unforgivable of him not to discuss it. His was not the only future impacted by it. "This endeavor will give you some freedom, Eve, and more choices. You may very well find that you could do better than a gentle-man who can't even be certain his parents will treat you with civility."

She shook her head. "You won't be ridding yourself of me that easily."

He stopped their forward movement. They were within a few steps of the cottage. "You think I want to rid myself of you?" He lightly kissed her. "Not even for a moment. I love you with every breath and every beat of my heart. I will miss you and long for you, but I won't ever stop loving you or wanting to have that life we're working toward."

She pulled him toward the cottage once more. "And what makes you think that I feel any differently, Dubhán?"

"Honestly," he said, "I'm not entirely sure. I don't doubt that you love me. I don't think you are flighty or insincere. Yet I cannot shake the concern that before all is said and done, you'll decide this isn't worth it." He feared she would decide *he* wasn't worth it.

"I know you well enough to have realized before now that you would struggle with that." She reached out and took hold of the door handle. "That is why I chose the chaperones I did for today."

Eve opened the door and led him inside.

Aunt Penelope, Uncle Niles, and Colm were waiting there. They weren't meant to know about her baking. It was being kept even from most of the Pack. Duke closed the door, shutting out the cold, all the while mired in confusion.

"I told them about my baking and our plans for the tea shop. I have been required to keep a significant secret from my sister lately, and I know how that burdens a person. I've had to watch everything I say and tiptoe through conversations with someone I would otherwise lean on for support and advice and encouragement. I don't want you to have to do that with your family. Now you won't have to."

A panic-edged worry grabbed hold of him. "I would not advise revealing this to my parents or grandmother."

Eve's smile turned laughing. "I have absolutely no plans to do so, I assure you. The Greenberrys are the family you will be surrounded by. They are the ones I want you to be at ease with. And their home needs to become home to you, which is unlikely to happen if you are constantly evaluating everything you say before you say it."

That was a painfully familiar scenario. "I lived that way at Writtlestone."

Aunt Penelope crossed to him and took his hands in hers. "We want Fairfield and our London house to be home to you. Even after you have begun a new chapter of your life elsewhere, when you come back to visit, we want you to feel that you are returning home."

"I am grateful that you are willing to make room for me—"

Aunt Penelope kept one of his hands in hers and pulled him to the sofa near the fire. She sat, tugging him to sit beside her. Uncle Niles sat on a nearby chair. Eve sat in another. Colm stood beside the fireplace.

The Best-Kept Secrets   251

"We are family, Duke," Aunt Penelope said. "Too many years of strain and tension have created a chasm that never should have been there. We have loved you your entire life from an unfortunately large distance. To have that distance shortened so much is a source of joy to all of us. Joy—not obligation or burden or annoyance or any of the other things you are likely worried about."

He was concerned about those precise possibilities. He'd often felt like a burden and annoyance in his parents' home.

"Before we leave for London," Uncle Niles said, "choose a bedchamber in the family wing. That will be yours whenever you are at Fairfield."

The family wing. Why that brought a surge of emotion to his throat, he couldn't entirely say.

"Eve had a brilliant idea not long after you and Father made the arrangements for you to make your home here," Colm said. "The coachman, team, and carriage you came to Fairfield in was still here but not needed. Clandestine instructions were given to the coachman to return to Writtlestone and gather all your possessions and have them brought here. If the task were seen to while your parents were still at Fairfield, the staff at Writtlestone would not have to combat the inevitable objections."

Duke looked to Eve. "You thought to have my possessions brought here?"

"This is your home," she said. "All the things that make a place feel welcoming and personal and . . . home need to be here. But if you had to gather them, it would place you back within range of your parents' barbed arrows and introduce the possibility that they'd withhold the carriage to prevent you from leaving. And if your parents were asked to gather and send your belongings, I suspect they'd either refuse or insist on making the journey themselves to make trouble for you."

"But it was a few days after my discussion with Uncle Niles before you began forgiving me for how abominably I behaved," Duke said. "You made the suggestion while I was still in your black book?"

"I believe I have told you before that I am a saint." Eve never failed to lighten his heart, even in difficult moments.

"I don't deserve you, Aoife O'Doyle."

"Yes, you do," she said boldly and unabashedly. "We are happy together. Joyful. Hopeful. And you deserve that, Dubhán."

Aunt Penelope put her arms around him. "You deserve to be happy and to feel loved without being made to think you have to continually prove that you deserve it."

"I won't likely know what to do with something so unfamiliar." He could hardly even smile a little.

"It's more familiar than you likely realize," Colm said. "The Pack and the Huntresses are family to each other in every way that matters."

"And"—Eve's voice had suddenly filled with an entertaining amount of mischief—"really delicious food is not entirely dissimilar to the joys of being surrounded by loving family. I think if we baked some shortbread this afternoon, that would be a great leap toward the familiarity you wish to build."

"I think you just want to bake shortbread," Duke said with a light laugh.

"Always." She grinned.

For the next hour or so, Eve talked them all through the tasks of baking shortbread as well as lemon biscuits. The Greenberrys were not merely tolerant of her *ton*-disapproved endeavor, but they were excited to be learning a bit of the art as well.

And there was laughter, smiles, easy interactions. Duke, just as Colm had predicted, found it more familiar than he'd expected. He hadn't experienced it with his parents or in the home where he'd grown up. But he had with the Pack for all the years they'd known each other at school. And he'd had it with the Huntresses in the year since they'd all become acquainted at the first house party.

And he'd had all of this and more as he'd fallen in love with Eve. Love. Acceptance. Encouragement.

And home.

CHAPTER FORTY

DURING THE FIVE DAYS SINCE Christmas, Artemis and Eve had spent a lot of time making plans and formulating strategies, determining what Eve ought to sort out and decide on before arriving in London and what could wait until she reached Town. Seeing her grow more excited with each conversation brought Duke every bit as much satisfaction as he felt choosing the bedchamber that would be his at Fairfield, placing his things in it when they had arrived the day before, and discussing with Uncle Niles the work and responsibilities that awaited him in London.

It was the last night of the house party. Everyone, aside from Eve, Nia, Mater, and Colm, would be leaving in the morning. Duke held out hope that this would not, in actuality, be the last time all of them were together.

The older generation was spending the evening in a sitting room, leaving the Pack and the Huntresses space to be together without disruption. Toss spent the evening playing the pianoforte while the group took part in country dances and general revelry.

Colm dropped onto the chair next to Duke's. "I'm beginning to suspect there isn't a tune Toss can't play."

"He is shockingly talented."

Colm nodded. "This is a remarkable group of people. Thank you for allowing me to become part of them."

"Allowing you?"

His cousin seldom looked uncertain or upended, but he did just then. "I worried when I was invited to one of your friends' gatherings that you would resent me being there. Considering the chasm between our branches of the Seymour family, I wasn't certain if I was permitted to cross it even that little bit."

"Much like I worried that you and your parents would consider me an interloper if I asked for houseroom," Duke said.

Colm nodded slowly. "We've both been rather carefully taught by our grandmother—you by your parents as well—to expect a shaky welcome from anyone we attempt to forge a connection with."

"I sometimes wonder how long it will take us to even discover the extent to which we were prevented from simply being family to each other." The more Duke realized the damage that had been done, the more heartbroken and disappointed he grew. But it also further demonstrated why caution was needed as he moved forward. He needed to make certain the life he built with Eve was placed on a sure footing, not the shaky one his parents had forced on him in the past.

"Once Nia is feeling well enough to return home, I'll be making my way to Town," Colm said. "We can work on closing that chasm then."

"I'd like that."

"As much as you'd like to dance with Eve? Because she has been watching you with unmistakable anticipation."

"There are few things I would enjoy anywhere near as much as being with her."

"I'm happy for you," Colm said. "Both of you. You've found someone worth fighting for."

"Remind me of that when you arrive in London," Duke said. "By then, I'll likely be nearly mad with missing her."

"I will." Colm set his hand on Duke's back and shoved him out of his chair. "Now, go dance with your lady."

Duke snapped a salute as if he were receiving orders from a commanding officer. Given that Colm had been an officer in the dragoons, it felt rather fitting.

He crossed to where Eve sat beside Nia. Illness had taken a toll on the younger of the sisters. She was clearly tired and had grown a little gaunt but was still eager to be among them, participating as much as she felt able to.

"Do you mind if I steal your sister for a dance?" Duke asked Nia.

"I don't think you'll have to 'steal' her."

Duke held his hand out to Eve. "Dance with me?"

"Always." She set her hand in his and stood.

Before they took a single step away, Nia spoke. "I'm glad you were the one who brought us here from Ireland."

Duke set his free arm around Eve and, to both sisters, said, "So am I."

Nia looked genuinely happy for them. "The O'Doyle family can be . . . overwhelming. I hope you're ready for that."

"More than ready."

Toss began a reel. Nia shooed them away to join those who had gathered in the open space to dance. Duke took his spot opposite Eve, unable to stop smiling whenever he looked at her.

A snort beside him pulled his eyes in that direction. "Did you have something you wanted to say, Charlie?"

"Only that you might find it difficult to manage your feet in a dance with your head in the clouds."

"And yet I predict I will execute the steps with greater skill than you will."

Charlie pretended to be shocked. "I am an *excellent* dancer."

"When you choose to be," Tobias said from his other side.

"Why choose excellent when comedy is so much more satisfying?"

And he lived up to that declaration. Within one minute of the first steps of the dance, chaotic hilarity had descended over the group. Charlie had managed to wreak more than the usual havoc. Scott, who'd not begun his time in the Pack as an obvious instigator of devilment, had shown himself of late to be a remarkably good match to Charlie and Toss in their tendency toward mischief. He did so again, helping pull the entire room into a state of uproarious laughter.

In the midst of it all, Duke set his arms around Eve, delighted at the wonderfully familiar sight of her smiling and laughing and being pleased with life. And she leaned into his embrace, so at home and at ease. They had a beautiful life to look forward to. Claiming it fully would take time. And it would be worth every moment of waiting.

February 1820
London

So very much had happened in the five weeks since Eve had last seen Duke. He'd written to her often, keeping her abreast of all he was doing, never failing to tell her that he loved her and missed her and looked forward to seeing her again.

Acting as lady's companion to Mater had proven the most wonderful arrangement. Eve was loved and cared about but was also inarguably useful and, she felt certain, brought actual joy and comfort to the lady.

Eve and Mater had just arrived in London. The journey had originally been planned for March, but along with most of the aristocracy, Mater had needed to be in Town for the funeral of the King.

They alighted at Lampton House. With efficiency as well as obvious warmth, Mater was welcomed to the home that had been her own and now was her eldest son's. There was likely no one who had ever met the dowager countess who didn't immediately love her.

"Have the earl and countess already arrived?" Mater asked as they were divested of their outer clothing.

"Yes, my lady," the butler answered. "They arrived this morning."

"Excellent."

"Someone else has been at Lampton House since this morning," the butler said, "and is waiting for Miss O'Doyle."

A bubble of excitement formed in Eve's chest. Though this 'someone' might very well be one of the Huntresses, she felt in her heart that he or she was not.

"And where is . . . *he* now?" Mater asked, a little too much laughter in her voice.

"The drawing room." The butler offered a little bow, not quite managing to hide his own amusement.

Mater nudged Eve in the right direction. "Go on, then. Put the poor young gentleman out of his misery."

Eve rushed toward the room that Mater, the butler, a footman, and two maids pointed her toward. This was, without question, going to be a very joyful house to spend the Season in. She spotted Duke in the room before he realized she had entered.

"Dubhán." His Irish name slipped from her lips in a jubilant whisper.

He spun around. The look in his eyes, she would never forget as long as she lived. Relief. Delight. The expression one wore when the world had just righted itself.

"My Aoife."

She didn't wait for him to cross to her but ran into his arms.

"Oh, how I've missed you." He held her so tightly, so close. "Six weeks without you was so long, my dear."

"We have six months of likely seeing each other every day," she reminded him as well as herself.

"My parents are likely coming to London as well."

She shook her head. "What matters is that we're here together."

"And that we'll face what comes together."

"Together," she repeated, looking up at him once more. "I can hardly wait."

He kissed her softly and tenderly and with the promise of forever.

ABOUT THE AUTHOR

Photo by Pepperfox Photography

Sarah M. Eden is a *USA Today* best-selling author of more than seventy witty and charming historical romances, which have sold over one million copies worldwide. Some of these include 2020's Foreword Reviews INDIE Awards gold winner for romance, *Forget Me Not*, 2019's Foreword Reviews INDIE Awards gold winner for romance, *The Lady and the Highwayman*, and 2020 Holt Medallion finalist, *Healing Hearts*. She is a three-time Best of State gold-medal winner for fiction and a three-time Whitney Award winner.

Combining her obsession with history and her affinity for tender love stories, Sarah loves crafting deep characters and heartfelt romances set against rich historical backdrops. She holds a bachelor's degree in research and happily spends hours perusing the reference shelves of her local library.

Sarah is represented by Pam Pho at Steven Literary Agency.

www.SarahMEden.com
Facebook: facebook.com/SarahMEden
Instagram: @sarah_m_eden